LEGEN I

STORM OF
SHADOWS

HOLLY ROSE

RED
SPARK
PRESS

LEGENDS OF IMYRIA

STORM OF SHADOWS

HOLLY ROSE

Cover artwork by Jay Villabos
Illustration by Kolarp Em

ISBN (hardcover): 978-1-914503-05-4
ISBN (paperback): 978-1-914503-04-7
eISBN: 978-1-914503-03-0

To my mum, for all your endless support.

BELENTRA

Ruins of Ithyr

Nimira

Aesari   Mithrys

LUMARIA   FENYR
WOODS

Shalandril

Olona Island

Verethia

Althira

Tarethel

Eldasil

ALANOR

Caelis

Talmira

The Shimmering
Isles

WORLD OF
IMYRIA

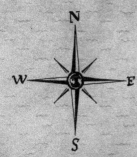

KRALAXXAS

TALIÐOR

Uldren Isle

Odela

VALKA

ÐROMGAR

Boldred

Zol Arrod

Arnvik

Jorga

Avrak

Ðalry

Gerazad

JEKTAR

Lowrick

NOLÐERAN

TIRITH

The Ghost
Woods

Ðul Kazar

Lenris Port

SELYNIS

Esterra

Nezu

Tuylon

Meran Island

CHAPTER 1

Rain drizzles down on the ruined streets of Nolderan, the heavens weeping for the thousands of lives lost. Blood streaks through the clouds as the first rays of dawn pierce the sky like a fan of daggers.

A new day.

I clench my jaw.

Two nights ago, Arluin and his necromancers stormed this city and laid waste to all in their path. Two nights ago, he stole everything and everyone from me, including my father and my best friend. Yet it feels like an eternity has passed since then. Now I can no longer imagine a Nolderan which isn't ravaged, a Reyna who isn't broken.

No.

I can't allow myself to be broken. I must fuse together the shattered pieces of my heart and force myself onward down this path I have already chosen. The path of vengeance. My choice was sealed when I sold my soul. All that remains is to put one foot after another until I reach my destination: Arluin's death and Father's freedom.

I tear my gaze down from the mournful heavens and look at the archway marking the Arcanium's entrance. The words etched deep into the stone stare back at me.

QUEL ESTE VOLU, PODE NONQUES VERA MORIRE.

That which is aether may never truly die.

A wry laugh bubbles in my throat at the irony, but I swallow it down in a thick lump, lest my new demonic companion hears it. I fear if it were to escape, it would sound more like a strangled sob than a laugh.

But Zephyr, the faerie dragon curled around my shoulders, seems to hear the noise. He lifts his head and peers at me. I say nothing as I pass under the archway. Zephyr nestles back into my neck, his serpentine body coiling around me like a scarf. The sharp tips of his folded wings poke into me, but I welcome the light pain. It reminds me I'm alive. That only I can avenge Nolderan and bring Arluin to justice.

I glance at the Void Prince reluctantly stalking behind me. His onyx horns glint in the emerging sunlight, and his cloven hooves clatter across the stone slabs. Crimson light snakes across the marble ridges of his torso, and rage smolders in the fathomless depths of his eyes. Those same eyes snap up to meet mine. His jaw tempers into steel. Hatred blazes across his expression in a storm of molten fury. His power lashes out at the invisible cord tethering our souls together, but even the mighty Void Prince of Pride can't overcome the dark magic binding us. The unrelenting chains only further enrage him. A murderous snarl writhes on his lips, silently promising me all the horrifying ways he will torture my soul upon my death, when I will belong to him as he now belongs to me. I can only hope his bindings will be strong enough to hold him until I kill Arluin. I dread to think what would happen if he breaks free. The threat he made when I summoned him rings in my ears as loudly as it did down in the small chamber deep within the Arcanium's vaults: *Little mage, I will tear you limb from limb, carve the flesh from your puny bones, and feed you morsel by morsel to my Void Hounds.*

Fear slithers up my spine, its icy touch more chilling than the frigid wind blowing over us. I shiver, unable to stifle my reaction. All I can imagine is the Void Prince breaking free from my command and tearing through me as if I am made from paper and not from flesh and blood. I wonder if he can see the fear in my eyes. If he can smell it.

Zephyr's whimper snaps me from my trance. He too must sense the terrifying dark power oozing from the Void Prince. The faerie dragon's fear reminds me of the need to banish my own. This demon is my weapon, and I must be strong enough to wield him.

I smother the dread swelling in my heart and desperately search for a reason to explain my staring. One which doesn't involve fear.

Though the Void Prince towers over me, he now stands three heads taller than me rather than thrice my height. In order to fit through the narrow staircases leading from the Vaults and up to the Arcanium's central atrium, the demon was required to use his magic to assume a stature more befitting of an elf than a demon.

"Your appearance," I begin slowly, at first not trusting my tongue to hide my unease.

The Void Prince's crimson eyes narrow, daring me to continue. I do.

"Since you could adjust your height, I assume you can alter"—I pause, wrinkling my nose at his draconic wings—"*other* aspects as well."

"What other aspects?" the demon growls, his words rumbling in the back of his throat.

My lips curl. I hope it masks my unease. "Everything."

I know my remark will shove more fuel onto an already roaring fire, but only by this way can I disguise my fear. It reminds me I'm in control. Right now, the demon is mine to do with as I please. Though I will bear the consequences of my actions in the afterlife.

Nonetheless, I decide not to push him too far. Just in case those magical restraints aren't quite strong enough.

"I say this only as a matter of practicality," I continue before the Void Prince can erupt. "There are few places in this world where demons are tolerated, let alone Void Princes. It's best you conceal your true nature to avoid drawing unwanted attention."

The demon glowers. "Unwanted attention is of no consequence to me."

"You forget your place, *demon*. You serve me now, and that which is of consequence to me is also of consequence to you."

"And you forget, *mortal*, that you will belong to me thousands of years longer than I will serve you."

"Then you should stop acting like a spoiled child, since this bargain is far more favorable to you than it is to me."

The Void Prince takes a step closer, his gnarled horns looming over me. I don't flinch and instead remind myself of the bond between us. Until it is broken, he can't harm me, his summoner. "What use do I have for the soul of a pathetic mage? Though I will certainly relish your eternal torture."

I don't know why I indulge him in his little speech when I can end it with a single word.

"Natharius Thalanor," I say, brandishing his name as if it were a weapon. In many ways it is. The Void Prince's true name is the greatest power I hold over him. "You *will* assume a far less conspicuous form. And that is an order."

The demon's expression warps into a vicious snarl, and I once more feel his power testing the extent of his restraints. His forehead creases as he battles the dark magic binding his soul to mine, but his resistance isn't enough. In the end, he is forced to comply with my demand. A perverted satisfaction trills through me, and I enjoy the demon's submission more than I should. Perhaps that makes me as monstrous as him, but how can it be wicked to force evil into servitude?

The shadows hiss as the Void Prince's form dissolves and is born anew.

Gone are his horns and wings and hooves. Now the creature standing before me is undeniably beautiful. Long silvery hair streams down his shoulders, softened by the amber rays of dawn. His near translucent skin is also tinged with a golden sheen and shimmers in the gentle light. His angular features are also less severe, though his chin is as sharp. The only remnants of his demonic corruption are his glowing red eyes and the markings entwining his arms and torso. Other than these, he appears exactly like the moon elven ambassador I remember Father meeting years ago.

A moment passes. Then another. I stand there and blink, unable to believe a being so horrifying could become so beautiful in mere instants. How can this be the same demon I summoned from the Abyss?

But the hatred carved into his otherwise flawless face undeniably belongs to the Void Prince of Pride.

His lips twist into a sneer. "Satisfied?"

I consider requesting him to conceal his blood-red eyes, but then I notice the rest of him. Namely, that he stands there barefoot, dressed only in a loincloth. I turn away from the nearly naked elf and remind myself of the draconic wings and fiendish horns present only seconds ago. His demonic appearance was less startling than this.

"Put some clothes on," I snap, and then continue down the street. I don't look back to see whether he obeys, but the swishing of shadows suggests he does.

Our footsteps echo like thunder through the deathly silence of Nolderan's ruins. Heaps of rubble blanket the lonely streets, and I pick my way around the broken glass. Zephyr's weight is distributed unevenly on my shoulders and makes nimbleness a challenge. Despite my efforts, a few shards find their way into the soft flesh of my feet.

The rain thickens, and fat drops splatter onto my tattered and bloodstained dress. It's the same gown I wore to the ball two nights ago—the ball which marked my transition from an adept to a fully qualified Magi of Nolderan. Achieving my dreams was supposed to change my life for the better. Instead, it ruined everything.

My steps falter. I grip my staff tighter, feeling the thrum of aether beneath my fingers. The staff which was once my father's, which distinguished him as the Grandmage of Nolderan, has now fallen to me. Along with this dead city I alone am responsible for.

I draw in a slow breath, filling my lungs with the bitter scent of destruction. I can almost taste the ash and embers whirring through the streets as they did on that fateful night. It's as if the dark magic which seeped through the city has left the white walls, dappled cobblestones, and cobalt rooftops stained with its touch.

I'm not the only one to suck in a sharp breath. The Void Prince's nostrils flare as he too breathes in the residue of Nolderan. Unlike me, he enjoys it so very much. Wicked delight sparks in his crimson eyes. I would expect one of the seven most powerful demons in the Abyss to revel in the taste of death and destruction, but this seems deeper. Unless the demon is merely relishing all his captor has lost and suffered.

He adjusts the top button of his high-neck robes. "After one thousand years, it appears Nolderan has received its due."

The demon's words shatter my thoughts, scattering them far and wide. At first my shock is so great that I can say nothing. Or do anything.

And then my shock melts away. With the dam breached, my fury rushes out in a violent storm of fiery waves.

Ferocious though my temper is, it only incites the Void Prince's laughter. That dark, velvety, *evil* sound is enough to shove me over the cliff and send me plunging into the blazing sea beneath.

Wrath consumes me, and the aether flowing through my veins ignites. Tendrils of flames lick at my fingers.

Once again, I have conjured fire without uttering a single spell-word. The resulting magic is wild and dangerous.

"You think it's funny," I seethe. Power pounds through me. "You think it's funny a cult of necromancers ravaged our city, slew all in their path, and raised them from the dead?" My brittle voice cracks at the end, revealing the well of emotion within. My fury, my grief, my hatred.

"Funny?" the Void Prince echoes, arching a silvery brow. His malicious sneer doesn't diminish. "No, I find it hilarious that Nolderan has been destroyed by the abominable magic it birthed. That the magi have finally paid the price of their many sins."

"You—"

I want to say so many things. That a demon as heinous as he, who traded the souls of his entire city for power because being the High Enchanter of Lumaria wasn't enough, has no right to blame anyone for their sins. That even if my ancestors are responsible for the curse of undeath, they have been dead for a thousand years and someone as bright and beautiful as Eliya, my best friend, never deserved to pay for their sins.

And yet I can say none of this. The words are tangled on my tongue, muddled in a knot too tight for me to unravel, and the rage drumming through me is so overwhelming it deafens my thoughts.

Fire crackles. It spreads from my fingers, desperate to escape the fragile cage of my remaining resolve and yearning for release.

Zephyr uncoils himself from my trembling shoulders and darts for safety. I barely feel the shift of his weight. I am a quaking volcano moments away from eruption. And when I explode, I want to take *everything* with me. Especially this demon and the ugly sneer on his face.

"Do it," he hisses, taking a forceful step closer. "Unleash all that wrath. End me, as you so desperately desire. Banish me from this mortal-infested world."

The last strands of my control nearly fray and free all this raging power within me. But then I remember who I am. What my purpose is. I see Eliya's too-still face as I lay her inside her crystal coffin, purple light brushing over her icy skin. My father's head turning toward me at an unnatural angle, the shadowy orbs of his eyes filled with ravenous hunger. Koby, a fellow adept who only wanted to help me save Eliya. His chest pierced by the bolt of dark magic conjured by Kaely, who was once my greatest rival but is now another scar which will never heal.

For all of them, I must destroy Arluin. But I can't do it alone. I am only an overgrown adept two days past her training. How can I slay the man who defeated the Grandmage of Nolderan? That's why I summoned this demon, why I bartered my soul. My power isn't enough to destroy Arluin. I need the Void Prince's strength. I can't lose my sole weapon by banishing him back to the Abyss.

But the power boiling within is too volatile to be smothered. No matter how much I will it, the inferno does not extinguish. My desperate pleas only further rile it. Then I'm bursting at the seams.

The firestorm breaks free.

The demon's grin stretches across his face.

No!

At the very last second, I use the last of my control to avert the spell's path. The flames skim past the Void Prince, singeing the sleeves of his dark robes and the silver thread woven through.

The fireball hurls into the wall behind him, shredding through the stone as if it were sand. Rumbling echoes through the city as the wall crumbles apart.

I clasp Father's staff and gaze at the destruction I have wrought. This is why magic should never be cast without spell-words. It is too unpredictable. Uncontrollable. And I can already feel the cost of its power gnawing on my consciousness. My body is far from recovered after all it has endured these past two nights, and the spell stole much of my remaining strength.

The ground beckons me, but I resist the claws of exhaustion. If I collapse, I'll prove to the Void Prince I really am a pathetic little mage who can't control her own measly magic. I dig my heels into the ground, ignoring the grit which presses into my skin. I don't let my face reveal anything but rage. And hatred.

For him.

For Arluin.

For myself.

The demon's smirk falters. Disappointment descends on his expression in a heavy shadow. Then it's gone, and the gleam in his red eyes is crueler than ever.

"Now, now," he chastises, his voice melodic, "that's no way to treat your precious city, is it?"

I don't deign to offer him the rebuke he desires. Nor do I let him see how his taunt crawls under my skin.

I hate him. His savage smirk, his silky voice, his murderous gaze—I hate them all. If not for Eliya, for Father, I would long banish this monster back to whence he came.

CHAPTER 2

THE ASHBOURNE MANOR IS AS I left it: the gilded gates swung wide open. Before, they were secured by a powerful enchantment, but now they're cut off from their power source.

I peer up at the empty Aether Tower standing sentry over the forsaken city. Two nights ago, it housed an enormous orb of humming magic and bathed Nolderan in its violet light. Now it's as dead as everything else.

I turn to my manor and stride through the magicless gates, passing the lion crest fixed to their metallic bars. The Void Prince's footsteps pound behind as he follows me through our ruined gardens.

The fountain's basin is smashed apart, and water leaks across the stone path, turning the grass into a marsh. Plucked flowers lie helplessly around their overturned and fractured planters. I don't stop to look, and neither does the demon. My bare feet squelch in the muddy puddles, as do his freshly conjured boots.

We reach the manor's entrance and ascend the chipped steps. The battered doors are open from when I stormed out last night, desperate to find a way to free Father from the shackles of undeath and to avenge the massacre of Nolderan. To find a way to make all of this *better*.

But I know I'll never find that.

I step over the fallen lion knocker and head through the doors. Zephyr unwinds himself from my shoulders and glides into the hallway, his left wing slightly crooked from where it was crushed under the weight of a heavy planter. Though I applied Blood Balm to his wound last night, it will take a few more treatments until it's fully healed.

I stop before the small table lying helplessly in the hallway. "*Ventrez*," I mutter, though it's a waste of my magic. Wind swirls from my fingers and blows the round table back onto its legs. But the spell does nothing for the smashed vase and torn lace cloth. The entire manor is in disarray. Even my mother's paintings haven't escaped the destruction. The one to my right, a depiction of pastel petalled roses amid an emerald field, has three scratches carved into the canvas. A ghoul must have clawed at it.

I scan across the rest of the devastated hallway, my chest tightening with grief. I don't know why I came back. Only misery can be found here.

As if to answer, my belly growls.

Food.

My body seems to be doing the thinking rather than my head.

I can't remember the last time I ate. It feels a lifetime since I did. I don't know how I will stomach anything, but I need every ounce of strength for the path ahead.

I head to our kitchen. It's large and would have plenty of room for servants but we never hired any, not even before my mother died. Our magic was always enough to make even the most tedious of tasks a breeze. We only kept faerie dragons to tend to our gardens and to ensure the enchanted brooms and dusters maintained their magic.

Like the rest of the manor, the kitchen is torn apart. Plates are smashed against the marble tiles, as are crystalline goblets. Mahogany doors hang limply from their hinges, shelves are severed in half, and drawers are pulled from their counters. Hopefully, enough plates and utensils will be usable. Though I've yet to determine the state of our pantry.

The Void Prince leans against the kitchen's door, his arms folded across his chest. "Do you want something to eat?" I force out, the words tasting like vinegar in my mouth. While I have no wish to be pleasant to the creature which mocked the slaughter of my people, this demon is my weapon and I must ensure my weapon is well-maintained.

"Eat?" His slender nose wrinkles. "Why would I eat any food sullied by your mortal hands?"

I draw in a deep breath and smother the spark of indignation before it can explode. "Do you require any sustenance at all, demon? Water?"

"I require nothing, mortal. Though I do have a taste for souls, particularly those formed from pure aether." His crimson eyes flicker over to the faerie dragon beside me.

Zephyr whimpers and cowers behind my skirts.

"You will not touch my faerie dragon," I hiss. "That is a command."

The Void Prince scoffs.

I extend my arm to Zephyr. "Let's see if we can find you a big bag of aether crystals in the pantry."

Though he crawls up my arm and perches on my shoulder, wariness remains in his amaranthine eyes.

I start to the door, but the Void Prince doesn't so much as twitch, let alone move out of my way. I step carefully around him, trying not to brush against him or the dark aura exuding from him.

When we reach the pantry, I find I can breathe easier without the Void Prince and his darkness clogging my throat. Out of habit, I reach for the switch on the wall, but without the Aether Tower's power, the crystalline sconces don't flicker on.

With a sigh, I hold out my fingers and let magic bubble at their tips. "*Iluminos.*" An orb of dazzling light radiates out, and I send it upward.

The pantry isn't as damaged as the rest of the manor, though a few shelves are broken. It isn't as full as I hoped, but at least none of the food looks as if the undead have bitten into it.

I set Zephyr on the nearest counter and rummage around for ingredients which will make a half decent meal. After all that has happened, it feels wrong to do something as normal as searching my pantry for food. I stare down at the onion clenched in my fist, its brittle skin cracking in my grasp, but then my starved body pushes me onward until I find sausages and potatoes. The large sacks of aether crystals in the far corner are also untouched, and I drag one to the center of the pantry. When I have everything I need, I murmur *ventrez* and conjure a breeze to blow everything up to the kitchen.

The Void Prince is where I left him, his arms folded and his expression loathsome.

I set the food and the sack onto the marble countertops and find two ceramic bowls for Zephyr. I fill one with a large scoop of aether crystals and another with water by using the spell *aquis*. He drifts over to them and clears all the crystals long before I've finished peeling my potatoes with a sharp wind spell, so I refill the bowl with a second helping of aether crystals. He takes a little longer to finish that one and soon floats back over to me, curling up on the nearby worktop and closing his eyes.

The Void Prince remains plastered to the door as I cook, his spiteful glare burning into my back. I ignore him and concentrate on using fire magic to keep the stove at the right heat.

When I finish boiling my potatoes and frying my onions and sausages, I find an unbroken plate to serve everything on and head into our dining room. Zephyr darts right after me, not wanting to be left alone with a murderous demon. The Void Prince peels himself from the doorway and follows me, though he keeps his distance.

Inside the dining room, many chairs are knocked over and the embroidered golden rug beneath the long table is folded back. The silk curtains are torn, and one window is smashed. I set my plate on the table and turn to the chairs.

"*Ventrez,*" I say, blowing them upright. I leave the carpet as it is.

I take a seat at the table and Zephyr perches beside me. The Void Prince takes the chair across from mine.

I stare down at the hearty serving of food on my plate. The warm smell wafts up into my nose. At first my mouth waters, but then nausea crashes into me. I hesitate before picking up my silver knife and fork, hoping the sudden bout of sickness will disappear. But it doesn't, even when my stomach growls. My body and mind are at odds with each other.

I take my first bite. The boiled potatoes taste like cardboard. As do the onions. I try the sausages last and wish I hadn't when I gag and cough. I take a big gulp of water to hide my reaction. I can't tell whether the Void Prince notices. His attention remains on the wall behind me, and his fingers rap incessantly on the arm of his chair.

Tap.

Tap.

Tap.

"Stop that," I snap.

"Stop what?"

"The tapping. It's annoying."

The Void Prince seethes, but his chains force him to do as I say and he ceases his tapping. "I hope you choke on your food."

I ignore him and try the sausages again, but soon realize it's useless. All I can see is Mrs. Baxter—the kind baker of *Flour Power*—gnawing on someone's severed arm.

I don't finish even a quarter of my meal, though my stomach remains hollow. I lay my knife and fork on the plate of unfinished food. The Void Prince doesn't comment on my lack of appetite when I push the plate away and lean back.

My gaze falls to my left wrist. A bandage made from scraps of my pearlescent dress is wrapped around it, concealing the mark of dark magic lurking beneath: a tracking spell. The dull ache seeps through my skin, making my arm weigh as heavy as stone.

I can't remove the bandage. If I do, Arluin will see me and enter my mind. But neither can I keep it on forever.

I hold out my wrist to the Void Prince. "A tracking spell was cast on me."

"I know. I sensed it the moment you summoned me here."

"Can you remove it?"

Slyness glints in his eyes. "Of course."

"How?" Whatever delights this demon can only involve my suffering.

He smiles. "I would merely need to divest you of your wrist."

I snap back my wrist and clasp it to my chest. "Absolutely not. Do you have another way which doesn't require the severing of my hand? Answer me truthfully, demon."

"I do not."

"Is there nothing at all that can free me from this spell?"

"Light magic. But in case you didn't notice, I am rather lacking in it."

I sigh. It seems keeping my wrist bandaged is my only option for now. "What about using the mark to our benefit? Is there a way to use it to pinpoint the caster's location?"

"No."

"Is that the truth?"

"It is."

"I thought you were a Void Prince, one of the most powerful demons of the Abyss. Yet it seems you don't know any useful spells."

"Send me back if you're having second thoughts."

"Not a chance," I say, drawing out every syllable to make my words abundantly clear. "But I find it hard to believe the so-called mighty Prince of Pride has no way of finding one man."

The Void Prince stares at me.

"Tell me, demon, do you know a spell which can locate the necromancer I seek?"

"Perhaps."

I lean over the table and narrow my eyes at him. "You will answer my question clearly. Yes, or no?"

His brow creases as he fights against the compulsion of my command, but there is no resisting. "Yes," he snarls with all the disdain in the world.

"Excellent. You will cast this spell."

"I cannot."

"Why not?" I grip the edge of the table, my fingers digging deep enough into the wood to leave imprints. "Tell me."

Each command causes the Void Prince's crimson eyes to burn with greater fury. "The spell requires an item."

"What item?"

"An object which belonged to them. I require traces of the person's soul to cast the spell."

"How recently must it have belonged to them?" I ask, thinking of Arluin's dusty robes hanging in the long vacant Harstall manor.

"A few months. After that, any traces will have faded."

I press my lips together. There goes my idea of using Arluin's old clothes. "Are there no alternatives?"

"No."

I sigh and run my hand down my neck. If there's no way of tracking Arluin, how will I find him?

My fingers snag on the delicate chain hanging around my neck. I lift the locket and roll the silver heart between my fingers. Until now, I forgot I was wearing it.

"What about an object enchanted with their magic?" I ask. "Even if it's been a few years?"

"It depends how much magic remains."

"What if the spell is active?"

"Then it's possible."

"Perfect." I sweep aside the long strands of my hair and unclasp the heart-shaped locket. "You will use this." I slide the necklace to the Void Prince.

"The spell will destroy the locket."

All I want is to see it burn. And if this treacherous item can further my path to vengeance, all the better. "That won't be a problem. You will cast this spell and locate the man whose magic resides inside this locket."

The Void Prince closes his eyes and inhales slowly. The locket bursts into obsidian flames. Dark plumes of smoke seep out. The demon reopens his eyes, and the haze sharpens, forming an image of a town with narrow streets and waves rolling in the distance. Arluin and his necromancers ride through the town, and the crowd parts to avoid being trampled.

The demon waves his hand, and the dark flames extinguish. Nothing remains of the locket. My only regret is I didn't obliterate it with my own flames.

"Where was that?" I demand.

"Lenris Port."

"That's east of here, isn't it? Along Tirith's western coast?"

"Indeed."

We magi can only teleport to locations we've previously visited, and I've unfortunately never been to Lenris Port. In fact, I've never once set foot off Nolderan's island, which means travel won't be easy. But maybe the Void Prince has visited Lenris Port. "Have you been there? Can you teleport us across?"

"No."

"Why not?"

"Do they not teach you anything in the Arcanium? It seems magi education has declined even more so over this past millennium."

"What are you talking about?"

"Teleportation only works with aether. As a demon, I cannot wield any magic except that of darkness. You do understand how teleportation works and why it can only be cast with aether, don't you? I would hope the magi taught you that much."

"Of course I know how teleportation works," I snap. "Aether flows in ley lines through Imyria, and this allows us to teleport. Light and dark magic exist only in the atmosphere since they originate from the Heavens and the Abyss." I'm not sure why I bother explaining myself; I don't care what the demon thinks of me. "But if teleportation can't be cast with dark magic, how do necromancers conjure portals?"

"I suppose you mean Death Gates, which don't require ley lines. A caster must be at both ends to tear a tunnel through the fabric of time and space. They also require a sacrifice at both ends, though a soul-gem is sufficient. It isn't dissimilar to the ritual you used to drag me here."

"I see." I lean on my elbow and rest my chin in my palm as I think. If we can't teleport to Lenris Port, we need another way of reaching it. Maybe some ships will be left in the harbor.

I drum my fingers on the table. I know where Arluin is, and I might have a way to reach him. Now all that remains is destroying him.

"I read that every Void Prince commands their own legions. How many demons serve you?"

"A hundred thousand."

I almost fall off my chair. A hundred thousand demons lie at his beck and call? Arluin and his necromancers won't stand a chance, even if they can raise the dead.

"Then we will find these necromancers and unleash your legions of demons upon them."

The Void Prince laughs.

"What?"

"Do you have a hundred thousand soul-gems?"

"No—"

"Are you willing to sacrifice an entire kingdom and use their souls to summon my demons?"

"Of course not!"

"Then those thousands of demons will remain in the Abyss."

"There must be another way."

"One soul, one demon. That is the price which must be paid. Unless you are willing to tear down the veil separating Imyria from the Abyss and unleash my brethren upon every mortal dwelling here?"

"Fine." I slump back into my chair. "We'll have to hope you alone are enough to defeat Arluin."

"One of me is more than enough to destroy a necromancer too big for his boots."

All I can hope is that his arrogance isn't misplaced and that I haven't sacrificed my soul for nothing.

"Very well," I say, rising from my seat. "We'll leave shortly. First, I have a few matters to attend to."

CHAPTER 3

AFTER CLEARING AWAY MY PLATE, I head upstairs. Zephyr follows me, while the Void Prince remains in the dining room.

The first thing I notice when I step into my room are the violet robes draped over the back of my armchair. This is the uniform all Magi of Nolderan wear to distinguish our rank. I don't know whether I deserve to wear them after everything I've done—whether I deserve to call myself a Mage of Nolderan—but I pull the robes from my armchair all the same.

Peeling off the bloodied and sweat-covered remains of my tattered dress takes me a short lifetime, and with every touch of the fabric, I relive the horrors of last night.

Once I'm free from the sullied silk, I turn to the golden full-length mirror in the corner of my room. My skin is marred with countless scratches and bruises, but it's the crimson line across my neck which captures my attention.

I reach up and run my fingers across the wound. The scab is coarse and painful to touch. It's the memories it stirs which hurt the most. In my reflection, I see Arluin beside me as he presses his dagger to my neck. As he drags it across my flesh. My father's shouts ring through my ears.

I can't bear looking at the bloody mark for a moment longer. I need it gone. I need *him* gone.

I tear myself away from the mirror and haul the violet robes over my head. I leave the buttons at the top undone and pace over to the counter beside my bed and retrieve the silver tin lying on it.

The ointment inside appears to be made from thousands of crushed rubies. I slather a thick layer across my neck, and the Blood Balm seeps into my skin. Aside from the tingling, I can hardly tell it's there. If only the ointment wasn't transparent and concealed the wound. I could use an illusion to hide the mark, but my strength is limited, and though I loathe seeing the wound, it would be a waste of magic. At least my robes will cover it.

I hurriedly button my collar, and most of the wound disappears beneath the violet fabric. With some luck, the Blood Balm will work quickly and not even the faintest trace of the injury will remain.

My attention snags on the rags around my wrist. The mark beneath is hidden, though the cloth does nothing to rid me of the wrongness crawling over my skin. If only there were a way of healing that, too.

I perch beside Zephyr, who lies curled up on the end of my bed, and dip my fingers into the Blood Balm. I go to rub it across his injured wing, but he shrinks away.

"It's only Blood Balm for your wound."

Zephyr doesn't inch closer. He looks up with an accusatory look in his bright, jewel-like eyes.

"I know you must hate me for what I've done, but what choice did I have? Arluin defeated my father so easily, and I don't possess even a fraction of his power. Without the Void Prince, I'll never stand a chance."

Zephyr only stares at me.

"He took everything from me, and he's still out there with his army of undead. There's no knowing what he will do next. Who else he will hurt. And he has my father. I can't let him be violated like this. He would never forgive me if he knew what I've let Arluin do to him."

My faerie dragon tilts his head, considering my words.

"As for the Void Prince, I promise he won't hurt you. He's bound to my will and must obey my every command. You're safe."

I reach out for him again. "Now let me rub some Blood Balm onto that wing. You're the only one I have left now, so I need you to be okay."

This time Zephyr doesn't move away from me and lets me apply a thick coat of Blood Balm to his injured wing. When I'm done, I screw the lid back on the tin and pause, peering down at the small container. I can see my distorted reflection in the metallic surface and the dark circles hanging from my eyes.

"And . . ." I whisper, not looking up as I speak. "And I hope in time, you can forgive me for the choices I've made."

Zephyr stays silent. He doesn't so much as growl. I know he's still furious with me.

And maybe he's right to be. I broke all the Arcanium's teachings by using dark magic to summon the Void Prince—I even forfeited my soul—and I don't know whether the demon will be enough to destroy Arluin, his necromancers, and all his undead. Maybe I've made a terrible mistake, but what else could I have done?

I haul myself from my bed and return the Blood Balm to the topmost drawer of my counter. I'm not sure why I bother tidying it away. Soon I'll be leaving, and this might be the last time I ever enter my room.

That thought hits me like a blow to the gut.

When I'm gone, what will happen to Nolderan? To my manor? Our home has been in the Ashbourne family for over a thousand years, as long as Nolderan has stood. What of my mother's paintings and the crystalline goblets that have been passed down generation after generation?

I cover my face with my palms, not wanting Zephyr to see my anguish.

Step by step, I led Nolderan to its destruction. My short-sightedness—my stupidity—caused all this. Why should I be allowed to live when someone as innocent as Eliya isn't?

Thick, hot tears swell. I bite them back with so much force it dizzies me.

I can't cry.

I can't break.

Through blurry eyes, I turn to the lonely city stretching out beyond my window. The cobalt rooftops merge into undulating waves.

I step forward and press my palm against the glass. It feels like a sheet of ice, but I don't pull away. I stand there transfixed, imagining it being torn apart by looters. I can't allow Nolderan to succumb to such a fate, but neither can I stay. Not when Arluin is out there, unpunished, and with Father's corpse under his thrall.

But I must do something for Nolderan. After all it has suffered because of me, it deserves that much.

I turn to the crystalline staff resting against my armchair, and the seeds of a plan take root.

Father used his staff to deactivate the Aether Tower, so the two must be linked. The only problem is I don't know how to activate it. In all my twenty-one years, I've never once seen the tower switched off. Maybe Father alone wouldn't have the strength to turn it on and would have needed all three Archmagi.

I'm not sure I'll be strong enough to reactivate the Aether Tower, but I must try. If I'm successful, power will spread across the city and all the enchantments will return, and my manor and the Arcanium will be protected. And maybe I can use its energy to activate more powerful defenses.

The best place to find such information is Father's office. I can't be certain I'll find the answers I seek, but I don't know where else will be better to look than there. I've never once set foot inside the Grandmage's office, and all I know is it's on the highest floor of the Aether Tower and Father used to spend much time inside it. I may find nothing, but I have to look before leaving Nolderan.

The plan now concrete in my mind, I retrieve the staff from my armchair.

"Wait here," I say to Zephyr. "I'll be back soon."

He lifts his head, his azure scales glinting in the morning sunlight pouring in through my window. His tail flicks out, making his disconcertion apparent.

"I won't be long."

His sharp gaze doesn't relent.

"We can't leave Nolderan to looters," I explain. "I'm going to see if I can activate the Aether Tower."

Zephyr drifts up from my bed and over to me, perching on my shoulder.

Since he's still annoyed at me for summoning the Void Prince, I don't shoo him away. Besides, there's a part of me which can't bear to be without him for even a few moments. As I told him, he's all I have.

"All right then," I say with a shake of my head. "I guess you're coming with me." Zephyr nestles on my shoulders, curling around them.

I clutch Father's staff. Magic buzzes beneath my fingers.

Closing my eyes, I draw aether from the surrounding air. My power needs recharging after all I've endured these past few days, but Father's staff acts as an amplifier, and my body is brimming with magic sooner than I can draw my next breath.

My thoughts turn to the Aether Tower, where so many awful things happened, and I begin painting the most detailed image as I can in my mind. Brushstroke by brushstroke, the tower becomes more real until I can feel the sting of its winds whipping across my cheeks.

When the image is alive in my mind, I release my magic.

"*Laxus.*"

A cloud of pale light washes over Zephyr and me. The spell seizes us, and my room vanishes. Then we're slipping through a void where neither time nor space exists, where we're as light as air. I wonder whether it's how Zephyr feels while flying.

Then the emptiness is gone. Magic pierces the darkness and sketches the Aether Tower in increasing detail until I once more feel the weight of gravity.

Winds howl and slam into me, threatening to shove me over the edge and into the dizzying wave of cobalt roofs below. On Monday, I threw myself from the tower to complete my first Mage Trial—the Trial of Heart—which required a demonstration of the faith and courage necessary to become a mage. Now it's Sunday. Not even a week has passed, and yet my entire world has changed.

I banish my thoughts, cleaving through the fog descending on my mind, and focus on what I came here to do. Cool stone kisses the soles of my feet as I pace across the platform. My toes feel like ice, but I push aside the feeling. It's not worth using my magic to ignite an inner flame and warm myself. Besides, I already feel numb all over, so the chill is easy to ignore.

I reach the center of the platform and stop where the enormous orb of aether should be thundering overhead. Despite the howling wind, it's too silent—too still—up here. Like the city below.

I don't stay much longer before heading down the winding staircase.

With the tower turned off, the crystalline sconces lining the stone walls are useless. The light filtering in through the narrow opening dims, shrouding my path in shadows.

A few steps later, I almost slip and grab the metallic handrail to steady myself. When I climbed these stairs for the Trial of Heart, I could see all the way down to the bottom, thanks to the violet light radiating from the sconces. The glittering floor at the base of the tower was so distant it appeared nothing more than a speck of magenta.

Deciding not to take my chances, I hold out my hand. "*Iluminos.*" I'd say avoiding falling to my death is reason enough to use my magic.

The conjured orb is bright enough to illuminate the first few steps beneath me. We continue down the tower's spiraling staircase, spinning faster and faster until we reach the top floor.

I step through the arched entrance. The corridor curves around the staircase, forming a perfect loop. Every floor is like this, aside from the lowest. That one is an empty crystalline floor with the staircase beginning at its center.

Father's office sits halfway around the looping corridor. The doors stand as tall and proud as Grandmage Telric Ashbourne did. They're crafted from aether crystals and shine with violet light. Like the Vault's innermost chambers, their magic is contained in their crystalline body, and they remain warded despite the Aether Tower being turned off.

"*Aseros*," I say, resting Father's staff against the crystalline doors.

At my command, their surface ripples and they swing open. I stride through and Zephyr swoops down from my shoulder and perches on Father's desk. It's made from mahogany with curved legs which look too thin to hold the weight of all the books scattered across the top. The desk is as Father left it, books wide open and arranged haphazardly.

I glance at the nearest book. Father's handwriting is scrawled across the pages. I can't tell what it says since his writing is intelligible—and that's being generous—but it appears to be some sort of log. My chest tightens. Unable to look at his handwriting for a moment longer, I hurriedly close the book.

But it does little to free my chest from the chains of grief. Wherever I look inside this room, I can't escape his presence.

I pace toward the large western-facing windows. Through them I have a clear view of Nolderan's cliffs and the sea beyond.

For a moment, I'm transfixed by the rise and fall of the waves. All I can see in their lull is Father. Arluin breaking him and raising his corpse.

Does even a shred of Father's soul remain within him? Is he at all aware of the fate he has succumbed to?

I pull away from the waves. I can't keep spiraling down into these dark thoughts. If they claim me, I'll never be able to scramble out of that bottomless pit. I must think only of my purpose and keep moving forward.

I head to the bookshelves lining the walls. They're made from mahogany like the desk and are curved to fit the unusual shape of the room.

A variety of books are featured on Father's shelves: biographies of famous magi like Grandmage Delmont Blackwood and Alward Ashbourne—the founder of Nolderan and an ancestor of mine who invented the spell *ignir'alas*, respectively; crusty scrolls containing detailed maps of every street in Nolderan; journals kept by long dead Grandmagi and Archmagi; and tomes on advanced spells I'll never master but take with me, anyway. I wave my hand over the three books I choose and murmur *evanest*, storing them in my internal aether. Since the books are heavy, I'm unable to carry any more. An experienced mage like Father could store ten, though. Maybe more.

Finally, after my search is starting to feel pointless and Zephyr appears to have drifted to sleep, I find the book I seek. It has a burgundy cover, and gold flourishes decorate the hardened leather. I lay it on Father's desk and peel back the cover. Clouds of dust billow out, and I cough as I waft them away.

The Defensive Systems of Nolderan is written on the first page in blotchy ink. I scan across the pages in search of anything I can use. There are diagrams detailing how to activate the turrets lining Nolderan's walls by the docks. They can fire beams of aether to blast enemy ships from miles away and repel naval invasions. There are also similar wards for the Upper City, designed either to secure the most important part of Nolderan if the Lower City is taken or to stop a civil war in case the non-magical population turns against us. To my knowledge, it never has, but I've read about a few street protests taking place centuries ago. Like most other wards and enchantments through the city, these are powered by the Aether Tower.

I also read that a thousand years ago, when the Lich Lord attacked, Nolderan was the only land his legions could not invade. This mechanism, combined with the defensive turrets lining the city's walls, prevented the undead from reaching our shores.

If only we didn't rely so heavily on the Aether Tower. That is the city's sole weakness, and Arluin exploited it.

At the end of the book, I find the mechanics of the tower itself. These pages are filled with maps showing the aether network from turret to turret across the city.

My earlier guess was correct. Father's staff is linked to the Aether Tower, and that's why Arluin needed him to deactivate it. The spell-word required to activate it is *incipiret*, the opposite of *terminir*, which Father used to turn it off. There's no mention of how many magi are needed or how much magic is required. The book only talks of the tower being the Grandmage's responsibility, but I'm not the Grandmage of Nolderan. I'm just his daughter.

Will it work? The book doesn't explicitly state one must be the Grandmage, and there's no one else to cast this spell. Surely the Aether Tower will recognize that?

I close the book and clutch it to my chest. Then I reach for Father's staff and start to the door.

Zephyr opens an eye and flutters up from the desk. I scan over Father's office one last time before shutting the crystalline doors behind us.

Each step is heavy as I march up the spiraling staircase. Dread weighs on my stomach like an anchor. What if I'm not powerful enough to cast this spell? What if I must leave Nolderan exposed to looters who will desecrate our church and our ancient library?

I reach the top and step out into the violent winds. I suck in a breath and take in the vastness of the lonely and broken and dead city. I won't allow vultures to descend on it. I will bury it with aether. If I fail to cast this spell, I'd sooner swallow it with fire than let it be further defiled by evil.

I halt at the center, directly below where the enormous orb of aether should be humming, and set the book down at my feet.

The first step is to conjure an aether crystal to act as the orb's core, so I raise Father's staff and follow the book's instructions.

"*Crysanthius*," I say, pouring as much magic into the spell as I can, while leaving enough for the activation.

The resulting crystal isn't as large as I intend, only the size of my fist, but it'll suffice.

Ventrez is my next spell, and the conjured wind rolls forth, blowing the crystal up to the orb's stone frame. It hovers there, suspended in mid-air. Before it can descend, I clasp Father's staff and call out: "*Incipiret.*"

The crystal explodes. Magic radiates out, filling the emptiness. It takes the shape of an orb, spreading further. My heart skips a beat.

It's working.

But before the magic reaches the stone frame, it starts to retreat. The power falters.

My heart plummets. I used so much power for this spell, and I don't have enough left for another attempt.

I squeeze my eyes shut and draw on the dregs of my power, emptying myself bit by bit. I channel all my power into Father's staff, and a beam of violet light transfers my magic into the orb. The energy stops retreating. But it doesn't expand.

Just a little more . . .

I fight the tide and force it back. The orb reaches its stone frame, but by the time it fills the tower, I've drained myself of so much magic.

The Aether Tower's orb roars overhead. I double over and clutch my knees, gasping for air and hardly able to believe I've succeeded.

I stay hunched over for a while, slowly regaining my strength. While I've depleted myself of magic, there are two more spells I must cast. First, I must activate the wards surrounding the Upper City so that no looters can disturb the Arcanium or our cathedral. Then I must teleport home or be forced to walk down each and every one of the Aether Tower's steps—a thought which helps to squeeze a little more power from my blood. Hopefully Father's staff will amplify it enough.

I crouch and flick through the book until I find the pages filled with protective barriers. The sketches show Nolderan's island surrounded in a bubble, and the paragraphs explain that the required spell-word is in fact *muriz*, a defensive spell I've used to shield myself countless times. The only difference is that this spell is far more powerful, fueled by the Aether Tower itself, so I only need a little of my own magic to cast it.

"*Muriz!*" I cry, thrusting the staff into the air.

Aether blasts up into the orb. Violet light washes over the city and solidifies into a crystalline wall. The protective bubble encases the entire island, even the cliffs. It blocks out most of the sun's rays, and the light which penetrates the barrier is stained with aether. The white walls comprising many of Nolderan's buildings appear lilac.

According to the book, the shield will last for as long as the Aether Tower remains active. Since I have the Grandmage's staff, no one can turn it off. And the tower won't run out of aether, since it draws on the magic running deep within the earth through ley lines.

"Time to go home," I say, beckoning Zephyr.

When he's perching on my shoulder once more, I raise Father's staff and call *laxus* to teleport us back.

CHAPTER 4

NOW THE AETHER TOWER IS reactivated, every enchantment in the city has returned, including those around my manor. Even I can't teleport through the gates' enchantment, so I target my spell outside them.

Zephyr and I materialize outside my manor, and the gilded gates stand as strong as they did before Nolderan's destruction. The same can't be said for the broken gardens.

I stare at the lion crest fixed to the gates and lift my chin. "Reyna Ashbourne."

The gates swing open at my command, and I continue through to my manor.

I don't bother checking whether the Void Prince is in the dining room and head upstairs. Thanks to the dark magic tethering us together, I can sense he's close and hasn't wandered off.

In my room, I find an enchanted leather satchel from the bottom of a drawer and search for everything I need for my journey: potions, clothes, the three books from Father's office, cloaks, boots, and gold. After laying them all out on my bed, I go downstairs to look for dried food and other non-perishables. I also grab a handful of aether crystals while I'm down there and take them upstairs with me.

I set the crystals onto my bed, and Zephyr eyes them greedily, so I scoop up a handful and hold them out for him to gobble up. I don't let him eat all of them, though, and keep some for myself.

Teleporting back and forth and activating the Aether Tower drained the last of my strength. The quickest way to replenish my magic is by swallowing aether crystals, but it's strongly discouraged by the Arcanium. If we misjudge how much we consume, it might be too much for our bodies to contain and cause us to implode, but it's a risk I'm willing to take. Unless I eat these crystals, I'll have no magic to pack my things. The satchel is enchanted, but the magic imbued within only prevents spells from unraveling. I must condense my belongings into orbs of aether so everything fits. I plan to take very few crystals, and I can't sense even a drop of aether in my blood right now. The risk is slight.

I lift a few crystals to my lips, and they instantly melt on my tongue, fizzling and crackling in my mouth. They taste sweeter than moon-blossom wine, which is imbued with aether, so it's no wonder Zephyr is addicted to them. Luckily faerie dragons are evolved to withstand high quantities of aether and aren't at risk of accidentally combusting.

It's hard to resist scooping up another handful, but I have enough magic flowing through my veins and I don't want to take another chance with the crystals.

I hold up a spare pair of boots and cover them in aether. "*Coligos.*" An orb of brilliant light devours them, and I squeeze until it's small enough for me to slip inside my satchel. Then I repeat the process for every item I've laid out on my bed, some bundled together for ease, and by the time I'm done, my satchel is crammed with dozens of humming orbs. It's a struggle to buckle it shut. I hope I'll have enough supplies for my journey, since I don't know how long it will take for me to reach Arluin. And destroy him.

The one item I'm unable to store inside my enchanted satchel is Father's staff. It's too powerful to compress into an orb. Since I've already placed the three books from Father's office inside my satchel,

I store it inside my internal aether with the spell *evanest*. With it contained in my blood, a heaviness washes over me. At least it's less cumbersome than carrying it in my hands.

I slip the satchel's leather strap over my shoulder and turn to the door.

Growing up, I imagined leaving home and exploring the world many times, but I never imagined it would be because of the destruction of my city.

I force myself to leave my room and motion for Zephyr to follow. I don't look back once as I shut the door behind me.

My steps are heavy as I descend the staircase. Every thud of my boots rings through my ears. I cling to the banister, my fingers digging into the wood.

It's too soon that I reach the bottom.

I don't let myself linger in the ruins of my hallway and continue to the dining room where the Void Prince waits.

He hasn't moved since I left him. He leans back in his chair, his arms folded across his chest and his foot tapping restlessly against the floor. "I was starting to think you had gotten yourself lost. Or killed."

"I didn't expect you to be so eager to leave, demon."

"The sooner we leave this wretched place," he sneers, peeling himself from his chair, "the sooner you'll die along the way."

"Natharius Thalanor," I say, narrowing my eyes, "you are bound to do everything in your power to keep me alive. And to kill Arluin, the necromancer responsible for Nolderan's fall."

His gaze sharpens as it meets mine. "Even if I'm forced to keep you alive, you mortals are so very fragile and always find a way to die. Disease, drowning, falling—you drop like flies."

"Don't worry about me." I pat my satchel. "I have plenty of potions to ward against disease. And I am more than capable of casting spells to save myself from drowning or falling. It's best not to get your hopes up. You're stuck with me."

"Even if disease, drowning, and falling won't kill you, there are thousands of other ways you mortals can find to die."

"And that's precisely why I ordered one of the most powerful demons in the Abyss to protect me. Really, I've never felt so safe."

The Void Prince glowers at me.

I turn and start out of the dining room. "Now, come along, Void Prince," I call back. "And don't make me issue that as an order."

The Void Prince snarls.

Once outside, I stop at the bottom of the chipped steps and gaze out at my ruined gardens. Long ago, my mother would plant every flower by hand and loved her gardens so very much. After Arluin's father murdered her, I vowed to tend to her flower beds and preserve her memory inside our gardens. But it seems I've failed at that, too.

Maybe one day, if I survive vengeance, I'll restore our gardens to their glory.

I tear my gaze away from the plucked pansies and march to the gilded gates. Zephyr drifts behind, his wings whispering against the wind.

The enchanted gates swing open as we approach and clatter shut once we're on the other side.

I don't look back at my manor. Or the Arcanium, when we pass that. I keep my eyes on the path ahead and pick my way through the debris littering the shattered streets.

If I stop for even a moment, I fear I'll never be able to leave Nolderan.

Soon we reach the Lower City, and the hardest part is over. I'm less familiar with this half of the city and have even less to leave.

Nolderan's docks come into view, and the ocean's brine fills my nose.

It's so quiet here. Until today, I've never seen the docks as anything but bustling. I didn't think Nolderan's harbor was small, but it feels enormous without all the dockhands and sailors and merchants hurrying about their business.

And the stench is worse than I remember. It must come from the barrels of freshly caught fish, which are no longer smelling fresh after being left out all day. At least it isn't Summer, or the stench would be worse.

At the center of the docks, I stop and scan across the vessels anchored here. There are galleons, their enormous masts towering high above, and also little fishing boats bobbing around. Then there are vessels of all sizes in between.

Aside from teleportation, there's only one way off Nolderan, and that's sailing. You could try to swim, but the currents are strong along the channel between us and Talidor's western coast. Unfortunately, my sailing experience is limited to rowing around the coast with Eliya one Summer. I only tried it once and hated it, so I never tried again.

The Void Prince's expression hasn't brightened since we left my manor, but I'm not surprised. He seems to be perpetually in an abysmal mood.

"Do you know how to sail?" I ask.

"No."

"Would you rather swim?"

His jaw tightens. I decide that's a no.

"Let me rephrase that," I say, placing a hand on my hip. "Either you think of a way for us to sail to Lenris Port, or else I will order you to swim me there. The choice is yours, Void Prince."

His nostrils flare. "Choose a ship and let us get on with it."

I return to the ships. One to my right catches my eye. It looks small and fast but sturdy enough it won't fall apart on our way to Lenris Port. A winged lion perches at the front, and its mouth stretches into a ferocious roar. *The Sea Lion* is painted across the bow's arch.

"We'll take that one," I say, pointing at it.

I don't wait to hear his response and stride over to *The Sea Lion*. The plank leading from the pier to the ship's main deck is rickety and wobbles as I ascend. I try not to look down into the water below and ignore the waves surging up to grasp me. Hesitation will make me look weak, and I can't afford to show this demon any weakness.

The Void Prince marches onto the main deck and waves his hand. The plank disintegrates behind him. He flicks his wrist, and the capstan turns. Metal grinds as the anchor hauls itself from the seabed. The sails billow out, freed from the ropes securing them in place, and shadows envelop the ship's hull. The dark magic is so dense it shrouds the surrounding water. Then we're rushing forth, sailing over a pool of black ink.

Nolderan drifts away, growing smaller and smaller. Grief swells in my throat. I bite it back.

There's nothing left here. How can a home be a home when it's missing those you love most?

My resolve is nearly undone when we burst through the aether shield encasing the island. I was so focused on the city behind I didn't realize we were sailing into it. I expected it to offer some resistance, but it's like passing through air. Highly energized air, though. Every inch of my skin tingles with aether, but it makes me feel no more alive.

On the other side, the barrier appears solid, and the silhouette of Nolderan's spires is faint. The island is already so distant, as if I'm stepping into a new world.

One where Nolderan no longer exists.

I don't let myself cry, though my heart weeps bitter, angry tears. I cling to the ship, fearing I'll fall if I let go. And not only because of my grief. There's a reason I never rowed with Eliya again. Every sway of the ship threatens to send my breakfast hurling up—or at least the little I ate. Now I'm grateful I barely touched it.

Zephyr settles onto the ridge beside me and stretches his forelegs, his scales rippling in the noon sun. I'm sure I'm terribly pale, and I wonder if he notices when he gazes up at me with his inquisitive eyes. I flash him a smile, and he must be satisfied with my expression since he lies down, resting his head in his tiny talons, and stares out at the endless blue around us.

Wind blows harder into our sails, and then we're hurling over the waves at an alarming rate. Sea spray splatters across me, soaking my cheeks with salt water, and my hair runs wild behind me, galloping through the breeze. Waves lurch upward, black as night thanks to the Void Prince's dark magic.

"If you fall overboard," he sneers, "I won't save you from drowning."

Seasickness makes snark a challenge. Nonetheless, I peel myself from the ship's side and lean against it, using it to support my weight. "It seems you've already forgotten the nature of our relationship. I only need to give the word, and you'll be unable to help yourself from saving me."

His expression creases into a snarl, and he whirls around. Apparently, the mighty Void Prince has no retort for that. The victory distracts me from seasickness for a short while.

CHAPTER 5

EVEN WITH THE VOID PRINCE'S magic, it takes the rest of the day for us to reach Lenris Port. The demon lets his shadows fade as we near the harbor, and we sail slowly into the port, propelled only by our previous momentum.

I turn to him and frown. "You should do something about your eyes."

He folds his arms across his chest. "There's nothing wrong with my eyes."

"Maybe you think that, but the people of Lenris Port won't. What sort of moon elf has red eyes? You'll draw too much attention."

"None of these peasants will be well acquainted with my kind. How will they know what color my eyes should be?"

"Your kind? Aren't you a demon?"

He glares at me.

"Touchy subject?"

"A subject which is none of your business."

"So, you *are* admitting you're touchy because I pointed out you're not a moon elf?"

"If I'm 'touchy', it is because I was dragged to this accursed world by a mage too pathetic and useless to save her city from a boy necromancer—"

HOLLY ROSE

"Stop." Blood pounds in my ears. I swallow back my fury, and it scalds my throat.

He isn't wrong I was too useless to save my city, but what he doesn't know is that it was far worse than that. I served Nolderan to Arluin on a silver platter. I destroyed my city. But I'll never grant him the satisfaction of knowing the sins which burden my soul.

He tilts his head as he considers my expression, a smirk curling onto his lips. "Touchy subject?"

Every moment I spend with this monster, I discover new depths to my hatred. "I commanded you to stop."

"I did."

"Be silent until I tell you to speak again."

His crimson eyes glint. I can't tell whether it's in delight at my rage or annoyance at the order.

"And while you're busy being quiet, I order you to change your eye color to something more appropriate for a moon elf. They should be iridescent, should they not?"

This time when the Void Prince's jaw tightens, there's no mistaking his emotion for anything but fury.

He raises his hand and covers himself in shadows. When they fade, his crimson eyes are an iridescent hue. I pause, examining the purples and pinks and teals rippling through his eyes and checking no hint of crimson remains. They shine brighter than the Lumarian ambassador I once saw meeting Father. I wonder if this is how Natharius's eyes looked before he became a demon. According to the ancient tome I read, he was a High Enchanter, and an incredibly powerful one at that.

Realizing I'm staring, I turn away and gaze out at the approaching port. There is nothing fascinating about him. He isn't even a real moon elf, and no aether shimmers in his eyes. It's only an illusion.

Neither of us speaks again before we anchor in the harbor. Since the Void Prince's magic puts us at risk of being arrested and marched to Tirith's capital, Lowrick, I use my magic to dock the ship. I whisper *ventrez* and send a gale blowing the capstan in the opposite direction.

The anchor rolls down beneath the waves, and after it plunges into the seabed, the ship feels more stable. But not nearly as stable as dry land.

I use the same spell to furl the ship's sails and then turn and march off the ship—

Except when I reach the edge, there's no plank. The Void Prince disintegrated ours.

"Can you resummon the plank?" I ask, gesturing to where it should be. "Or conjure a new one?"

He shrugs.

Our pier is on the outskirts of the port, and we're a fair way out at sea. None of the nearby ships have anyone onboard, and it's nearly nightfall, so no one will notice a few more shadows. The demon should be fine using his magic—as long as he's quick.

"Well, summon it back then," I say. "Or else you'll have to carry me down to the pier."

He rolls his eyes and waves his hand. The plank emerges from black dust, spanning the side of the ship and down to the pier. I wonder whether his spell is like *evanest* and whether it too has a name in Abyssal, the language of demons and dark magic. Maybe the plank was stored inside the dark magic coursing through his veins (if he even has them), or maybe it was banished to the Abyss. I'm curious, but not nearly curious enough to ask and permit him to speak. Unless he suffers his punishment, he'll continue to taunt me about Nolderan's destruction.

I don't thank him before heading down the plank. I owe him nothing but my hatred.

Zephyr flutters after me and perches on my shoulder. For a moment, I feel rather like a pirate captain striding down from their ship with a parrot on their shoulder. Except mine is a faerie dragon, and I'm also wearing violet magi robes.

Lenris Port is as cold as Nolderan, if not colder. Frost sheens the pier, and I take care not to slip and tumble into the dark waves on either side. The Void Prince would only laugh at my expense before I forced him to pull me out.

A man hurries toward us, his lantern swinging back and forth. With his speed, it's surprising he doesn't slip on the frost.

"Evening, good sirs!" he calls out. I don't bother correcting him, and when he reaches us, he adjusts his spectacles on his nose and squints at me. He straightens and clears his throat. "I beg your pardon, miss. I believe my eyesight must be getting worse."

"It's not a problem." I flash him a quick smile and hope he will step out of our way, but he doesn't.

He cranes his neck as he peers behind us at *The Sea Lion*. "Where's the rest of your crew?"

"It's just the two of us," I say. The man glances between us both, so I gesture to my robes. "I'm a Mage of Nolderan, and he's an Enchanter of Lumaria. What use do we have for a crew?"

"I see," the man replies, dipping his head. "So, did the two of you come to import goods? Or perhaps you're seeking exports to take back to Nolderan?"

"We came to visit."

"In that case, how long do you intend to stay? There is a fee for our port, charged by the day for—"

"We won't be needing the ship again, so you can keep it. Perhaps that will free us of any fees?"

He blinks at me. "How peculiar. Why, that's the second time this week I've had a ship donated to me. Well, not personally to me. Of course I give it to—"

"The second time this week?" I blurt. "Who else has given you a ship?"

The man frowns. "It was yesterday or the day before that a ship anchored here with a crew all wearing black robes. What an odd-looking bunch they were."

"Where did they go? Do you know?"

"They asked for the nearest tavern, so I directed them to *The Laughing Gull*—just over there." He points in the distance to the few buildings overlooking the sea. Light radiates from their windows. "Why do you ask?"

"I'm looking for them." When his curious expression doesn't relent, I add: "One is an old friend, and I owe him a favor."

The man nods, appeased by my answer, and glances at the Void Prince. "Does your companion speak? I've never met a moon elf before and—"

"He isn't well versed in Common."

The Void Prince scowls at me.

"Oh, that is a shame. I've always wondered what Lumaria is like."

"I would stay and translate, but I really must find this old friend of mine." I stride forth, and he thankfully steps aside to let me pass. "Thank you for your help, and I hope you find a use for our ship!"

He raises his hand in acknowledgement as we leave.

The Void Prince's glare burns into the back of my head.

I roll my shoulders in a shrug. "And here I thought you didn't wish to interact with any more mortal scum than necessary."

His glare intensifies.

"Besides, I much prefer you with your mouth shut."

The Laughing Gull is a far cry from Nolderan's finest establishments in the Upper City. The tavern sits along a row of run-down buildings with streaks of algae staining the stone walls. The tiles forming its roof are weathered and some have broken off, though there's no trace of them. The windows are cracked and cloudy, and it's hard to glimpse inside, especially with it being dark.

A gull is painted onto the wooden sign swinging overhead, its beak stretched open and eyes narrowed into a scowl as ferocious as the Void Prince's. It looks more like a screaming gull than a laughing one, and the owners of this tavern could do with a new sign.

The demon's foot taps against the cobblestones. If he could speak, he'd complain I'm wasting time standing here and admiring the shabby tavern. I push open the door, and it creaks, its hinges in dire need of oiling. I don't hold it open for Natharius. Unfortunately, it doesn't swing back into his face.

The inside of the tavern is no better. The floor is filthy, and my boots squelch in thick layers of ale. I pass many tables of rowdy sailors, their clothes full of holes and loose threads. Their raucous laughter thunders through the small building. I head for the counter at the back of the room. A man with grease-stricken stands behind it, pouring ale into a tankard for a patron.

I lean on the counter and watch the barkeep hand the tankard to the customer and collect several copper coins. He turns to the Void Prince and me. "Can I help you?"

"We're looking for a party wearing black robes. I believe they came in here yesterday."

The barkeep eyes my robes. "Might have seen them. Might not. Hard to say with so many folk coming in and out all day."

"I was told they definitely came here. Surely they can't be difficult to remember?"

"What can I say? My mind has a habit of playing up these days. I vaguely recall such a group, but it's hard to say with nothing to jog my memory."

I sigh and unbuckle my satchel and sift through the orbs until I find the one containing my purse. I hold it flat on my palm and murmur: "*Acoligos.*"

The orb expands, and the light fades to reveal my purse. I pull it open and retrieve a single silver coin and place it on the counter. The barkeep's greedy eyes light up, and he picks it up and examines it so closely his bulbous nose touches it. "Ah," he says, depositing it into the pouch secured at his waist, "now that I think about it, I do remember such a group of strange people. Definitely the shady sort, and they insisted on hiring our largest room. It's not small, but it's not large enough for ten. Didn't fancy arguing with them about it, though. Weren't the friendliest looking folk I've ever seen."

"Are they still in town?"

"Afraid not. Heard they took the eastern road out of town this morning."

If they left this morning, they could be anywhere now. Even if we follow the eastern road out of Lenris Port, we have no way of knowing which route they took after that. We need to figure out where their destination is. Perhaps the room they stayed in will hold some clues. If we can discover their destination, maybe we'll be able to follow them.

"Can you show us the room they stayed in last night?" I ask.

"It's available for the night, if you'd like to rent it."

"That's all right, thank you. We'd only like to look."

"How's four silvers?"

"No, no. We just need to see if they left anything in their room."

He holds out his hand. "Four silvers then."

"That's not—" The barkeep's expression hardens, and I cut my words short. Arguing with him will achieve nothing. If I want to look around, I have no choice but to rent the room for the night.

I reluctantly pick out four silvers and hand them to the thieving barkeep. At least I left Nolderan well prepared and filled my purse with all the gold I could find, as well as a few silvers. Since a hundred silvers make one gold coin, I estimate I'd have enough to rent the room for an entire year, but it's a matter of principle. I'm careful not to let him see any of the golden coins inside my purse, or else he'll demand even more for the room.

The barkeep retrieves a ledger from beneath his counter and dips a quill into a pot of ink. "Your name?"

Is it wise to give him my real surname? This is the first time I've left Nolderan, and I've no idea how much the rest of the world knows about us. If they know the Grandmage is—or was—an Ashbourne, will I draw unnecessary attention to myself? And I don't know whether Arluin has any spies lurking here. If I give my true name, he might discover that I'm pursuing him.

"Whiteford," I say instead.

The barkeep nods and scrawls Eliya's surname across the page. "There's also a deposit of two silvers, which will be returned to you in the morning in exchange for the key. The cost of any damage, however, will be deducted from this amount."

It's hard not to scowl as I reach into my purse for a second time. I place two silvers onto the counter with the rest of my coins. Only the gods know whether I'll see my deposit again.

The barkeep swipes the six coins from the counter and puts away his ledger and hands me a key. I take it from him before he can rob me of any more silver.

"Oi, Melaine," he shouts over to a barmaid laughing with a table full of sailors. "Take these two to room six."

The barmaid looks displeased at being forced away from her acquaintances but doesn't argue with her employer. She gestures for us to follow her upstairs. "This way," she says.

The wooden stairs creak as we ascend them and feel far from sturdy. The owner must be too greedy to pay a carpenter to check the rungs. Zephyr at least has the sense to drift behind me, rather than adding extra weight to my shoulders and further unbalancing me.

Thankfully, I make it to the top without falling through the steps and hurry after the barmaid who's already waltzing down the corridor.

"Here's the room," she says, stopping at a door with a metal six nailed onto it. "Make sure you return the key to Darius in the morning."

I assume by Darius, she means the barkeep. She hands me the key, and I take it from her and unlock the door.

While the room is spacious, there's only one bed. The blankets don't look expensive, but at least they aren't moth bitten. Zephyr drifts past me and onto the bed. He pads around before settling down and curling up.

Chests of drawers sit on either side of the bed, and one handle looks like it will fall off if pulled with too much force. Candles perch on top of the drawers, and a fireplace lies along the left wall. The only decorations in here are the plain circular rug lying at the foot of the bed and the mountainous landscape hanging above the fireplace.

"*Ignis*," I say, igniting all the candles. Their warm light illuminates the room.

Natharius remains in the doorway, his eyes narrowed.

It seems I have no choice but to free him from my command of silence, or else he won't be able to tell me if he finds a clue, and he'll certainly revel in that. "You may speak again."

He doesn't and remains by the door, glaring at me. With how murderous his scowl is, I expected him to take full advantage of his freed tongue and start hurling threats at me. I suppose they'll come later.

I scan across the room. If we can find anything the necromancers left behind, the Void Prince can use it in another tracking spell. "Start searching, demon. If you find anything of note—particularly anything belonging to the necromancers—you'll bring it to me at once."

His iridescent eyes simmer. I imagine his true crimson eyes are burning as brightly as wildfire beneath. The tendons in his neck tighten as he battles with the power of my compulsion. But as always, his resistance isn't enough. He drags himself from the doorway and stalks across the room to the chests of drawers, without uttering a single word. Somehow, his silence is more frightening than his insults. Like the calm before a storm.

I turn to the wardrobe on the right and swing open the oaken doors. Must wafts out and burns my nostrils. I exhale sharply through my nose, trying to banish the smell, and reach inside. I feel through the darkness, but my fingers only find dust. The drawers at the foot of the wardrobe are as empty. I sit back on my heels and sigh. When I glance at Natharius, it seems his search isn't faring much better as he tears open empty drawer after empty drawer. But it's not time to admit defeat yet. There are plenty of other places to search. Like under the wardrobe.

I drop to a crouch and press my cheek to the damp floorboards. I can see nothing but darkness through the gap between the wardrobe and the floor, so I draw aether to my fingers and murmur *iluminos* to conjure a radiant orb. It slots through the narrow gap and makes the area as bright as day. Other than dead spiders and their long-forgotten webs, there's nothing under the wardrobe.

I haul myself up and search the bed as thoroughly as I can, hoping to find even a loose thread—though I'm unsure whether that would be enough to fuel the Void Prince's tracking spell. Zephyr growls when I try to lift the bed sheets. I give him a pointed look. "Don't you dare growl at me," I scold. "Not when you aren't even helping us."

He tilts his head, considering my words.

"This search would go a lot faster with an extra pair of hands. Or talons."

Zephyr hesitates for a moment longer before surrendering his spot and fluttering over to the fireplace to search there. His talons claw through the ashy remnants of firewood.

I find nothing in the bed or beneath it, only more dead insects and dust.

I survey my surroundings, wondering if there's somewhere we've missed. But then I notice Zephyr nuzzling something in the rug. Whatever it is, he can't pick it up.

I hurry beside him. He uses his talons to point at a long white thread caught in the rug's fibers.

No, not thread—hair. It's so thick it's no wonder I initially mistook it for thread.

My heart skips a beat. I pry the strand from the rug's grasp and pinch it in my fingers, holding it high to the candlelight.

There was an orcish woman with Heston years ago. I don't remember seeing her two nights ago in Nolderan, but that doesn't mean she wasn't there.

I take it to Natharius, who is unenthusiastically searching a windowsill.

"Can you identify whose this is?" I ask, holding out the strand.

He stares at me.

Fine. He wants to do it like this.

"You will take this and see if you can identify what sort of person it belonged to."

The Void Prince has no choice but to obey the command and take the strand and hold it to his nose. He sniffs it. "Orc. Female. Dark magic."

It seems my guess was correct. "Perfect. Now you will use a tracking spell on it and locate this necromancer."

Begrudgingly, he conjures his shadows and the white strand bursts into obsidian flames. In the dark smoke, rolling hills spread out into an emerald sea. A campfire flickers. Ten silhouettes clad in black robes are gathered around it.

The vision sharpens. I can make out the orcish woman whose hair we used for the spell. She stands next to Arluin and the bald man I saw him speaking with when I hid myself and Eliya's body behind an illusion. The three of them are consulting a map, and Arluin's fingers trail across it, heading east. The path he traces goes through Tirith then across northern Selynis, winding around a forest labeled the Ghost Woods, and finally up to the orcish region of Jektar. His finger stops at a city called Gerazad. I can't hear their conversation; I can only see their lips moving. But it is clear this is their destination. Arluin folds away his map, and the smoke fades, taking the image with it.

Whatever wicked plans Arluin has, they must involve Gerazad. Maybe he intends to destroy it like he destroyed Nolderan. To fuel his army with more corpses.

I must stop him before he can succeed. I must reach Gerazad before he and the necromancers do.

"They're headed for Gerazad," I say.

"What an excellent deduction."

I ignore his jab. This matter is too important to waste time by arguing. "We must reach it first, or intercept and destroy them on the way."

Natharius says nothing.

"How long will it take to reach the city?" I ask.

He remains silent.

"Tell me how long it will take for us to reach Gerazad."

"Two weeks."

That isn't the answer I hoped to hear. We're already two days behind the necromancers. "Are there any faster routes? What if we cut through the Ghost Woods, rather than going around it like they intend?"

"Ten days," he replies, and then by some miracle adds, "perhaps even less."

"Then that's the path we'll take."

He lets out a dark laugh. "If that's what you wish."

"The only thing you find humorous is my doom, so spit it out."

"The Ghost Woods is home to all terrors of the night, feared by many mortals." Zephyr lets out a squeal, and the Void Prince's iridescent eyes glint. "I'm surprised you haven't heard of it."

"We spent more time learning about magic than geography in the Arcanium. Though I do vaguely recall the mention of such a region. Are the stories true or exaggerated?"

"Quite true. The last time I entered the Ghost Woods was over three hundred years ago, and there was all manner of undead there. Some serve their long dead master, while others owe allegiance to no one but themselves."

I swallow. The path Arluin traced was around the Ghost Woods. If even the necromancers have decided to avoid it, the danger must be real and not just one of Natharius's taunts. But if we follow the same path as Arluin, there's no hope of reaching Gerazad first. My only choice is to go through the Ghost Woods and hope this demon is powerful enough to defeat whatever monstrosities lurk inside.

"I don't fear the dead," I say, lifting my chin. "We will pass through the Ghost Woods."

His lip curls. "If that is your decision, then I look forward to your demise."

CHAPTER 6

SINCE THE BARKEEP ROBBED ME of several silvers for the room, I decide to make the most of it and stay the night. We're on a tight schedule and can't afford to waste any time, but my body needs the rest. I haven't slept properly since the night Nolderan fell, and I'm running on low energy. The more strength I have, the faster we'll be able to travel. And I suspect this will be my last night sleeping in a bed for some time.

Zephyr curls up against me, and it's almost like we're back inside my room. That illusion is shattered before it can truly take root. The bed is cold and hard, and the sheets are itchy and unfamiliar. I stare up at the ceiling. The moonlight illuminates the empty room. I'm grateful the Void Prince isn't here to see me tossing and turning. I did offer for him to sleep on the floor—only to be polite—but he wrinkled his nose and said he doesn't require sleep like us mortals. I don't know where he went after that, but I ordered him not to stray too far. Just in case.

The thoughts of Arluin and what lies ahead gnaw on my mind. As do the images of what unfolded on that fatal night. I try to shake away the memories, but they only cling to me. I roll onto my side and hug the lumpy pillow, silent tears streaking my cheeks. Zephyr is too busy snoring to notice. Only the darkness is there to witness the night-mares haunting me.

Eventually, my body drags my mind to sleep. But it isn't a restful one.

In my dreams, I'm standing in a meadow, the sky violet with aether. Threads of darkness taint the light, thin as spider silk. They're so faint I almost missed them at first glance, but they're undeniably there.

"Reyna," says a familiar voice.

I whirl around and find myself face to face with Arluin and his raven hair and gray eyes.

I want to scream. I want to cry. But I can do nothing except stare at him, icy claws squeezing my chest until I can breathe no more.

He has stolen everything from me, and now he steals my dreams too.

When I don't move, he reaches for my cheek, and as his fingers trail over my skin, it feels like spiders are writhing their way up my spine. In the shadows of his eyes, I watch him plunge his dagger through Father's heart.

"I was so scared, Reyna," he whispers. "When our connection was severed, I feared the worst. I searched for you everywhere, but I couldn't find you." He takes my wrist and presses his thumb against the mark branded into my skin. Now in my dreams, the rags have disappeared, leaving the dark eye exposed. The force of his thumb sends pain jolting through me, breaking me from my trance.

"Get off me!" My breaths are labored as air rushes back into my lungs. "Don't touch me!"

"You might hate me now, but given enough time you'll learn to love me again—"

"I'll never love you," I spit. "I'll destroy you."

"Then come and destroy me," he says with a soft smile. "There's no one I'd rather destroy me than you."

I pinch myself hard, willing myself to wake up. If I'm forced to look at him for a moment longer, I fear I'll finally break.

Arluin gazes at the violet sky. "Your soul feels different." He tilts his head, examining the dark strands laced through the aether. "Darker. What have you done?"

"I summoned the means to destroy you," I snarl. This time, when I pinch myself, it's hard enough to wake me up.

The meadow and Arluin dissolve into darkness, and then I'm back in the cold, hard bed with Zephyr.

I bolt up and gasp for air, tearing my fingers through my hair. My left wrist throbs where Arluin grabbed it. I glance down, and maybe it's my imagination but the rags seem to have loosened. I lift my wrist to my mouth and bite down on one end of the makeshift bandage and pull with my free hand to secure it. With how much the mark aches, I fear what I experienced wasn't merely a dream. Maybe it really was Arluin, communicating with me through his spell. The realization makes me feel violated.

I roll back the blankets, slip out of bed, and pad over to the counter where I left my enchanted satchel. I browse through for my bundle of potions and hold the humming orb flat on my palm.

"*Acoligos.*" The orb expands into a small bundle. I rummage around until I find the potion I'm searching for—a glass vial filled with indigo liquid, which is as dark as the midnight sky. This sleeping potion is so powerful even my mind will be unable to resist it. Research from the Arcanium shows those under its influence don't dream. The consequence of it is they don't wake well rested, and its long-term use is discouraged as it can cause dependence on the potion, but this is the only way I can sleep without Arluin haunting my dreams.

I count three vials in the bag. Hopefully, I will have enough to last me until I can remove this tracking spell.

I pull out the cork and drink precisely a third. The entire vial would render me unconscious for up to twenty-four hours. I estimate this will last for approximately eight hours, and even that might be too long.

The potion tastes bitter, but it's far from the worst I've drunk. I return it with the rest of my potions and ointments in my satchel and climb back into bed. Zephyr doesn't stir.

This time when I fall asleep, I don't dream.

It's already dawn when I wake. Sunlight pours in through the moth-bitten curtains. I leap out of bed and yank them aside. The sky is heavy and overcast, but there's no denying it's already late morning.

It's my first day of pursuing Arluin and his necromancers, and I've already slept in. I'm not sure whether it's because of the sleeping potion or my exhausted body, but regardless I must hurry. At this rate, Arluin will reach Gerazad long before we do.

I tear off my nightgown, replace it with my magi robes, and shove my feet into my boots. When I'm changed, I hurry over to Zephyr and nudge him awake. I mustn't be very gentle, since the faerie dragon opens an eye and growls. Either that, or he's even more exhausted than me.

"We need to get going," I say.

He still doesn't stir, so I'm forced to pick him up. With my free hand, I grab my enchanted satchel and hook it over my shoulder. I almost forget the key lying on the mantelpiece and sigh as I shut the door.

Zephyr yawns and wriggles out of my arms as we're going down the stairs, startling me and almost causing me to trip. I glare at him, but he's drifting on ahead and doesn't notice.

I find the Void Prince sitting in the far corner of the tavern. Though it's morning, the sun doesn't reach this part, leaving him cast in shadows. He appears to have conjured himself a cloak, black like the rest of his attire, and the hood is pulled up over his head, covering his silver hair and pointed ears. A mug of ale sits in front of him.

"And here I thought you wanted to leave at dawn," Natharius says as I slide onto the chair opposite him.

Before he left last night, we agreed to leave Lenris Port at dawn. Of course, I shouldn't have expected him to come and wake me up. I roll my shoulders back. I'm don't intend to tell him I took a sleeping potion last night—nor the reason I did.

"And here I thought you didn't like mortal food or drink," I say, pointing to his ale mug.

The demon lifts it by its wooden handle and tilts it toward me. The mug is mostly full. "I never said I didn't like mortal food or drink. Only that I do not require it."

"I didn't take you for being an ale drinker."

"I'm not. And this is easily the worst ale I've drunk in a millennium."

"Then why order it?"

He jabs his finger toward Darius, the greedy barkeep. "I was told to order a drink or leave."

"The mighty Void Prince of Pride allowed himself to be bullied by a barkeep?" I say, leaning over the table and lowering my voice.

His lip curls. "Next time, I'll threaten to feed him to my Void Hounds. Would that be more to your liking?"

I have no retort and can only sit down. The Void Prince smiles triumphantly.

"How did you pay for your drink, anyway?" I ask to interrupt his gloating. "I doubt they'd accept demon currency, whatever that is. Unless you happen to use gold?"

"Gold?" he scoffs. "What use do we demons have for gold?"

"Then what do you use?"

"We pay with blood."

"Blood?" I exclaim.

"Power resides in blood. Did the magi not teach you that?"

"What I mean is it isn't normal to trade with blood. Though I can't say I'm at all surprised. You demons probably drink it."

The Void Prince frowns. "I prefer wine."

I don't know whether to be relieved or disgusted. The fact he knows he prefers wine means he's tried drinking blood at least once. I wonder if it came from a demon or a mortal. Maybe the blood came from a mage like me.

"And if you were wondering," Natharius continues, "I didn't pay for my ale with my blood."

"Then how did you pay for it?"

"I put it on your tab."

I roll my eyes. Of course he did.

After I order something for breakfast and pay for everything, we leave the tavern. The bill is higher than I hoped, especially Natharius's ale. At least I see my deposit of two silvers returned.

We find a stable on the outskirts of town and buy two of their fastest horses. I'm not sure I pay a reasonable price for the horses, since I've never bought any. In fact, I've never ridden one. With Nolderan being a small island, there was no need to learn.

That makes mounting my horse quite the challenge. Natharius slips onto his with regal grace and makes it look easy. I suppose he's had over a thousand years to practice. I also wonder whether Void Princes ride horses in the Abyss, or whether they ride some sort of fire breathing demonic steed.

I try to mimic the same movement and hook my boot through the left stirrup and hoist myself onto the saddle. Unfortunately, I lack Natharius's grace and end up falling in a mound of hay. Thankfully, it's fresh and I don't end up covered in horse poo.

Natharius brings his horse to a halt outside my stable. His dappled mare looks over the door and snorts, looking just as unimpressed. At least Zephyr, who perches on the edge of the water trough, looks concerned for my wellbeing.

"Having some trouble?" Natharius asks.

"Not at all." I push myself onto my feet and try to mount the horse again. This time I'm successful, even if it's far from elegant.

My gelding seems a lot taller now I'm on his back. The hay sways beneath. I reassure myself I've jumped off the Aether Tower twice, which must be at least a thousand times his height, and give his flanks a sharp kick. Apparently it's much harder than I intend, since he bolts through the door and Natharius has to move his horse aside to avoid our collision. I pull and pull on the reins, and eventually my horse halts at the end of the street.

I grimace. Riding will be much harder than I expected.

Natharius trots up to me on his mare. He raises a silvery brow, his eyes glinting with amusement. "You can't ride."

"Of course I can't ride," I snap. "I grew up on a small island."

"Oh dear," he says with mock pity. "It seems all your plans are thwarted by your inability to ride a horse."

I grip the reins and glare at him. My plans will not be ruined by something so trivial.

"You'll ride for us both," I say through clenched teeth. Having to ride with such a loathsome creature is far from ideal, but I will do anything to destroy Arluin and free Father.

The Void Prince heaves out a sigh. "How bothersome."

I go to slide off my saddle, but then realize I'll probably fail at dismounting as well and end up landing facedown on the cobblestones. So, I teleport off my horse.

The sudden burst of aether sends my horse into a frenzy, and he rears up. I barely catch his reins before he gallops down the street. Luckily, he calms down after a few strides. When I look back, Natharius is even more amused.

I storm over to the stables with my horse in tow, and Zephyr follows me, not wanting to be left alone with the Void Prince. Thankfully, the stable master refunds me the silver I paid him when I explain I can't ride. Then I have the humiliating task of walking back to Natharius and extending my hand to him so he can help me up.

The Void Prince hauls me up onto his mare, his slender fingers pressing into my waist, and sets me down in front of him.

He flicks his reins, and then we're off, riding through the streets and out of Lenris Port.

CHAPTER 7

BEYOND LENRIS PORT, THE TERRAIN turns into plains. Our mare's hooves beat against the dirt track, which is wide enough for oxen bearing wagons. We pass plenty of travelers on our way, and they carry an assortment of goods: from grain to spice to silk. Sometimes Zephyr flies behind us, other times he perches on our mare's back, behind Natharius and the saddle.

It doesn't take long before my legs ache. A burning sensation scorches my thighs. If I were to check, I'm sure I'd find my legs severely bruised. And that's only from a few hours of riding. To reach Gerazad, I have at least ten days of this. I can only hope my body will become accustomed to riding long before then.

I'm probably making it all worse by trying to keep still. Mostly because if I fidget, the Void Prince will know how uncomfortable riding makes me and will mock me for it. Or worse yet, he'll start riding erratically to torment me with every bump and sharp turn. Another reason for my stillness is because I wish to touch him as little as possible. The dark magic oozing out of him is so unbearable it makes my skin crawl. At least he doesn't smell awful. I was expecting him to give off the scent of death and destruction, but he smells like charcoal and myrrh.

Soon the road steepens and then we're riding up rolling hills. Rain drizzles down and quickly turns into a heavy downpour. The thick drops splatter across my robes, turning the indigo fabric to an inky shade and making it stick to my skin. My hair clings to the back of my neck with the dampness. A winter wind rolls over us, sharp and bitter. I suppose I should be glad the sky isn't attacking us with hail.

Not once do I complain about our travel conditions. I could conjure an aether shield to shelter us from the rain, but neither Natharius, Zephyr, nor our horse seem bothered by the weather. I don't want to be the only one who can't tolerate a bit of rain.

We stop at late noon, when the heavy clouds are darkening and the sun waning, and let our mare drink from the gentle stream trickling past. The water is almost bursting from the banks from all the rain. Natharius dismounts first and casts me an exasperated look before helping me down. Despite his expression, I consider this to be a major improvement. After all, he helped me without any orders. He doesn't comment on it, and neither do I. He gathers our mare's reins and leads her down to the stream to drink.

I make for the nearby oak and stand beneath its thick canopy of leaves and branches to get a moment's respite from the rain. Zephyr perches on the branch above and gazes down at me with his bright eyes.

While Natharius isn't looking, I rummage around in my enchanted satchel until I find the potion I'm looking for. The vial is cold to the touch, thanks to bright blue liquid inside. Ice Honey is one of the most dangerous potions Nolderan's alchemists manufacture, since drinking too much can freeze your heart. It's also incredibly addictive. The Arcanium recommends only taking a small dose for a few days at a time and to never take it with any other potions, in case there are adverse side effects. I'm not sure whether the sleeping potion has yet left my system, and I'll need to take more tonight if I wish to sleep without Arluin intruding in my dreams, but I don't hesitate to pull out the small wooden cork and take a small sip. What choice do I have? I can barely walk as it is, and once our horse has had sufficient rest, we'll be riding until nightfall.

The potion is cool and sweet as it slips down my throat. I opt to drink a small amount and hope it'll be enough to take the edge off my pain. I return the vial to my satchel before the Void Prince can notice and lean against the oak's trunk, its damp bark pressing into my back.

Zephyr growls above me. It sounds like one of his hungry growls, even though I already fed him this morning before we left the tavern.

I hold out my hand, and aether blooms. "*Crysanthius.*" The magic solidifies. Zephyr swoops down and gobbles up all the crystals faster than I can blink.

When our mare has had her fill of water from the stream, Natharius leads her up the bank and allows her to graze on the grass. I'm not sure how she finds any fresh grass to nibble on, since the ground is so clogged with mud, but she seems to manage. Natharius holds her reins, keeping them slack enough while she grazes, and doesn't tie her up to join me under the shelter of the oak tree. I can't say I mind. Perhaps he wants a break from me as much as I do from him. I watch him from the corner of my eye. The rain seems to hit him and roll straight off, barely touching him at all. Even the rain is repulsed by his murderous aura.

We leave half an hour later, and this time I manage to mount by myself, though Natharius has to steady me before climbing onto the saddle himself. Then we ride across Tirith's plains, our horse's hooves splashing through the muddy puddles. Thanks to the Ice Honey I took, the pain in my leg fades to a dull ache and riding isn't quite as unbearable.

By nightfall, the rain relents. We stop when the sky is pitch black, and the moon is peeking through the thick clouds. Though the drizzle has ceased, the ground is too wet to sleep on, and we venture from the road in search of shelter.

It takes us another hour before we find a cave wedged into the hillside, and we dismount to lead our mare up its narrow slope. The cave overlooks a forest to our left, and we're so high up the treetops stretch on around us like a leafy sea.

Natharius ties our horse near the cave's entrance, and we head inside. It reaches farther than I thought, but it's too dark for me to see how deep it is. The steady drip of water echoes all around.

"*Iluminos.*" I raise my fingers and aether bursts from them. The orb radiates through the cave, making the stone glisten like diamonds. Bats swarm from the very back, and Zephyr ducks behind me as they flap around the cave. I lower the orb until the bats settle down. Aside from them and a few rats, there's nothing else. While I'm fond of neither, it isn't as bad as I feared. I was worrying that there might be a large grizzly sleeping somewhere in here.

I crouch and press my palm to the stone. It's cold, and is made even more so by the constant draft blowing in, but it's better than sleeping in mud. And if we can light a fire, it'll be warm enough. While I can conjure flames with my magic, they'll soon burn out with no fuel and I can't cast the spell while sleeping. The same goes for lighting an internal flame to warm myself.

"We should find some firewood," I say to Natharius, though the campfire will be for my benefit alone. Since demons don't need to eat or sleep, I doubt the cold bothers them.

"Good luck finding any. Everything will be soaked through from the rain."

"I can dry it out. That won't require much magic."

Natharius shrugs.

I head out of the cave and pause at its entrance. Zephyr follows me. With the forest right beneath us, it should be easy enough to find some fallen wood. The main issue will be how many trips it'll take me to bring back enough to build a campfire. Zephyr will be able to bring some as well, but it'll take us a while without Natharius's help.

I glance back to where Natharius leans against a stone wall. "You'll help too."

He says nothing.

"You can either help out of your own will, or I can issue it as a command—though I don't imagine the constant compulsion is pleasant. The choice is yours."

He glares at me but peels himself from the wall and joins us at the cave's entrance. "It's a rather long way down," he says, peering over the edge at the forest beneath. "Especially for your mortal legs."

"Then it's a good job I didn't intend to use my legs." With that, I weave aether into air magic. "*Nimbus*." At my command, the spell expands into a cloud and wraps around my feet. Then I jump off the edge. Zephyr dives after me.

Gravity doesn't take a hold of me, thanks to my flight spell. Instead, I slowly drift down toward the trees and steer my cloud to avoid being speared by sharp branches. When I look up at the cave, Natharius has assumed his demonic form—complete with wings and horns and hooves. His size doesn't change, but he looks every bit as monstrous as when I first summoned him. His draconic wings spread open, and he too leaps off the edge.

He soars through the air, his wings beating back and forth. Though it isn't a competition, I have the sudden urge to fly faster than him and reach the ground first. I urge my cloud to descend quicker, narrowly avoiding the branches as I weave through the thick canopy of treetops. I'm certain the Void Prince is flying faster, too.

But I can't tell who wins, since we both land at what appears to be exactly the same time. And the winner could also very well be Zephyr.

Natharius folds away his wings and, without a word, stalks off through the trees in search of firewood.

I wave my hand to dismiss my cloud and beckon for Zephyr to follow me. "Let's see what we can find."

We begin our search and soon find plenty of branches and logs. Most are muddy and soaked through, but some are a little drier since the rain didn't reach them. Zephyr blows a cloud of aether around his firewood, and they float up through the air with him. I try a similar technique, but extend the cloud around me to also include my branches. It requires more concentration than on the way down here, especially while taking care not to crash the wood into any trees and have it all fall everywhere. And trying to avoid hitting my head isn't easy, either.

Luckily, I make it back to the top without hitting myself or losing all my firewood. I'm the last to return. Both Natharius and Zephyr have deposited their wood at the center of the cave. I blow mine into the same heap and kneel before it as I cast the spell *calida* to dry the wood. Our pile is hefty and it'll take a while to get through, so I touch two branches at a time as I speak the spell-word. My magic instantly evaporates the moisture, and steam fills the cave.

When I'm done, I heap all the firewood together and let flames spark in my fingers. "*Ignis.*" The wood catches fire. It burns at a steady rate, providing enough warmth without burning all at once.

I flip open my satchel and search for the food I bundled up. I don't bother offering Natharius any, but Zephyr comes sniffing for more aether crystals and I indulge him.

"Are you going to stand there all night?" I ask Natharius before biting into a chunk of jerky.

"I will stand where I like," he replies, "and for however long I like."

I shrug. If that's what takes his fancy, so be it.

Natharius stays there for some time, but not all night. By the time I've finished eating, he deigns to grace me with his presence at the campfire.

He doesn't make conversation, and I don't either. He leans back on his elbows and stares into the flickering embers. I wonder what thoughts are currently going through that wicked mind of his. Maybe he entertains himself by thinking of all the awful ways he dreams of torturing me.

I pull out one of the books I found from Father's office and flick through it. Zephyr nestles into the excess fabric of my robes, using it as a makeshift blanket. Remembering I packed one inside my satchel, I sift around for the orb I stored it as and say *acoligos* to expand it to full size.

The blanket is made of violet brocade and is lightly padded. I spread it on the ground beneath us, and Zephyr wastes no time in making himself comfortable. He bites a corner and pulls it over him.

"I have a spare one," I say to Natharius, though I'm not sure what possesses me.

The Void Prince raises his hand and conjures a blanket of his own from the shadows. It matches his tunic perfectly and appears to be from the same black silk with silver thread weaved through.

"Suit yourself," I say.

After that, I spend the rest of the night reading notes on the advanced spells recorded in Father's book until my eyes blur from fatigue. I return it to my satchel and pull out a sleeping potion. The Void Prince is staring into the flickering flames, so silent and still I'd think he's sleeping with his eyes open if I didn't know any better. Since he's so focused on the campfire, it's easy for me to sip the potion and return it to my satchel without him noticing. I sip even less than I did last night, conscious of the Ice Honey flowing through my veins, though I'm not sure if it will be enough to stop me from dreaming.

It turns out it is. I dream a dreamless sleep until dawn.

CHAPTER 8

I WAKE TO AN AGONIZING ache across my legs. The Ice Honey has finally worn off.

For a while, I lie there and stare up at the cave's stone ceiling. But then that proves unbearable, though I'm not even moving, so I push myself upright and end up disturbing Zephyr who's nestled into my side. My muscles scream in protest, but I ignore them and glance around the cave.

Our campfire has burned out, but it mustn't have died long ago since faint plumes of smoke waft upward. Surprisingly, the Void Prince appears to be asleep. He doesn't look comfortable though, and his body is stiff, the silken blanket tucked around him. His arms are even crossed across his chest. It's a wonder he's fallen asleep in such an awkward position.

Except, I'm not sure he really was asleep. His eyes open as soon as I drag myself onto my feet. His eyes are crimson, but he's at least rid himself of his wings and horns.

I frown at him. "You should change your eyes back."

"Good morning to you, too," he snaps.

"All I meant is your glowing red eyes will be problematic if we ride through a town."

"We're not riding through a town now," he retorts.

"Fine. But if we pass through any towns—or go anywhere near them—then you'll change your eyes back. And that's an order."

He glares at me.

I pull out some cheese and crackers to eat for breakfast and use the spell *ventrez* to slice my cheese. I'm not as hungry as I expected to be after enduring an entire day of riding, but I make myself eat enough. When I'm done, I discreetly sip some Ice Honey and apply Blood Balm to Zephyr's wing. It's almost entirely healed, and I might not need to apply any tomorrow. I treat him to a large handful of aether crystals, and our mare watches longingly, so I offer her an apple. Natharius neither drinks nor eats and simply sits there on his blanket, drumming his fingers against his knee until I'm ready to leave.

Then onward we ride, soon finding the eastern road and continuing along it. The landscape flattens, and after a few hours, we ride past a small town in the distance. It's so far away I have to squint to make out the roofs. We don't pass anyone on the road though, and Natharius's eyes remain crimson. We ride long and hard and stop twice throughout the entire day—and that's only so our mare has time to rest. Otherwise, we'd have kept on riding. Our pace is so frantic that later in the afternoon, even Ice Honey isn't enough to keep the pain at bay. Thankfully, it dulls it enough that I can walk.

We ride late into the evening and only stop for the night when the sun has long set. Tonight, we don't find a cave or anywhere else for shelter, but at least it isn't raining. Since we stop in the middle of a forest, the trees keep the howling wind at bay. The only issue is the ground being waterlogged from yesterday's torrential rain. I press my palm to the grass and cast the spell *calida* to drain the excess moisture from the soil. In some places, I accidentally drain too much and the grass shrivels up. The spell requires much concentration and energy, but my body has recovered and my blood is once more plentiful with aether.

When the earth is dry, we build another campfire. As usual Natharius says little, and our silence is filled by the crackling of flames and the hooting of owls. The wind rustles through the leaves high above. I pull out the book I started studying last night and continue reading it.

I must become stronger. I can't rely on the Void Prince in the battle to come. To face Arluin, I must further my knowledge of magic.

One spell which catches my eye is a chain lightning spell called *folmen*. I learned how to manipulate aether into lightning during my third year at the Arcanium, but this is a more advanced version which allows me to summon multiple bolts.

I read the pages over and over, but there's only so much reading I can do. In order to master this spell, I must practice casting it.

I stand and hold out my hand. "*Conparios.*" Magic bursts in my palm, and violet light stretches into the shape of Father's crystalline staff. I step away from the campfire, so my practice doesn't disturb Zephyr, and place the book at my feet. I scan over the instructions again and use the spell *tera'ortis* to raise a ring of stones around myself. They're tall enough to reach my shoulders and will make perfect practice targets.

Raising my staff, I draw on aether, and magic radiates in its crystalline surface. I stare at the stone target directly ahead while keeping the targets on either side in my peripheral vision.

"*Folmen*," I hiss.

Magic surges from the staff in a lightning bolt, striking the stone. The rock absorbs all the energy and there's none left to bounce onto the other targets. I must be faster at splitting the aether before it reaches the first target. Maybe if I power it with more magic, enough will be left after the first strike to create a chain.

I clench my jaw and attempt the spell again. This time, the lightning rips through the air and scars the stone with its intensity. I also succeed in splitting the aether. One bolt strikes the leftmost stone with perfect aim, though it's lacking in power. The other bounces back at me. I have to duck to avoid being electrocuted. The bolt continues out my ring of stones and toward the campfire. It almost strikes Natharius, but he raises his hand and blocks it with shadows. The bolt bounces off as if it were only a pebble, and the spell doesn't tax him in the slightest.

"What a pitiful attempt," he says, snapping his fingers. His shield dissolves into ash. "It appears aim is yet another thing they failed to teach you in the Arcanium."

My face burns. I hate how visible my reaction is, especially knowing how much it will satisfy him to see, but I can't stop the embarrassment from branding my cheeks. I hope it's dark enough he can't see the redness of my face. "Then why don't you grace me with a demonstration?"

He gets to his feet. "If I must." At first I'm surprised he would offer to help me but then again, the Void Prince of Pride would hate to miss an opportunity to show off.

Natharius joins me at the center of the ring and conjures shadows into his hand. I take a few steps back to avoid being struck by his spell.

He requires only a single heartbeat to prepare his spell. His magic bursts into a bolt of dark lightning and strikes the stone target opposite him. Then it bounces off the first target and hits the next. Every target is struck, forming a perfect loop. What makes it all worse is he didn't need to utter a single spell-word, and yet he had full control over his spell.

His lips curl with smugness. "Was that demonstration sufficient?"

I try not to let his arrogance ruffle me and fold my arms across my chest. "I suppose."

"If you require another, I'll be more than willing to oblige."

"I'm sure you would," I scoff. But then I bite my tongue. After all, he was once the High Enchanter of Lumaria, and apparently an incredibly powerful one at that. Perhaps even more so than Father. Even though he now wields dark magic, he will be well acquainted with the manipulation of aether. Maybe I'll even be able to learn a spell or two from him, or maybe he will be able to guide me in mastering the techniques recorded in Father's tome.

If becoming stronger means swallowing my pride, then so be it.

"You'll teach me," I say.

He blinks at me, and I find satisfaction in knowing I've caught him off-guard.

"I suppose you remember how to wield aether from when you were an enchanter?"

He lifts his chin. I take that as a very much insulted yes.

"Then you can teach me some moon elven spells."

"Or perhaps I can teach you more dark magic," he says, his crimson eyes gleaming.

"I'll pass on that one."

"Does dark magic frighten you?"

"I've seen for myself how corruptive it is."

"And yet you used it to summon me."

"That's different."

"How is it?"

"I only used it once. It would take repeated use for me to be affected. As long as I never use it again, the aether in my blood won't fade."

"Is that what you believe? That you could summon a Void Prince from the Abyss and emerge unscathed? Little mage, your soul has already been marked by darkness."

When Arluin invaded my dream, the violet sky in the meadow was laced with shadows. He said my soul felt different and asked what I had done. I thought it was from the darkness binding Natharius to me, but what if my soul has been irreversibly scarred by the summoning? What if it leads me to madness and ruin?

I do my best not to flinch.

"Then that's all the more reason to avoid using it," I reply as stoically as I can.

"Suit yourself," he says with a shrug, "but it is far more efficient to fight darkness with darkness. Shadows feast on aether."

This I know to be true. When we fought Arluin atop the Aether Tower, he was powerful enough to corrupt Father's spells and use them to fuel his own magic. That's why Natharius's words almost tempt me. Or perhaps that's the shadows within me speaking.

"Are you willing to teach me?" I ask after a moment. "Spells involving aether, I mean."

"What choice do I have? If I refuse, you will only force me to do so."

"That's why I asked if you were willing or not."

He heaves out a sigh. "Sit."

I do as he instructs and sit opposite him, cross-legged on the grass.

"Close your eyes." When I do, he takes my hands in his. The shadows wash over us, and the sensation of the grass beneath fades. As does the wind brushing my cheeks. I can't feel myself breathe. My body is a distant memory.

The darkness clears, and I find myself standing in the same meadow as the one from my dream with Arluin. The sky above, which I suppose reflects the aether in my blood, is tinged with darkness like before. At least it hasn't spread.

Thankfully, Arluin is nowhere to be seen. Only my demonic companion. "Where are we?" I ask.

"Inside your soul."

"We're inside my soul because . . .?"

"Because I cannot cast aether in the material plane of existence. Everything here, however, exists only in your mind."

"Then I suppose it's a little like a mind-link spell."

"Perhaps, but the spell is far more powerful and does not require a connection between two individuals."

"What do you mean?"

"One could reach this state of transcendence alone—provided they are powerful enough to cast it. Many skilled enchanters, including myself, use it to master spells which would otherwise take years to practice. How slowly time flows in this state depends on the strength of the one casting it."

Now that he's explained it, I recall reading about such a technique in the Arcanium. But only the most powerful of magi can reach this meditative state. I'm not sure whether Father practiced it, but it would certainly be useful to someone as busy as the Grandmage of Nolderan.

"How slowly would you estimate time to be passing for us now?" I ask.

"At approximately a tenth of the usual speed."

"So, ten hours here would be only one in the physical plane?"

"Indeed. Now, I would recommend we first work on your pitiful aim."

I wrinkle my nose. "There's nothing wrong with my aim. Not usually, anyway. It was only with that spell. I've never tried to cast it before tonight."

Natharius waves his hand. Six obsidian statues surround us. Their silhouettes are humanoid but lack any detail to distinguish what race they're modeled after. "I will demonstrate the spell again, but now with aether." Violet light sparks at his fingers. It's odd to watch the Void Prince draw on aether rather than dark magic. The crimson glow of his eyes fades to the iridescent hue of a moon elf's, and his clothes change to teal robes decorated with magenta thread. Even his hair seems to shine brighter.

I'm so busy examining the changes to his appearance that I forget I'm supposed to be watching his demonstration of the spell. All I notice is aether bursting through the six obsidian targets.

"Your turn," he says.

I give him a nod and focus on the target opposite us. This time when I cast the spell, I'm pleased to note there's nothing wrong with my aim. It lacks the power to go all the way around the circle of targets, but at least the attempt is decent enough Natharius can't mock me for it. He makes me repeat the spell over and over, instructing me to adjust my angle and timing. He also refines the way I pronounce the spell-word *folmen*, forcing me to slowly repeat each syllable after him.

There's no way of sensing time inside this meadow, but I'm sure it takes me a thousand tries before Natharius is satisfied.

"Will I be able to cast the spell in the physical realm as well as I'm able to here?" I ask.

"It might take a few attempts for your body to adapt to the spell, but it won't be too difficult since your mind already knows how to cast it."

"And what would you suggest I learn next?"

"I don't know which spells the magi have already taught you."

"Suggest something, and I'll tell you."

He pauses, and his silvery brows pinch together as he thinks. *"Gladis?"*

I conjure a crystalline sword and hurl it at the nearest target. The sword fractures the obsidian before it shatters and disperses.

"What about *astrombis?*" he asks.

I frown, not recognizing the spell. "Is that the Medeican or Lumarian name?"

"Medeican," he replies.

"Then no, I don't know that one. What does it do?"

"In Lumaria, we have a similar spell called *reiltinnara*, meaning 'star fall.' The spell causes shards of aether to rain on its victim."

"It sounds rather like our blizzard spell, but with aether. I don't see what new advantage this spell will offer me."

"Knowledge alone should be advantageous enough," he replies with the shake of his head. "But the fact this is cast with aether rather than ice means it will be more powerful. Energy is lost when converting aether into the elements, and in this case, it means transferring aether into both water and air. This is why we enchanters favor aether above all else. It is far more efficient."

I don't point out his mention of 'we enchanters.'

"But aether is easily corrupted into dark magic," I say. "As it stands, my blizzard spell will be far more effective against the necromancers. Or perhaps you know a fire equivalent? Fire fares best against dark magic and the undead. And I'm sure I saw a spell of the sort in my father's book."

"Ignir'tempis?"

"That's the one. Do you know how to cast it?"

"Of course," he replies. "I know every spell both Lumaria and Nolderan have ever invented."

"But surely not the ones invented after you became a demon?"

"No, not those."

"What about the flaming wings spell? Do you know that one?"

"You'll have to tell me the Medeican name."

"But then the spell might be activated."

He casts me an exasperated look. "Do you really possess that little control?"

"Well no, but we're taught not to say the names unless we intend to use them. Don't the enchanters encourage a similar approach?"

"Indeed, but only those lacking any skill at all would be required to follow such a ridiculous rule."

I press my lips together. "*Ignir'alas.*" Thankfully, no flames burst from my fingers, proving I do have at least some control over my magic.

It takes an age for him to say: "No, I do not know that one."

"I didn't think you would," I reply. "One of my ancestors, Alvord Ashbourne, invented the spell five hundred years ago."

"A spell invented by the magi can hardly be consequential."

I turn to the nearest obsidian target and call flames to my fingertips. "*Ignir'alas*," I say, spreading the flames into wings and launching them upward. They descend on the target at a furious velocity. The spell is far more effective than the aether sword I conjured and melts half the target. The obsidian rolls down like thick ink.

No one can deny I possess a natural affinity for fire magic.

Natharius hesitates. "A trivial spell," he finally says. "*Ignir'tempis* is more efficient and has a larger radius."

"But wasn't *ignir'tempis* also invented by the Arcanium? I read the Founder of Nolderan developed most elemental magic, since Lumaria cares little for it."

"Perhaps." His nose creases. "Now, I will demonstrate *astrombis*, so you can see how it is cast."

"I'd rather learn *ignir'tempis* first."

"First you will learn *astrombis*, since it is one of the earliest spells taught to enchanters."

"See? I knew it was a basic one."

"All magic requires a solid foundation," he says. "You will learn *astrombis* first."

In the morning, the Void Prince is back to his usual silent self. I wasn't expecting to wake up and find us best friends, but I thought that our civil conversation from last night would have continued.

Apparently not.

We leave shortly after dawn, continuing through the forest. We pass tree after tree and little else. Sometimes we pass a fallen log.

By noon, we leave the woods behind and the terrain turns into gravelly crags. The path narrows until it's too difficult for us to ride, and we're forced to dismount. Natharius marches on ahead, guiding our mare up the steep incline. I trail behind with Zephyr.

The wind becomes more relentless the higher we climb. I keep my head down to stop it from whipping across my face.

There's little shelter up here, but after a few hours we take a break against a nearby cliff face. I'm not sure our mare needs as much of a rest now that both mine and Natharius's weight is off her back, but when the Void Prince stops out of habit, I don't protest. I need the rest myself, especially since my legs are unused to walking after two solid days of riding.

We don't pause for long before resuming our climb. And after what must be another hour, we finally reach the top.

This peak is far from the highest here, and behind I can make out the looming silhouette of a mountain range. Beneath is more woodland, but the landscape gradually changes in a gradient of deep emerald to yellow-green.

Natharius also halts and scans the area. The wind blows his silver hair around him like a storm.

"Where are we now?" I ask.

"The very edge of Tirith. We will enter Northern Selynis by nightfall."

"And we're still on schedule to reach Gerazad before the necromancers?"

He gives the slight inclination of his head and continues on.

I take one last look at Selynis's plains before hurrying after him.

Our path soon takes us downhill, and the incline is as steep as when we were ascending. I almost skid over loose stones but manage to stop myself before crashing into Natharius. In some places, I'm forced to take tiny steps to avoid my boots losing grip, but both the Void Prince and our horse continue down with ease. Zephyr doesn't seem to want to take his chances on my shoulder and opts to flutter down after me. If only I had his wings.

Eventually our path flattens, and we enter another forest. The trees here look no different to the ones before the crags. When the track widens, Natharius mounts our horse again and holds out his hand to help me up. Then we ride on through the trees, our surroundings as riveting as ever.

"What's Lumaria like?" I ask after a while, bored with the endless scenery of leaves and branches and bark.

"Dark," comes Natharius's reply from behind me.

I roll my eyes, though the effort is wasted since he can't see my face. "Of course it's dark. Lumaria is the land of eternal night."

"Then what do you wish to know of it?"

"I don't know . . . Maybe what the cities are like? How about Shalandril? That's the capital, right?"

"Shalandril is made from moonstone, like all Lumarian architecture."

"Moonstone?"

"It is a substance not unlike marble, but far more luminous. It is the aether imbued inside which makes it shine."

"Do the enchanters pour magic into the stone?"

"No, it is found like that naturally," he replies.

"Where are you from in Lumaria?"

"Ithyr."

"What's it like there? And don't say 'dark' again."

"Ruins," he says instead.

"Ruins?" I repeat. "Why? What happened to it?"

"I destroyed it."

I suppose that's one answer. Now he's said it, I remember he bargained his entire kingdom to the Void King. "For power?"

He doesn't answer. Our mare's hooves clomp across the muddy dirt track, and Zephyr's wings beat behind us.

"What about your family?" I ask, though I suspect it might be an insensitive question. Not that he deserves such consideration. He's made worse comments about Nolderan. "What were they like?"

"My family . . . They deserved their fates."

"I take it you didn't see eye to eye then?"

"My mother cared only for her beauty, and my father only cared for his reputation."

"And your siblings? Or were you an only child?"

"I had four," he replies. "Two sisters, and two brothers."

"Older or younger?"

"Older."

"All of them? So, you were the youngest?"

"Indeed."

"I didn't expect you to be the youngest," I say.

"Why not?"

Because he's so ancient and terrifying, I suppose. But I don't tell him that. He would only take it as a compliment, and his arrogance is insufferable enough.

"I just find it hard to imagine."

"It's my turn for a question," he says. "How was Nolderan defeated?"

"By the necromancers."

"How?"

"They deactivated the Aether Tower."

"I'm not blind," he retorts. "My question is how did they deactivate it? Even Kazhul the Lich was unable to overpower Nolderan's Aether Tower, as it is fueled by the cluster of nexuses beneath the island."

"They forced the Grandmage to turn it off," I say through my teeth.

He pauses, considering this for a brief moment. "Why would he be stupid enough to do that?"

Blood hums in my ears at his remark, but I swallow back my rage. I will not let him see how easily his words rile me. "As I said, they left him no choice."

"And why is it the only survivor is a weak little mage?"

"That's none of your business," I snap.

"I ask only to better understand my enemies."

"Don't you mean *my* enemies? Or are you now resigned to your fate?"

He doesn't reply, but I feel the heat of his glare.

"And why don't we carry on talking about why *you* destroyed your city? If you truly were such a powerful High Enchanter, why would you need to sell your soul and the souls of your entire kingdom to the Void King?"

I dare to glance at him. Anger blazes in his crimson eyes. "Mortal," he seethes, "you know not what you speak of—"

An arrow whizzes past us.

It darts so close it almost scrapes Natharius's cheek, but he leans back before it cuts him. Zephyr gives a frightful growl and ducks behind us.

The arrow slams into the nearest tree trunk. Its ivory white head digs into the bark. All of the arrow is made from the same white substance.

My stomach twists.

Bone.

Natharius's jaw tightens. "Goblins."

CHAPTER 9

A FLURRY OF ARROWS RACES for us.

Natharius leaps from our mare in a single, fluid movement and lands as gracefully as a cat. He raises his hands, and dark magic swells. It forms a formidable storm of shadows, and the arrows bounce off it. They race back toward the trees, where they came from.

There are a few cries, but not as many as I'd like to hear.

Another volley is launched from the left. Our horse rears beneath me and charges in the opposite direction. I jump off, but not nearly as elegantly as Natharius. I miss my footing and tumble to the ground. Loose stones graze my hands and dig into my back. But I barely register the pain. Three bone arrows descend on me.

There's no time to roll away.

I thrust out both hands. Aether surges.

"Muriz!"

A shield encases me. Two arrows hit it and fall to the ground. But I'm not fast enough to block the third.

Just as the violet light spreads over my left arm, the third arrow slips through. I lurch away. The arrow misses my shoulder but skims the top of my arm. The sharpened bone tears through my robes and my flesh, cutting deeply enough to draw blood. My focus is shattered, and my shield fizzles out.

I hiss in pain and clasp my injury, my fingers coated in blood. At least it isn't too deep.

I glance down at the fallen arrow. The bone white head is coated in a viscous substance reminding me of tar.

A dozen green figures burst from the bushes. Their skin camouflages with the leaves so perfectly I didn't realize they were there. They are so short they barely reach my waist, and their heads are larger than their sinewy bodies. Their gnarled fingers clutch maces and axes and daggers made from black wood and sharpened bone. I don't want to know whether those ivory blades were carved from beasts or people. A dozen pairs of yellow eyes fix on me and narrow into cat-like slits. They all grin at me, revealing rows of pointed teeth.

Though I've never met a goblin, I've seen plenty of sketches during my time at the Arcanium. They didn't look particularly friendly in those books, but the illustrations failed to depict exactly how horrifying these creatures are. From my studies, I recall they dwell in caves—meaning they've likely been following us since we entered the crags and were waiting for the opportune moment. And the most important fact of all is that their favorite delicacy is unaware travelers.

They may have caught me by surprise, but this is the only blood they'll draw from me. I have no intention of being the centerpiece of their banquet tonight.

The horde of goblins is almost upon me now, their ivory weapons swinging dangerously close. Another barrage of bone arrows launches from the bushes. I dread to think how many of these creatures there are.

"*Laxus!*"

Before they can reach me, I disappear into violet light. Their weapons strike air.

I reappear several paces away, in front of Zephyr. "Stay behind me," I say to him, and he does as I instruct, cowering behind the length of my indigo robes.

Natharius is also surrounded by goblins, far many more than me. His dark magic bats them away as if they were flies but whenever one falls, another springs from the trees to take its place. Even a Void Prince of the Abyss can't defeat all these goblins in one strike. I'm on my own (unless Zephyr counts), but that's fine. I won't rely on him or anyone else any longer. If I can't defeat a mere pack of goblins, how will I ever stand against Arluin and his necromancers and their legions of undead?

Aether radiates from my hands. "*Conparios.*" At my command, Father's crystalline staff emerges from violet light, and I clasp it tightly. Through its touch, all the magic in my blood sings louder.

"*Folmen!*" Aether sparks into lightning and strikes the nearest goblin. Then it splits and bolts across to six more. The first goblin is struck by so much power he's instantly killed, while the others are left momentarily stunned. The highly charged current causes their sparse strands of hair to stand up and frazzle.

But my spell only succeeds at dazing half my attackers. The rest continue toward me at full speed. My retaliation has only made them fiercer. Hungrier.

"*Gelu'vinclair!*"

Frost bursts from my fingers and spreads across the dirt track. Ice spirals up to their knobby knees, shackling them to the ground. They writhe against their frozen bindings, swinging their bone weapons manically. But my frost only holds them tighter. They are at my mercy.

And I intend to show them none.

I raise Father's staff, preparing to cast a spell devastating enough to destroy them all in one strike. But before I can finish it, another round of arrows rushes from the trees.

I alter the spell, redirecting my aether and transferring it into earth magic. Emerald light glows in my palm, and I send it forth. "*Terra!*"

A wall of stone erupts from the earth. Only one arrow is fast enough to make it past, and it lands several paces away from me. The earthen wall continues upward until it reaches the tree tops. Even if the goblin archers try to shoot over it, they will be completely blind.

Ice cracks. I glance back at the goblins caught in my frozen snare. One has freed his leg. He kicks at the frost around his other, and icy shards flake off. Seeing his progress, the rest of the goblins are spurred on. They too begin to break through the ice.

Soon they'll all be free. I must strike now while I have the upper hand.

"*Gelu'tempis!*" I cry, flinging a giant ball of ice high into the air.

Before it reaches the treetops, the ice shatters and a thousand frozen needles rain on the goblins. They cover their enormous heads with their thin arms and double their efforts to free themselves. The shards of ice rip through their lumpy skin, and green blood spurts out. Some are struck by fatal wounds and slump over, their slack bodies held upright by the ice shackling their knees to the ground. They don't twitch. The rest are covered in wounds, but otherwise look only enraged.

I prepare a second spell to take care of the survivors, but Zephyr growls behind me. I whirl around to see him spewing balls of aether at the two goblins behind us. The magic strikes them and leaves them briefly dazed.

If not for Zephyr, they'd have reached me before I realized. But I have no time to thank my faerie dragon. The goblins behind are breaking free from the ice and these two are returning to their senses.

I launch the first spell which comes to mind. Fire, of course. "*Ignira!*"

Since Father's staff allows me to draw more aether than I naturally can, the resulting fireball is enormous. It erupts from my fingers and slams into the two goblins. They shriek but the flames devour them, and the smell of charred flesh wafts through the smoke. I don't wait to watch their ashy remains emerge from the embers. Cracking sounds as the other goblins break from their icy chains. They charge at me, their weapons glinting in the dying sunlight filtering through the trees.

"*Astrombis*," I call, unleashing the spell Natharius taught me. Last night, I was debating the point of learning *astrombis*. It seems I've now discovered the unique advantage it offers: a fast spell with a large enough radius to strike multiple enemies.

A ball of aether launches into the air and rains on the crowd of goblins like falling stars. The violet bolts strike them over and over, and many more goblins collapse. Only a few make it onto their feet.

A shadow looms over me. I glance left to see Natharius assuming his true demonic form. He's tall enough that his obsidian horns skim the treetops. Branches snap as his draconic wings spread out. The crimson markings across the alabaster planes of his torso hum with raw power, and his eyes gleam with the same frightening magic. He strides forth, the ground breaking beneath his hooves. He raises a hand, and a dark iron sword appears from the shadows. The weapon is almost as tall as him.

The goblins are like ants beneath him—even I am. Natharius grins, revealing fangs, and his grin is far more terrifying than the one the goblins offered me.

Natharius lifts his enormous sword, and the goblins have the sense to run. But they don't flee fast enough, and his reach is too great.

His blade comes crashing down. It pierces the ground, tearing apart the earth. The resulting quake is powerful enough to throw me off my feet and causes my stone wall to shatter. Rock rains on me. I shield my head. The large pebbles smack into my arms, but at least it isn't my head.

The few goblins left are also thrown off balance. They also try to shield themselves from the quaking wall, but they're nearer to it than I am and some are far less fortunate. Larger boulders tumble down and crush them.

The barrage ceases. I raise my head.

Natharius yanks out his obsidian sword, and the earth is left scarred by a deep chasm. The ground rumbles again as his blade leaves the earth, but not as viciously as when he struck it.

Three goblins evaded being felled by his sword. They scramble upward and race for the trees, but Natharius doesn't allow them to escape. Dark magic swirls in his left hand, and he unleashes black flames on the goblins. They fall.

The ones near me also try to flee, sprinting through the rubble. Maybe I should let them go, since their surrender is clear. But had our places been reversed, they would have shot me down and eaten me. And I am determined to be as vicious as a Void Prince of the Abyss.

So, I burn them all.

"Ignir'alas!"

Flames surge from my fingers, rising upward and spreading into fiery wings. Then they descend on the fleeing goblins and scorch everything in their wake, including the bushes and the trees. All is charred by my flames. Smoke rises into the treetops, carrying ash with it.

I look back at Natharius and catch him watching, a curious glint in his eyes. When he notices my gaze, he breaks his stare. Shadows wash over him as he returns to his moon elven form. I can't help from smirking. He was lying last night when he called *ignir'alas* a trivial spell. He's too proud and stubborn to admit how powerful it is, especially since it was invented by one of my ancestors.

I turn to Zephyr and examine him carefully, my fingers tracing his wings as I inspect them for any injuries. "Are you hurt?"

He shakes his head, and I help him crawl onto my shoulder. Then I head over to where the Void Prince stands, peering down into the chasm he carved through the earth.

"What is it?" I ask.

He points to the ruins beneath. Goblin blood is smeared across the stone, and the green substance appears luminous in the low light. There are severed limbs and heads, and some of their remains are so pulverized they look like squashed insects.

The old Reyna would have been so disgusted she vomited all over Natharius's shiny leather boots. But I have seen far worse sights since then, and all that disturbs me is my own indifference.

It takes me a moment to realize Natharius is pointing at one goblin in particular. This one is trying to push himself upright, but his limbs are too broken. He's the only one that survived, but half-dead would be a better descriptor.

"So what?" I say. "One goblin survived. What's so fascinating?"

"Have you ever wondered how soul-gems are created?"

"Not really."

He tilts his head, regarding me carefully. "Not really?"

"I mean not at all," I blurt.

"You were willing to use one in order to summon and bind me here, but you have no wish to know how they are created? What will you do if I am banished to the Abyss and you find yourself without another soul-gem to summon me back?"

"If I didn't know better, it sounds like you would want to be summoned back to serve me. Besides, why would you be banished?"

"If I am struck by a mortal wound, I will be returned to the Abyss," Natharius replies with a grin. Though his fangs are now gone, his expression is no less menacing. I suppose he's counting on my refusal to learn dark magic and is enjoying taunting me with it. I've not given much thought until now about what I'll do if Natharius is forced back to the Abyss. I could try to find another soul-gem, though I'm not sure it'll be easy to find someone selling them since dark magic is shunned through all of Imyria. Then again, I think there were a few more soul-gems inside the Vaults beneath the Arcanium. If it comes to that, I can teleport myself back to Nolderan and use another to summon him. Since I have the Grandmage's staff, I should be able to bypass the ward surrounding the island.

I shrug. "I have plenty more soul-gems. Don't worry, you wouldn't miss me for long."

Natharius doesn't rise to my taunt. Shadows surge from his hands and across to the dying goblin. A specter-like form of the goblin ascends into the air, and dark chains wrap around him. I suppose the ghostly being I'm seeing is the goblin's soul.

The shadowy chains tighten around the goblin, shrinking until his soul is condensed into a shard. The stone is mostly ink black, but a few strands of violet and gold run through it. The goblin's soul must be predominantly dark magic.

Natharius gives the chains a sharp pull. They come racing back at him with the soul-gem in tow.

He snatches the glittering shard from the shadows and holds the soul-gem high, admiring its jagged edges. Before I can demand for him to hand it over, he opens his mouth and eats it. He swallows it whole, like a snake devouring its prey. Shadows swirl from his nostrils as he exhales. "How refreshing. Though I doubt it will taste as sweet as your soul." His crimson eyes flicker across to Zephyr. "Or your faerie dragon's."

Zephyr hides behind me.

"I thought you intend to torture my soul," I reply, keeping my tone as indifferent as I can. "Not eat it."

"I'll torture it for a hundred years, perhaps two, and then I'll eat it."

"Charming," I say and turn away. Mostly so he can't see my expression, in case my face betrays my horror. Though we've been through what he intends to do to me a thousand times already, it still unsettles me. Especially after watching him eat a soul.

I hurry down the path, where our horse disappeared. I have no idea if she's there, or whether she was captured by the goblins.

After a few paces, when our horse is still nowhere in sight, I glance back at Natharius. "Can you sense our horse anywhere nearby?" Since he doesn't look ready to answer, I add: "Or else you'll need to carry me all the way to Gerazad."

He halts and inhales deeply. "Not far ahead."

With that knowledge, I double my pace, hoping to reach her before she can flee again. But the world spins around me. Fatigue fills my limbs.

I force myself onward, even when nausea hits me. Our mare's dappled coat emerges through the trees, and I hobble toward her with renewed effort. I stumble on a loose rock, and Zephyr goes flying off my shoulder. He looks up at me. I don't know if the Void Prince notices, but he doesn't comment on my stumble.

My sight blurs. Three identical horses stand ahead of me. I continue on with wobbly knees and manage to reach our mare. She doesn't jolt away from me, and I clasp her saddle, using it to steady myself.

Pain shoots through my temples. I draw in a deep breath and press the back of my hand to my forehead. I'm burning up.

"What's the matter?" Natharius asks. "Dying or something?"

I ignore him and grit my teeth. Then I tackle the saddle.

I manage to get one foot into the stirrup but then my leg gives way, and I lose balance. I fall but barely feel the impact. My entire body is so very numb. I try to push myself upright, but my limbs are too weary.

Natharius peers down at me. "Definitely dying," he purrs. "You look as pale as a corpse."

His voice sounds hollow and echoey. I rub my ears, trying to clear them.

Is it fatigue? Did I somehow use up more magic than I realized while fighting those goblins?

A sudden jolt of pain erupts down my left arm. I glance over at it, and my gaze snags on the tear through my robes where the arrow struck me. I'm no longer bleeding, but the cut has turned black. Then I remember the tar-like substance coating the arrowhead.

Poison.

My heart hammers.

I don't know what poison the goblins used. Maybe it's paralysis, or maybe it's deadly. Since Natharius said I look like I'm dying, maybe it's the latter.

"Healer," I gasp. Forcing out words is becoming increasingly difficult. I don't know how much longer I'll remain conscious. "Take me to a healer. I command you to do everything in your power to save me." My words grow quieter, and I'm not sure whether he hears me over the wind rustling through the trees. But he must, since he lets out a heavy sigh and grabs my waist and hauls me up onto the saddle.

I barely feel him as he climbs on behind me, my senses almost completely dulled by the poison.

The last thing I hear is the sound of hooves beating furiously against the earth. And even that fades into silence as the poison claims me.

CHAPTER 10

"Reyna," Arluin says. I'm back in that meadow beneath a violet sky tinged by darkness: the place Natharius explained is my soul. "You're hurt." His gray eyes fix on the wound running across my arm. The cut is as black as night.

That's right. I was poisoned. And then I fell unconscious. The fact my arm hurts even in this place means I'm alive.

I think.

Arluin holds out his hands. I step back.

"I told you to stay away," I snarl. "I want nothing to do with you."

His brows draw together. "I'm sorry you feel that way."

"You're sorry?" A hysterical laugh escapes me. "You're sorry you took everyone and everything from me?"

He shakes his head. "You don't understand. I made a bargain."

"A bargain?"

"I had to, Reyna," Arluin continues. "Otherwise I'd have never been powerful enough to return to Nolderan. For us to be together. Your father would never have allowed it. I tried to explain, but you wouldn't listen and jumped off—"

"Nothing can ever excuse what you've done," I hiss. "There's nothing more for you to say. I will never forgive you. Not even in ten thousand years."

"Reyna—"

"Save it," I snarl. "*Ignira!*"

A fireball erupts from my fingers, and I banish him from my dreams. All I wish is that he was real, and that I really did destroy him.

Warmth brushes my cheeks. Slowly, I open my eyes. The sunlight is so bright it momentarily blinds me, and I shield my eyes with my hand.

When my vision adjusts, I lower my hand and glance over at the tall window a few feet away from where I lie. Silken curtains flow down either side, swaying back and forth in the gentle breeze. They're pulled open wide enough for sunlight to pierce through into the room.

I push myself upright, and the mountain of pillows behind me supports my weight. Thin sheets cover me and the strange, circular bed which I'm lying on. I roll back the blankets and peer down at what I'm wearing: a silken dress.

Where are my robes? Where is this place?

I scan the room, hoping to find some clues to explain my whereabouts. Zephyr is snuggled up at my feet and doesn't appear disturbed by our current location. If he were, he wouldn't be sleeping so soundly right now. A golden tapestry hangs on the right wall, forming an abstract depiction of dawn, and my enchanted satchel sits on the white cupboard beneath it. The room is too empty for me to piece together where I am. My robes are also nowhere in sight. Neither is the Void Prince.

With a frown, I reach over to my injured arm. My fingers find only smooth skin. I pull my arm closer and inspect it. There's nothing there, not even the faintest of scars to show I was injured.

Natharius must have found me a healer in time. Unless I'm dead and this is Heaven. But that would be nonsense. The Gods only permit their most pious followers into their celestial palaces, if at all. For us magi, the afterlife consists of our souls becoming one with aether. And I'm very much corporeal right now.

I throw aside the blankets and climb out of bed. My footsteps are quiet across the strange, marble floor. Zephyr doesn't lift his head. My

legs are shaky at first, unused to walking, and I wonder how long I've
been unconscious. I make it to the door but as I reach out, it swings
open. I stumble back.

A girl appears, wearing white silk like me, and her dress contrasts
her dark skin. Her eyes shine with golden light, brilliant like the noon
sun. She grips my shoulders and steadies me before I can topple over.

"You're awake?" she says. "I was just coming to check up on you."

Still disoriented and half-asleep, I blink. The girl takes my arm
and guides me back to the circular bed. "Who are you?" I ask as she
pulls the thin blankets over me. "Where am I?"

"You're in Esterra City," she says.

I clutch my temples, trying to remember where that is on a map.
Geography was never my strong suit. "Esterra?"

"Northern Selynis."

"Oh."

"And I'm Yadira, a priestess of this temple."

"We're in a temple?" I ask.

Yadira nods. "You've been here for two days. The High Priestess
of Esterra assigned me to look after you."

"Two days?" I exclaim, my eyes widening with horror. By now,
we should be passing through the Ghost Woods. I need to find
Natharius and leave. At this rate, Arluin and his necromancers will
destroy Gerazad long before we arrive.

"You need to rest," Yadira says when I try to get up. She holds
my shoulder down with surprising strength. Or maybe my body is
that weak. "You nearly died from poison, and you're still afflicted by
dark magic."

"Dark magic?"

She gestures to my wrist. The tattered rags from my ballgown
have been replaced by white silk. I hope the priestesses changed the
bandage quickly enough that Arluin didn't have the chance to glean
my whereabouts. Maybe that's how he knew I was injured when he
appeared in my dream. "Even the High Priestess could not cleanse the
mark," Yadira continues. "She's been looking through even the most

ancient scrolls we have here in the temple, but she hasn't found anything to cure you yet. She said you need to rest until she finds a solution."

My jaw tightens. I want to tell her I must leave, but what excuse can I give? If I tell her the truth about Arluin and his necromancers, she'll send for the High Priestess who will want to ask me questions. That'll waste more precious time.

Yadira dips a cloth into a bowl of water and wrings out the excess. She dabs it across my brow and inspects my now healed injury. Once satisfied, she turns to leave. I grab her wrist before she can escape. "The one who brought me here," I say, "where is he?"

"Don't worry," she replies gently, lifting my fingers from her wrist and freeing herself from my grasp, "you needn't ever worry about him again. The temple has already dealt with him."

"Dealt with him?" I echo, my throat closing around the words. "What do you mean 'dealt with him?'"

"You're safe now. That demon will never again hurt you."

Panic rages through me, heightening my pulse to an alarming rate. Natharius is dead?

The priestess peers at me, examining my expression. She's likely wondering why I'm horrified a demon has been defeated. I must relax. I can't afford to reveal my fear.

Besides, Natharius can't die. At worst, the priestesses will have banished him back to the Abyss. And I've already considered this outcome. If he's truly been defeated, I'll teleport back to Nolderan and find another soul-gem in the Vaults to summon him again. It'll delay us further, and I'd risk dark magic consuming all the aether in my veins by invoking the ritual again, but at least not all hope is lost.

I exhale deeply and allow the tension in my shoulders to slip away. The priestess's confusion disappears, and she seems to interpret my reaction as relief for my safety. She gives me a nod and turns away, leaving me to sleep.

"Zephyr!" I hiss once she's gone. He doesn't reply. I crawl across the bed and prod his azure scales until he wakes. He sleepily blinks at me. "Where's Natharius? Is he alive?"

Thankfully, the faerie dragon nods.

"Do you know where he is?"

He shakes his head.

I sigh and sink into the pillows. At least he's alive, even if I don't yet know what has happened to him and what the priestess meant by him being 'dealt with.' Maybe I can try reaching out to him with a mind-link.

I draw aether into my hands and imagine the Void Prince as vividly as I can. I'm not sure which form he will currently be in, and I don't know whether his appearance will make a difference to my spell. My tutors at the Arcanium never taught me how to forge a mind-link with one who can change their forms. Maybe I ought to go with his demonic form, since I think that's his true appearance. Or is it? After all, he was born a moon elf.

In the end, I settle for his moon elven form since that's what I'm more familiar with.

I paint a portrait of him in my mind, and he becomes more real with each brushstroke. I imagine his silvery hair, as bright as the moon, and the sharp angles of his unyielding face. His crimson eyes burn with wrath, and a hateful smirk writhes on his lips as he laughs at something to do with my demise. I can almost feel the aura of dark magic exuding from him, and a chill crawls over my skin. When he becomes so real that looking at him angers me, I release my spell.

"*Aminex*," I say softly, not wanting the priestess to hear the spell-word and return to my room. I hope she can't sense my use of magic.

"*Little mage*," comes his velvety voice. "*You aren't dead after all.*"

"*If I were dead, you wouldn't be here.*"

I can almost hear his resulting scowl.

"*Are you here in Esterra City?*" I ask.

"*Unfortunately.*"

"*Where?*"

"*In their temple.*"

"So *am* I." I frown, though he can't see it. "*Where exactly are you in here?*"

He pauses. *"The dungeon."*

So, that's what Yadira meant about him being 'dealt with.' *"You're in their dungeon?"* I repeat, my tone incredulous.

"That's what I said," he growls. *"Are you deaf or just stupid?"*

I consider telling him deafness can't possibly have anything to do with it since he's thinking his thoughts into my mind, but I have far more pressing matters than provoking the demon. *"And why is it that the Void Prince of Pride has been captured by a bunch of priestesses? If you can be defeated so easily, perhaps I should be concerned by your ability to defeat the necromancers."*

"It was because of your orders," he snarls. *"If not for your command to do everything in my power to find a healer and keep you alive, I wouldn't have been captured. I couldn't kill them, or else they wouldn't have been able to heal you."*

After seeing how he shattered the earth to defeat a pack of goblins, I'm inclined to believe him. If he'd fought the priestesses with his full strength, this temple would likely be in ruins. *"Perhaps,"* I say, and I can feel his wrath through our mind-link at that single word. *"Now, if I were to give you the order to do everything in your power to break out of the dungeons, would you be able to do so?"*

"No." He only sounds angrier by the suggestion.

"Why not?"

"They've subdued my power with manacles forged from their wretched light."

"Then it appears you're in need of saving, Void Prince. Unless you'd prefer to spend all of eternity caged beneath a temple?"

"Be quick about it," he snaps. *"The sooner I escape these bindings, the sooner I can unleash my wrath upon these light worshipping imbeciles."*

"I think not."

"Why not?" he seethes.

"Because I'm disinclined to order the execution of those who have saved my life."

"You do not understand the nature of these zealous fools. Showing them mercy will prove a costly mistake."

"*Sit tight and be good,*" I say. "*I'll come and fetch you soon.*"
He only snarls at me.

CHAPTER 11

SHORTLY AFTER SPEAKING TO NATHARIUS via a mind-link, I end up falling asleep. It isn't what I intend, but it seems my body has other plans and is determined to make a full recovery. And I suppose Yadira is right. I did almost die from the goblins' poison.

I'm not sure how long I sleep, but it must be a few hours since I feel much better when I wake. I sit up and notice my robes are laid neatly at the end of the bed and Zephyr has nestled into them.

I try to shake him off, but he doesn't budge. After much wriggling, they come free from beneath him, and he rolls onto his side and continues to snore.

I hold up my robes and inspect them. They look brand new. Even the tear in the left arm has vanished, and the indigo material is free of all dirt and bloodstains. It seems the Priestesses of Selynis are as skilled at mending fabric as flesh.

I hastily change out of my silk dress, worried Yadira will reappear and insist I return to bed. But I can't afford to sleep for a moment longer. We've already wasted enough time. I must find Natharius and leave Esterra City as soon as possible.

"Don't tell me you're still sleeping," I say to Zephyr when I'm back in my magi robes. He doesn't so much as open an eye in response.

"All right, suit yourself. I'm leaving as soon as I find the Void Prince. If you don't wake up, you'll have to stay here and learn to eat light magic instead of aether crystals."

Since he springs up at that, I'm certain he was only pretending to be asleep.

I march across the room, and Zephyr flutters behind me. When I reach the door, I pause and glance back at him.

"Do you know where the dungeons are?" I whisper.

He tilts his head to either side as he thinks.

"You have an idea, but you're not entirely sure?"

Zephyr nods.

"Right, we'll have to look around the temple." I glance across at the window beside the bed. The sun is dipping low in the horizon and casts crimson streaks across the sky. "If the priestesses ask where we're going, we'll tell them we're hungry and are looking for food."

I slip through the door and step out into the corridor and pause, holding my breath. Nerves hum through me, even when I repeat the excuse I suggested to Zephyr.

Luckily, there are no priestesses here. The corridor is empty. Pale rock stretches out either side of us. The temple must be built from limestone.

"Which way?" I hiss to Zephyr.

He darts right and I follow, keeping my pace brisk, but not too quick that it'll raise suspicion. On the next corner, we pass two priestesses but they're too busy in their conversations to notice us. Like Yadira, their eyes are golden and they're wrapped in white silk. The hems are decorated by an ornate gold trim and matching circlets halo their heads. Sandals peek out from beneath their flowing skirts and the leather bands look like little cages around their toes.

As we head deeper into the temple's complex, the corridors become busier. We pass maids, as well as priestesses. At least I think they're maids. They wear simple muslin dresses, and their brows are without circlets. Their eyes also aren't golden, showing their lack of light magic, and they brush the white floors with their brooms. I suppose they could also be priestesses in training.

Some smile at me, and I return the gesture before hurrying after Zephyr. With how busy this part of the temple is, I don't know how we'll break into the dungeons and free Natharius. Hopefully we'll find the dungeons on the other end of the temple, where there will be few priestesses around.

"Oh, there you are!"

I glance back to see Yadira hurrying toward me.

I groan inwardly. It seems we'll have to wait for another opportunity to search the temple. Maybe it'll be better to search later tonight when most of the priestesses are asleep.

"Zephyr!" I hiss and hold my arm out to him. He scrambles onto my shoulder.

I smile as brightly as I can at the priestess, hoping my expression won't betray my nerves.

"I was about to head over to your room and check up on you," Yadira says.

"I slept for a bit after you left, but I'm feeling much better now. Someone put my robes at the end of the bed for me. Were you the one who cleaned them?"

Yadira shakes her head. "We gave your robes to some of the initiates to practice on." She gestures to a few of the younger priestesses passing us, and they look barely old enough to be in their teens. Their eyes are golden, but they don't shine as brightly as Yadira's and the other more experienced priestesses.

"Oh, well thank you. They did a marvelous job. I didn't realize you're able to heal clothes, as well as people."

"Mending clothes requires less strength, and the techniques aren't dissimilar. We also send our younger priestesses out into the city to help the poor repair their clothes, as well as minor ailments."

"I see," I say, and then my stomach growls. Though it's embarrassingly loud, at least I don't have to tell Yadira my excuse as to why I'm wandering through the temple instead of staying in bed.

She laughs. "You must be hungry. We'll all be eating in the hall soon, and the High Priestess will be there, too. She wishes to talk to you."

"She does?"

Yadira nods but doesn't elaborate. I frown as she leads me through the temple. What does the High Priestess want to talk to me about? Yadira said the High Priestess was the one who healed me and is trying to find a way to cure Arluin's tracking spell, so maybe she wants to discuss that. Or maybe she wants to question me about Natharius.

We soon reach the tall doors leading to the hall. The walls slope into a high, arched ceiling, and long wooden tables run either side of the room, filled by dozens of priestesses. At the end lies a single table on a dais. The priestess sitting there wears a circlet far grander than the others, and her robes are so heavily decorated by golden thread, it's as if she's wearing a tapestry.

Yadira bows her head when we arrive at her table. I decide it's best to do the same. "High Priestess," she says, gesturing to me, "here's the mage you healed."

The High Priestess scans over me. She's a tall, lithe woman with tiny creases marking her brow and beneath her eyes. When her observation is complete, her lips draw out into a smile, and her golden eyes radiate with warmth. They shine brighter than any other priestess I've seen so far. She must have spent decades practicing light magic.

"You're finally awake," the High Priestess says. Her voice carries through the hall and all the priestesses fall silent.

I dip my head. "It is only thanks to your kindness that I am."

Her smile grows. "It is through the Mother's Light that I healed you. You owe Her your thanks."

I'm not sure how to respond to that, and whether I ought to drop to my knees and offer the Mother Goddess a prayer of gratitude. In the end, I opt to keep my head lowered and hope it appears respectful enough.

"What is your name, mage?" the High Priestess asks.

"Reyna."

Should I tell her exactly who I am, the Grandmage's daughter? Despite what Natharius claimed, the priestesses seem gentle and healed me without any request of payment. Light and dark magic are natural enemies, so maybe the priestesses would help me if I explain I'm hunting a cult of necromancers. But for that same reason, I must be careful to avoid them discovering my association with Natharius.

If the High Priestess notices my inner debate, she doesn't comment on it. "It is a pleasure to meet you, Reyna. I am High Priestess Ahelin, and I welcome you to Esterra City." She gestures to the long table on our left. "Do sit. You must be hungry."

Yadira guides me to my seat and the priestesses slide down the bench to make room for us. Zephyr crawls off my shoulder and sits between Yadira and me.

Maids hurry into the hall with arms full of stew and bread. They leave the dishes at the ends of the tables, and the priestesses distribute the food. Yadira slides me a bowl and spoon and then hands me a thick slice of bread. I can't tell what's in the stew, but the steam wafting up into my nose smells so good. I'm dying to eat but none of the priestesses pick up their spoons, so I force myself to wait.

The High Priestess stands. Every priestess falls silent and looks at her. She bows her head and clasps her hands together, and the priestesses all mimic her gesture. Not wanting to be seen as rude, I do the same. Even Zephyr has the sense to dip his head.

Ahelin starts to speak in a language I don't recognize at first but suspect to be Old Selynian. I don't understand any of the words, but I remember reading that the Priestesses of Selynis use their old language for prayer rather than Common. At various intervals, the High Priestess pauses and the priestesses echo her lines. Yadira repeats them next to me, but the syllables are too strange for my ears to decipher, so I'm forced to keep my head lowered and do my best to ignore the ravishing smell of my stew and my growling stomach.

Finally, Ahelin reaches the end of her prayer and returns to her seat. The priestesses lift their heads and begin to eat. I don't hesitate to pick up my spoon and dig in.

"It has been long since the Magi visited our city," the High Priestess says to me, resting her spoon against the delicate rim of her bowl. "What brings you to Esterra?"

I make a show of chewing my bread to gain me a few extra moments of thinking time. What should I tell her?

Think, Reyna. Think. What reason would a mage have to come to Esterra City?

Would it be easier to tell her the truth than to risk being caught out on my lies?

I swallow my bread and say, "I'm searching for someone."

She raises a brow. "Who are you searching for? Perhaps I can help."

"Um," I say, this time having no bread to excuse my hesitation. I'm such a horrible liar. "A group of necromancers."

I'll tell her the truth. Then I'll deal with breaking Natharius out of here. One hurdle at a time.

Ahelin's expression darkens. "Necromancers?"

I give her a small nod. "They . . . they destroyed Nolderan."

"Impossible!" the High Priestess exclaims, her golden eyes widening. The entire hall quietens, and the priestesses listen to our conversation. Yadira goes rigid beside me.

Maybe I should have left that part out. I pray I'm not making a mistake by telling the priestesses the truth.

I draw in a deep breath. "Six nights ago, this cult of necromancers stormed Nolderan with their army of undead and razed the city. Only I escaped the massacre." I hope she doesn't ask me how I survived. I have little desire to explain why I'm the reason my city was destroyed.

Murmurs ripple through the hall. The High Priestess narrows her eyes as she examines my expression. I can't tell whether she believes me, but it doesn't matter. It's the truth.

"If this is true," she says after a moment, more to herself than anyone else, "then we all face a grave threat. Perhaps the demon which attacked you is under their command."

"Maybe," I say, keeping my face as straight as I can.

Now she looks fully convinced of my words. "That means they could be close. We will search the city for them and double our security."

My stomach sinks. This is going to make escaping with Natharius much more difficult. "I believe they are heading for Gerazad."

"Gerazad?" Ahelin says with a frown. "What do they want with the orcs? Are they working with them, or do the necromancers intend to destroy them?"

That's a possibility I didn't consider. What if Arluin is working with the orcs?

"I don't know," I say.

Ahelin drums her fingers on the edge of her table as she thinks. "The Grand Priestess must be informed immediately. Perhaps she has foreseen such things." With that, she rises and steps down from her platform, leaving her untouched stew. "Yadira, show Reyna back to her room when she has finished. We will discuss these matters in the morning. Tonight, I will ensure our city is secure."

CHAPTER 12

AFTER DINNER, YADIRA INSISTS ON escorting me back to my room, and though I'm certain I can find my own way there, the priestess will hear none of it. When we're back in my room, she fusses over me and my injured arm, though I tell her I'm already much better after many days of rest and all her hard work. It takes much persuasion before I convince her I'll be fine without her supervision, and then she finally leaves Zephyr and me to rest.

But I've no intention of resting. Not when I have a Void Prince to rescue.

I don't begin my search right away and remain in bed for a long while, tucked up in all my blankets like Yadira left me, waiting for the right moment to begin my rescue attempt. Every time I consider throwing aside my blankets and getting to work, footsteps pace outside my room. I knit my fingers and continue to wait, doing my best to stay patient and not to torment myself with thoughts of Arluin and his necromancers and how they may have already reached Gerazad by now.

It takes several hours for the temple to fall silent, and by then I've almost drifted asleep. Moonlight pours in through the window, casting the rug in a silver tint.

Purple light glows in my fingers as I gather aether. I cup my hands and squeeze the magic into a ball. When the light is compressed into a small orb, I press it to the center of my brow and close my eyes. Aether hums. I focus all my thoughts on the orb.

"*Oculus.*"

Light bursts, transferring my mind into the orb.

With the Mind's Eye spell cast, I see the surrounding room while my eyes are closed. Through the orb, I gaze at where my body sits cross-legged on the bed. Zephyr snores loudly beside me and doesn't seem at all disturbed by my magic. When I first learned this spell in the Arcanium, seeing myself from outside my body was unnerving, even more so than *speculus*, a cloning spell. *Oculus* isn't spell I've often used since mastering it during my studies, and I was half expecting for it to fail on my first attempt.

I direct the orb forth, and it crackles like lightning as it drifts through the air. When it reaches the door, I focus all my thoughts on forcing it through the wood. With enough effort, the orb slips through the door.

The corridor is empty, like I hoped. I follow it left, gliding weightlessly through the temple, and cling to the shadows. When footsteps sound, I dart behind the nearest wall or pillar and hope the approaching priestesses don't glimpse the pale glow of my orb. While they can detect dark magic with ease, they're less sensitive to aether. That's what I read in the Arcanium, anyway. As long as I keep out of their sight, they shouldn't be able to detect my spell.

The orb moves faster than I ever could through the temple, allowing me to map my way through the complex. I explore every turn, making a mental note of how all the corridors connect so I can retrace my steps later.

I find the dungeons deep in the heart of the temple, at the end of a long, spiraling staircase.

Torches lit with golden light perch along the walls. In Nolderan, we instead use aether crystals and fuel them with the Aether Tower's power. As far as I'm aware, the Priestesses of Selynis haven't constructed a system to enable ordinary citizens to use light magic and to enable enchantments to continue running without needing maintenance. I doubt they've ever tried creating such a thing, since they see their magic as Goddess-given and too sacred for the uninitiated to harness. All of this means these torches, few though they are, must be manually lit by priestesses, and I can't tell how long it'll be before they run out of magic and someone comes down here to light them again. There are also few hiding places.

That means I need to be quick.

I race down the long, dark corridor, and the air hums with aether as my orb pierces it. At the end, I come to a heavy iron door and force the orb through. It requires much more concentration to penetrate than the wooden door in my room. Once I'm through I emerge to a few steps, and the orb drifts down them. The dungeons are small, containing only three cells in total. Either Esterra has even less crime than Nolderan, or these cells are reserved for powerful enemies while regular criminals are contained elsewhere in the city.

I find Natharius in the farthest cell, manacles binding his wrists. Runes are carved into their shiny surface, emitting golden light.

He sits away from me with his back pressed against the metal bars. I drift closer so I can see him, and the glow of my orb reaches into his cell. His eyes open.

His lip curls. It's more a sneer than a smile. "Now you know where I am, hurry and release me from this wretched place." He holds up his golden manacles, and the chain linking them together clinks with the motion.

Unfortunately, I can't speak while in this orb form and therefore can't offer him one of my finest retorts. I consider delaying to annoy him, but that would waste precious time. Even annoying the Void Prince isn't worth that.

"*Terminir*," I say in my mind. I vaguely have the sensation of my lips moving, but the feeling is distant. The orb bursts, and my entire world is shattered by violet light. The brilliant rays last for only a brief moment before fading to darkness.

I once more feel the weight of my limbs and the softness of the silk blankets beneath me. When I open my eyes, I see my room through my own eyes rather than through the orb.

I don't hesitate before scrambling from where I sit, and I reach over to Zephyr and shake him twice. He opens an eye but otherwise doesn't move.

"I found where they're holding Natharius. We need to hurry and get him out of there."

Zephyr closes his eye again and has the audacity to snore. Loudly. I roll my eyes. Not even my exceptionally lazy faerie dragon can fall asleep that quickly.

"I know, I know," I say, emphasizing my words with a heavy sigh. "I'd much rather leave him to rot in this temple, too."

His head perks up, and he peers up at me with an extra shiny glint in his amethystine eyes.

"But we can't."

He snorts in protest.

"Look, we've already been through this. I can't defeat Arluin and his necromancers and all his countless legions of undead alone."

He puffs out his chest.

"Yes, yes. Of course. I mean, *we* can't defeat him alone."

Zephyr doesn't look convinced by that, but I don't bother debating his ability to destroy Arluin by spitting little balls of aether at him.

"Anyway, we need the Void Prince and his dark magic, even as loathsome as he is, so we can't leave him here."

Zephyr lets out a heavy exhalation that sounds like a sigh, makes a show of stretching his forelegs, and then reluctantly hops off the bed.

I grab my satchel from the counter, check the room for any other belongings, and when I find nothing else, hurry to the door.

I turn the handle slowly and am even more cautious while pushing open the door. I wait with bated breath and tilt my head to either side as I listen for any footsteps, no matter how distant. Even after waiting several minutes, I hear nothing except the gentle rhythm of Zephyr's wings as they keep him midair and my own racing heart. I take the plunge and dart from the safety of my room. Zephyr follows me as closely as if he were my shadow.

While I have the sudden urge to sprint all the way to the dungeons, doing so will only raise more suspicion if I'm found wandering the temple in the dead of night, and I force myself to walk. I keep my pace brisk, but not too brisk that my footsteps are loud. And I'm grateful for that decision because halfway to the dungeons, we pass a priestess tending to the torches along the walls. I hear her strides long before she comes into view and have plenty of time to grab Zephyr and pull him around the nearest corner. I mutter *alucinatus*, blanketing us with aether and creating an illusion to blend us in with the wall. The priestess takes her time lighting all the torches, and I grimace as she lights the torch beside us. She comes within touching distance when passing between the torches on either side of us, and I try to calm the frantic rush of my pulse, half expecting her to turn and glare at us and demand to know what we're doing sneaking around the temple. Thankfully she doesn't, and it seems my illusion is flawless. Eventually she finishes lighting the torches here and disappears down the corridor and into the darkness. I hope no other priestesses are lighting the torches leading to the dungeons, since there's nowhere to hide down there. My illusions can only be cast while standing still, so they will be of no use. Perhaps Natharius will know a more advanced version of the spell which doesn't require being stationary. I'll have to remember to ask him another time when I'm not busy trying to break him out of a temple.

I wait a few minutes to be certain the priestess is long gone, and then end my illusion spell and hurry toward the dungeon. My pace is slower than before, fearing we'll run into more priestesses.

Luckily, we make it to the dungeons without being caught.

I race down the spiraling staircase, taking two at once. Now I'm not traveling in a ball of magic, I take thrice the time to reach the bottom, and when I do, I realize how dark it is down here without the pale glow of magic. I hold out my fingers and cast the spell *iluminos*, conjuring an orb which emits brilliant light.

The iron door is as I left it, with no sign of priestesses. Before I could penetrate it while in an orb form, whereas now I will have to unlock the door. And I don't have the key.

A critical oversight.

I groan. As if all my plans are now in jeopardy because of a mere key.

I tap my finger against my chin as I consider my options. Teleportation is out of the question. Though I've been inside the dungeons while in my orb form, my physical body hasn't and therefore, according to the laws of magic, I can't teleport myself straight in there. I need to think of something else. But what?

I glance across at Zephyr. "Any ideas?"

My faerie dragon tilts his head as he thinks and then nods.

"What?"

He opens his mouth and spits a ball of aether at the door. Nothing happens when the magic reaches it. The spell is only small and the violet light soon fizzles out. Zephyr does the same again and jabs the sharp end of his tail at me.

"Use my magic to blast through the door?"

He nods.

"That won't work. If I try throwing aether at it, my spells will only wake the entire temple, and then the dungeons will be swarming with priestesses. How will we get the Void Prince out of there then?"

Zephyr says nothing. He doesn't look too concerned about the current state of my rescue plans. If anything, he looks pleased by the possibility we may fail to retrieve Natharius.

"No," I continue, "I can't force the door open through sheer strength, but I suppose using my magic isn't a bad idea." I step closer to the door and run my fingers over the hinges to inspect them. They're strong and won't easily give way. However, they are by far the weakest part of the door and the best place to concentrate my efforts. It requires flames of enormous temperatures to melt metals like iron, but luckily my tutors at the Arcanium taught me just the spell in my fifth and final year.

"*Ignira.*" Flames bloom from my fingers, amber as usual. I raise my hand and hold the flames to the hinges. "*Incendius.*" The small flames burst into blue light. So much heat radiates from them that Zephyr darts away. I press the flames to the middle hinge, level with my shoulders, and hold them there until the metal glows red. It takes several minutes before the entire hinge glows, and then I move to the lowest hinge, which reaches my ankles. I crouch there with my blue flames pressed to the iron until it too glows, and once done, I straighten and peer up at the final hinge. It lies half a foot above my head, so I have to stand on my tiptoes and try to reach the topmost hinge. My fingers come half an inch short. I groan. Not only has a key thwarted all my plans but also my height. I'm not short for a Nolderan woman, though I'm certainly not as tall as an elf or my demonic companion sitting beyond this door, anxiously awaiting his rescue.

I push myself a little higher, standing on the very tips of my toes. My fingers brush the bottom of the hinge. It will have to be enough. I focus on making the flames as powerful as I can, and they intensify, encasing most of the hinge. It takes longer than the others to become malleable, but at least I succeed.

By the time I'm done, the first two hinges have begun to cool, so I give them another blast of heat. When they're glowing vibrantly again, I glance back to check no priestesses are racing down me and then nod to Zephyr.

"Stand back."

Though the faerie dragon has edged closer to examine the hinges, for a change he obeys my instruction without question and twirls away from the door.

"*Ventrez.*"

A gale slams into the iron door. With the hinges weakened from the heat, the door lifts away from its frame, and I push it through into the dungeons and guide my wind to lower the door as quietly as I can.

I release the spell and hurry through. Zephyr flutters after me.

Natharius is as I left him, facing away from the entrance with his back pressed against the bars. Even as I approach, he doesn't turn.

"Took you long enough," he says.

"Be grateful I'm here at all. I won't deny I didn't consider leaving you here to rot in this temple."

"You wouldn't dare. You need me."

"I could summon another Void Prince. I have another six to choose from."

"They wouldn't be even half as charming as me."

"'Charming' is one word for it. I bet other Void Princes aren't as insufferable as you."

"I would say I am the most reasonable of my brethren. Besides, you cannot summon another Void Prince."

"Why not?"

"Your soul belongs to me and me alone."

"I could make another deal and overwrite this one."

"You cannot."

I frown. That wasn't something I read in Nolderan's Vaults, where tomes containing forbidden magic are kept, but I didn't spend long researching demonology before deciding to summon a Void Prince. "What about if I made a deal with the Void King instead? Surely that would take precedence over ours?"

At this, Natharius finally turns to face me. His blood-red eyes meet mine. It's only been a few days since I last saw the Void Prince— and I was unconscious for most of them—but I already managed to forget how unsettling his crimson eyes are.

"You would not."

"I wouldn't?"

He lifts his pointed chin. "I should clarify what I meant: You would not be able to. The Lord of the Abyss would have no interest in a puny little mage like you. He is only interested in making deals with those whose souls are abundant with power, those who would make demons strong enough to rule his seven domains."

"Like yourself."

His lip curls. "Indeed, like myself."

I decide to leave our argument at that. It isn't as if I have any interest in summoning the Void King. From recent experience, Void Princes are infuriating enough. I don't want imagine what their king would be like. Besides, we have much more pressing matters to contend with right now. Such as the matter of how to break this Void Prince from his bindings of light magic.

"You can save your bragging for later," I say. "Unless you actually want to stay here and rot."

"No," he growls. "I do not."

"Then we need to hurry and find a way to get you out of that cell. I don't know whether the priestesses have placed wards over the dungeons—"

"They have placed many here."

"Fantastic. Then they could already be alerted to my presence and be racing down here as we speak."

"They could."

"And yet you don't sound concerned."

"If you fail and the priestesses execute you, then I shall be freed from this wretched world and will enjoy torturing your soul in the Abyss to repay you for the humiliation you have caused me to endure at the hands of these zealous fools. And I would say the odds are stacked in my favor."

"Or they could capture me and leave me to rot in the cell beside you. The average lifespan for a mage is approximately three hundred years, so you would get to enjoy up to three centuries of my company."

"I can't think of anything worse," he says with a grimace. "Stop talking and hurry up."

Of course, I have no wish to endure potentially three centuries in the cell beside this loathsome demon, so I don't argue over the fact that *I* am the one who issues orders and not him.

"How do I get this open?" I ask, prodding the lock on his cell door.

"With a key."

"How very helpful," I retort. "Was the prospect of spending the next three centuries with me not motivating enough?"

He sighs. "Unless you can retrieve the key, you will have to force open this door like you forced open the last."

"Fire it is then."

Just as I'm about to conjure my flames, Natharius adds: "The cell door is warded with light magic."

"How wonderful of you to neglect to mention it."

"I didn't neglect to mention it," Natharius says. "I told you, did I not?"

"You could have told me sooner."

He shrugs.

"Is there any other way to get this door open, demon?"

"Not unless your magic is considerably stronger than their High Priestess's and you blast it open with aether."

Even with Father's staff, I'm not sure I can conjure such a powerful spell. And if I do succeed, the impact will disturb the temple, even without considering the ward, and I won't have enough time to get Natharius out.

"Or you could use dark magic."

"I would never use it."

"Of course not. After all, you are a high and mighty, upstanding Mage of Nolderan who didn't decide to defy all her teachings to use dark magic to summon a Void Prince of the Abyss—"

"Shut up."

As my words are a direct order, he has no choice but to obey my command. Any other time, I'd gloat over the infuriated look on his face. Instead, I press my hand to the bars to test for the wards Natharius claims High Priestess Ahelin has placed over it.

Golden light ripples across the bars, the ward becoming visible to the naked eye. The magic feels different to both aether and dark magic. Aether fizzes and crackles like lightning, whereas dark magic is like ice seeping through your veins. Light magic is warm and soothing, like a gentle stream on a bright summer's day.

I don't dwell on the sensation of the strange magic and hold out my fingers, pulling aether toward me. "*Ignira.*" Violet light bursts into crackling flames. "*Incendius.*" The plume of fire intensifies to roaring blue flames, and I waste no time in pressing them to the hinges. The barrier of light magic holds fast, and I focus on fueling my spell until I penetrate it. Slipping through the barrier like a needle requires less power than shattering the entire thing, but it costs enough that I have to fuel the flames with more aether. If the High Priestess wasn't already alerted to my presence when I entered the dungeons, she will be now I've penetrated this barrier. I must work quickly and crack this cell door open faster than the last.

Heat billows out. Zephyr drops to the ground, shielding himself with his wings. The Void Prince doesn't flinch at the heat.

When the first hinge is glowing, I move to the others. Like before, I blow it open with the spell *ventrez,* but now I focus the wind on the hinge, turning the door anticlockwise like a torque. The High Priestess's spell is powerful and resists my magic. I fuel it with increasing amounts of aether until the barrier finally gives way, and the door is torn aside.

With the cell cracked open, the barrier's circuit is broken and falls away, disappearing into glittering dust. I stride through into the cell, and Natharius holds up his wrists and gestures to the golden manacles binding him.

Of course. The manacles.

I run my hand down my face. These will be more challenging than the dungeon and cell doors combined.

"Any suggestions?" I ask.

"If I knew how to remove them, I would have broken out of this wretched place and unleashed my wrath upon all those priestesses days ago."

I step closer to the demon, though every instinct screams to stay away, and examine the golden manacles around his wrists. The metal is thicker than the steel hinges, and I doubt I will be able to melt through them. Even if I succeed, it'll take me all night and we don't have that sort of time.

There is one other option, however. It isn't one that concerns me, but I suspect it'll concern the Void Prince.

"How well do you heal?" I ask.

"Well."

"How well is 'well'?"

His crimson eyes narrow. "Whatever you are considering, I will not agree to it."

"I don't need you to agree to it," I point out. "I only need to issue the order."

The tendons in his neck pulse, as if he's fighting to break free of our bond so that he can end me in so many terrifying ways.

"Anyway," I say, indifferent to his wrath. "If you were to lose a hand or two, would they grow back?"

"Grow back?" he roars. "You're asking if my hands will grow back like a tree?"

"I wasn't of thinking a tree in particular, but now that you say it . . ."

"No."

"'No' what?"

"You have already caused me to endure such humiliation at the hands of these priestesses. I will endure no more."

I place a hand on my hip. "Your injured pride is the least of my concerns right now, demon. If I cut off your hands to remove the manacles, will you be able to restore them? From what I've seen so far, your physical form is fluid and you can change your form at will—provided your magic isn't bound. If you are released from the bindings and your magic is freed, it stands to reason that you should be able to conjure yourself new hands as easily as you can conjure clothes, blankets, and wings."

He seethes with rage.

"Fine, we'll do it this way. Tell me, Natharius, is what I say the truth?"

He grinds his teeth together but is unable to keep his mouth shut. Our bond compels him to speak. "Yes," he hisses with all the hatred in the world.

"Perfect." I roll up my sleeves so they don't get splattered with the Void Prince's blood, especially since my robes look new thanks to the priestesses cleaning them.

Natharius closes his eyes. I imagine he's picturing in vivid detail all the ways he will torture me in the Abyss upon my demise. I know I'm playing with fire, but if all goes well then my death won't be for another three centuries and I won't have to bear the consequences of my current actions for a very long time. Besides, there's no other way to break Natharius out of his bindings. Once the Void Prince is freed, hopefully his power will allow us to escape even if the priestesses catch us down here. They might have taken him prisoner, but Natharius claimed he was unable to cause any fatal damage because I commanded him to do everything in his power to find me a healer and keep me alive. I can only hope that claim is true.

"Look away," I say to Zephyr. He doesn't, and his bright eyes glitter. Apparently my faerie dragon has a vicious streak. I suppose this must be payback for Natharius threatening to eat him.

"Hold up your wrists," I instruct Natharius. He has no choice but to obey.

"Make it quick," he snaps.

"Don't you want me to go so very slowly? It's only fair I get to torture you a little if you plan on torturing me for the rest of eternity."

His lip curls into a snarl. I decide not to push him any more, since I don't have the time either to make the severing of his wrists slow, anyway. Luckily for him, it'll have to be quick.

"*Conparios*," I say, and Father's staff materializes in my hands. I gather more aether and shape the magic into a wind spell. "*Vent—*"

Before I can finish, a shout shatters my concentration.

"You!"

I whirl around.

High Priestess Ahelin stands there, flanked by dozens of priestesses.

CHAPTER 13

"Step away from the demon," the High Priestess commands.

Zephyr is the first to react. He darts into the cell and cowers behind Natharius and me. I'm sure the demon poses more of a threat, since the priestesses wouldn't hurt a harmless faerie dragon. I think.

I glance between the High Priestess and the golden manacles binding Natharius and his magic. I could step away from the Void Prince and see if I can reason with the priestesses, though I'm not sure I'll manage to explain myself out of the situation. My actions are incriminating enough. I could attempt casting *ventrez* again and hope Natharius quickly regains his magic once his hands and the manacles are removed, but the High Priestess could kill me before I finish the spell. Or maybe she won't deal a fatal blow. Can I afford the risk?

Unfortunately, I don't have time to debate the risk of defying her. Already her patience is thin.

"I said step away from the demon," she booms. Golden light flares in her hands. The surrounding priestesses all follow suit, prepared to strike.

Now one thing is certain. There won't be time to conjure a wind spell to sever Natharius's hands and for him to regain his magic. I'll be blasted apart with light magic long before then.

I take a step away from the Void Prince and raise my hands, though I certainly don't put down Father's staff. "I can explain."

The High Priestess doesn't want to hear whatever sorry excuse I can come up with. Her brow creases with fury. "When I sensed my ward being broken," she says, her voice carrying through the dungeons, "I did not expect to find *you*. We healed and fed you. We showed you kindness, and yet you repay us by freeing a demon of the Abyss?"

"I have my reasons—"

"There are no reasons to excuse unleashing a demon on our city. Do you know how many innocent lives your actions put at risk?"

"You don't need to fear him raging terror through your city," I say. "No innocent lives are at risk. This demon is strictly under my control."

Apparently that's the wrong thing to say. Ahelin's golden eyes sharpen. "You are the one who summoned this demon. The one to whom it is tethered. I thought it strange for a demon to be strolling our streets without its summoner in sight, but not once did I consider that a Mage of Nolderan would be responsible. Though the magic you wield is much different to ours, I have always considered the magi to be noble folk. How wrong I was."

"You don't understand. Nolderan is gone. What other choice did I have?"

"Lies! The story you told us earlier this evening, all of it must be lies! Upon reflection, such news is too shocking to believe. How can Nolderan, a city which has stood for over a millennium, cease to be overnight?"

"It's the truth!"

"No. What I believe is that you came here to gain our trust and infiltrate our ranks, all so that you could unleash this demon upon our city. I do not know your motives, witch, but I do know that you will not succeed. The Mother will ensure your failure."

What can I say to convince her that Nolderan's fall is the truth? That I summoned Natharius out of desperation?

I turn to the Void Prince, wondering if he might have anything to add, but he only smiles at me. Of course, he's pleased that I'm surrounded by countless priestesses and must face them alone. Ahelin seems enraged enough to kill me where I stand, and then Natharius will be freed from our bond, and I will get to enjoy an eternity of torture at his hands.

Wonderful.

"Surrender," Ahelin demands. "Come peacefully. I have no wish to fight you, but I will if I must to protect the people of Esterra. Do not force my hand."

The magic radiating from all the priestesses glows brighter at her words.

Right now, it looks as if I only have two choices: to fight or to surrender. Will I be able to defeat all these priestesses, some of whom appear to have been practicing light magic for longer than I've been alive? Most likely not. But do I plan on surrendering? Not at all.

I could try to free Natharius, but it's unlikely I'll manage in time. And now that Ahelin knows I am his summoner, she would rather kill me and banish him back to the Abyss than risk Natharius storming her city. I can't waste my first move. Whatever I choose, it has to stack my pitiful odds in my favor.

Fortunately, I have just the spell in mind.

I cast as quickly as I can, weaving together all my strands of aether, and I speak the spell-word only at the very last moment, when the spell is almost birthed.

"*Speculus.*"

Four bolts of aether radiate from me. They take physical form, manifesting into mirror images of myself.

The most I've ever conjured at once is two clones. I wasn't sure I'd succeed at creating double the amount I was taught to at the Arcanium, and sustaining them will require much concentration. The fact the spell worked exactly as I intended is either out of sheer desperation, luck, Father's staff—or all of the above.

Ahelin doesn't hesitate to launch her magic at me, calling out *mizarel*. Her priestesses take that as their signal to strike, and beams of golden light hurl at me from every direction.

"*Laxus*," I cry before they can reach me. All my clones teleport with me to the corners and far walls, where the paths of light can't reach us. The beams follow a straight trajectory and don't curve around to us.

I begin casting as soon as I materialize. Ahelin and her priestesses only begin preparing their next spells a moment later, briefly confused by my teleportation spell. Hopefully they have no idea which of the five Reynas I am. By their expressions, they all seem to be intent on striking any one of me and hoping they get lucky. A few are looking at the real me. At least Ahelin herself isn't.

"*Folmen*," cry all my clones and I.

Violet lightning bolts at the nearest priestess and jumps to the next, forming a chain. All my clones mimic my spell, sharing a portion of my strength. The power is evenly distributed, meaning the priestesses won't be able to identify which among them I am. It does, however, mean each individual bolt isn't as powerful as if I were to cast it without my cloning spell. Only a few priestesses are struck multiple times, enough to daze them. But my aim was to divert their attention and force them onto the defensive.

As expected, they panic and conjure a wall of golden light around themselves, forming an enormous bubble. Even Ahelin follows suit. She drops hers as soon as she sees both she and all her priestesses are protected by their shield.

This gains me several precious seconds. Enough to conjure my next spell.

"*Telum!*"

Aether blasts from my fingers, the spell mimicked by my clones. Every blast is directed to the same point in their shield. I aim for the weakest area, where the barrier is maintained by a young priestess. Her brow creases as she struggles, but she isn't strong enough to withstand the blow. My magic tears through her shield, sending her flying back into the wall. Priestesses hurry to her side, though enough remain to hold the rest of the shield.

I don't know how badly my magic struck the young priestess, and I can't let myself dwell on it. I must focus on fighting the rest of them, fighting for my chance to destroy Arluin and avenge Nolderan.

"*Mizarel*," the High Priestess shouts, and a spear of light blazes toward the nearest clone. The rays pierce the clone's chest, and it disintegrates into violet dust.

Four Reynas remain.

A priestess strikes the clone to my left.

Three Reynas.

Even though I split myself into five, my clones can only cast the same spell as me. I can't cast both defensive and offensive spells, whereas the priestesses are so many in number that they can do both with ease.

At this rate, I will be defeated. I must do something. But what? Their shield is so strong, and targeting the weakest priestess only pierced their defenses for a fleeting moment. Now the other priestesses have covered the gap and made the wall even stronger.

An idea flashes in my mind. A way to shatter their ranks. It is reckless, but I have no other options.

I drop to my knees and slam my palm against the stone. "*Terra!*"

Green light bolts across the floor, heading to where Ahelin stands at the center of the priestesses. The ground quakes, my magic ripping it apart. The temple shakes with the disruption. Dust billows out as the walls and ceilings grind against each other. Zephyr whimpers. I don't turn to see where he hides. Judging by where the sound comes from, he must be cowering in Natharius's cell.

The priestesses shriek as the floor gives way. The crack isn't wide enough for them to fall through, though the chasm plunges countless feet underground. I can't risk making the earthquake any more violent without causing the entire temple to collapse on us. Even now, the walls tremble enough that I fear I may have miscalculated my spell.

Though the spell inflicts no immediate harm on the priestesses, it achieves what I intend. Their concentration is shattered, their shield with it. They are also momentarily surprised by the chaos. Even Ahelin is caught off-guard for a second. And it's a second long enough for me to cast my next spell.

"Ignir'alas!"

Flames burst from my fingers, rising into the wings of a phoenix. The inferno crashes down on the priestesses. Ahelin has enough time to throw a hasty shield around herself. Other priestesses react quickly enough to protect themselves, but a few are left exposed and suffer the full impact of my spell.

They scream as the fire consumes them. The smell of burning flesh fills the dungeons. It isn't a smell I miss. It reminds me of the night Nolderan fell, when I used my flames against the undead—the reanimated corpses of those I knew.

I banish the memory as quickly as it rises. I dull my senses and rid myself of the smell. I cannot afford any weakness. My past will not cripple me. Not now. Not ever.

Some priestesses fall. The others race to their allies and smother them with golden light, desperately trying to heal them.

Rage blazes in the High Priestess's eyes. "You will pay for this, witch."

Shards of golden light rip through the air. Her attacks are focused on one of my remaining clones, but a few shards scatter through the dungeons and fly dangerously close to me. I lurch away, and the bolt skims my cheek. Though the ward of light magic felt soothing, this spell feels far from it. It scorches my flesh, leaving a burning line in its wake.

A similar line appears on my clone's cheeks, though the one Ahelin struck is already fading away. The High Priestess's attention snaps to me, the real me. The fact my clones now bear my injury is enough to reveal me as the true Reyna.

The High Priestess gathers magic into her fingers, as do all her unwounded priestesses. I clutch Father's staff and draw on all the aether I can.

"Muriz!"

My shield barely manifests in time to stop me from being immolated by their holy fire. Golden flames lick at the violet walls encasing me. I grip the staff tighter, throwing more aether at my shield. With my concentration devoted to the barrier, the mirror image spell shatters and my last clone disappears.

Holy fire licks at the violet light. A hole emerges overhead. I focus on mending that part of the shield, but with my attention diverted there, the rest of my shield unravels.

No!

The priestesses unleash another barrage of golden flames. My shield struggles to withstand it. Flames pierce the barrier. They lick at my sleeves and the ends of my hair. I pour every ounce of strength into the shield, using Father's staff to pull more aether toward me. But the magic in my blood is almost drained, and I lack the strength to weave the aether in the air into my shield.

A scream rips from my throat. Though its incoherent to my ears, my magic understands the spell-word *quatir*.

My shield explodes. Aether devours the holy fire. Golden and violet ash scatter through the darkness. The shock wave is powerful enough to throw back Ahelin and her priestesses. But I don't have the strength to take advantage of it. The explosion used up every remaining drop of aether in my veins, and now I don't have the strength to pull any more from the air.

I drop to my knees, exhaustion weighing on me like an anchor. Father's staff rolls from my fingers and clatters onto the stone floor. I know I must get up and fight, but an invisible force pushes me down. My limbs refuse to obey.

"Seize her!" Ahelin shouts.

I struggle to my feet. It's a battle that costs me even more strength.

The priestesses grab my arms. I shake them off and desperately call on my magic. There's no answer. Until I rest, there will be no more casting spells. I kick at the priestesses and manage to throw a few of them off me. But there are too many. They come at me from all angles.

Light blooms in Ahelin's hands, and she sends golden chains spinning toward me. "*Alsila.*"

I try to lunge away, but the priestesses hold me in place. The light wraps around my legs and coils upward, squeezing tighter and tighter. Then I can't so much as kick at the priestesses.

Ahelin retrieves a set of golden manacles from the dungeon's far wall and marches toward me. I try to pull my arms away from the priestesses, but it is no use. I can do nothing but watch as she approaches.

"Her wrists," she says to the priestesses holding me.

They pull my arms in front and roll up my sleeves, exposing my wrists.

Ahelin opens the manacles, slots them around my wrists and then clicks them in place. The markings glow with golden light. Though little aether remains in my blood, I could sense that which lies in the air. Now I'm cut off from it entirely, and the air is devoid of magic.

"Put her in that cell," Ahelin instructs, pointing to the cell beside Natharius.

I scream and kick, but it does nothing to stop the priestesses from shoving me into the cell. They slam the door shut behind me.

"What should we do with this creature?" one priestess asks, peering at Zephyr who's huddled in the very far corner of Natharius's cell.

"It's a harmless thing," Ahelin says. "Take it out of the dungeons and give it to the younger priestesses to look after with the doves."

The priestesses glance at each other. None of them seems to want to step inside the cell and pass dangerously close to Natharius, who is sitting to the left with his back against the bars. When it's clear no one will volunteer, Ahelin sighs and marches into the cell. She doesn't so much as look at Natharius as she strides past him, but the Void Prince lifts his head and wrinkles his nose.

Ahelin crouches in front of Zephyr. He covers his head with his wings.

"Come now, little one," she urges.

Zephyr doesn't stir. He remains frozen in place.

"It will do you no good to stay in here with this monster."

Natharius seethes at that.

After considering her words, Zephyr lowers his wing enough to reveal one crystalline eye. His attention flickers between Natharius and Ahelin as he weighs his options.

"You will be well cared for," Ahelin continues, holding out her hand.

Zephyr lowers his wing a little more and looks back at me. As much as I hate to admit it, Ahelin is right. It will do Zephyr no good to rot down in these dungeons with us. He deserves better than that.

I give him a quick nod, and he unfurls the rest of his wings. He tentatively climbs onto Ahelin's hands, and up onto her shoulder. Pain shoots through my heart at the sight, but I tell myself this isn't a betrayal. I failed Zephyr by getting us all caught.

He looks back at me as Ahelin strides out of Natharius's cell, and I force myself to meet his eyes, though it hurts. Zephyr is all I have left, and now I have lost him too.

The High Priestess shuts Natharius's cell and places her hand over the doors, conjuring a ward of light magic. She does the same to mine. I don't look at her and draw my knees up to my chest.

I know I must be strong, but it's hard when defeat weighs so heavily on my shoulders.

"You two," Ahelin barks as she leaves the dungeons. She gestures to two of the priestesses. "Guard both of the prisoners with careful diligence. I will send replacements to take your posts in the morning. You are not to set foot outside of the dungeons until then. Is that understood?"

"Yes, High Priestess," they both reply, dipping their heads.

With that, the other priestesses flock out of the dungeons with Ahelin, leaving Natharius and me and our two jailors.

CHAPTER 14

I STARE DOWN AT THE golden manacles binding my wrists. Light flickers across the runes engraved into the surface, pulsing with a steady rhythm like the ebb and flow of the tide. Ahelin pressed them so tightly together the metal pinches my skin.

The two priestesses Ahelin ordered to guard the dungeons stand sentry like statues. They don't move even once from the dungeon's iron doors and rarely blink. I wonder whether stoicism is a part of a priestess's training. I do my best to think about that rather than my much more terrible thoughts.

Like Arluin. His necromancers. Father's corpse enslaved to his will. Legions of undead storming the world.

My failure.

But when I fall asleep, I'm unable to stop all those terrifying thoughts from invading my mind. My dreams are haunted by fragmented images of Arluin and his undead, some from the night Nolderan fell, others from a future which has yet to pass but is now cemented by my failure.

Everything I've done so far—wielding dark magic and bargaining my soul to summon a Void Prince—has been in vain. And I didn't even make it past the Ghost Woods.

In my nightmares, Kaely laughs at me. Her features are twisted by the taint of undeath. My flames slam into her and consume her reanimated corpse, and her taunts turn to screams.

Eliya is there inside her crystal coffin, clasping an illusionary rose to her chest. Her eyes snap open. She asks me why I let her be killed. Why I failed to bring her murderer to justice. Then her face is replaced by Father's, and his eyes are filled with dark magic. He shakes his head and tells me what a disappointment of a daughter I am. That he should have disowned me years ago when it was clear how useless I am.

Finally Arluin appears, and he sneers at me and says how easy it was to fool me. How lonely and broken I was and how I jumped at the affection he showed me while pretending to be Nolan. How blindly I trusted him.

When it all becomes too much, I'm torn out of my dreams and wake to tears spilling across my cheeks. And Natharius staring at me. I wonder whether I made any noises while weeping in my sleep.

The Void Prince says nothing. He hasn't said a word since the priestesses threw us in here. When I lift my head and meet his eyes, his attention flickers across to the bars behind me.

I bite my tongue to hold back a wry laugh. How unexpected. I thought he would mock me to no end for my tears, but it's as if he didn't notice them at all. Unless perhaps the demon is too busy feeling sorry for himself for being caged beneath this temple.

I lift my hands. The manacles clang together. It's a struggle to wipe away my tears with the back of my hand, and it involves contorting my wrists at an odd and painful angle, but I succeed in the end. Then I sit there and stare at my manacles again, contemplating my failure. At least the Arluin who appeared in my dreams wasn't real and was only a figment of my imagination, terrible though he was. It seems these holy manacles are suppressing Arluin's tracking spell, as well as my magic. Either that or he wasn't available tonight to torment me in my dreams.

I'm not sure how long I slept, but both priestesses are still standing guard at the door and haven't yet been replaced, so I doubt it's morning yet. With the dungeons being so far beneath the temple, there are no windows. The only light comes from the torches scattered across the walls.

How long will they keep me inside this dungeon? For eternity, as I joked to Natharius? Will I have to spend the next three hundred years inside here? Will my only escape be death from old age? Then I'll have more imprisonment awaiting me, coupled with the eternal torture of my soul at the hands of the demon in the cell next to mine.

In the end, all I traded my soul for was a few days of journeying through Tirith. Maybe that's all I'm worth.

But I won't let myself cry again. I dig my nails into my palms as deeply as I can. The strain causes the manacles to pinch my wrists harder. I focus on the pain until the urge to cry fades into bleak despair.

I peel myself from the bars behind me. I've been sitting against them for so long they've imprinted themselves into my back. My limbs are stiff, but I make it to the center of the cell, and I lie there on my back, pressing it against the cold stone floor to relieve the ache. I stare up at the ceiling and spend a while longer contemplating all the consequences of my defeat.

Maybe my imprisonment won't last three hundred years. Maybe Arluin will conquer the world before then. Maybe he and his undead will tear apart the city and find me down here afterward. Or maybe I won't live to see Arluin conquering the world. Maybe the priestesses will execute me first.

I don't know which future fate has planned for me and I can contemplate it all I want, but it will bring me no closer to knowing the truth.

Somewhere amid all those bleak thoughts of my demise, I fall asleep again. This time, my dreams are empty and no one enters my mind. Not Arluin, not Eliya, not Father.

After some time, I wake to creaking. It must be morning now since two new priestesses enter the dungeons to replace the others. They are accompanied by a third priestess who bears trays filled with food and water. At first I don't recognize her but when she draws nearer, I realize it's Yadira.

I scramble forth to my cell's door and cling to the bars. "Yadira!"

She doesn't look at me as she retrieves a key from her white robes and uses it to unlock Natharius's cell. The demon doesn't lift his head. Or so much as twitch. I'd think him asleep if his eyes weren't open. He hasn't moved at all.

"Yadira!" I try again. She takes a cautious step into Natharius's cell and places the tray close to the entrance. Then she leaves and swiftly locks the cell behind her. Golden light ripples across the bars as the High Priestess's ward restores itself.

"You have to listen to me!" I continue. "Everything I said about the necromancers, about Nolderan's fall—all of it is the truth!"

Yadira stops in front of my cell and lifts the key. "Step away from the door."

"If you leave me locked in here and no one stops the necromancers, then it won't only be Nolderan that falls. It will be the entire world!"

"I said step away from the bars, witch. If you don't, I'll be forced to leave without giving you this." She uses her golden key to point at the water and stew on the tray.

"I'm not a witch," I grind out through clenched teeth. "I'm a Mage of Nolderan. Your High Priestess has gotten this all wrong."

"Do you deny summoning that wicked creature?" She nods to Natharius, who snarls in return.

"No, but I had my reasons—"

"Do you deny harming my fellow sisters only a few hours ago?"

"You make it sound as if I hurt them in cold blood. Is that what lies the High Priestess has been spewing?"

"Blasphemy! The High Priestess does not lie."

"But she certainly tells half-truths. I needed to escape, to save the world, and they stood in my way. Tell me, which is the greater sin? One who fights for justice, or one who enables a monster to destroy the entire world? What is the wellbeing of one or two priestesses when, as it stands, the entire world will be destroyed and countless innocent lives will be lost—"

"Save it," Yadira snaps. "I was instructed to come down here with food and water, not to debate what kind of monster you are. Whatever reasons you claim to have, they do not change the fact that you summoned this demon and harmed my sisters. Now, step away from the bars or I will leave without giving you water."

I grit my teeth and do as she says, only because my words are falling on deaf ears and I'm so thirsty it's as if my throat is filled with sand.

Yadira unlocks my cell and places the tray at the entrance and locks the cell behind her. She stares me down from the other side of the bars. "The High Priestess also instructed me to tell you your execution will be held later this afternoon. She already announced it to the citizens of Esterra this morning."

Execution.

My execution.

My knees slacken and crumple beneath me.

"No," I gasp. I shuffle forth on my knees and grasp the bars. "No, this can't be true!"

But Yadira isn't fazed by my protests. She deposits the golden key back into her robes.

"You can't do this!" I shout after her. "If you kill me, you won't know where those necromancers are! Nor what they intend to do! All of Imyria will suffer the consequences of your actions!"

Yadira doesn't look back as she steps out of the dungeons. The doors close behind her, and with them the tiniest seed of hope I had—the hope I could convince Yadira to appeal to the High Priestess on my behalf—dies with it.

I scream, but the doors don't open. The guards look over at me for a few moments and then resume their statuesque vigil. I scream until my throat is raw, until my voice breaks, and only when I can scream no more do I slump back onto my heels and stare uselessly at the golden manacles around my wrists.

Before the priestesses caught us, I joked to Natharius about divesting him of his wrists, since it was the only way I could think to free him and because he could conjure back his hands. My magic is incapable of growing back any body parts, save for as an illusion, and yet if I had a blade inside this cell, I would use it on my wrists without hesitation.

If I can't find a way out of this cell, I'll be executed before the day is up. It must be morning now, but I don't know if it's late or early morning. I don't know how many hours I have left to live.

And even though I knew Yadira for less than a day and I'm the one who is indebted to her and not vice versa, her betrayal stings.

"Think of it this way," Natharius's silky voice comes from my right, pulling me from my thoughts. I almost forgot he could speak. His crimson eyes gleam. "Now you won't have to spend the next three hundred years in here with me."

"No, I will just get to spend an eternity being tortured by you before you grow bored and decide to consume my soul instead."

"I will never grow bored of torturing you," the demon purrs.

"Wonderful."

I lie back on the floor and stare up at the stone ceiling, which has a crack running through it—perhaps from when I summoned that earthquake to shake the temple. Then I stay there for a long while and contemplate which is worse: having my soul eaten by the Void Prince or enduring endless torture. Probably the latter.

When I grow tired of staring at the ceiling, I haul myself up to a sitting position and stare at the tray Yadira brought. I don't try eating the stew, knowing I'll be unable to swallow a single mouthful, but I have a few sips of water. It does little to relieve my parched throat or the nausea washing over me, and it's more difficult to swallow than I anticipate, so I cough most of it up. I don't bother trying to drink again.

Time drags on, and I run out of things to stare at to stop my thoughts from spiraling out of control. A few times, I stand and pace around my cell, looking for any potential weaknesses in the walls or bars, but I find none. There is no way out of this cell, other than the key Yadira used. And that will have long been returned to the High Priestess.

"Void Prince," I hiss, shuffling close to the bars separating us. He doesn't lift his head. I don't dare raise my voice any more, as our guards can likely hear me as it is. "Natharius, look at me."

Despite the holy manacles shackling our wrists, the dark magic tethering us together is as strong as ever. The demon is forced to raise his head and meet my eyes, though his lip curls from having to do so.

"Tell me," I continue, lowering my voice, "is there any way out of these cells? You will answer me truthfully and tell me any suggestion you can think of."

The demon pauses and then smiles. "There is no way of escaping your death, if that is what you wish to know. If a Void Prince such as myself cannot escape these chains, how could a puny little mage ever hope to?"

I stare at him, hoping that the manacles have somehow weakened the compulsion of my command. That Natharius has resisted enough to lie. Because if these bindings haven't subdued the dark magic between us, the Void Prince is telling the truth. And there's truly no way out.

Desperately, I try squeezing my hands out of my wrists. I don't know what enchantment Ahelin has placed over them, other than it suppressing my connection to aether, but the metal seems to cling tighter to my wrists the more I struggle. Either that, or trying to force my hands out of the manacles has caused my wrists to swell considerably.

When it becomes clear yanking my hands out of the manacles will do me no good, I instead try bending the steel bars of my cell. The two priestesses standing guard by the dungeon's doors briefly look up as I attempt to wrestle with them, but then they lower their heads and resume their silent vigil. And they have no reason to interfere. Golden light blooms across the cell, preventing me from moving them even a hair's breadth. I don't have the physical strength to bend steel to my will. My magic would be a different question—if I could currently use it.

I give up trying to force apart the bars sooner than I gave up wrestling my hands out of the manacles. The only crack I can find in the surrounding stone of my cell is the one running through the ceiling, but I can't reach it. I doubt even Natharius would be able to in his current form.

When the doors finally open once more, I'm lying down in the center of my cell and staring up at the ceiling. My blood runs cold at the sound of voices and footsteps, and I bolt up to a sitting position.

A flurry of white and gold silk filters into the dungeons. Countless priestesses swarm forth. At their helm is High Priestess Ahelin.

CHAPTER 15

THE HIGH PRIESTESS MARCHES FORTH. My heart pounds at a frightening tempo.

This is it.

Soon I will meet my end.

Ahelin's gaze sweeps between Natharius and me. She presses her hands together and closes her eyes. "*Sohira.*" Golden light pours out of her and spirals into both of our cells. The wards dissipate into glittering dust and both doors swing wide open.

She turns to her entourage of priestesses and gestures to us both. "Seize these wretched creatures," she commands. "By the Mother's light, we shall purify the world of their evil."

The priestesses swarm into my cell and drag me to my feet. They're more cautious about entering Natharius's. One of the older priestesses seems bolder and leads the way. Though Natharius snarls at the priestesses manhandling him, he offers little resistance. Not like me. I scream and kick, refusing to let them escort me to my death. But without my magic, my efforts are futile.

The back of my head slams into a priestess's jaw, and the room spins. Dark splotches gnaw at my vision.

The priestesses seize the opportunity. While I'm momentarily disoriented, they wrap cloth around my mouth and my next screams come out muffled. They also secure their grasp on me, holding my arms in place. I kick out as best as I can while they shove me out of the cell.

High Priestess Ahelin watches my struggle, and her nose wrinkles. "I suggest you come quietly, witch. Or else we will bind your legs and carry you to your execution."

My execution.

A tiny part of me clung to the hope that perhaps Yadira was exaggerating. That perhaps the High Priestess didn't really intend to execute me in front of all her citizens. But hearing those words from her mouth leaves no room for doubt. They slam into me like a sudden blow to the chest.

All I can see is Father's face. Eliya's. I have failed them both.

My knees threaten to yield, but the priestesses hold me too tightly for me to sink. Numbness washes over me as they lead me out of the dungeons, up the many stairs, and out of the temple. I'm so focused on the dark thoughts of my demise that I barely notice the shift of my surroundings.

How can this world be so cruel? It already snatched away those I loved. Why won't it even allow me to avenge them?

A breeze washes over my cheeks, somewhat stirring me from my daze. We're on the streets now and the citizens hurry to the sides, allowing our procession to pass through.

The crowd jeers at Natharius and me. The news of a demon and its summoner must have spread. People hurl rotten food at us. Mostly vegetables.

A tomato slams into my cheek. The blow doesn't hurt, but the impact catches me by surprise. The tomato bounces off my cheek and falls to the street, sticky juice oozing out of it. I turn to look in the direction it came from, to see who threw it at me.

A boy stands there, no older than nine. His clothes are covered with holes, some clumsily patched up, and many loose threads hang from the stitches. His expression is brave at first—until I meet his eyes. Our gazes lock together, and his lower lip trembles with fright. His mother's face creases into an ugly scowl, and she pulls her son away, safely behind the crowd. I don't catch another glimpse of them.

I stand and stare at where they disappeared. Am I truly that frightening?

What sort of monster have I become?

But these questions don't matter. Not when I'm being marched to my death.

"Get a move on, witch," a priestess snarls. She shoves me forth. The force is great enough for me to almost collide with the priestesses escorting Natharius ahead.

The demon's gaze sweeps over the crowd as they hurl rotten food at him. With his poor temper, I expect him to react more volatility and, at the very least, offer the people of Esterra one of his finest scowls, but his expression looks bored. Maybe this isn't the first time townspeople have thrown rotten vegetables and jeered at him, or maybe he's only thinking of what is to come.

My demise. His freedom.

The priestesses lead us farther into the city. With every corner we turn, my once magnificent magi robes become more sullied. A mockery of the mage I am. Maybe this is what I deserve for my sins. For enabling Nolderan's destruction by handing the city to Arluin on a silver platter. For dishonoring Nolderan's memory by breaking the Arcanium's teachings and wielding dark magic to summon a Void Prince.

Our destination is the city's square. Many are crowded here, eagerly awaiting our arrival. The townsfolk who watched us pass on the streets trail behind us and spill into the city's square. At the center stands a large stone platform with many steps leading up to it. Priestesses are gathered at the base of the platform, forming an impenetrable ring around it.

The masses part way at the sight of the High Priestess, and their heads bow so deeply it's as if she's the incarnate of the Mother Goddess herself.

With each step we take toward the platform, my insides knot a little more. The High Priestess will execute me up there. How will she choose to end me? Will she smite me down with her golden flames?

My mind flashes back to the night Father executed Heston Harstall. Stone chains bound him to the street, preventing his escape. Flames licked the flesh from his bone, and his screams pierced through the night.

Will I die like him? To these people, am I as monstrous as him?

The priestesses push me up the platform. The steps sway. I stumble. A shove from behind keeps me moving.

When we're on the platform, the priestesses separate Natharius and me, positioning us at either end. A priestess unbinds the cloth from my mouth. I wish she hadn't. Now the entire city will hear my screams as the High Priestess's magic consumes me. As it ends me.

Ahelin raises her hands. "*Alsila*," she cries. The crowd falls silent, spellbound as they watch her. Golden light blooms in her hands, taking the form of chains. They shoot across to Natharius and me, wrapping around our legs and fixing us in place. I struggle against them, desperately try to kick my legs free, but the chains don't budge. Even if they did, there would be no escape. The platform is surrounded by hundreds of priestesses, all dressed in their silken robes. I wouldn't manage even a step into the city's square. Satisfied that the High Priestess's chains will secure me in place, the priestesses holding me draw away. Then only Ahelin, Natharius, and I are left on the platform.

Natharius's expression is one of disinterest, not fear. For him, execution means returning to the Abyss, back to where he belongs. For me, execution means death.

And eternal torture.

I squeeze my eyes shut and will myself not to cry in front of all these people. It's all I can do not to picture Father's face. Eliya's. And the face of the man I wish nothing more than to obliterate from this world.

Today I will die. Never will I free Father's soul. Never will I bring Arluin to justice.

My legs quake beneath Ahelin's chains. If they weren't there, I'm sure I'd fall to the platform in ultimate defeat. All I can hear is the pounding of my heart and the frantic gasping of my breath. The High Priestess's words are almost inaudible.

"Today we gather in the Mother's Light to purge our city of the evil which plagues our streets!" Her voice rings through the square and echoes off the rooftops beyond.

The crowd is silent as she speaks, listening intently to the revered High Priestess. No one questions the fact that neither Natharius or I received a trial. To the citizens of Esterra City, the High Priestess's word is the law of heaven.

"These vile creatures harmed my fellow sisters, loyal servants of the Mother."

Nausea washes over me. I could try to argue with her words, that I didn't *want* to hurt anyone. That I did only what was necessary to escape, to bring about Arluin's end and save the world from his darkness. But I've already tried to convince Yadira with the same argument and received only her scorn. If she wouldn't listen to me, why would any of these strangers in the crowd below listen?

"In order to remain in our plane of existence, a demon must be tethered to a mortal soul." The High Priestess gestures to me. "It is to this witch the abomination is bound—"

"I've seen some abominations in the Abyss," Natharius says, "and I can assure you they aren't half as pretty as me."

"Silence!" the High Priestess roars. "*Shadela!*" Light magic springs from her fingers. At first, I fear she intends to execute Natharius on the spot. But I'm wrong. The light magic stretches into a golden ribbon and wraps around Natharius's mouth.

Though the Void Prince hurls what is undoubtedly all manner of threats and curses at the High Priestess, his words are indecipherable thanks to the golden ribbon around his mouth. Until now, he hadn't looked too bothered about his imminent execution—if anything, he'd looked excited—but now he looks incredibly vexed. The last time I remember seeing him this furious was when I first summoned him in the vaults beneath the Arcanium.

To say his pride has been injured would be an understatement.

Fire burns in his crimson eyes. If his power wasn't cut off by the light imbued manacles around his wrists, he would unleash the most wicked magic he knows upon the High Priestess.

With Natharius silent, the High Priestess turns to the crowd once more. "Before you stands a mage who misused her power to summon a vile creature from the Abyss. Purging her from this world will also send this creature of darkness back to whence it came."

Natharius says something again, or at least tries to. What exactly, I can't tell.

"Do you have any last words?" Ahelin asks me.

There are a thousand things I could say. I could try to convince her that Nolderan's fall is no lie, that there truly are necromancers whose darkness threatens the safety of the entire world. That summoning a demon to aid me in defeating them and fighting fire with fire can't be considered a sin.

But with death looming over me, all I can think about is how the High Priestess will execute me. How it will feel to die. How Natharius will torture me for the rest of eternity.

"No?" the High Priestess says, raising a brow. "Then so be it. Today I shall grant you mercy with a quick end."

She raises her hands. Golden light pours from them. I close my eyes, preparing to feel the blast.

Flames crackle.

But before the High Priestess can utter the spell-word and unleash her magic upon me, before death can embrace me, a cry rings out from the crowd. It echoes through the square louder than the High Priestess's voice did, and this shout commands far more power.

"Stop this madness at once!"

CHAPTER 16

A YOUNG WOMAN STRIDES THROUGH the crowd. Her robes are grander than the other priestesses from the temple, and they flow from her elegant form like molten gold. Glistening bracelets spiral up her bare arms. Her hair billows behind her, pale as the moon, and her skin is as dark as midnight. But it's her eyes which make me pause. They shine a far brighter hue than even the High Priestess's—like orbs of pure sunlight.

She's flanked by two guards clad in leathers. Gold adorns their boots and bracers and shoulders, and from both that and the way they hold themselves, it's clear neither are common swords for hire.

The three of them march through the crowd, ignoring the murmurs rippling around them. High Priestess Ahelin whirls around to face them, her eyes blazing with fury. "Who dares to intervene with the Mother's justice?"

The white-haired priestess isn't fazed by Ahelin's wrath. Her face remains a serene mask. She halts at the base of the platform and stares up at the High Priestess, Natharius, and me. She raises her hands and golden light erupts from them. "*Arandir!*" Bolts of light hurl toward both Natharius and me.

My blood chills. I brace myself for the incoming blast. Does this new priestess also seek to destroy me? But why stop my execution?

When the light touches me, coolness washes over me. Fear floods from me, and in its place there's only calmness. It only lasts for a fleeting moment and then it fades, taking Ahelin's chains with it.

With my legs freed, I stumble and struggle to regain my balance. The chains around Natharius are also gone thanks to the priestess's magic, and so has the ribbon of light which bound his mouth. The demon says nothing, though. He watches the newcomers through narrowed eyes.

"Guards!" the High Priestess shouts. The city guards step forth at her command.

The white-haired priestess raises her head as she regards the High Priestess. She reaches into the pouch at her belt and retrieves a golden seal and holds it high. The metal is engraved with the image of a rising sun, light magic radiating from it. "It has been years since we last met, High Priestess Ahelin of Esterra City, but I would have hoped you'd remember my hair at the very least."

At the sight of the seal, the entire crowd falls to a bow. The people of Esterra City press their foreheads to the stone in utter reverence for this girl. She looks only a few years older than me but whoever she is, it's clear she's even more divine than the High Priestess.

Ahelin's eyes widen with horror. Golden light floods her palms. "*Mizarel!*" A bolt of light surges toward the white-haired priestess.

"*Zire!*" A glistening wall surrounds the young woman and the two warriors at her side. Both their weapons are drawn: thin sabers with runes carved into the blades. The markings look similar to the ones engraved into the manacles around my wrists and also glow with golden light.

Ahelin's attack hits the shield, and the barrier ripples as it absorbs the magic. The white-haired priestess barely blinks. Blocking Ahelin's spell has cost her little strength.

Ahelin staggers back. Her hands tremble. She glances around in search of allies, but there are none. Every other priestess is bowing to the young woman in golden robes.

"Guards!" the white-haired priestess calls. Her calm voice rings through the city's square. She waves her hand, and the shield falls away around her and her allies. "Seize this sinner!"

The High Priestess's eyes remain on the golden seal. "S-sinner?" she echoes. Then, like everyone else in the city's square, she falls to her knees and drops to a low bow.

The guards obey the command without question. They march up to the platform and grab the High Priestess's arms, dragging her to her feet.

"I am exacting the Mother's will!" Ahelin protests. "I have served her dutifully for over four decades! How can I be a sinner for eradicating evil from this world?"

"Firstly," the white-haired priestess begins, gliding up the platform's steps. She comes to a stop before Ahelin and clasps her hands. "This is not the Mother's will."

"Impossible! Demons and dark magic are abominable! Those who serve Her are bound to carry out her will in cleansing this world from shadow."

"High Priestess Ahelin, do you claim to know the Mother's will better than I?"

Ahelin's gaze lowers.

"Secondly," the white-haired priestess continues, "you have cast a spell with the intention to bring harm to me, the First Disciple. This crime is great enough to warrant your arrest."

"No!" Ahelin shouts, her voice shaking. "You don't possess the authority to command such a thing! I'm a High Priestess. You aren't the Grand Priestess yet!"

"Indeed, I am not yet the Grand Priestess, but I can assure you my position as the First Disciple is more than sufficient to place you on trial."

Ahelin's fists tighten, but she doesn't dare to further argue.

"High Priestess Ahelin of Esterra City, on behalf of Grand Priestess Elunar, I am arresting you for the crimes of attacking the First Disciple, and for interfering with the Mother's will."

Shock plasters across Ahelin's face. She struggles against the guards as they lead her down the platform and through the city square but doesn't use her magic to save herself.

The First Disciple doesn't watch Ahelin leave and instead paces over to me. Her lips pull upward into a warm smile. "It is a pleasure to meet you, Reyna Ashbourne, though I wish we'd met under different circumstances. The turn of events following the goblin ambush wasn't the path I hoped the future would take."

I can only stand there and blink, so many questions racing through my mind. How does she know my name? How does she know about the goblin ambush? What does she mean by the path the future would take? And most of all why did she, a devout follower of the Goddess Zolane, intervene with my execution at the hands of another priestess and save my life?

The question I end up blurting out is: "You know my name." Though I suppose it comes out as more a statement than a question when it leaves my lips.

Her smile only grows. "I do. And I know a great many more things about you. I'm sure you must have plenty of questions."

I nod. "You might know my name, but I don't know yours."

"I am Taria Aram, First Disciple of the Grand Priestess." She gestures behind to her two guards—first to the woman, and then to the man. "This is Caya and Juron." Juron dips his head in acknowledgment, whereas Caya's only reaction in the slight narrowing of her eyes.

I'm not sure exactly how to exchange pleasantries with my saviors, especially given the fact I'm in chains, so I opt to ask another question. "Why did you—"

Taria raises her hand and the elegance with which she does it silences me before I can realize. "I will answer all your questions, but I hardly think this is the right place to do so." She gestures to the golden manacles around my wrists. "And I would much rather not have this discussion with you in chains." She turns her gaze to the priestesses flocked around the base of the platform. "Is there a key to release our guests from their restraints?"

No one questions the fact that only a few moments ago we were prisoners to be executed and not guests. Yadira is the first priestess to answer, and she retrieves a golden key and hurries up the platform to Taria. The key she bears resembles the one which she used to unlock our cells this morning. Hopefully it'll work on our manacles, as well as our cell doors.

Yadira stops before Taria but doesn't draw any closer than two arm lengths. I can't tell whether it's out of respect or fear. Perhaps both.

Taria nods to her female bodyguard. "Caya, if you will."

Caya takes the key from her and strides toward me. A scar runs across her cheek, trailing up to her dark, feline eyes. She lifts my bound wrists with her callused hands and slots the key into the manacle's lock. A click sounds and the metal bindings fall loose. The light fades from the runes etched into their surface, and I slip my hands out of them. Immediately, my connection to aether rushes back in an overwhelming wave. All around me the air feels energized and tingles my skin, and when I breathe in, it smells and tastes sweet. I've grown so accustomed to living with my connection to aether that I've never noticed how potent the air is with it. This is by far the longest I've ever been shut off from my magic, and I wonder how long it will take before it stops being a novelty.

Once my manacles are off, Caya stalks back over to Taria. "And what of the demon?"

"Free him as well," Taria replies. "He too is destined to play an instrumental part in Imyria's fate."

Caya doesn't look pleased by Taria's orders, but she doesn't argue with her. From her hesitation to release Natharius, I expect her to approach him with unease like the priestesses did while entering his cell, but she saunters over to him and her hips don't lose their sway. Her nose wrinkles, however, as she reaches for his manacles and slots the key inside. She had no problem lifting my wrists to more easily unlock mine but is careful to make no contact at all with Natharius. With the proud and confident way she holds her shoulders, I doubt she does so out of fear. It's more likely out of repulsion.

As Caya slots the key into Natharius's manacles, the Void Prince's calculating eyes sweep over the crowd and settle on the High Priestess, who has almost disappeared into the streets beyond the city's square, flanked by dozens of guards. From his expression alone, I can guess his intentions.

"Natharius," I call over as the key clicks. "I order you not to lay harm to anyone here. Especially not the High Priestess."

It's a bold statement, especially if Taria and her friends end up being as zealous as the High Priestess and march us back here to our execution a few hours later. However, I'm hopeful the fact Taria claimed saving me was her goddess's will means she won't be smiting me down any time soon. And if Natharius maims a priestess or two, even if they're deserving of it like Ahelin, I doubt it will earn me any more allies.

And I'm in dire need of all the help I can get.

Natharius scowls, but I'm more than used to his wrath, and now the imminent torture of my soul isn't so imminent after all. Hopefully I've postponed that for at least a few more years.

Taria turns to me, her gaze trailing over my sullied robes and hair, which are splattered with rotten food. "Let us return to the Temple," she says. "We shall talk after you've freshened yourselves. And eaten. I suppose you must both be hungry."

I can't argue with that, not when I'm ravenous. I follow Taria and her guards down the platform and into the surrounding crowd.

"I am a Void Prince of the Abyss," Natharius growls. I run my hand down my face and hope he doesn't start spewing out a mouthful of terrible insults. One threatening word out of him and I'll have no choice but to silence him. "I do not require mortal sustenance."

Taria pauses and glances back. I wonder how insulted she will be by his sharp tone and whether I should opt to issue a command of silence. Thankfully, when I peer at Taria more closely, I notice her golden eyes twinkle with amusement. "I know exactly who you are, Natharius Thalanor, Void Prince of Pride, Former Prince of Ithyr, High Enchanter of Lumaria, and third son of King Vastiros the Second."

Crimson flames simmer in Natharius's eyes. "You know not what you speak of, priestess."

Taria returns his burning glare with a smile. "Oh, but I do. The Mother has ensured I know every detail of your past and precisely why it makes you so instrumental to Imyria's fate. I'm sure you're aware there are very few others of your kind the Mother smiles upon."

"Lies," he hisses. "You cannot know my past."

"Do you not believe me? If you prefer, I can announce to all of Esterra City why Prince Natharius of Ithyr, High Enchanter of Lumaria, sacrificed his kingdom?"

"I will carve the flesh from your bones, priestess," he spits. "Do not threaten me again."

"That's enough, Natharius," I say, though I have to bite my tongue to stop myself from asking Taria what she knows of the Void Prince's past and why his temper is even more volatile than usual at the mention of it.

Natharius's wrath doesn't diminish as he turns to me. It only intensifies. "And you," he snarls. "For this humiliation you have forced me to endure, you will suffer an eternity of the most excruciating torment the Abyss has to offer."

"I thought that was already on the table, Natharius. You need to think of some new threats because I'm growing tired of hearing the same ones."

The demon glowers.

"Now, let's return to the temple," I say. "Even if you don't require food or drink like us mortals, you can do with freshening yourself up." I give his dark tunic a pointed look, as it's as covered in rotten tomatoes as my robes, though the darker shade helps to disguise the stains.

He inhales sharply and shadows swarm in his hands. Panic seizes me, and I desperately run back over the command I issued him. I'm certain I gave explicit orders for him not to harm anyone here in Esterra City. But what if he's found a loophole in my words and is preparing an attack to murder these innocent people in the square—even if they were jeering at me minutes ago?

I open my mouth to stop him, but then darkness washes over him and I realize the intention of his spell. When the shadows fade, his clothes are clear of all stains.

I'm not the only one who appears to have assumed the worst about Natharius's spell. The crowd around us has shrunk back, and people are cowering in fear. Both of Taria's guards have drawn their swords, the golden runes engraved into the blade shining brightly. Only the priestess herself seems to be the only one who isn't unsettled by Natharius's use of magic.

He arches a silvery brow. "What? You would all be long dead by now if I were able to kill you."

"Natharius," I snap. "I order you to keep your mouth shut and follow us back to the temple."

The Void Prince snarls at me and is no doubt considering all the wonderful ways he longs to torture me, but he has no choice but to remain silent and follow me to the temple with Taria and her two guards.

The crowd parts for us as we pass through the city square, and many of the citizens drop to a low bow at Taria. While many gazed upon me with hatred when we entered the square, now I seem to be invisible. Natharius receives plenty of fearful glances, though.

The priestess exudes grace as she smiles upon the people of Esterra, and she blesses the forehead of more than one baby. Her two guards do their best to usher people away, but they aren't able to stop the hands grasping for Taria's flowing silk robes. Natharius rolls his eyes at every interruption, but he says nothing thanks to my command. Though I'd be lying if I said I'm also not growing impatient with how long it takes us to leave the city's square. I'm desperate to return to the temple and sit down and discuss with Taria everything she knows about me and why she saved me and a demon from execution.

Once we're out of the city's square, there are fewer people to obstruct our path. The crowd trails after us, but the entourage of priestesses behind stops them from reaching us. A few streets away from the temple, Taria takes an odd turn which I'm certain will lead us farther away from our destination. My suspicions are confirmed when her two guards glance at each other, but they don't question her change in direction and hurry after her. I do the same, curious where she's heading.

Taria's path takes us through a tangle of narrow streets, and we venture farther from the temple. The flock of priestesses doesn't follow us, and the crowd from the city's square seems to have lost sight of us. I wonder whether that's Taria's intention, as I can think of no other reason that one of the most deified priestesses in all of Selynis would want to wander down such run-down streets. A few shady looking men eye us with interest, but it only takes one glance at Caya and Juron's shining swords and Taria's bright eyes for them to scarper down the street.

I find the answer to why Taria has come here in a shadowed corner. A young girl is slumped against the wall, her arms so thin she looks like a bag of bones. Taria stops before her and crouches to inspect her. The girl doesn't look up. Her eyes remain shut.

"She's barely breathing," Juron says, peering at the girl from over Taria's shoulder. He isn't wrong. I have to stare at the girl for several moments before I notice the slight rise of her chest.

"It's a wonder no one has tried selling her," Caya says, shaking her head. "Though perhaps for her luck, I doubt she'd be any use to anyone. She looks like she won't last another morning."

Taria draws her lips into a thin line and presses her hand to the back of the girl's forehead. Her white brows knit together. "She has a fever." Taria presses her palms together in a silent prayer, but Juron grips her shoulder.

"Taria," he says softly. "Death will soon claim her. Healing her will cost you too much strength."

Taria lifts his hand from her shoulder. "The Mother guided me to this girl because she knows I alone possess the strength to heal her. It would be sinful of me not to carry out the Mother's will."

Juron's jaw clenches, but he says nothing more. Caya doesn't object either, but the frown she wears is indication enough of her concern.

I watch as golden light radiates from Taria's hands. While we Magi of Nolderan are far from religious, we acknowledge the existence of the gods. They are, after all, the counterpart of the Void King and his demonic lieutenants. I've always been convinced that the gods care nothing for us mortals, and I'm not alone in that belief. Yet here I stand, watching this strange priestess use her powers to heal a peasant girl by the Goddess Zolane's instruction. And there is also the fact Taria interrupted my execution. Does the Mother Goddess care also for my plight? Or perhaps she isn't as concerned by my pursuit of justice as she is by the threat Arluin and his necromancers pose to the world.

I wonder what exactly the goddess has shared with Taria.

The priestess closes her eyes, and an aura of light washes over her. Her brows furrow with tiny lines of concentration. The surrounding light grows with intensity until it becomes blinding enough that I have to look away, and so does Natharius. Even Taria's two guards are forced to avert their eyes.

"*Tamiliya,*" the priestess whispers. The light erupts. A beam shoots forth and slams into the sickly girl.

The girl jerks backward from the force. Magic pours from the priestess and into the peasant girl. Beads of sweat emerge on Taria's brow. Her hands tremble, and her magic falters. The strain in her shoulders is clear.

"Taria!" Juron calls over to her. "That's enough! If you use any more magic, you could kill yourself!"

If Taria hears his warning over the buzz of magic, she doesn't heed it.

"Leave her be," Caya says to Juron, her voice cold and firm. "The Mother guided her to this girl for a reason. We cannot know what part she may have to play in the future and why the Mother asked Taria to heal her. Perhaps one day she shall become a priestess or a chancellor. It is not our place to intervene."

Juron lowers his head.

Impatient tapping comes from behind. I turn to see Natharius looking exceptionally irritable. Since he can't currently speak, I suppose he feels the need to communicate his displeasure in a different way. I flash him a glare and hope it reminds him I've already silenced his tapping before and that I'm prepared to do it again. Given how he wrinkles his nose and stops, I'm inclined to believe he understands my silent warning perfectly well.

The excursion of healing a peasant girl isn't one I had in mind, especially not when it risks killing the priestess who possesses the many answers I seek, but we can't leave her here to die. Though Natharius would advocate for that option if he could speak.

I have no choice but to wait until Taria finishes healing the girl. Luckily, it only takes a few minutes more.

The girl's eyes flutter open, and she looks up at the five of us and blinks several times. "I . . ." The syllable comes out hoarse, as if she has drunk nothing for days, but she doesn't finish her sentence since Taria topples backward. Juron lunges forth and catches her before she slams into the street.

"Taria!" he exclaims.

The priestess murmurs something, but I can't make out her words.

Juron clasps her delicate face in his hands, his dark eyes filled with panic.

"She'll be fine," Caya says. "She's used up more of her magic than this before. All she needs is rest."

Juron lifts Taria into his arms as if she were a porcelain doll. The priestess looks even more serene with her eyes closed and her chest steadily rising and falling.

"What of the girl?" I blurt, when Caya and Juron turn away. "We can't leave her here." Especially not after Caya mentioned the possibility of the girl being sold. If this part of the city is as dangerous as that, Taria's effort to heal her will be in vain.

"We don't know what vision the Mother granted Taria," Caya says, placing a hand on her hip. "She knew how much strength it would require to heal the girl and that it would more than likely result in her being rendered unconscious. If she intended for us to bring the girl back to the temple with us, she would have told us to do so before beginning her spell. Though I can't claim to know the Mother's Will like Taria does, I've learned enough to know the future is a tangle of hundreds of different threads and any slight ripple can cause the entire world to plunge down a dark path. I'm also sure this is something you have recently experienced for yourself."

"What—"

"This isn't the place to have this discussion with you, nor should I be the one to do so. Taria will once she's well."

Caya's expression is stone, and her tone is ice. I doubt words alone will pry the truth from her lips. But after what she has said, all I can think about is whether Taria has seen a vision where Nolderan did not fall. Were my choices those tiny ripples which Caya alluded to? Could my actions have prevented all that death and destruction?

Caya plucks a golden coin from a leather pouch among the many blades sheathed at her belt and holds it out to the girl. She shuffles back into the shadowed corner as Caya approaches and regards the rest of us warily—particularly Natharius. I suppose even a child can tell there's nothing natural about blood-red eyes. She doesn't seem too trusting of Caya either, but her face isn't much more welcoming than the Void Prince's. And that's no easy feat.

"Here," Caya says, tossing the coin onto the street. "Take this and buy yourself something to eat tonight. You'll have more than enough for clothes as well. Spend it quickly, or it'll end up in someone else's pocket."

The girl creeps forth on her hands and knees and snatches the coin. She lifts it to her mouth and gives it a single bite and, once satisfied, darts around the corner and out of sight.

"You could have at least given her two," Juron says.

"Then it would draw twice the attention," Caya replies. She gestures toward the temple in the distance. Its limestone pillars peek out from the rusty roofs of the city. "Let's get a move on. Taria needs to rest, and one of our guests is in desperate need of freshening herself." She gives me a pointed look and wrinkles her nose as if I stink. I probably do.

I shrug. "Fine by me."

CHAPTER 17

THE ENTOURAGE OF PRIESTESSES FROM the square awaits us at the temple's entrance. They hurry to us as we turn the corner, their faces growing concerned at the sight of Taria's small body in Juron's arms.

"The First Disciple!" they exclaim.

A senior priestess turns to Juron and frowns. "What happened? Has she been injured?"

Juron shakes his head, but it's Caya who answers.

"The First Disciple over exerted herself while carrying out the Mother's will," she says. The priestess narrows her eyes at this, so Caya adds: "There's no need for alarm. It was only a healing spell."

The priestess peers at Taria more closely and then nods. "We shall find her somewhere to rest." She orders three priestesses to help Juron escort Taria into the temple, and once they're gone, she turns to Natharius and me. "Did the First Disciple give instructions for what we should do with our . . . guests?"

"Bathe and feed them," Caya replies. "Though apparently the demon requires neither."

Still under the command of silence, Natharius can only glare at her.

"Right this way then, witc-" She coughs and eyes the indigo fabric of my robes beneath the layers of rotten food. "Mage." The priestess extends her arm and gestures to the many steps leading up to the temple's enormous doors.

"What of my faerie dragon?" I ask the priestess as I hurry up the steps after her.

"Faerie dragon?" she says, glancing back at me. "Oh, of course. You mean the small creature which accompanied you here? Forgive me, I've never heard the name before."

"Yes, that's who I mean. Do you know where he is?"

"He's with the temple's doves. I'll send a girl over with him while you're in the baths."

I give her a nod. "And my staff? Do you know what happened to it after I was locked in my cell?"

"It's safe in our vaults. I'll have it sent to you with your pet."

We reach the top of the steps and slip beneath the large, arched doors. The temple's courtyard stretches out before us, bustling with maids and priestesses.

"Natharius," I say, turning to the Void Prince. "I permit you to speak once more."

The demon scowls at me.

"I assume you aren't planning to come to the baths?" At least, I hope he wasn't planning to do so. I'm not sure what the temple's bathing facilities are like, but if there's only one communal bath then I certainly have no desire to strip off before the Void Prince. Nor do I have any desire to see him naked—

I decide it best to stop that ridiculous chain of thoughts before they start conjuring images of the Void Prince I would very much rather not see.

Natharius scowl doesn't relent.

"I'll take that as a no then." He doesn't correct me, so I continue: "I won't be too long, though there's little we can do until Taria is awake. Try not to stray too far."

Natharius wrinkles his nose and turns on his heel. The ends of his long, silvery hair flash out like a fan of swords with the sharp motion.

"Actually, let's make that an order!" I call after him. "Natharius, you are not to leave this temple."

Though I'm certain his keen elven ears won't have missed a single word, he offers no indication of hearing me.

"Shall we?" The priestess gestures to the left of the courtyard.

The baths are in the eastern wing, and when we reach them, the priestess utters the spell-word *nesimti* to conjure a golden breeze and blow open the heavy wooden doors.

Steps lead down to a rectangular pool with water trickling from the various tiled pipes situated around its perimeter. White petals float across the rippling surface, and an aroma of heavy perfume greets me. Jasmine and lychee, I think. Not that I've ever been exceptional at identifying key notes in perfume. That was one of Eliya's particular skills. Her heart-shaped face and crimson locks flash through my mind, and a sudden stabbing pain shoots through my chest.

I mask my expression as best I can, and if the priestess notices the fleeting shadow of anguish across my face, she says nothing of it.

"You may help yourself to our facilities," the priestess says. "I'll send a maid in with a towel and fresh robes for you to change into. If you leave your clothes to one side, she can collect them and take them to be washed."

"Thank you," I reply. "I appreciate it."

The priestess nods and leaves, shutting the wooden doors behind her.

Bright mosaics cover all the walls, their images depicting various interpretations of the Mother. The sun and sky are also frequently featured, which is to be expected since the Goddess Zolane is closely associated with them.

I peel the layers of sullied indigo fabric from my body, my nose creasing at all the stains. I'm sure my robes stink, but the fragrance wafting from the pool is strong enough to mask all other scents. I pull off my boots, which also didn't escape the barrage of rotten food, and leave them beside my folded-up robes. Even my undergarments somehow received a few stains.

Once I've shed my dirty clothes, I step down to the pool of water. I reach the last step and gaze into the water. My reflection is distorted by the rippling surface and floating petals, but it's clear enough to see the tomato juice on my cheek and matted in my hair. I crouch and dip my hand into the pool and use the water to wipe the stain from my cheek.

Those people in the streets hated me today. I've never seen anyone look at me with so much loathing—except perhaps for the Void Prince—and all those people were strangers. I've done nothing to harm them personally, and yet they hated me for the fact I used dark magic to summon a demon from the Abyss.

If the people of Nolderan could see me now, would their eyes hold the same burning hatred as the people of Esterra City? Would they ever forgive me for leading them to their deaths and mutilation? For abusing my power as a mage and breaking the Arcanium's teachings by summoning a Void Prince?

My father wouldn't. Would Eliya? She was the most understanding person I've ever known, so maybe she would forgive me even if I don't deserve to be forgiven.

I swirl my finger in the pool and watch the surface ripple around it.

What Caya said earlier about slight ripples entirely changing the course of the future echoes through my mind. In the water, images flash by of a different world where Nolderan isn't destroyed. Where those I love are living and breathing. Where the boy I knew since childhood didn't shatter my heart.

If I made wiser choices, would the present be completely different? Instead of being here in this strange land of sun and sand, would I be giggling with Eliya over a bottle of moon blossom wine?

I draw out a heavy sigh and slip down into the water. It's cooler than I expect, so I hold out both hands underwater and let aether gather in them. "*Calida.*" Warmth blossoms through the water and caresses my skin. When the water is a more comfortable temperature, I tilt back my head and gaze up.

The ceiling has been carved out to reveal the open sky. Night has not yet fallen, but the clouds are tinted with a rosy glow and amber light streaks through them. I shift backward so I'm partially floating and stare at the sky.

It has been two weeks since Nolderan fell, and yet the pain in my heart hasn't at all diminished. How many months—years—will it take before the wounds are no longer raw? Will I ever be able to think of those I love without tears pricking my eyes, without the anchor of guilt weighing on my heart?

Will I ever again feel *normal*?

The young, carefree Reyna died the night Heston murdered my mother. The grief of losing my mother—*watching* helplessly as she was killed—was unbearable. Continuing to live my life after that was almost impossible, but I managed by throwing myself into my academic studies and vowing to become the best mage I could be. Now I don't have my lectures to distract me. I only have vengeance and a loathsome Void Prince. I don't know how I will ever heal and become whole again.

The shuddering of the doors from the other side of the room interrupts my thoughts. I flop back with a splash, scattering petals across the pool, and swivel around. A maid hurries in with a fluffy towel, fresh robes, and my staff, and Zephyr flutters behind her.

My fragile heart surges at the sight of Zephyr. Not only do I have vengeance and a Void Prince but also my faerie dragon. He's the last little piece of home I have, and a weight is lifted from my shoulders at the sight of him fine and well. Though the priestesses may have marched Natharius and me to our execution, it doesn't seem they've inflicted their wrath upon my faerie dragon.

He zips through the air and does a loop before coming to a stop before hovering over the water's surface. He stares at me with his glittering eyes.

"Miss me?" I ask.

He answers by nudging my shoulder with his muzzle, and I run my fingers across the smooth scales on his forehead.

"I'll leave everything here," the maid says, her small voice barely reaching across the room. She places the towel, robes and my staff atop the steps leading to the pool and scoops my sullied clothes and boots into her arms.

"Thank you," I call after her.

She dips her head. "Do you require anything else?"

Zephyr snaps his teeth together and snorts.

I laugh. "Food and drink, please."

She frowns as she looks at Zephyr's hungry expression. "We tried feeding your pet berries, seeds and grains like our doves, but he would hardly touch any of his food. We weren't sure what else to feed him."

I laugh and hold out my hand. "*Crysanthius*." Aether solidifies into crystals, and Zephyr's eyes widen at the sight. He swoops down to my hand and gobbles them up. His forked tongue flicks out and licks every trace of aether from my palm.

"Zephyr is quite the fussy eater," I say to the maid. "He won't really eat anything other than aether crystals."

"I'm not sure we'll be able to accommodate for aether crystals, but it looks like you already have that covered. Shall I send for your food to be brought in here?"

"To my room, please. I won't be much longer in here."

The maid gives a nod and leaves, taking my robes and boots with her.

CHAPTER 18

Scrubbing the rotten food from my hair takes longer than I expect. Zephyr tries to help, but his talons only jab my scalp. When I let out a yelp of pain, he stops and tries to nudge my locks with his muzzle, but it accomplishes little. In the end, he gives up and perches on the pool's tiled wall while I wrestle with my hair.

By the time all the dirt is out, I'm sure I've left half a head's worth of hair in the pool. I dry myself with the towel the maid gave me and drape it over the side of a ledge. Once I've changed into fresh silk robes, I stride out of the baths and head for my room.

I find Natharius sitting in the corner of my room, his arms folded across his chest and his crimson eyes burning into the wall opposite him. Food is already laid out on the small table in front of him, though none of it has been touched. The maids have brought enough for two people, though Caya mentioned to the priestesses Natharius neither needed to bathe or eat. There's also a colorful bowl full of water, which must be for Zephyr.

"What are you doing here?" I ask, slipping onto the chair across from him. Zephyr perches on its wooden arm. I push the bowl of water toward him, and he crawls to the edge of the arm and leans forth to drink, his forked tongue lapping up the water.

Natharius tears his gaze from the wall and looks at me. "What?" he growls. "Am I *forbidden* from coming here as well as being unable to leave this damned temple?"

My question wasn't at all accusatory, but the Void Prince must still be sour about the command I shouted down the corridor. I don't have any regrets about doing so. If I hadn't ordered him to stay put in the temple, Natharius could be anywhere in the city, and we're already behind schedule for reaching Gerazad. We can't afford to waste any more time. As soon as Taria wakes, I must speak with her and discover what the Mother Goddess revealed to her. And though I loathe to admit it, the Void Prince has a millennium's worth of knowledge and his insight is nothing to scoff at. Even as insufferable as he is. That's why I'd prefer him to be present when I talk to Taria.

"No," I reply, lifting the goblet of wine poured for me. While it's far from as exquisite as moon blossom wine, I have drunk nothing all day except for a few sips of water while in the dungeons, and it tastes like honey as it slips down my throat. I place the goblet back on the table. "I just didn't expect you to willingly seek my company when you have an entire temple's worth of places to choose from."

"This is the only place in the entire temple free from light wor-shipping fools. You are slightly more tolerable than them."

"That sounds like a compliment coming from you," I say, in between biting into my food.

"The reason you are more tolerable is because I merely remind myself of all the ways I shall torture you upon your demise."

"Ah. That's more like it. But your reason for choosing to come here doesn't stand."

"Why not?"

"I can think of one place in the temple with neither me nor priestesses."

"Where?"

"The dungeons."

"I have spent long enough in that vile place."

"I thought such a dark and morbid place would be right up your alley."

He glares at me.

I take another mouthful of food and ask, "Anyway, how many days was I unconscious?"

He doesn't reply.

I lower my fork and draw out a sigh. Surely he isn't that worked up over my comment about him preferring dark and morbid places? Or perhaps he holds a grudge over the command I gave him to not venture out of the temple's walls. But when he acts as stubborn as this, what choice does he give me than to assert my power over him?

"That was an order," I say.

"What was an order?" he grinds out.

I pinch the bridge of my nose. "Natharius, if you were more co-operative then I wouldn't have to keep doing this."

He stares at me, his unnatural crimson eyes pinning me in place.

"I don't actually enjoy stripping you of your free will all the time." Maybe that's a slight lie. But if I do enjoy it, it's only because he deserves it for being so obstinate.

"You seemed to enjoy yourself before."

"I only ordered you to stay put inside the temple because I knew you'd vanish from here at the first opportunity you got and then I'd have to order you to return via a mind-link, anyway."

He lifts his chin. "I might have returned willingly."

I give him a dubious look. "Would you?"

"That's not the point. You didn't give me the opportunity to prove otherwise."

"Then I offer my sincerest apologies. Next time I will ensure I offer you amble opportunity to prove that you aren't always so insufferable."

Zephyr lets out a snort that sounds very much like a laugh. Natharius shoots him a murderous glare, and my faerie dragon falls silent.

"Besides," he continues, "that wasn't the only command you issued today."

The Void Prince of Pride certainly is touchy about being ordered around, though that isn't surprising, given his title.

"You threatened to tear Taria to pieces because she mentioned your past."

"I didn't threaten to tear her apart," he says. "I offered to carve the flesh from her bones."

"That's the same thing."

"It isn't," he replies. "It is very much possible to skin someone whole. I am willing to demonstrate should you find a suitable subject."

"I don't require a demonstration, thank you very much. I'll take your word for it."

Natharius shrugs.

"But regardless of whether you threatened to tear Taria to pieces or carve the flesh from her bones, you left me with no choice but to silence you."

"I will not allow these fools to humiliate me any more than they already have."

"Taria saved you from humiliation at the High Priestess's hands."

"Saved?" he repeats. "She did not save me. Though she may have saved you, she has prevented my freedom. Now I do not know how long it will take for you to die."

"I'm hoping a long, long while."

"I am not."

"No offense taken."

"How unfortunate," he says with a sigh.

"Anyway," I say, finishing the last bite of my meal and pushing the plate away, "you didn't answer my question."

"What question?"

"Do you really not remember what I asked, or are you just trying to be difficult?"

He doesn't answer, so I decide it to be the latter.

"Natharius," I warn.

"Do it. You will prove my point."

"And you are just proving why I have to order you around."

He stares at me.

"Fine." I suppose when he's this annoying, I don't feel the slightest bit guilty about exerting my will over him. "Natharius Thalanor, I order you to truthfully answer the following question: How many days was I unconscious for? And while you're at it, I also command you to truthfully answer this other question: Do we have a chance of reaching Gerazad before Arluin and his necromancers?"

Natharius clenches his jaw, visibly fighting against the compulsion of my command. "Three days," he finally snarls. "As for your second question, it is possible, but the chance we will reach Gerazad first is slimmer than before. And it was already exceptionally slim."

"But possible," I say.

"Are you deaf? That is what I just said."

"It wasn't a question. I was thinking out loud."

"Well, don't."

I ignore him and turn to the window, considering his answer. Hopefully it's possible for us to stop whatever destruction Arluin intends. While the Void Prince isn't omnipotent, I do trust his judgement. In this regard, anyway. Even if the chance of us succeeding is incredibly thin, the odds have been stacked against me from the start. I'm not about to give up now, just because we may be three days behind schedule.

"Of course," Natharius continues, "the only way we have the slightest chance of reaching Gerazad before the necromancers is by passing through the Ghost Woods and that region is filled with—"

"All horrors of the night which will attempt to murder and devour me in more ways than I can imagine."

"Exactly," Natharius says with a smile.

Zephyr squeals at that and scratches my silken sleeves with his talons.

"You can stay here if you would prefer," I say, staring down into his fearful eyes. I hope he can't see the truth in mine: that I would much rather him stay by my side, even if that is a selfish thing to want.

Zephyr shakes his head and crawls onto my lap and curls up there. From all Natharius has said, the Ghost Woods is no place for an innocent faerie dragon but I'm relieved I won't need to part ways with him.

"I wonder how long Taria will need to rest," I muse aloud, though I already know Natharius couldn't care any less.

"Leave without her," the Void Prince says.

"Why would I leave without her? You yourself said that light magic is most effective against dark magic. From what I've gathered so far, she's also the second most powerful priestess in all of Selynis and would prove an invaluable ally. Besides, I also want to know what the Mother Goddess has revealed to her. She might hold vital information on defeating our enemies."

"*Your* enemies."

"My enemies are your enemies, Natharius. Until they are defeated, I cannot allow you to return to the Abyss."

"These priestesses cannot be trusted."

"You're only saying that because you are a demon."

"I am not. Have you forgotten that only a few hours ago, you were almost executed by one of them?"

"That was Ahelin's doing, not Taria's. She proved her intentions when she stopped my execution."

"That doesn't make her trustworthy."

"Perhaps not, but I certainly trust her more than I trust you."

His temple twitches at that. I can't quite read the emotion on his face, however. Surely those words won't have stung him? How can he possibly be surprised that I don't trust him when all he's ever done is wish for my demise and tell me all the horrifying ways he plans to torture my soul?

"No one can know what schemes lie in the minds of these vile creatures," Natharius says. "Not that there can be possibly much in their minds, seeing how they place all their faith in an absent goddess. Their precious Mother Goddess doesn't give a single damn about them, just as she doesn't with any other human which has ever existed."

After all I've suffered, I'm inclined to agree that the Mother Goddess must be either absent or callous, but then I can't deny she sent Taria to save me. And she also guided her to save that peasant girl. Was that foresight Taria's own magic or was the goddess guiding her?

"It is said the Mother Goddess created all of mankind," I say, reciting what I learned during my lectures at the Arcanium. "How can she not care for us?" Of course, most of us magi believe that the gods no longer involve themselves with mortals, except for their most devout followers, but my words are chosen to provoke Natharius. I'm curious how much knowledge he holds regarding the Heavens.

Natharius laughs darkly. "Care for you? She and the other gods stopped caring for you humans tens of thousands of years ago. Your kind have long served your purpose for them."

Now that is something I've not heard before. I sit up in my chair. "Our purpose? What are you talking about?"

"I'm talking about the reason you humans were created."

"Every child knows that legend. Meysus created the earth and sky, and Zolane filled the world with elves and men."

"Zolane did not create us elves."

"Then why don't you share your version of the creation myth?" I say. "If the Goddess Zolane did not create elves then who did, and for what purpose did she create us?"

"What do you know of the War of the Gods?"

I hesitate and press my lips together, reluctant to admit my ignorance.

"Nothing, as I thought," Natharius continues, his silky tone laced with smugness. "You humans are so useless that you cannot even record your own origins."

"And how do you know Lumaria's version of the creation of Imyria and all its creatures is the truth?"

"Because it is. Even the Abyss records it as so."

I suppose I can't argue if the Abyss has recorded the creation of the world. I imagine it would be as accurate as that which is recorded in the Heavens—that is, unless the Void King has twisted it.

"Fine," I say, folding my arms across my chest. "Tell me then."

"Long ago," Natharius says, leaning back in his chair and curling his slender fingers around the arms as if he were instead sprawling across a throne, "no barriers lay between the Heavens, the Abyss, and the mortal plane. Gods and demons were free to pass from their realms and into Imyria whenever they pleased."

"Yes, I know that," I interrupt. "Meysus created barriers between all planes of existence to save mortals from the Void King's evil."

"No, he did so to protect his own, the Caelum," Natharius says. "In the war between the Caelum and Malum, the Void King recruited some of the original inhabitants of Imyria for his army."

"Who?"

"Goblins. They seduced some of the primitive tribes with the promise of power and warped them into beings of terrible strength. You know them as orcs today."

"Orcs were created by the Malum?" At least that explains why orcs have always been more closely aligned with dark magic than any other race.

"Indeed, though their power has vastly diluted through the millennia. Now, the Caelum had no army of their own, so Meysus shaped his soldiers from the earth and Zolane breathed life into these statues. That is how humans were created."

I suppose this version isn't so different from the one I know.

"You humans were created for war," Natharius continues. "That fact alone explains many of your race's shortcomings."

"Our shortcomings?"

"Throughout the ages, humans have always sought conflict and power. I suppose you cannot be blamed. It is in your nature."

I lower my gaze and stare at the scraps of food remaining on my plate, though I left little. If we humans were born for war, then does that explain monsters like Heston and Arluin? Are there monsters inside us all?

Not wishing to dwell on such thoughts, especially not in my current company, I lift my head and look at the Void Prince. "And what of the elves? How were they created? You've explained how both humans and orcs came to be, but not elves."

"We were not created. We descend from the Caelum."

I tilt my head and regard his expression. He persistently includes himself in the mention of elves. Though he has been a demon for over a thousand years, he clings to his identity as an elf. I can't help but wonder what exactly Taria knows of the Void Prince's past. I could order him to tell me the truth, but that's a line I have no wish to cross, even if he is a hateful demon.

"If elves descend from the gods," I reply, "why are they mortal?"

"Our ancestors were locked out of the Heavens for so long that their powers diminished."

"Why? What happened for them to be locked out of the Heavens?"

Natharius pauses, his shoulders tensing. Whatever the truth is, he's reluctant to admit it.

Before I can probe any answers out of him, a knock sounds at the door.

"Come in," I call.

The door swings open to reveal a maid. She's young, perhaps not even sixteen, and she doesn't dare to step foot inside the room. Her shoulders tremble. Is her fear for the Void Prince or for me as well?

"T-the First Disciple has requested to see you," she squeaks, keeping her head down and not looking either of us in the eye. "Both of you."

CHAPTER 19

WHEN WE REACH TARIA'S CHAMBERS, the maid wastes no time in knocking on the ornate, white door. "First Disciple," she calls. "I have brought the two guests, as requested."

Zephyr narrows his eyes at her, but she doesn't correct herself.

The door opens, revealing Caya's scarred cheek. Her dark eyes flicker across us all. "Good. You may leave."

The maid doesn't need telling twice. She flees down the corridor as quickly as her legs can carry her. Not once does she glance back over her shoulder.

Caya opens the door wider for us. "You can come in." She turns to Natharius, her eyes narrowing. "But threaten the future Grand Priestess again, Void Prince, and I will give you a taste of my blade." Her hand shifts to the hilt of her sword, her fingers dancing around it in anticipation.

Natharius's lips twist into a menacing snarl. "I'd like to see you try, mortal."

Caya's hand tightens around her sword, her shoulders taut with tension. Before either of them can threaten each other again, I step between them.

"He's under my control," I say to Caya, hoping I sound more confident than I feel.

The warrior meets my gaze with a stern expression and, after scrutinizing me for a long moment, offers a single nod. She whirls around and strides through the room.

"One threat," I hiss to Natharius, "and I'll have you silenced like before."

Natharius shoots me an icy stare in return. I doubt the Prince of Pride enjoys being silenced by a mere mortal.

I follow Caya into the room and find Taria perching on a golden chaise. She sits there cross-legged, her hands resting on her knees and palms facing the ceiling. An aura of golden light surrounds her, and her chest rises and falls to a slow, steady rhythm as she meditates.

Juron stands behind the priestess, his gaze never leaving her. Not even when the three of us approach. I cast my gaze around the room, my brows raising at the lavish decorations. The rectangular rug at the center is a finely embroidered tapestry of the sun, and the white tiles across the floor are so polished they glitter like crystals.

We stop before the chaise, and Taria's eyes flash open. Despite having been deep in meditation, the priestess's senses appear sharp. Her lips pull upward into a light smile as her gaze falls on me.

"It is good to see you again, Reyna," Taria says, her voice exuding warmth. "Please, take a seat." She gestures at the cushioned chairs across from her.

"Thank you," I reply, sitting down. Zephyr swoops down and perches on my shoulder. Though there's an empty chair beside me, Natharius doesn't sit. His body stiffens with tension, as if being so close to the priestess causes him great discomfort. As Taria's golden eyes drift over him, she does not display the same uneasiness as he does. I wonder whether she will again urge the demon to sit, but she doesn't.

"Back in the city square today," I say after a moment, when the priestess remains silent, "you mentioned Imyria's fate. That both I and Natharius play an instrumental part in it."

Taria gives a single, swift nod. "While you both do, your part to play is far greater, Reyna. Imyria's fate revolves around you. Along with another."

"Arluin?" My voice is but a breath as I say the name of the man I hate most in this world. The man who once held my heart.

"Indeed. Your destiny, and Arluin's destiny, are both connected by the threads of fate to each other and to Imyria. If you are to die, the hope of Imyria's survival will die with you. If Arluin Harstall dies, then Imyria will be protected from the threat he poses. In short, everything rests on you. And Arluin, too."

With Taria's words comes a heavy burden that I do not know how to bear. Already I can feel its weight on my shoulders, threatening to crush me. "Why me?" I choke, not liking how small my voice comes out.

"From the moment you became an integral part of the necromancer's life, you sealed this path for yourself," Taria replies.

"You mean I chose this for myself by becoming close to him?"

"Indeed."

"Would . . . would everything still have happened like this?"

"Are you asking whether Nolderan would have fallen if you did not know Arluin?"

I manage a small nod, not allowing myself to imagine the possibility of a different reality.

"I don't know," she says. Is that the truth or is the priestess hiding the truth to spare my feelings? "What I do know, however, is that in every future I see where this evil is vanquished, it is you who brings the new dawn. In the futures where you fall, eternal night reigns over Imyria. And death with it."

How can someone as useless as me be so important? Other than the fact Arluin and I tied our fates together, how else do I qualify for this enormous responsibility?

"Priestess," Natharius demands from behind me. "Do you know what this necromancer ultimately intends?"

Taria shakes her head. "Unfortunately, I do not. My visions are never clear. I only see fragments of many possibilities and must piece them together through meditation."

A solemn expression shadows Natharius's face. Why does the demon care about Arluin's intentions for this world? He belongs to the Abyss, not Imyria, and he hates mortals us and revels in all our suffering.

He must feel my gaze on him, since his crimson eyes flicker from the priestess and down to me. "I hate necromancers," he growls.

I watch him for a moment longer, though his expression reveals nothing more, before turning back to Taria. "We've learned that Arluin and his necromancers are heading to a small orcish settlement in Jektar called Gerazad, but we don't know why he wishes to travel there."

Taria presses her lips together as she thinks. Neither of her guards offer any suggestions, though Caya is more focused on Natharius than the conversation which is unfolding. Her fingers drum on the hilt of her sword. Meanwhile, Juron watches Taria carefully—as if she may fall unconscious at any moment.

"I'm not sure either," Taria replies. "I haven't seen Gerazad in any of my visions."

"You haven't?" If Taria hasn't seen Gerazad in any of her visions, then does that mean we won't reach it in time? That we will fail to defeat Arluin?

Taria must notice the disappointment in my expression. "My visions are fragmented," she says softly, "and they are not exhaustive of every possible future."

"But a future remains where Arluin is defeated? It's a possibility?"

"Yes, it is. However, the odds would have been more stacked in our favor if I'd reached you sooner. For that, I apologize."

"You have nothing to apologize for," I say.

The snort that comes from Natharius says otherwise. Caya grips her sword and her eyes narrow, ready to strike the Void Prince if needed.

Taria lowers her head. "I owe you a great debt, Reyna."

"You owe me?" I exclaim, bewildered by her words. "You're the one who saved my life today. The debt I owe you is unmeasurable."

"I first started having these visions a month ago."

"Before Nolderan's fall?"

"They were fragmented at first, nearly impossible to piece together," Taria says. "The Mother was trying to warn me of what was to come, yet I lacked the wisdom to see what she wanted me to see. Even up until that very night, I was blind. I only realized the truth when the Mother granted me vision through your eyes."

Natharius scoffs. "Then maybe your precious goddess should have supplied you with clearer guidance."

I shoot him a warning glance. The demon merely shrugs in response.

"Do not speak of the Mother in such a way!" Caya hisses.

Even Juron looks away from Taria long enough to wrinkle his nose at Natharius in disgust.

Taria raises her hand before he too can add to Caya's words. "That night, the goddess sent me a vision through your eyes," she continues. "I was there with you when Nolderan fell. I . . . I saw everything."

I avert my gaze from her and swallow back the lump of grief swelling in my throat, threatening to overwhelm me here in front of the demon, the priestess, and her two guards.

"If I had been less foolish and had understood the visions sooner, then perhaps Nolderan could have been warned. Perhaps—"

"Don't," I choke. I can't bear for the priestess to say it. That there could have been a future where everyone wasn't dead. Where my home wasn't destroyed. Where the man I once loved didn't steal my best friend from this world and reanimate Father into a monstrosity. My hands tighten around the silken fabric of my robes, and I will myself not to cry. Not here.

Zephyr seems to notice the emotion swelling within me, since he nuzzles his nose against my cheek. I rub the soft scales on the top of his head and pull him a small smile.

"I am sorry. I did not mean for my words to come across so insensitive."

"They weren't," I say. "I'm fine."

Taria dips her head, thankfully seeming to take no offense to my outburst. The priestess is silent for a moment, most likely giving me time to recompose myself. But time is not something I have. Not if I want to defeat Arluin. To free Father. To avenge Nolderan. To save Imyria.

"Though you haven't seen Gerazad in your visions," I begin, keeping my words steady as I speak, "that's where Arluin is heading. We intend to follow him there, unless you have another suggestion?"

"I do not," Taria replies. "If Gerazad is his destination as you say, then it seems following him there is the only possible course of action."

"I don't know why he's traveling there, but it can't be for any good reason. I was hoping to arrive there first and warn the orcs, so that a catastrophe can be averted. But even with a Void Prince on my side, I can't be certain I have the means to destroy the necromancers. Would you be willing to travel with us to Gerazad?"

"I have told you already," Natharius says with a sigh, "I am more than capable of obliterating a puny necromancer who is too big for his boots."

"Though I have little doubt you would be an equal match for Arluin—"

"I am the Void Prince of Pride and a former High Enchanter of Lumaria during its most glorious days. He is not my equal, and you insult me by claiming as much."

I roll my eyes. "Sorry for insulting your greatness. Besides, it isn't only Arluin I'm concerned with you defeating, but also his necromancers and thousands of undead. Even you can't possibly face that many enemies. And you were bested by the priestesses here at the temple. Why shouldn't I be concerned by your capabilities?"

Natharius's temple twitches. Perhaps I should have kept that last remark to myself. "Had you not gotten yourself poisoned, we would not have needed to come to this temple."

"Had you been able to defeat that band of goblins more quickly, I wouldn't have gotten myself poisoned in the first place."

Taria lets out a gentle cough. Remembering that the priestess hasn't yet answered my question, I turn back to her and offer an apologetic look.

"I will accompany you on your journey to Gerazad," the priestess says. She gestures to her two guards. "As will Caya and Juron."

I glance between the two warriors. Their eyes aren't golden like Taria's, and I'm not sure how much light magic they can wield—if at all. But their swords shone brightly in the city's square today, and every blade is needed to sway the odds of victory into our favor. "Thank you. For being willing to help us."

"No thanks is needed. The Mother showed me those visions, and she chose me for this task. As the future Grand Priestess of Selynis, it is my responsibility to protect Imyria from evil."

A part of me wishes my motivations were as noble and pure as the priestess's. Mine are instead fueled by hatred and wrath. The burning desire to see Arluin pay for all the atrocities he committed.

"I was hoping to leave tonight," I reply. "Time is not a luxury we have." Though Taria looks weary from the healing spell earlier this afternoon, she looks a little more rested.

"I understand," Taria replies. "If we can reach Gerazad before the necromancers, then not only will we be able to warn the orcs of the impending danger, but we will also be able to set up wards around the city."

With how easily Arluin shattered Nolderan's defenses, I hadn't thought about setting up wards. In fact, I haven't thought much at all about what will happen when we reach Gerazad. If the wards are actively channeled from inside the settlement, they'll be harder to break than turning off the Aether Tower. Though I doubt my magic will be enough, the priestess's entire being is brimming with holy magic. And light is far more effective than aether against dark magic. Her wards would stand even stronger than Natharius's would, since his would only be born of the same shadows which the necromancers wield themselves.

"Then it's settled," I say. "We'll leave immediately."

"Taria—" Juron begins.

"It's fine." The priestess doesn't look at him.

Juron must want to remind her of how much strength she used earlier today in order to save the peasant girl. Though I feel a small twinge of guilt from knowing Taria isn't fully recovered, time can't be wasted.

"We will leave shortly," Taria continues. "We will need a few moments to gather our belongings and replenish our supplies."

"As will we," I reply.

"Take what you need from the temple. We are setting out to exact the Mother's will. Our quest is a sacred one, and the temple will offer us all the resources we need."

I dip my head, while Natharius scoffs. He thankfully spouts no more blasphemy. Yet his expression doesn't go unnoticed by Caya, whose hand hasn't left the hilt of her sword.

"Nonetheless, I'm grateful for any aid the temple can offer," I reply, rising from my seat. Zephyr hops off my shoulder and flutters behind me as I start toward the door. Natharius trails after us a little more enthusiastically than usual. He must be eager to escape the priestess and her blinding aura of golden light.

Halfway to the door, I pause. "There was another matter as well," I say to the priestess.

"Yes," Taria asks, "what was it?"

"High Priestess Ahelin. I was wondering what will happen to her."

"You needn't worry. She attacked the First Disciple of the Grand Priestess Elunar. She will be dealt with according to the law, and undoubtedly stripped of her position as the High Priestess of Esterra City."

"How will she be punished? She won't be executed, will she?"

"That is for the law to decide," Taria replies. "A trial will be held to determine her fate."

"I see . . ."

"Do you wish for her to be executed?"

I shake my head. "When I arrived, she cleansed me from the poison running through my veins and saved my life. Though she later tried to execute us, I can't deny that Natharius is a Void Prince of the Abyss and that I'm the one who summoned him, though I wouldn't call myself a witch by any stretch of the word. Ahelin was only doing her job as the High Priestess of this city. She couldn't have known the Mother would send you here to carry out her will." I don't add how I explained the threat Arluin and his necromancers pose to Imyria and how Ahelin believed me until she discovered my connection to Natharius. Doing so may result in more evidence against Ahelin, and I don't believe she deserves to be executed. Maybe being stripped of her title and responsibilities, but not death.

"You're quite correct. Natharius is a Void Prince, and you are his summoner. In usual times, that would warrant your execution. That's why Ahelin won't be tried for this. She will instead be tried for the crimes of striking me, the First Disciple. Her intent was clear to all who witnessed her actions earlier today."

At least if Ahelin is executed, it won't be because of me. That may be a horrible thought to think, but there's already enough blood on my hands. I don't need any more.

I give her a nod. "When you're ready, I'll meet you outside the temple."

"We won't keep you waiting for long," Taria promises.

CHAPTER 20

AN EVENING BREEZE ROLLS OVER me as I gaze up at the twinkling stars. Natharius stands to my left, leaning against one of the temple's pillars, and Zephyr hovers on the other side of me, his wings beating back and forth. The Void Prince's arms are folded across his chest, and his foot taps against the stone. Over and over. With so few outside the temple, it would be peaceful if not for the incessant tapping of his foot.

"Stop that," I snap, glaring at his foot.

"Stop what?" the demon asks, raising a silvery brow. His foot pauses, offering me a moment's respite. Then it continues louder than before.

"Your foot. You have an awful habit of tapping it whenever you're waiting. It's irritating."

"Don't blame me," Natharius replies. "Blame the priestess and her friends. We have been waiting out here for almost an hour. If they were here already, I wouldn't need to tap my foot."

I heave out a breath. Unfortunately, he has a point. We've been waiting outside the temple for a while, though Taria promised she wouldn't be long. I fed Zephyr more aether crystals and filled my enchanted pouch with more supplies before we came out here to wait. I expected the temple's maids to protest when I headed down to the kitchen, but they saw to my request quickly. They must have wanted me to leave the temple as soon as possible. And to take the Void Prince with me.

Regardless, the priestess's lateness doesn't excuse Natharius's annoying habit.

"Why are you so eager to leave, anyway?" I ask. "I didn't think you'd be in such a hurry to be reunited with the priestess."

Natharius wrinkles his nose. "I'm not in a hurry to reunite with that light-worshipping fool. We should leave her behind."

"That doesn't answer my other question."

"Which other question?" he growls.

"Why you're in such a hurry to leave?"

"I've already explained this before," Natharius says, casting me an exasperated look. "The sooner we leave, the sooner we reach the Ghost Woods and you die."

I don't need to glare at him, since the one Zephyr casts him is scalding enough. Natharius offers him a venomous scowl, and my faerie dragon's resolve crumbles and he cowers behind me.

I sigh and stroke Zephyr's head, though it does little to calm his nerves. "I wouldn't count on it though," I say to the Void Prince. "There's always the possibility that I'll make it through the Ghost Woods alive."

"Indeed," Natharius says with a sigh. "And perhaps I will be forced to remain in this wretched place for decades."

I pray it won't take decades to defeat Arluin. I can't allow Father to be enslaved to his will for that long. Nor can I allow Nolderan to go unavenged.

I say none of this and continue stroking Zephyr. "Anyway," I say, "I don't believe you."

"What don't you believe?"

"That the only reason you're eager to leave is so you can return to the Abyss sooner."

"Returning to the Abyss is my only interest. What could possibly make you think it is not?"

"Oh, just the part where you were intrigued as to what Arluin intends for Imyria. And where you said you hate necromancers."

The Void Prince turns away, his gaze settling on the quiet streets in the distance. His jaw tightens.

"Didn't you say before that you hate necromancers?" I continue, peering at him.

"I did."

"And why would a fearsome Void Prince like yourself hate necromancers? Do you not wield the same dark magic as each other?"

"Though we demons wield the shadows as necromancers do, that does not mean that our magic is the same, like how the magic of magi, enchanters and stormcallers differs, despite all wielding aether."

"That answered my second question, not my first. Why exactly do you hate necromancers, Natharius?"

"I do not wish to discuss this matter with a puny mage like yourself."

"All right," I say, raising both hands in surrender. "It was only a simple question. There's no need to get so angry about it."

Natharius doesn't reply.

"I would wager that the reason you hate necromancers is the same reason you wanted to bite Taria's head off earlier today. I think the reason you hate necromancers has something to do with why you became a demon. Why you sacrificed your entire kingdom, your family, to sell your soul to the Void King in exchange for power."

"Stop," he snarls. It seems I've touched a nerve.

I would continue to probe the demon, to uncover what truths he hides, but beneath that snarl I swear I hear the twang of pain.

If it were anyone else, I might apologize. But not to him. Back when we emerged from Nolderan's Vaults, he took delight in my suffering, in my people's suffering. He doesn't deserve my sympathy. He's only lucky I don't take delight in his misery.

"Fine," I say. "Suit yourself."

Natharius turns away from me once more, this time gazing up at the stars. I do the same. There's no moon, and it makes the stars shine brighter.

Even several minutes later, when I return my attention to Natharius, his furious expression hasn't relented. He looks even angrier with me than he did with Taria earlier in the city's square. And I didn't even threaten to reveal his past to all of Esterra City.

Maybe Taria will tell me. I doubt Natharius will ever reveal the truth to me, and I don't want to stoop so low as to order him to tell me.

Not that the Void Prince's past matters so much to me, of course. I'm merely curious why he's so bad tempered whenever it's brought up. Then again, Taria alluded to it being the reason he has an instrumental part to play in Imyria's fate.

By the time Taria and her guards finally show up, Natharius is still riled. Seeing the three of them only seems to infuriate him further, if that's at all possible.

"I apologize if we kept you waiting," Taria says as she approaches us.

"It's fine. We weren't waiting long."

Natharius scoffs, but at least he doesn't make none of his usual remarks.

The priestess is dressed in the same sleeveless robes as before, and they flow from her lithe form like molten gold. Though I also wear robes, the indigo fabric isn't as billowy and is less likely to get snagged on twigs and branches. Then again, it's hard to imagine the priestess getting tangled in foliage. She is too graceful for that.

I also wonder about Taria's arms being bare and whether she feels the cold. While I'm not sure what the climate is like in the orcish land of Jektar, I doubt it will be as warm as Selynis, the Kingdom of Sand and Sun. Maybe the priestess has a fur-lined cloak inside a saddlebag her guards carry, but they all look too small. Perhaps the holy magic radiating from Taria's entire being prevents her from feeling the cold. Even from several paces away, I can feel the warmth exuding from the priestess. She is like the sun in mortal form.

"Come," Taria says, continuing past us and gliding down the temple's steps. Her guards follow closely behind her. "We will find some horses in the stables."

I waste no time in hurrying after her. While Natharius complained about the priestess's lateness, he seems to be in no hurry as he trails behind us. Perhaps he's trying to put as much distance as he can between himself and the priestess's overwhelming aura of light magic.

We select the fastest horses from the temple's stables, and the stable hands help us prepare our chosen mounts for riding.

Though I've only had a few days of riding experience, I'm determined to manage by myself rather than having to ride with the loathsome Void Prince. I suppose I could ask Taria or Caya if I can ride with them, but I don't want my new allies to think me a burden.

I choose a dappled mare, who appears to be of a mild temperament, and do my best to mount her as gracefully as I can. Natharius watches me, most likely hoping I'll land on my backside again or crack my head open and die, but by some miracle I don't fall. I still have a long way to go though, especially when compared to Caya, who slips onto her horse with even more grace than Natharius.

I lead my mare through the stables and out to where the others wait, Zephyr sprawled out behind me and taking up half the saddle. He refuses to budge.

The horse Natharius chooses is a stark difference to mine. The ebony stallion kicked and reared when we arrived, the stable hands struggling to get him under control. Natharius just stood there and glared and now his horse is even more docile than mine. It seems even horses can sense the Void Prince's murderous aura.

Once we are all mounted and outside the stables, Taria turns to me. "Which road will we be taking out of Esterra City?"

Unsure, I press my lips together. Since I've only ventured between the temple and the city square during my time here, I have little idea of the city's layout.

"The northern one," Natharius replies.

"North?" Taria asks, her pale brows pinching together in confusion. "Would it not be best to leave the city through the Eastern Gates in order to reach Jektar?"

The demon shakes his head. "Gerazad is in Northern Jektar."

"Even so," Caya says, "wouldn't it be best to follow the Great Road that cuts across Selynis and into Jektar in the east?"

"That is the path Arluin and his necromancers are taking," I reply. "But it is not the way we will take to reach Gerazad. Not if we wish to arrive there first."

"Then you intend to travel through the Ghost Woods?" Taria asks.

"We do."

"The Ghost Woods?" Juron exclaims. "Only fools travel through there, never to be seen again."

Maybe I am foolish to think we can travel through the Ghost Woods, but what alternative is there? We're already three days behind Arluin and his necromancers. Unless we take a shortcut through the Ghost Woods, reaching Gerazad first will be impossible.

"It is said that the trees are filled with ravenous spirits," Juron continues, "all waiting for the opportunity to devour your soul, and that no life dwells there. Only the unliving."

Even the necromancers chose not to travel through this realm of the dead. I shiver and tell myself it's the evening breeze and not Juron's words.

Zephyr huddles into the back of my robes. I wonder if I should ask my faerie dragon again whether he wants to stay here, far away from danger. Out of selfishness, I don't.

"If we don't go that way, we'll never reach Gerazad before Arluin," I say, clenching my jaw. "Yes, it might be foolish, but we have the Prince of Pride and the First Disciple of Selynis. As well as myself, a mage of Nolderan and the daughter of the Grandmage, and both of yourselves. If anyone can navigate through those woods and come out the other side, then it is us."

Juron looks unconvinced, however. As does Caya, her fists tightening around her horse's reins. Juron glances over at Taria. The priestess's face is a mask of serenity.

"Reyna is right, Juron," Taria says after a moment. "There is no alternative. Though Selynis and Jektar have never been on particularly friendly terms, it would be wrong for us to allow the orcs to succumb to such a terrible fate. But I understand if you choose not to accompany us on this journey. Your fears are not misplaced." She turns to face Caya. "I will also understand if you choose the same."

Caya snorts. "Unlike Juron, I am no coward. I would follow you even into the Abyss itself."

"I am no coward either," Juron grinds out, glaring at her. "I do not fear for my own life but yours, Taria. I fear that if we enter such an ungodly place as the Ghost Woods, I'll be unable to uphold my oath to protect you from all dangers."

"Juron, you don't have to come," Taria says gently. "I promise I will not think less of you for it."

Juron shakes his head. "If you insist on traveling with the mage and the demon through the Ghost Woods, I also must follow you. I would never abandon you."

Taria dips her head and grips her reins. "Then let us ride."

CHAPTER 21

Hooves clatter across the street as we ride out of Esterra City. The streets are quiet at this late hour, but the few people around drop to low bows upon seeing Taria's flowing golden robes and white hair.

All which illuminates the streets are small round lanterns hanging to walls and roofs, tiny flames filling their ceramic interiors. We ride fast enough that it's hard to inspect them, but it doesn't seem light magic keeps them lit and only regular fire. The lanterns sway from their ropes as we charge past.

We soon reach the city's northern gates, and we don't need to stop to ask the guards to open them. At the sight of Taria charging forth, they roll open the stone gates and the path is clear long before we pass through them. Once we're on the other side, the guards close them behind us and then we're riding across the barren plains surrounding the city.

Now we're beyond the city's walls, the wind is free to blow at us with all its might. I clutch my reins and dig my heels into the stirrups to stop myself from being blown off my saddle. My other companions also adopt a similar posture, huddled over to reduce the wind's impact. Though Zephyr flew behind me as we rode out of the city, he now perches at the front of my saddle, using my arm and shoulders to shelter himself from the wind. Only Natharius seems unbothered by the conditions. He sits tall in his saddle, his silver hair streaming behind him. A bit of wind isn't enough to defeat the Void Prince of Pride.

Long, yellowed grass stretches into an expanse as vast as the sea surrounding Nolderan. Only a few trees dare to grow here, scattered sparsely across the unforgiving land. Their trunks and branches are hunched over, cowering from the brutal wind and blistering sun. Judging by how dry all this land is, the sun must be even more relentless than the wind and I'm very glad we left Esterra City tonight rather than in the morning. By the time dawn arrives, these plains will hopefully be long behind us.

The road soon becomes little more than a dirt track and is almost impossible to make out beneath the long, yellow grass. The darkness doesn't help, either. Both the moon and stars are too far away to supply us with enough light. I would offer to use my magic and cast an illumination spell, but Taria and her guards seem to have no difficulty navigating our path. They must be familiar with this area.

We ride through the entire night, and though our pace is frantic— even more so than when I traveled across Tirith with Natharius—I barely notice the ache in my legs. All I can think of is reaching Gerazad before Arluin, of defeating him and freeing Father.

None of us speak as we ride, even as the hours stretch on. I doubt we'd manage a conversation above the roaring wind, anyway.

The winds die down a little as night slips away. Yet they're soon replaced by the sun, which is as scorching as I feared. At least the savannahs are mostly behind us now. Emerald plains lie ahead, and thick patches of trees are clumped together here and there. The heat worsens as morning wears on and the sun climbs higher in the sky. When I tilt my head back and peer at the sky, not a single cloud lies in sight. Not so long ago, Eliya and I would have dabbled with dangerous magic for a spell which could conjure such a glorious sky. Now all I want is for it to rain.

Sweat gathers on my forehead and the back of my neck. I reach behind to feel the hair there and it's so hot it's as if the strands are on fire. I doubt my dark shade helps. I wipe my brow on the back of my sleeve, though it doesn't do much since more sweat replaces it several minutes later, and I'm sure my pale skin must be burned bright red. No one else appears to be affected by the heat. Zephyr's azure scales seem to be immune, since they're cool when I reach out and brush the top of his head. Though the wind has disappeared, he sits at the front of my saddle as we ride. Taria looks completely unfazed by the sun, and I wonder whether the Mother Goddess has also gifted her this resistance along with healing and foresight. Caya and Juron are a little more affected, but not as much as me. And as for Natharius, I doubt his expression would be much different if he were riding through a blizzard or a volcano. Even if the heat bothers him, he'd be too proud to admit it. He doesn't look at all burned, though his skin is several shades lighter than mine.

While I consider conjuring ice more than once, I don't want Natharius to mock me for my weakness. I have no choice but to endure the sun and hope the worst of it is already behind us.

Fortunately, we come to a stop around half an hour later. It's Taria's idea to take a break, though I'd have liked to take one hours earlier. I can't tell whether the reason she suggested we stop is because she noticed my reddened cheeks and sweat-soaked brow or because she's worried about the horses. We rode them throughout the entire night and now, judging by how high the sun is, it isn't many hours away from noon. I dread to think how hot it'll be by the time the sun reaches its peak.

As I struggle out of my saddle, I realize why my legs aren't hurting. It's because I can't feel them at all. And that makes dismounting gracefully a challenge. Actually, it makes dismounting at all nearly impossible. I slide one boot out of the stirrup and then scoop my hand under my thigh to force my leg upward and over. The result is unsurprisingly disastrous. I tumble off my mare and land on the grass with a mighty thump. The only saving grace is that I land on my stomach, which I decide isn't as nearly as embarrassing as landing on my backside, and my mare is mild-mannered enough that she doesn't so much as nicker at the commotion. She just starts nibbling away at the grass. Maybe my riding was so awful that my fall doesn't surprise her.

The others dismount with fluid grace I'd need to spend years practicing to achieve, and not a few days of riding with a grumpy demon. In all fairness, I'm rather pleased with myself for getting onto the saddle in the first place and to keep up with everyone while riding. My mare should probably take most of the credit for that, though.

I roll onto my back and stare up at the sky, which remains cloudless. Zephyr floats onto my chest. He pads forth and licks my cheek with his slobbery tongue. It isn't done entirely out of concern, either. I can tell by the glint in his eyes that he wants more aether crystals and right now I don't know how I'll be able to sit up, never mind conjure more or root inside my satchel for the ones left in there.

"Not now, Zephyr," I say, wiping his saliva from my cheek. His tail flicks out in annoyance. "Yes, yes. I'll get you some in a minute." He narrows his eyes at me and then hops off my chest to lie in the sun.

Grass crunches as Juron approaches. He peers down at me and frowns. "You look worse for wear."

Apparently I look as awful as I feel. Marvelous. "I'll be fine," I insist.

"You don't look it."

"Juron," Caya snaps, casting him a stern look.

"What?" Juron says with a shrug. "I'm only saying it out of concern. She looks like she's going to collapse if we ride much more."

Caya shakes her head and crouches beside me. "I'm sorry about my brother," she says, holding a hand out to help me up. Though I had no intention of getting up for several minutes more, I accept her help, if only to ease Juron's concerns. Even if he means it out of goodwill, I don't want him to convince the others they need to slow for my sake. Not when we need to reach Gerazad as soon as we can.

"Brother?" I repeat, grateful for the opportunity to turn the conversation from me. From the corner of my vision, I see Natharius watching me through narrowed eyes and no doubt considering how useless I am.

Caya nods. "We're twins, actually."

"But you can't tell," Juron says, wrapping his arm around his sister's shoulders and pulling her into a clumsy hug. She bats him away. "Not when I got all the looks."

Caya rolls her eyes at him. "And none of the brains."

"We can't all be as clever as you," Juron protests.

She snorts at him. "And some of us can't be clever at all."

We rest a while longer before resuming our furious pace. We ride through the rest of the afternoon, stopping once for food and to let the horses rest. Only when the sun has long set do we make camp for the night. Though we mustn't be too far from the Ghost Woods now, it's warm enough that we don't need to huddle around a campfire. The twins roll out padded blankets from their saddlebags, and Juron lays one down for Taria between both of theirs. I too rummage inside my satchel and find my blanket.

Juron frowns as he watches me use the spell-word *acoligos* to expand the orb into my blanket and drape it across the grass. It isn't as thick as the others' padded blankets, but hopefully the grass will be soft enough. At least it'll be comfier than that cave Natharius and I slept in.

"That looks like a useful spell," Juron says. "How much can you carry in there?" He gestures to my satchel.

I open it wider to show him all the orbs humming within. "This one is a bundle of a food," I say, picking up one and holding it out. I replace it and select another. "And this one is a spare pair of boots."

"And all those other orbs are completely different things? By the Mother, you must have nearly two dozen of them in there!" He holds out his hand, his fingers tentatively hovering over the orbs. "May I?"

"Sure."

His fingers brush over a few orbs. His frown hasn't lessened, but I can't tell what he's thinking. I wonder whether he's ever felt aether before and whether it feels as foreign to him as light magic feels to me.

"Did you say this one was a spare pair of boots?" He points to an orb. I nod and he continues, "How can you tell which is which? All I can feel is tingling. Like lightning."

"How can you know what lightning feels like?" Caya scoffs, sprawling out on the padded blanket next to Taria's. The priestess has already assumed a meditative position, her eyes closed and her hands folded on her lap, oblivious to our conversation. "You've never been struck by it."

"All right then," Juron says. "It feels like how I imagine lightning would feel."

Caya shrugs and doesn't seem to have an argument for that. She reclines on her blanket. Natharius sits a few paces away with his back to us. He has said little since we left Esterra City, and tonight is no different. Though I by no means miss the demon's company, it feels odd to interact so little with him after having to endure countless days of his endless taunts and threats. In comparison, the company of my new allies feels like a breath of fresh air.

Zephyr swoops down and makes himself at home on my blanket, deciding to curl up in the middle of it. I shake my head at him, knowing I'll need to move him later, but say nothing and turn back to Juron.

"I suppose aether must feel like lightning," I say, though the only lightning I've ever experienced is that which I've conjured from aether. I'm not sure whether my magic feels like real lightning, but I suppose Juron is right. The fizz and crackle of aether can only be described as lightning. "And as for being able to tell which is which," I continue, "I'm simply able to sense them."

That doesn't seem to appease Juron's curiosity. "Sense them? How?"

"I just know, in the same way you know whether something is warm or cold when you touch it," I reply. "It's only because I'm the one who cast the spell, though. If I were to touch another mage's, then I'd only feel the hum of aether like you did."

Juron nods at that and judging by the fact he asks no further questions, my answer must be satisfactory enough.

He starts over to his blanket on the other side of Taria but stops and frowns when he reaches it. "Here," he says, gesturing to his blanket. "You should have mine."

"I'm all right, thank you," I reply. "I already have one."

"Yours isn't very thick."

"Honestly, I'll be fine with this one."

Juron doesn't look convinced. "You need to rest more than I do." He doesn't say why, but I know he's thinking of how riding all day has exhausted me. On the last break we took, it was a struggle to climb back onto my saddle, and it was only through sheer willpower that I succeeded. I refused to injure my dignity by someone having to lift me onto my saddle. Natharius's eyes burning into my back also provided me with an extra dose of motivation.

"Really, I promise I'm fine."

Juron opens his mouth to say something, but Caya cuts him off.

"Oh for Light's sake, Juron," she says with a sigh. "Leave the poor girl alone. She said she's fine, all right?"

Juron looks like he's about to protest, but then seems to think better of it and clamps his mouth shut and slumps onto his blanket.

"Don't worry," Caya continues, "he's like this with everyone. It's a persistent problem."

"No, it's not," Juron protests.

She casts him an exasperated look. "Have you already forgotten about the rats?"

Juron lowers his gaze, his ears burning.

I arch a brow at Caya, and the corners of her lip curl up.

"When we were nine, Juron decided to save and raise three baby rats," she explains. Juron doesn't look up as she speaks. "Never mind the fact that we were starving on the streets and couldn't even feed ourselves."

"Oh," I reply, not sure what else to say. Only now do I realize what a privileged upbringing I've had, even if all of it has come crashing down around me. If only I realized at the time and savored every moment. Never did I have to go hungry or fear freezing on the streets. My greatest concern was passing classes with the least effort required. Perhaps all this is retribution for my shortcomings.

I dearly hope Caya won't ask me to share my background, though I wonder how much she knows. How much has the Mother Goddess shared with Taria, and how much has the priestess shared with the twins?

Fortunately, Juron changes the conversation to save his own dignity. "I'll take first watch tonight."

"It's all right," I say. "Natharius can."

The Void Prince's head whips over his shoulder. "I can do what?"

"You can take first watch," I reply. "Actually, you can keep watch all night. You don't need to sleep like us mortals, do you?"

He glowers and turns back around, staring at the rolling hills stretching around us.

I consider issuing him a command to keep watch and wake us should any threat arise, but I already ordered him to protect me and he will be forced to dispose of any enemies. Of course, they may pose a threat to my new companions, and Natharius may opt to take no action, but I'm sure Taria is more than capable of defending herself.

After feeding Zephyr aether crystals and eating something myself, I lie back on the blanket and stare at the stars. A small slither of moon has been carved from its luminescent form. Zephyr curls up into my side, and it isn't long before he's snoring away. As loud as he is, no one comments on his snoring.

I close my eyes and will myself to sleep. While my body is exhausted, sleep doesn't come easily to me. And when it does, it isn't a restful one.

Once again, I find myself in that meadow with black threads lacing through a shining violet sky. Arluin's form fades into view, his raven curls gleaming in the purple radiance.

"Reyna," he says, stepping closer. "I've been trying to speak to you these past few nights. If not for the tracking spell remaining intact, I'd have feared for the worst."

I scramble back, almost tripping over my feet in my haste. "I thought I made myself clear last time," I grind out. "I want nothing to do with you, except your demise. You're not welcome in my dreams. Not now, not ever."

Arluin frowns. "How can you say never? No one can know the future."

"No." My fist clenches. "I *will* hate you forever, Arluin. I can promise you that."

He says nothing, but his frown doesn't relent.

"Leave."

"Reyna—"

"I said leave!"

Arluin doesn't disappear, not even when I demand it over and over, and I'm forced to pinch myself hard.

My eyes flutter open to the twinkling stars. I let out a deep breath, the tension slipping from my shoulders now I'm rid of Arluin and his torment. Zephyr is nestled into me, snoring away. I'm not sure how long I've slept, but Juron and Caya appear to be fast asleep. Taria hasn't moved, remaining cross-legged in her meditative position, and Natharius is nowhere to be seen. I roll my eyes, though the moon is my only witness. I should have issued the Void Prince with a strict order to keep watch. After how much he complained about being ordered to stay put inside the temple, I gave him the benefit of the doubt. So much for that.

Though I'm annoyed by him being unable to co-operate even once, I'm grateful for the distraction from Arluin. I imagine the Void Prince's silver hair, angular features and crimson eyes in as much detail until I've painted his portrait in my mind.

"*Aminex*," I whisper softly, careful not to wake the others. My magic takes shape, connecting my mind to Natharius's.

"*What is it?*" comes his growl.

"*You're meant to be keeping watch.*"

"*I am.*"

"*You're nowhere to be seen.*"

"*It isn't my fault your mortal senses are lacking.*"

I sigh loudly and hope he can hear it in my mind. "*Where are you?*"

"*Above.*"

I tilt back my head and stare up at the midnight sky. It isn't until I squint that I notice movement, a shadow flickering across the stars. It descends a little lower and then I can make out the silhouette's curved wings and the flash of silver hair. I can almost feel his crimson eyes burning down on me, even from this height. "*Make sure you don't fly too far away. Or else I'll have to issue a command to make you watch over our camp.*"

Natharius makes his contempt clear through his silence. Having no desire to engage with the loathsome Void Prince for longer than is necessary, I release the spell tethering our minds together.

I return my focus to our camp. The others haven't shifted since speaking to Natharius; Juron and Caya appear to be fast asleep, along with Zephyr, while Taria continues her meditation.

Arluin didn't intrude on my dreams last night or the night before, but that's because I spent the first shackled with light infused manacles, which may have stopped him from connecting to my mind, and I spent the second riding through the entire night. Sleeping remains a problem.

I rummage inside my satchel for my bundle of potions and hold out the orb and whisper *acoligos*. The bundle appears in my hands and from it, I retrieve a bottle of sleeping potion. I raise the vial to the moonlight, the deep indigo hue glittering in its radiance.

Taking sleeping potions carefully to ensure I only sleep a certain number of hours was how I endured Arluin's torment before Esterra City. Right now it seems sleeping potions remain my only solution, but I only have a few bottles with me and I don't know where I can find the herbs I need to make a new batch.

Even if I had an unlimited amount of sleeping potions to take, it isn't a long-term solution. If I can destroy Arluin in Gerazad then I'll be freed from this spell, but there's always the possibility he will escape justice. Then I don't know how many months—years—it will take for me to defeat him.

My gaze trails across from the sleeping potion to Taria, her face serene and her white hair glowing in the moonlight. When I summoned Natharius, I asked him if he could remove Arluin's spell and he said he couldn't cleanse it with his dark magic. But maybe Taria's light magic will be powerful enough to cleanse it. While I'm loathe to interrupt her peaceful meditation, I decide this matter is urgent enough to disturb her.

I return my potion to the bundle and slip off my blanket as best I can without waking Zephyr. One of his talons snags on my robes, but I manage to unhook the fabric and free myself. I tiptoe over to where Taria sits.

Though the priestess appears to be in deep meditation, her golden eyes snap open as soon as I crouch before her. She scans over my expression, her white brows drawing together. "Is everything all right?" she asks, her voice as gentle as a summer breeze.

I sit opposite her on the other end of the blanket and hold out my bandaged wrist. The fresh silk the priestesses at the temple used to secure it remains in place. "Do you already know what's under this?"

Her frown deepens, and she reaches forth to take my wrist but doesn't loosen the bandage. "No," she replies softly, "though I can sense powerful dark magic here." She taps my wrist precisely where the dark magic is embedded into my skin. The mark burns in response to her touch. "Is it not part of your connection to Natharius?"

I note she calls Natharius by his name rather than 'Void Prince,' but why Taria is sympathetic to such a fearsome demon isn't my most pressing concern right now. "No," I say, "it isn't Natharius's magic. It's Arluin's."

Her expression darkens. "Arluin's?"

"On the night Nolderan fell, he placed a tracking spell on me."

Taria draws her lips into a thin line. "Then he can sense your current location? Does he know we're pursuing him to Gerazad?"

"No, it doesn't seem like he can. The mark on my wrist is an eye, and as long as it's covered, he isn't able to enter my mind. At least not while I'm awake."

"And it isn't the same case while you're asleep?" she presses.

"No, it seems he can communicate with me through my dreams."

"Does he appear every night?"

"Every night that I dream."

She raises a brow.

I'm hesitant to admit the truth, that I've been taking sleeping potions religiously to cope with Arluin entering my dreams. It isn't my fault he does, yet I can't help from being ashamed by this truth. It makes me feel so helpless, the person I vowed I'd never be yet constantly seem to be.

I'm not sure how much Taria knows of Nolderan's potions, or whether the Priestesses of Selynis have their own version of alchemy. In Nolderan potions were originally invented to enable the non-magical population to access certain perks of aether—though they certainly have their benefits for magi—and I doubt the priestesses would allow their divine light to be easily distributed among the general population.

Thankfully, Taria doesn't press me for an explanation.

"The dark magic I sense from the mark is great indeed, but perhaps I can dispel it," Taria says.

"Thank you," I say. "The High Priestess noticed it when she healed me from poison and another priestess said she was looking for a way to cure it, but then I ended up in a cell."

"The only way I can think to cure this mark is through *arandir*. I imagine the High Priestess will have tried this, though."

My stomach sinks. "Is there no other spell you can think of?"

"Let's see if it works first. It is possible the High Priestess's magic wasn't enough to remove the mark."

"But yours might be?"

"The Grand Priestess's certainly would be. However, there is a reason I will succeed the Grand Priestess and not any of the High Priestesses."

"Because you're naturally stronger with light magic?"

"The Mother chose me from birth," Taria replies, lowering my wrist. "From the moment I entered this world, my golden eyes marked me as chosen by our goddess. The Grand Priestess was outside my mother's house at the very moment I was born, having seen my birth through the Mother's vision, not a minute early or late."

I wonder what it feels like to shoulder such an enormous burden since birth. Maybe that's why Taria seems decades older than her years, though she appears to be close to my age.

"Anyway," she continues. "Let's see what we can do to rid you of this dark magic."

"Arluin will see us both as soon as we remove the bandage," I warn as her fingers reach for the silk binding my wrist.

"I will be quick to blink the mark with my light magic."

I give her a nod and then she pulls the bandage from around my wrist.

I haven't seen the mark since the night Nolderan fell, since I threw myself off the Aether Tower to escape Arluin, and now the sight of it causes my breath to hitch in the back of my throat. An eye is etched deep into my flesh, animated as if it belongs to a person. At first the eye is closed, but the lid twitches and it opens. Taria presses three fingers to it, and then barely a second passes before golden light radiates out. The magic builds in intensity, becoming so blinding I have to look away. If it becomes any brighter, it'll wake Juron and Caya. Even Zephyr.

"*Arandir*," Taria whispers.

Heats spikes across my skin, cutting into the mark. The invisible blades plunge deeper, scraping out the darkness. The mark begins to yield to the light magic, but then it clings on tighter to my flesh. Then the light fizzles out. Night blankets us once more.

Taria slumps over, her back bowed. Her exhaustion is clear from the lines etched into her brow and the beads of sweat tracing her temple. Despite her fatigue, she doesn't release my wrist. Her fingers remain pressed tightly to my skin, concealing the eye beneath.

"I'm sorry," she says. With her free hand, she reaches up and wipes away the sweat from her forehead. "It appears I too am not strong enough to banish the mark."

I lower my head. How powerful has Arluin become? Taria is to become the future Grand Priestess of Selynis, and light magic is far more effective than aether against dark magic, and yet her magic is no match for Arluin's.

I shiver, though there's no breeze blowing through the trees. Even if we reach Gerazad before Arluin and his necromancers, will the five of us be enough to defeat him? Six, if you count Zephyr. Though my faerie can be valiant when he wishes, I doubt he'll be much help against the legions of undead. And what worries me most of all is whether even Natharius will be powerful enough.

"I can try again," Taria says when I don't reply.

She already looks exhausted. I doubt she has much more strength to offer, and if she tries, she'll only drain herself more than she did while healing that girl on the street. "It's all right. You've done more than enough."

"I'll try again another time," she promises, a fierceness in her golden eyes. "My strength hasn't yet fully recovered, but I'll try again when I'm back to my usual self. Perhaps if I meditate long enough, I'll be able to recall another spell from the depths of my mind." I frown at that and she adds, "Perhaps you magi don't have an equivalent. We priestesses can use light magic to absorb the entire contents of a book, but we can only retrieve that information through a spell which requires meditation."

"That sounds useful."

"It is, until the tomes start muddling together. I would trade the skill for your ability to conjure objects from aether." Her gaze returns to her fingers on my wrist and the bandage beneath. "I suppose we'll need to be quick with tying this again."

I nod.

Taria grabs the bandage with her free hand and removes her fingers from my wrist. She works swiftly to secure the silk, but it isn't fast enough. The eye opens quicker this time, and it stares at the two of us.

"*Reyna.*"

Arluin's voice echoes through my mind, drowning out all of my thoughts.

Taria presses the silk to the eye before he can say anything else. And hopefully before he can make sense of our surroundings. While Taria's golden eyes mark her as a priestess of Selynis, it's doubtful he will recognize her as the future Grand Priestess.

She frowns at my strained expression. "Were we not quick enough?"

"We were, I think. He called my name, but I don't think it was long enough for him to know where we are."

"Good. That's fortunate."

After thanking her for attempting to cleanse me of Arluin's spell, I head back to my blanket and retrieve the sleeping potion from the bundle, careful to only take enough for a few hours of sleep. The moon is long past its apex, and I doubt dawn is far away.

I curl up next to Zephyr and stare up at the stars. There's no way I'd be able to sleep tonight, not naturally. The worry of whether we're powerful enough to defeat Arluin claws at my heart. Luckily, the potion soon hits me and I fall into a dreamless sleep, free from any intrusion.

CHAPTER 22

WE REACH THE GHOST WOODS two days later. No one announces our arrival, but no one needs to. Gnarled branches reach for the miserable sky. Few leaves cover them, and the ones which remain are shriveled up. An ominous mist drifts from the woods, sending a chill across me. Never have I seen a landscape as ghastly as this. The thought of stepping into those trees sends fear slithering up my spine. If not for avenging Nolderan and freeing Father, I might be tempted to turn back.

I'm not alone with my nerves. Caya and Juron both look as disconcerted by these woods and Zephyr lets out a squeak. Even Taria's mask of serenity cracks. Her brows pinch together as she surveys the trees ahead. Only Natharius doesn't look unsettled by the Ghost Woods. He stares at the trees with a bored expression. If we weren't mounted on our horses, I'm sure his foot would be restlessly tapping against the dirt track.

"Having second thoughts?" the Void Prince hisses over to me, a smirk dancing on his lips.

The others look over at me. Juron's expression is particularly hopeful.

"No." I hope the word doesn't betray the lie. Then again, it isn't as if I'm reconsidering entering these woods. Yes, they terrify me, but I won't let this obstacle hinder my pursuit of justice.

"As you say," Natharius replies, his annoying smirk not faltering. I briefly consider wiping it away with my fist or flames, but decide he isn't worth the effort.

I fix my gaze on the eerie trees ahead and urge my mare forth. She only manages three strides before coming to a halt. I frown at my mare and urge her on with a sharp kick to her flanks. Still, she does not budge.

Gritting my teeth, I try more forcefully. This time, my mare takes three slow steps.

A crunch sounds from somewhere amid the trees. My horse rears in terror, sending Zephyr and me flying from the saddle.

The back of my head smacks the grass with a thud. The trees ahead sway, dark blotches forming at the edges of my vision. In my daze, the Ghost Woods seem even more fearsome.

Zephyr flutters down and nudges my shoulder, while Taria leaps from her horse and hurries to my side. "Are you all right?" she asks.

I rub my eyes until the trees stop spinning and my vision returns to normal. "I'm fine, thank you."

Taria helps me back onto my feet, and we turn to face the direction my mare fled in. The horse is already far away now, galloping over the grassy plains as quickly as her hooves can take her. So much for her being mild-mannered. Though I suppose the Ghost Woods really are that terrifying.

I groan and run a hand down my face. Now I have no horse. Hopefully Taria will suggest I ride with her; I have no wish to ride with the Void Prince again.

But when Taria returns to her horse, she doesn't grab the reins. Nor does she offer for me to ride with her. Instead, she whistles and slaps her horse across its flank. The beast whinnies and flees from the Ghost Woods, like mine.

I flash the priestess a bewildered look. "Now we're two horses down?"

"It would be cruel to force these animals to enter the Ghost Woods," the priestess says. "It is best we enter on foot."

I'm not sure how much farther Gerazad will be on the other side of the Ghost Woods nor how much time we'll lose from traveling on foot rather than horseback, but before I can explain my reasoning to the priestess, Caya and Juron are already dismounting their horses and letting them flee the area. Even Natharius follows suit.

I sigh. On foot it is then. I suppose horses would be more trouble than they're worth here.

With our horses long out of sight, the six of us enter the Ghost Woods. The heavy mist envelops us, and I can barely see my hand in front of me.

The dirt track weaving through the mass of gnarled trees narrows until we have no choice but to travel single file. Taria leads the way, an orb of golden light humming in her fingers. Her magic cuts through the darkness in a way even my most powerful spells couldn't. The surrounding haze is unnatural, the result of all the dark magic clinging to the trees. Even detecting aether in this suffocating air is nearly impossible, and I'm not sure how Taria summoned enough light magic to conjure her orb. Maybe her blood contains far more magic than mine and so she relies less on drawing power from the world.

Caya is next in line, her fingers resting on the hilt of her blade. Every time a twig crunches beneath us, she grips her sword and glances around at the trees. Since I'm walking behind her, I worry the warrior's nerves are so taut my throat might be accidentally sliced open if I breathe too suddenly.

Zephyr sits coiled around my shoulders like a scarf, though I'm sure he'd hide under the length of my robe if he could.

Natharius and Juron bring up the rear, with the Void Prince behind me. His expression is the opposite of Caya's. He may as well be strolling through tranquil gardens instead of the Ghost Woods. Maybe the dark energy helps to dampen Taria's brilliant aura of holy magic.

After we've been walking through the Ghost Woods for what must be an hour, the air cools considerably. It's hard to believe that we're only a three days' ride from Esterra City, where the sun is as sweltering as a furnace. When my breaths come out in wispy clouds, I find myself missing the scorching sunlight of the savannahs.

I wrap my arms around my torso, pulling my robes tighter around me and doing my best to keep from shivering. But it does little to warm me. The frigid wind is unbearable, its touch threatening to turn me into a block of ice. It's no wonder this forest is so desolate. Life can't flourish in frozen winds. Only death.

I close my eyes and draw what little aether I can from the darkness, hoping I won't trip over any protruding roots while my attention is on my magic instead of the path. "*Calida.*" My magic blooms, and my hands glow red. I press them to my shoulders, allowing the warmth to seep through my body.

Though the spell treats some of my physical symptoms, it doesn't stop me from shivering. There's no way to remedy the suffocating darkness around me.

Natharius breaks into a whistle. I can't tell what the tune is. It's either elvish or demonic, though it sounds far too cheery to be the latter. Maybe being surrounded by dark magic has improved his usually abysmal mood. Or maybe he's thinking about what evil lurks inside these woods, waiting to tear me apart. I shudder. Thanks to the dark turn of my thought, the cheery tune now sounds as if it has an ominous note to it.

"Stop it," I hiss, glaring back at the Void Prince. Despite my irritation, I keep my voice low, not wanting to disturb the deathly silence engulfing the trees.

"Stop what?"

"The humming."

"Why?"

"It's annoying."

Natharius scowls, but is forced to do as I say and ceases his humming. After that, the only sounds echoing through the Ghost Woods are the howling wind and our footsteps. Everything else is so unnaturally still.

The sea of trees stretches on, seeming to have no end. How long will it take to reach the other side? One day or several? I'm not anxious only over reaching Gerazad before Arluin, but also over the fear of what other monstrosities lurk here. Maybe it's my imagination, but I can't shake away the feeling of being watched. Yet I can't see anything but trees and mist, and no one else comments on feeling the same strange sensation. I decide it must be my paranoia.

"We should take a break," Taria says after a long while, when our path opens to a glade. The grass is sparse, and frost coats the fallen leaves.

I raise my head, turning my gaze upward. Beneath the thick canopy of branches and mist, there's no way to tell what time it currently is. But I suspect we've been walking for hours, given the tiredness which has set into my legs, and I'm certain it must be nearly nightfall.

Though I stifle a yawn at the thought of it being nightfall in the world beyond these deadly woods, resting here isn't a suggestion I find appealing. The hairs on my arms crawl with the sensation of being watched, and I don't want to close my eyes for even a moment, let alone long enough for sleep to claim me. But I can't deny we need a break. Especially me.

"Just a short break," I reply.

Juron sets down his belongings against a nearby tree trunk and scans the glade. "Maybe we should build a campfire to warm us and keep the mist away. I think the chill has already got into my bones."

"Are you sure that's a good idea?" I ask. "It could act as a beacon to all the creatures lurking here—"

"Wisps, ghouls, and dead necromancers," Natharius declares. "This isn't called the Ghost Woods for nothing."

Wisps don't sound particularly dangerous, and at least ghouls are a familiar enemy, not that I fancy running into any. It's the latter which concerns me the most. "Dead necromancers? Or *undead?*"

He flashes a grin, his teeth glinting in the low light. "Who knows?"

"Wouldn't undead necromancers be liches?"

"Necromancers can only become liches if they place their soul inside a phylactery," Natharius replies.

"So, these would be wights?"

"Correct," Natharius says. "Except any undead we find here will be bound to no master. They'll have been risen from the dark magic lingering in these woods."

That explains why Arluin avoided the Ghost Woods. Rogue undead must be problematic for necromancers as well.

I turn to Juron. "On second thought, I think a campfire would be a good idea." One thing I've learned from Heston's and Arluin's attacks on Nolderan is undead don't fare well against fire. Though even with a campfire, I won't sleep well, not especially after Natharius enlightened me on the horror lurking in these woods.

"I'll find us some firewood," Juron replies.

"I'll come with you," Caya says. "It's best we don't wander off alone in this place."

"Do you want me to help?" I ask.

Juron shakes his head. "The two of us will manage. It's best for you to stay here and guard Taria."

The priestess smiles as she paces across the glade and sits cross-legged on the grass. "I'll be fine."

Juron frowns but doesn't argue with her.

"All right," I say to Juron, "I'll stay with Taria." I'm not sure what use I'll be in defending the priestess should any undead monstrosities ambush us, but I'd much rather stay near her since her magic can cut through the darkness.

The two warriors start through the trees, rummaging through the foliage. I place down my belongings and heave out a sigh, perching on a nearby rock. Zephyr curls up at my feet, trying to make himself as small as possible. He flinches at every sound which comes from the trees, even when it's only Caya and Juron.

It doesn't take long for Taria to fall into meditation. Her midnight skin glows with golden light, and her magic is like a lone candle amid the darkness.

The howling wind rustles through the sparse leaves decorating the thick canopy of branches. I mutter *calida* again and press my hands to my chest. Renewed warmth spreads through me.

Juron and Caya soon leave our sight, though I hear their footsteps in the distance. Natharius wears a bored expression, as if he's disappointed none of us are dying yet.

"How many times have you been here?" I ask to relieve the silence.

"Once," he replies. "A few hundred years ago."

"And are the Ghost Woods as you remember?"

"It is mostly unchanged. However, I feel a shift in the atmosphere."

"A shift?"

"Last I was here, the trees were more abundant with darkness. It is as though the shadows have lessened."

"Lessened?"

"Indeed."

I stare at the gnarled trees. How could these suffocating shadows possibly be any worse? They already feel as if they could choke the life from me. "How did this place become so filled with dark magic?"

"Long ago, the Lich Lord made this area his foothold in Talidor when he sought dominion over the world. He and his armies of undead tainted these woods with their blight. Over time, the shadows fed on the aether living inside the plants and creatures here, corrupting it into more dark magic."

Natharius's explanation only makes me feel worse about this place. Now I'm even less sure camping here for the night is a good idea, even if my legs are exhausted.

I close my eyes and try meditating like Taria does, drawing on the little aether I can find in the air. But concentrating is difficult when I feel the creeping sensation of being watched—and not by the Void Prince.

Caya is the first to return. I open my eyes at the sound of her footsteps approaching, and Zephyr jolts up, only settling down once she comes into view. Her arms are full of dried wood, plenty to build a small campfire. We won't need Juron's share with how much she has.

She glances across at us. "Juron hasn't returned?"

Since Taria is deep in meditation and Natharius is, well Natharius, I'm left to answer her. "No," I reply. "The last time I saw him, he was disappearing into the trees with you."

"Hm, strange," Caya says, dumping her firewood in a pile at the center of the glade. "One minute he was behind me, and the next he was gone."

"I'm sure he'll be back soon," I reply. "Maybe he noticed a rabbit or deer and is busy stalking it through the trees?" I certainly hope he is. Though it's only been three days since I ate a fresh meal in Esterra City, my stomach rumbles at the prospect of warm food.

To my dismay, Caya scoffs. "More like he's having a piss somewhere."

"Actually," Natharius says, "he's probably dead by now."

"Don't say such things," she snarls. "My brother is more than capable of handling himself."

"Maybe," Natharius replies with a shrug, "but this forest is also very good at handling itself. Can you not feel the shadows around us? Though it has depleted over the centuries, this place was once as abundant with dark magic as the Abyss itself."

Caya swallows at his words, any rebuke dying in her throat.

"That's enough, Natharius," I say, narrowing my eyes.

The demon only arches a brow in response.

We wait a while longer, minutes turning into several dozen. The tension in Caya's shoulders tightens. I don't blame her. Juron should have long returned by now, and his current whereabouts is also concerning me.

Finally, when Caya can't bear waiting any longer, she leaps to her feet and strides across the glade, passing Natharius and me. "I'm going to look for him," she says, her mouth set into a firm line of determination. "My brother's sense of direction is horrific at the best of times. I'd better find him before he gets himself any more lost." With that, she starts toward the trees.

"Are you sure—" I begin, but my words are cut off by Natharius.

"Watch out for the ghouls and ghosts," he calls after Caya.

I glare at him.

"What?"

Before I can scold him, Taria speaks.

"Caya," she says, her golden eyes flicking open. The priestess pushes herself onto her feet. "Don't go."

"Why not?" Caya challenges, folding her arms across her chest. "We don't know where he is, nor do we know what monstrosities lurk in these woods."

"It is for this very reason that you mustn't go alone."

"But Juron is out there!" Caya thrusts a finger at the trees. "He's my brother—the only family I have in this world!"

A glimmer of pain flashes across the priestess's serene face. The fleeting emotion vanishes so quickly I can't be certain whether I imagined it. "He's like family to me too," Taria says softly, her voice barely audible over the wind roaring through the trees. "All I'm saying is that you mustn't go alone. Let me come with you."

I scoop Zephyr from my feet and rise from the rock I'm sitting on. The last thing we need right now is to split up and lose each other in these woods. Even if we stay together, finding Juron will have us drifting farther from the main path weaving through the Ghost Woods and possibly losing our way.

"I'll come with you," I say.

"What an excellent idea, mortals," Natharius says. "Let us go gallivanting into these woods at the dead of night when all the ghosts and ghouls have come out to play."

"Why do you care?" I demand. "I thought you spent your every waking moment wishing me to drop dead?"

"That's true. The sooner you die, the sooner I may return to the Abyss."

"Then what are you complaining about?"

"Very well," he says, standing and straightening the creases from his dark tunic. "I look forward to seeing how long it takes for you to get yourselves killed."

CHAPTER 23

We gather our belongings from the glade and divide Juron's things between us. Noticing Natharius carries nothing, I offer him a broad smile and hold out Juron's bow and quiver. "This is for you."

His eyes narrow, glancing between me and the weapons. "Why would I want these?"

"Because you're not carrying anything else," I reply. "And because I say so."

Grumbling various curses and ways of torturing me under his breath, Natharius takes the bow and quiver and slings them across his back.

With our camp cleared, we start through the trees, heading deeper into the woods and farther from the safety of the path.

The mist is denser in this part of the woods. A howl comes from deep within the trees, ringing out like distant thunder. My skin crawls. Though it at first sounds like a wolf, the howl is too low and guttural. I don't allow myself to imagine what else it might be. I instead focus on the back of Taria's golden robes as she and Caya lead the way through the trees.

As irritating as he is, I'm grateful for Natharius's presence behind me. Being sandwiched between the future Grand Priestess of Selynis and the Void Prince of Pride makes me feel marginally better about wandering through these ungodly woods.

Caya stops at a tree stump and scans the area. A layer of frost covers the stump's bark, and cobwebs hang from the surrounding branches, dancing in the wind and twinkling in the low light. "Here," she says. "This is where I lost him."

"Maybe we can find footprints?" I suggest. An idea strikes me, and I turn to the Void Prince. "Or maybe if you have something he won't mind parting with, Natharius can use a tracking spell to pinpoint his location."

"That will be of no use," Natharius interjects. "The spell will only show an image of the idiot wandering past trees which look identical to the ones around us. Pinpointing his location will be impossible from that alone."

"But it could help," I protest. "And we might be lucky enough to spot a landmark or two." Or if he's dead, then we'll know for certain. I don't say that thought aloud.

Caya's nose wrinkles. "I have no use for your heinous magic anyway, demon."

Natharius offers her a lavish smile, pleased he won't have to lower himself to use his magic to find her brother.

"Let's start by looking for footprints and any other sign of him," Taria says.

"The two of us can take the right," Caya says to Taria.

"All right," I reply. "Natharius will stay with me and Zephyr. Let's not wander too far from each other though, or Juron won't be the only one lost."

Caya and Taria start over to the trees to the right, scanning the foliage for any clues as to Juron's whereabouts. Zephyr and I take the trees to the left, Natharius trailing behind us.

"My bet," he says, once we're out of earshot of Caya and Taria, "is that he's already long dead."

I whirl around to reprimand him, but there's no amusement dancing in his crimson eyes—though it would be a stretch to say the

Void Prince looks concerned. Mildly serious is more like it. "What makes you say that?"

"He doesn't exactly look like the sharpest tool in the shed, does he?"

I shake my head at him and continue searching the area. I crouch and examine the grass and push aside brambles and branches, Zephyr helping me as best he can. Natharius follows us, standing behind as we search high and low for any sign of Juron. Though I'm not too happy about the fact that he isn't assisting in our search, I'm grateful for his presence. Wandering through these woods with only Zephyr wouldn't be much fun.

Just when I'm about to give up, Caya's shout comes from the trees. I break into a run, my boots trampling over fallen twigs and Zephyr's wings beating behind me. Natharius's footsteps pound after us, though his pace doesn't sound half as frantic as mine.

I find Caya and Taria staring down at a few footprints printed into a patch of mud. They glance over their shoulders as the three of us approach.

"Here," Caya gasps, pointing at the trail. "He came this way!"

We waste no more words before following the trail of footprints, charging through the foliage like a hurricane. Caya draws her sword and slashes at the thickets in our way.

Juron's tracks lead deep into the trees, and we must end up sprinting for at least half an hour, seeing how my chest burns. While Natharius and Caya show no sign of fatigue, Taria does, and I'm glad I'm not quite as unathletic as I fear.

The footprints soon end. The damp mud dries up and spreads into a patch of grass. Though a faint indentation of boots is pressed into the soft grass, determining which route Juron took through the trees is now difficult.

We stop and squint at the trees in the hope they'll reveal some sign as to his whereabouts. But even after several minutes, none of us spots any clues.

We've strayed far from the main path through the forest now, and navigating ourselves through the Ghost Woods won't be easy. If we spend hours, or even days, trying to find Juron, it'll deal a costly blow to our quest to reach Gerazad before Arluin. But I can't think like that. Juron is family to Caya and Taria. Even if he's now an obstacle to my path to vengeance.

"What shall we do now?" I whisper when no one speaks. My words don't inspire any words, though.

Caya grits her teeth, while Taria closes her eyes, seeming to briefly meditate upon our situation. Natharius, of course, says nothing and wears his usual bored expression. Even Zephyr seems to understand the graveness of our situation, since he doesn't let out a squeak or pester me for aether crystals.

I heave out a sigh and start over to a nearby fallen tree trunk, deciding to give my body a moment to rest while we decide what to do next. But I only manage threes strides before stopping in my tracks.

A pale light flickers in the trees.

I frown and continue toward it, taking a large step as I walk over the fallen tree. The blue light dances in the shadows, shining brighter as I draw nearer. It lets out a tinkering which sounds like a thousand tiny wind chimes all singing at once.

Then it lets out a very different noise. One which sounds human.

"Reyna?" a woman calls.

I stop. The hairs along my spine shiver at the familiar voice.

"Reyna? Is that you?" the woman continues, her voice echoing through the trees. "Come over here so I can get a good look at how you've grown."

The blue orb intensifies. Beneath its hazy glow, I can make out the shadowy silhouette of a woman. Her long hair sweeps through the breeze. I can't distinguish any features beneath the brilliant light, but there's no doubt as to whom the figure belongs.

"Mother," I gasp, my throat constricting around the word. I stumble, almost tripping over fallen branches in my daze. She seems so close but with every step I take, she drifts away. "Please! Don't go!"

Cool fingers close around my wrist, like ice on my skin.

I jolt and tear my gaze away from the blue light to see Natharius staring down at me. I can barely tell that his crimson eyes are narrowed. His silver hair and alabaster face are blurred.

Zephyr hovers behind him, peering at me. He must be very concerned for my wellbeing if he's willing to venture so close to the Void Prince.

I blink several times, rubbing my eyes with my free hand. Maybe staring into the blue light for too long has affected my vision. "Let go." The Void Prince has no choice but to obey the command. "My mother, she—"

"Is dead," Natharius interrupts. "That thing you saw was not your mother."

"It . . . wasn't?" I don't like how my voice raises a pitch as I speak that final word, exposing my vulnerability to the demon.

"No," he says softly, "it was not."

That's right. My mother died years ago, long before the fall of Nolderan. Her soul was scattered into aether and returned to the world when Father destroyed the wraith Heston warped her into. How could I have possibly seen my mother's spirit?

"It sounded just like her," I say, my voice small. I keep my head lowered, not looking up at Natharius. As if by averting my gaze, I can hide the emotions churning within me. "If it wasn't my mother, then what exactly was it?"

"A wisp," Natharius says.

Taria and Caya come to a stop beside us. It's the priestess who offers me a proper explanation.

"A wisp is a type of undead," she says, her golden eyes gazing past me and into the dark trees ahead, where the blue light disappeared. "They are formed from the souls of the deceased, much like wraiths. The difference is that wisps are tiny fragments of souls, whereas wraiths are formed from an entire one. They are as mindless as ghouls and as hungry to consume the living. Except since they lack teeth, they seek to siphon away your energy and turn the fragments of your soul into one of them."

I swallow, staring into the shadowy trees ahead. If Natharius didn't stop me, I might be moments away from turning into one of them. "How long does that take? To be turned into one of them?"

"It depends on how many wisps are feasting on your soul," Natharius says. "If it's only one, it might take days. If it's dozens of them, your soul could be siphoned away within minutes. Usually it is the latter, since they lure mortals toward their lairs by conjuring illusions of those their victim has lost."

I shudder. The illusion of my mother felt so real. Maybe the enchantment the wisp cast over me confused my senses. Even my vision became blurred.

A sudden, horrible thought strikes me.

"Do you think that Juron might have also seen a wisp?" I say each word slowly, worried how Taria and Caya will take the suggestion. "Maybe it lured him farther into the forest?" After all, the footprints leading us here looked hurried. Maybe he was chasing after an illusion of someone he lost?

Caya's throat bobs, but she doesn't argue with my suggestion. The priestess's expression falls solemn, and she offers me a grave nod.

"I fear you might be right," Taria replies. "If you are, then perhaps the wisps have led him to their lair."

Which, according to Natharius, could mean he's dead already. His soul siphoned, and the fragments warped into more wisps to fill their ranks.

Though I've only known Juron for a matter of days, this isn't a fate I want to imagine anyone succumbing to.

Caya's fists tighten. "Then we must hurry."

I avert my gaze, worrying that my expression will reveal my suspicions and crush Caya's hope. But perhaps that would be kinder than allowing her to believe her brother is alive. That he can be saved. Maybe I should tell her, but I don't have the heart to. Neither does Taria, though maybe the priestess is as hopeful as Caya and is willing to believe in the impossible odds. Even Natharius surprises me with his silence.

I lift my head, peering into the dark trees once more. As much as I doubt the fact Juron is alive, I can't be certain he isn't. We have to try to save him. Even if it risks reaching Gerazad in time.

"It seems our best chance of finding Juron is to find the wisps' lair," I say. "But since the wisp has disappeared, I'm not sure how we'll find it?"

"Indeed," Taria replies, "and it might not return. These creatures rarely prey on large groups and prefer to ambush lone travelers."

"We could split up," I say, "but then we risk losing each other."

And time is ticking away. If we lose each other, it might take too long to regroup. Then reaching Gerazad before Arluin will be a hopeless endeavor. Even now, I can't be certain we'll reach there first, not with the countless days we spent in Esterra City.

Neither Taria nor Caya add anything else, seeming to have no idea how we can force the wisps to show themselves. And if they don't appear, there's no hope of finding their lair and saving Juron. If he isn't already dead.

Or undead.

A dark voice whispers in my mind, advising me to abandon Juron and my new companions. That the Void Prince alone will be enough to defeat Arluin.

I close my eyes, doing my best to silence the voice. This isn't me. I'm not someone who sacrifices others to aid my own goals. Even if the fate of the world rests on my achieving those said goals.

I run a hand down my face. I have absolutely no idea how to solve any of this.

Surprisingly, Natharius does.

"I might have an idea," he begins, his voice a purr, "but I doubt you will be fond of it."

As pleased as I am that the Void Prince has a suggestion, I can't help my suspicions from growing. When does the demon help anyone except himself? If we find Juron dead in these woods, he'd only laugh.

Still, I can't deny my curiosity. Though Natharius's plan will somehow benefit him, it isn't as if we have any other ideas. Hopefully his suggestion will prove a plausible plan.

I fold my arms across my chest and examine Natharius carefully through narrowed eyes. He looks far too gleeful. "Why don't you think I will like your idea?"

He smiles. "While I'm confident of its effectiveness, I'm also confident you'll die."

CHAPTER 24

Natharius is right. I don't like his plan one bit.

I'm to be wisp bait.

I don't know how I ended up agreeing to this plan, but I do know I'm already regretting it. If only we had an alternative.

I inhale deeply and continue through the shadowy trees. The others are so far behind I can no longer see or hear them. Caya assured me she wouldn't let me out of her sight, so I hope her vision is superior to mine. Taria also promised that at the first sign of danger, she would unleash the Mother's wrath upon the wisps. And Zephyr also nodded, silently pledging his support.

As for Natharius, he just smirked.

My thoughts are interrupted by a crunch beneath my boots.

I jolt so violently my bones almost spring from my skin. I raise my foot carefully, wincing as I dare to peer at what lies beneath it, fearing I will see bones. Someone's bones.

Fortunately, I find only twigs under my boots.

I continue through the trees, shoving away the branches which threaten to gouge out my eyes. Despite my efforts, the sharp edges scrape across my cheeks.

Leaves riddle my hair, but I don't have time to care. I'm too busy scanning the trees, my eyes darting frantically between the shadows in search of blue light. But no matter how many steps I take, the wisps refuse to show themselves.

And I'm certain I've already spent an hour strolling through these woods as wisp bait.

I groan. We really can't afford to waste more time. The sooner I find another wisp and follow it back to its lair, the sooner we can continue on our way to Gerazad. Not that I'm looking forward to another run in with the ghastly creatures. Knowing my luck, I'll stumble upon something even more dangerous than wisps. Maybe an enormous undead abomination which can swallow me before Taria or the others can save me.

I also try not to think of what Natharius said about dead necromancers. Or about what else could lurk within these woods, monstrosities even he isn't aware of.

I shake my head. I need to focus on the wisps. Though they too can kill me, at least I know what I'm up against. Their visions are illusions, no matter how real they seem, and I won't fall for their petty tricks a second time.

At least, I hope I won't.

I pull the bravest face I can muster as I traipse through the foliage. With every step, I frantically glance in every direction.

Still, there are only trees to be seen.

"Wisps, where are you?" I call into the darkness, hoping my words won't be lost to the wind. I also pray they don't come out as shaky as they sound in my head. "Where've you gone? Hurry up and show yourselves already." If I don't find a wisp soon, I'll be driven to madness in these ungodly woods.

The wisps don't answer my call, and they remain in hiding. No blue lights flicker amid the shadows.

My throat rumbles with a growl of impatience.

When I didn't want to find them, one revealed itself to me. And yet now I'm desperately seeking them, none will appear. Just my luck.

While Taria claimed wisps are mindless beings, I'm not so sure about that. Right now, it seems they're watching me from afar, laughing as I stumble through the darkness.

I look back over my shoulder and mumble a curse to my invisible companions.

If they get me killed from a lack of attentiveness, I'll come back to haunt them. And the dark magic in these woods will ensure I'm brought back from the dead.

Then again, I can't blame them. Caya and Taria, at least. It's my fault for agreeing to this plan. And Natharius's for suggesting it.

When he first proposed the idea of me venturing alone through the woods as wisp bait, I protested vehemently. Taria offered to take my place, but the demon argued her aura of holy magic would cause the wisps to give her a wide berth, meaning she's no good as wisp bait.

Caya also offered, seeing as it's her brother who was whisked away by the wisps. Though I thought it an excellent idea, Natharius countered it. Unsurprisingly.

Firstly, he argued, we can't be certain the wisps will choose to target her. Their preferred victims are those whose minds are easily penetrable and susceptible to visions of grief. While her brother was targeted, that doesn't mean Caya would be as well.

I suspect his argument is nothing more than an excuse to ensure I'm the one who is wisp bait. That I'm the one at risk of dying so he has a greater chance of returning to the Abyss and torturing me for eternity.

I suggested for Natharius to go in my place, but he said the wisps wouldn't bother him. A demon's soul can't be warped into a wisp, since it belongs to the Void King. Besides, their physical bodies disintegrate on death as their souls return to the Abyss.

So that's why I'm here, stumbling through the woods all by myself. No one else makes good wisp bait.

Everywhere looks the same, the next trees identical to the last. It must be close to an hour now that I've been searching for the wisps.

This really is proving to be a futile endeavor.

I halt, a thought striking me.

Maybe the reason I'm not finding any wisps is because I'm trying so hard. Natharius mentioned about them selecting their targets with care. If I'm desperately looking for them, maybe my senses are too alert for them to worm their way into my mind. Before, when the wisp appeared to me, I was exhausted from sprinting through the forest and was planning on sitting down so I could rest. Perhaps pausing my search and forgetting about the wisps for a short while will prove a more effective approach. An hour of stomping through the woods has achieved nothing.

A few paces later, I arrive at three large rocks and perch on them. The cool stone seeps through my robes. I go to warm myself with magic but think better of it. The more helpless the wisps believe me to be, the sooner they'll show themselves. I'll just have to freeze until they do.

I sit there for a long while, resting my head in my palms. What time is it in the world beyond these woods, where the sun rises and sets? We must have spent several hours searching for Juron, and it's likely late at night or very early in the morning. The lack of sleep weighs on me. I could meditate and draw on aether to lessen my fatigue, but again that means deterring the wisps with my magic.

I shut my eyes, allowing myself to rest as much as I can here in these terrifying woods. I wonder whether the others will burst through the trees and demand to know what I'm doing, but hopefully they'll see the wisdom in my plan.

Time stretches on. The night wind rustles through the sparse leaves overhead. Aside from that, the woods are deathly silent.

Until a tinkling comes from the trees.

I don't stir at the sound. Sleep already has me in its clutches.

"Rey-rey!" Eliya's voice chirps.

I bolt upright.

A blue light flickers by the nearest tree, only a few feet away. As my sight adjusts, so does the orb. Like how the wisp assumed my mother's form, Eliya's features appear beneath the spectral light. Though she's cast in shadows, there's no denying it's her.

Well, not her. An identical, phantom version of her.

But that doesn't lessen the grief in my heart.

I leap up and start toward the wisp, chanting over and over that this isn't the real Eliya. My best friend died in Nolderan, her soul scattered into the atmosphere. The real Eliya slumbers inside a crystal coffin in the Upper City's cathedral.

The spectral Eliya lets out a giggle. Shadowy limbs gesture for me to follow. "Come on, Rey-rey!" the wisp exclaims in Eliya's voice. "I've a stash of my uncle's finest moon-blossom wine waiting for us to drink it! Come and look!"

My breath catches in the back of my throat.

It sounds so much like Eliya.

I shake my head, clutching my temples. My nails claw into my skin.

Not Eliya.

Not Eliya.

Not Eliya.

Despite the reminder I chant, it seems I'm not entirely immune to the wisp's enchantment. I stumble after it, my vision blurring like before.

No.

I can't let myself be disarmed. I must keep my wits, or else Natharius's wish will finally come true.

The wisp dances between the trees, leading me along a winding path through the forest. There's no rhyme nor reason to the route it takes, seeming to choose its direction at random.

What if there's no wisp lair like we suspect? What if this creature leads me to a cliff or a river and pushes me over the edge?

I let out a deep breath, doing my best to expel my fears with it.

I'm a mage. I can manipulate the air and water around me. Falling and drowning are of no concern.

The trees spin as the wisp's spell secures its grasp on my mind. I can't let it consume me, but I also can't give so much resistance that

I scare it away. Maintaining that delicate balance is becoming more challenging by the minute.

Another wisp appears in the trees, its blue glow flickering in the shadows. It joins the first, once more taking on the image of my mother.

"Come over here, Reyna," the second wisp calls. "Let me get a good look at you."

"Rey-rey!" the other chimes. "The wine won't drink itself!"

I tighten my fists as the two wisps bombard me with their haunting voices. As I follow the specters through the trees, I fight to stop my mind from being stolen.

Time becomes a vague concept as I battle for control of my mind.

After we pass many more trees, a third wisp joins us. Their assault on my mind grows in strength. This one takes the image of Father, complete with his crystalline staff beneath its eerie blue light.

My sense of touch dulls. The wind's chill fades on my cheeks, as do the gnarled branches tearing into my indigo robes and scraping the skin beneath. Even if these trees leave me battered and bruised, I won't notice beneath the wisps' bewitchment.

"Reyna," Father says, his voice as stern and commanding as always. "You let me down. You let all of Nolderan down."

"No," I gasp. "It wasn't my fault . . . I . . ." Yet there's no reason why I'm not to blame. I was the one who trusted Nolan, who forced Father to deactivate the Aether Tower, who enabled Arluin's undead to flood through their death gates.

I was the one who killed Father. And Nolderan with him.

I stop and cradle my face in my palms.

The sins I've committed are unmeasurable. How dare I believe I can atone for my actions by bringing Arluin to justice. Obliterating him and his necromancers from this world won't wash away my sins, nor will it resurrect the dead.

"Rey-rey," Eliya's voice chirps, her words echoing through the shadows. "Aren't you coming? Aren't we friends anymore?"

My jaw tightens. The wisps are wearing down my resolve, attacking my most vulnerable weaknesses.

While defeating Arluin will neither reverse what happened nor clear me of guilt, Father's soul—his corpse—is chained to Arluin. I must free him.

And that means facing Arluin in Gerazad.

I push myself onward through the trees, stumbling after the wisps. They all call to me, taunting me with their haunting voices.

They aren't real. I can't forget that, no matter how familiar they seem. The real Eliya is dead, as is my real mother. And Father's soul is bound to Arluin.

None of them can be here. I can't allow the wisps' enchantment to capture me. To make me forget my entire self.

Soon my vision blurs so much I can no longer discern the trees, even when they're close enough to touch. They're nothing but a mass of shadowy leaves. Only the wisps' blue light is visible in the darkness.

More wisps join, feeding on my memories. Their forms warp into those who fell in Nolderan. I see Eliya's father, her uncle, her siblings. I see the three Archmagi. I even see Kaely.

I sprint after them. There are dozens now. That must mean I'm close to their lair.

After many more strides and frantic breaths, the wisps become so many they're like a sea of twinkling sapphires. In their flickering blue lights, I see all the images I witnessed on the night of Nolderan's fall. The images which haunt my most terrifying nightmares.

The wisps cluster around me. Their enchantment tightens its grasp on my mind. They merge in a cloud of blue light. The surface ripples, forming the image of Nolderan.

At the far end of the street lies Eliya, her broken body slumped against the wall. Her expression is so still. Ghouls stalk toward her, their rotten hands reaching out and ravenous teeth grinding together.

"Eliya!" The last of my resistance shatters at the sight of my best friend's corpse. "Eliya!"

I hurry forth, muttering *ignira* and summoning flames to eradicate the undead seeking to consume her flesh.

"Eliya!" I cry once more, sliding across the cobblestones as I frantically reach down to clutch her.

Her skin is ice cold. Her pulse doesn't beat.

"Eliya!" I wail, thick tears rolling down my cheeks. I grasp Eliya's shoulders, shaking her desperately. "Eliya, don't go! Don't leave me!"

Eliya doesn't respond.

My hands tremble. The rest of my body is frozen solid. I can't feel the ground beneath me, nor the evening breeze. All I can feel is Eliya's icy skin against my fingertips and the weight of her lifeless body in my arms.

Until even Eliya slips away.

Then I'm alone in the darkness.

I stare down at my hands. They're translucent and glow with pale blue light.

What am I doing? How did I get here?

It feels like the answer is there, lost somewhere in the depths of my mind. No matter how much I try, I can't locate it.

I rub my temples and shake my head, trying to clear it.

Who was that girl lying in my arms only moments ago?

My fingers sweep across my cheeks, feeling the tears dried on my skin.

I was crying.

Why was I crying?

I close my eyes, the weight of those questions pressing down on me, and lie on the ground. I can't tell whether it's grass, stone or sand beneath me. Actually, it's more likely to be cloud or smoke, since the surface has an airy quality to it.

My breathing slows. Darkness washes over me.

I'm tired. So very tired. I've never felt this peaceful. Though I can no longer recall a time before this tranquility, I'm certain painful memories lurk somewhere in the depths of my mind. If those experiences brought me so much anguish, isn't it best to forget them? To let go of the past and allow myself to fall into this nothingness?

A smile plays on my lips. Coolness washes over me. If I can, I want to stay here for eternity, free from all worries and fears.

A tinkling chimes around me. The melodious sound is one of agreement, urging me to drift deeper into the tranquility they offer.

And I may have, if not for a sudden force crashing into me.

The ground gives way, and I fall. Shouts pierce the darkness. Voices which sound vaguely familiar, though I can't pinpoint to whom they belong. They all shout the same strange word.

"Reyna!"

CHAPTER 25

I BLINK. The shadows blinding me give way.

A cave surrounds me, its stone walls looming over me. I'm sitting on the floor, the wisps circling me closely. They draw nearer, sweeping me up and lifting me into the air.

Once more, their enchantment seeks to capture my mind. Panic wells in my chest. I fight them off, my limbs flailing at them with all my remaining strength. But my physical attacks do little to harm them. My arms and legs pass through them. In my struggle, I glimpse the cave's entrance.

Natharius stands there, along with Taria and Caya. Zephyr perches on Caya's shoulder. Darkness swirls from the Void Prince's hands, holy magic in the priestess's. Caya has drawn her sword, golden light shining across the runes engraved into her blade, and violet light glows in Zephyr's mouth.

The demon and the priestess launch their magic on the wisps. Light and shadows erupt, slamming into the wisps. Blue sparks drift through the cave as the wisps caught by the attack are obliterated.

Shaken by the blow, they release me. I fall to the stone floor with a thud. The impact reverberates through the back of my shoulders and arms. The pain lasts mere heartbeats before it's drowned out by horror.

Without me even realizing, the wisps lured me into their lair and started consuming my soul, warping me into one of them.

How much longer before I'd have been past saving? While I'm grateful the others arrived in time, I wish they'd arrived sooner.

I scramble upright. The wisps nearest me sense my movement and drift toward me, seeking to prevent my escape. My senses are muddled from their magic. My surroundings are blurred, and the wisps' tinkling sounds hollow in my ears. It'll be a miracle if I don't topple over.

Not only did the wisps begin devouring my soul; they also fed on the magic flowing through my veins, leaving me fatigued. When I weave aether into flames and call *ignira*, the spell is a fraction of its usual size and the attack barely reaches the wisps. At least it keeps those nearest me at bay while my companions continue their barrage of magical attacks against the wisps.

The undead swarm to the cave's entrance. Though vastly outnumbered, the others seem to be slowly pushing through our enemy's ranks. The wisps retaliate by spitting out balls of blue fire. Though each wisp's attack is tiny, there are hundreds of them, and as their flames collide midair, they grow substantially in size. Even my own spells, when at usual strength, pale compared to the wisps' attacks.

A volley of large blue flames hurls at my companions. Taria clasps her palms together and squeezes her eyes shut. Her golden robes billow out in the darkness as holy magic radiates from her hands. "*Zire!*" she cries. The golden energy bursts, sweeping over her and the others.

The wisps' blue fire slams into the shield. The lines on Taria's forehead deepen with concentration as she clenches her jaw, holding her defenses against their attacks.

The golden barrier stands fast. The blue fire dissipates, fading into the darkness.

With their attack nullified, Taria lowers the shield. Natharius spins shadows in his fingers and sends a bolt of darkness rushing at the wisps. Since he had plenty of time to conjure the counterattack while Taria held the shield, the spell he launches upon the wisps is devastating.

Darkness cleaves through the sea of blue light, wiping out a substantial number of wisps.

A few dart behind them, somehow bypassing both Taria's and Natharius's attention. Caya takes care of those, her sword sweeping out furiously, while Zephyr spits balls of aether at them. The wisps lurch away from them, dancing around their strikes.

With my allies plowing through the wisps, more rush forth to take the places of the fallen. Though there seems to be an endless number of wisps, fewer are left around me. I blast the surrounding wisps with aether and flames, freeing myself from their clutches.

"Reyna!" Caya calls over, having noticed my advantageous situation. "Is my brother with you?"

I spin, examining the cave behind. It stretches far through the darkness. I can't see the blue light of any wisps. They must all be at the front of the cave now, battling the others.

Except for one.

A stray wisp drifts toward me, spitting tiny blue flames. "*Telum*!" Aether slams into the wisp, extinguishing it. I return my attention to the back of the cave.

"*Iluminos*." An orb shines from my fingers, illuminating the darkness. With how much magic the wisps siphoned from me, the spell lacks its usual brightness. But it will suffice.

The cave reaches farther back than I expect, but the far wall isn't more than a few dozen strides away. Bones lie heaped across the stone floor, both animal and humanoid remains.

Nausea washes over me, and I swallow. I can't let the morbid sight distract me from the task at hand. I must find Juron.

I scan across the heaps of remains. No fresh corpses lie among them, only the ivory white of bones.

I kneel before the most recent looking pile of bones, examining them for any sign of Juron. Along with what looks like rabbit bones, I find human skulls. And what I also suspect are goblins' skulls.

How I'll identify Juron's skull, I have no idea and can only hope none belongs to him.

As I lean over to inspect a skull, two wisps drift toward me. I notice their attacks in time to draw aether into my palms. *"Ignir'muriz!"*

A wall of roaring flames wraps around me. The wisps' spells hurl into it, fizzling out the moment they touch my shield. I don't hesitate to launch my counterattack.

"Ignir'quatir!"

The fiery shield explodes. Flames slam into the wisps, devouring them.

I turn to the nearest heap of bones, resuming my search. I hope I find nothing. Or else I'll have to be the one to tell Caya her brother is dead. To snuff out her last bit of hope.

I find nothing in the first pile of remains, even when I muster enough courage to sift through the bones with my fingers. I straighten and turn to the other heaps. Though there's no trace of Juron in this pile, it doesn't mean I'll find nothing among the others.

I start over to one lying a few strides away, though I doubt I'll find anything among it. The bones here are old, their ivory white surface dirtied and yellowed with time. I suspect they've lain here for several decades.

Metal glints to my left. I hurry toward it, crouching before the metallic object.

A sword. Its hilt has a familiar gilded pattern.

My throat dries at the sight.

This belongs to Juron.

My fingers close around the sword's hilt. I stare down at the blade, the brilliant rays of my illumination orb gleaming across its surface. Behind, the sounds of the others fighting the wisps continue.

I grip the hilt. Juron was here. Why else would his sword be in this cave?

My gaze trails across to the most recent pile of bones. My stomach knots as my eyes fall upon the human skulls.

Is one of them his? Have we arrived too late?

"Reyna?" Caya calls. She must have noticed me peering at something. Urgency fills her voice, raising it by several pitches.

I can't bear to look at her expression, let alone tell her that her brother is dead.

I simply remain there, clutching the sword's hilt as I search for the right words. None come to me.

Soon the fighting quietens. With the wisps defeated, hurried footsteps approach.

"What is it?" Taria asks, halting beside me.

I turn slowly and hold out the sword.

Caya takes one look at it and lets out an anguished cry. She doubles over, clutching her chest.

Taria closes her eyes, placing a hand on Caya's shoulder. I don't miss the tear tracing her cheek.

"No," Caya gasps. "This can't be right. My brother . . . He can't be . . ."

"I'm sorry," I whisper, looking away from her. Guilt snakes around my chest, constricting so tightly I fear my heart will stop beating. I know Caya's pain all too well. The agony of losing those held dearest.

It was my choice to cut through the Ghost Woods. If I hadn't insisted on us taking this perilous path, Juron wouldn't be dead.

Silence stretches between us, filled only by Caya's ragged breaths. Taria gently tugs Juron's sword from my hands. She clutches the hilt, her golden eyes squeezing shut and tears flowing down her cheeks. I lower my head, shame weighing heavily on my shoulders.

Out of cowardice, I turn away and start out of the cave. Natharius and Zephyr trail behind me. The demon says nothing as we walk.

Cool air slams into my cheeks, jolting me awake. Since the wisps cast their bewitchment over me, I haven't felt this aware of my surroundings. Their magic must have now completely lifted from me.

I let out a deep breath. Zephyr flutters down and rests on my shoulder. I tilt back my head and peer up at the canopy of gnarled branches hanging overhead and shutting out the sky. The tiniest rays of sunlight slice through the branches, and they're all which prevents darkness from entirely consuming these woods.

I suppose it must be morning again.

Even after standing here at the cave's mouth for a long while, Natharius remains silent. Though I can't say the demon is usually chatty, I'm surprised he hasn't uttered a single snide remark about Juron's death, but I'm glad he's kept such hateful thoughts to himself, for once.

"Do you know where we are?" I ask, desperately seeking a distraction from my guilt.

Natharius gazes at the trees ahead of us. "Somewhere deep inside the Ghost Woods?" he offers, a smirk etching onto his lips. It disappears as soon as I cast him a stern look. I'm in no mood for playing these games with him.

"Do you honestly not know?" I demand, my patience already thin.

He pauses for a moment. "It was long ago that I was last here."

"Does that mean you don't remember the way through to the other side of these woods?"

"I vaguely recall the way out. Maybe the route will come back to me. Or maybe it won't."

I sigh. If Natharius doesn't know the way out of these woods, we could wander through the trees for weeks. And that's if we don't run into any more undead—ones which may prove deadlier than wisps.

"Can you try to remember?" The thought of wandering through these woods for eternity makes my words tremble. "Please?"

The demon blinks. I suppose he's more used to me barking orders at him than making polite requests.

For a moment I think he might laugh at me for the weakness but he doesn't, surprising me as much as the lack of snide remarks over Juron's death.

"I can try," Natharius says after a moment. There's a softness to his crimson eyes, or at least I think there is. With how quickly it vanishes, I decide I must imagine it.

I give a small nod and dare to glance into the cave. Caya is on her knees, clawing at the floor. Taria hasn't moved since we left. The priestess's shoulders are stiff, and she clasps the sword as if it will slip through her fingers.

Swallowing, I turn to the trees ahead and reach up to stroke the soft scales on Zephyr's head. I can only hope that their loss won't be for nothing. And that Natharius will succeed in navigating us out of this wretched place.

CHAPTER 26

I'M NOT SURE HOW LONG the three of us are outside the cave before Caya and Taria emerge. The priestess wears a stern expression which masks her grief. Caya's grief, however, is clear. Her eyes are bloodshot and swollen.

"Come on then," Caya murmurs, her posture as lethargic as her words. "He . . . he wouldn't want us to rot in here for his sake."

She doesn't wait for our response before pressing on through the trees, clutching her brother's sword as she steps over the protruding roots in her path.

We follow her, and Natharius soon takes the lead as we navigate through the endless maze of shadowy trees. After facing the wisps, it seems Zephyr has become a little braver since he neither curls around my shoulders nor huddles beneath my robes. Instead, he flutters behind me, though he's careful to stay close.

Despite her initial resolve, Caya eventually trails far behind us. Taria's pace is almost as slow, barely a few strides ahead of her. Natharius doesn't wait for them, and I call for him to stop when they drift too far back.

Natharius's route doesn't return us to the main path, and my concern grows with every step we take. With no tracks and only identical trees around us, it's impossible to tell whether we're heading in the right direction or venturing farther into the forest.

"Do you remember the way?" I ask him after a dozen more strides.

The demon shrugs.

I wish I didn't ask.

I draw in a deep breath and continue after him, praying he has at least some idea of where we're going.

It may be hours or half a day that we walk before Natharius halts. He tilts back his head as he gazes up at the two tall trees towering above us. These look somewhat different to the ones behind us, but only because of their enormous height.

"What is it?" I ask, stopping beside him.

"I remember now."

"The way out of these woods?"

"Indeed."

"Thank aether for that," I say with a sigh of relief. "How much longer before we reach the other side?"

"At least a day."

How much time have we lost from searching for Juron? The words are on my tongue, yet I can't bear to ask such an insensitive question. Not with Taria and Caya so close behind. Caya's eyes are puffy and red. I suspect she's been silently weeping while following us through the trees.

"Do you think there's a chance we might reach Gerazad before Arluin?"

"I'm a Void Prince, not a seer. Why don't you ask the priestess?"

I turn and peer at Taria expectantly.

"I can't be certain," she replies, shaking her head. "I haven't had the chance to meditate since a few nights ago. Even then, I didn't glimpse any visions of us in Gerazad."

"It's all right," I say. "We have no choice but to keep pressing on, anyway."

Taria nods and glances at Caya. Though Caya watches the three of us as we speak, I'm not sure she's paying attention to our words, seeing how unfocused her gaze is. She follows us silently as Natharius continues to pave our way through the trees.

All I can hope is that we'll reach Gerazad first. Or else we won't be able to warn the orcs of their impending doom. If we arrive too late, I don't know when I'll next have the opportunity to defeat Arluin.

If ever.

With every step we take through this ghastly forest, I allow thoughts of Arluin to drive me forth. Natharius's pace is relentless, but neither Taria nor Caya complain. My legs ache with fatigue, but I fill my mind with the vengeance I will claim in Gerazad. Of Father, whose corpse and soul are enslaved to that monster.

Finally, the trees open to a sprawling lake. Its waters are murky, though I expect nothing less in woods as shadowy and eerie as these.

Natharius stops, and his crimson eyes darken. If I didn't know better, I would say the Void Prince looks horror stricken.

My brows furrow together as I examine Natharius's expression. I go to ask him what's wrong but before I can say anything, he breaks into a sprint.

I blink at him, watching him bound toward the water's surface. "Natharius?" I call after him. "What is it?"

The demon doesn't respond. He doesn't once pause, and his pace is frantic until he reaches the lake. He halts at the edge and stares into the depths below.

"Natharius?" I repeat, hurrying after him. But he doesn't seem to hear me. His gaze remains on the murky lake. A very mortal emotion is plastered across his face, though I can't pinpoint what exactly. It almost looks like fear. Dread. What could cause the Void Prince of Pride to feel such emotions?

Zephyr doesn't draw near the water's edge. He keeps a few paces away from the lake and watches it cautiously.

Natharius raises his hands. Darkness swirls out, reaching across the lake. His spell sweeps across the water's surface, capturing every drop in a shadowy net. Once the entire lake is covered by his magic, he pushes his hands together. The water follows his command, constricting and forming an enormous orb. Natharius's jaw clenches as he pushes the gigantic bubble through the air, exposing the bottom of the lake.

With all the water hovering in the air, the lake is now but a crater. It runs so deep into the earth, it's impossible to see anything in the darkness.

Lines of exertion are etched into Natharius's forehead. "Illuminate the bottom of the lake with aether," he says to me.

My brows shoot up. He's the one who's bound to my will and not the other way around. I almost go to remind him of that fact and of his place in our relationship, but something in his expression silences the words on my tongue.

He's scared: something I thought to be impossible until this very moment.

And if the Prince of Pride is scared, then I should be as well. Even if I don't yet know what the threat is.

"*Iluminos.*" A radiant orb springs from my hands, drifting into the darkness below. The rays shine across the moist soil, making it glitter like thousands of diamonds.

As the light reaches the bottom, a shadowy object comes into view. I narrow my eyes, squinting to better determine the item.

It's an altar of some form, too wicked to belong to a church. Skulls are etched into its obsidian sides. Though it's tiny from where we stand high above, my throat dries at the sight. Its appearance alone makes one fact evident: It's an object of dark magic.

"It's . . ." Natharius starts, his voice breathless and barely audible over the wind. "It's gone." The tremble in his voice makes me shiver.

"What's gone?" I ask. My stomach churns at the horror plastered across his face.

Taria comes to a stop beside us. "Here the darkness in these woods is at its strongest," she whispers, her words sending a chill across my skin. "I have never felt air this suffocating."

I don't look at the priestess as she speaks. My eyes stay on the Void Prince. "Natharius," I say, my pitch rising with fear, "what's gone?"

He remains silent for another moment. Then he drops his hands. The darkness swirling around us fades, as does the magic holding the lake overhead. The orb shatters.

Water descends, crashing into the crater below. With the tremendous force, it splashes out and soaks me from head to toe. Zephyr has the sense to dart away, narrowly avoiding the water.

Though Natharius ends up as drenched as me, he doesn't seem to notice. His gaze remains on the water's surface, staring at the spot where the altar lay beneath its murky depths.

Normally I would scold him for soaking me, but both his and Taria's words have sent panic coursing through me.

"Natharius?" I try again. Must I command him to answering my question? Before I can make my decision, the demon finally speaks of his own accord.

"This lake was frozen when I was last here," he mutters. From how low his voice is, he might be talking to himself.

"Well, now it's clearly not," I scoff, pointing to the water's very liquid surface. "What's the problem with a bit of ice melting?"

Natharius shakes his head. "The problem is that things which have long been laid to rest now rise once more."

I turn to Taria, hoping she'll offer a clearer explanation, but she doesn't meet my gaze. Her eyes are fixed on the lake, and her pale brows are knitted together. Maybe she's as in the dark as I am, and Caya's blank gaze suggests she also has no idea, though I'm not sure she's thinking about anything other than her brother.

"Things like what?" I demand to Natharius.

"Things like Kazhul Nightbringer, the Lich Lord."

I stare at him, wishing I imagined those words. That name. The wind rustles through the canopy of gnarled branches overhead. For several heartbeats, no one speaks.

"The Lich Lord?" I echo, repeating each syllable slowly. I hope Natharius will tell me I've somehow misheard him.

To my dismay, he nods. "Though the Lich Lord was defeated over a thousand years ago, he was not entirely destroyed. Only sealed away in the far reaches of Kralaxxas."

"Why would an enemy as dangerous as him not be completely obliterated from this world?" I ask with a frown.

"Because a lich is only truly defeated when all remnants of their soul are destroyed," Natharius replies. "And the Lich Lord, the first lich, was able to divide his soul into three parts. Each he placed into a separate phylactery. We could not find them, and there was little time to act. Already, the Lich Lord's crusade on the living had wiped out most of Imyria. The only hope was to seal him away with the most powerful sorcerers from each race of man, orc, and elf."

I peer at Natharius, not missing the 'we' he used. I shouldn't be surprised, since the Void Prince is old enough to have been alive at the time of Kazhul Nightbringer. The question is whether he was a demon or an elf then, but I strongly suspect that it was the latter. Is the past Natharius didn't want Taria to reveal in Esterra City linked to this? It would explain his horrified expression over the lake.

Though I want to ask, I know he'll refuse to answer, and I don't want to stoop so low as to command him to tell me.

"What has the Lich Lord got to do with this lake?" I ask.

Natharius turns to the water, a shadow drifting over his expression. "Three centuries ago, I was summoned to Imyria by an orcish necromancer. He sought the Amulet of Kazhul, and his quest led him here. To this very lake."

My heart skips a beat.

An amulet?

It can't be . . .

I swallow. "The amulet was here? You saw it for yourself?"

"I did," Natharius says. "I used my magic to shatter the ice, and the two of us ventured into the frozen water. Hundreds of undead lurked in the lake's depths, and the warlock who had summoned me was defeated by them. Before I returned to the Abyss, I glimpsed the amulet on the obsidian altar below. There was no denying that the Lich Lord's soul, or at least part of it, dwelled within."

"This amulet," I begin, the words grating across the back of my throat, "what did it look like?"

"A skull of obsidian like its altar, with a blue stone hanging from its jawless mouth."

The blood drains from my face. A wind rolls over me, almost shoving me into the lake. My legs offer little resistance against its might.

In the water below, my reflection distorts into the streets of Nolderan. I see Eliya's lifeless body slumped against the wall. I see Father atop the Aether Tower, his dead eyes burning into me.

My fists tighten. The Lich Lord's Amulet—it explains everything. How Arluin could defeat Father so easily, the Grandmage of Nolderan.

I squeeze my eyes shut, fighting past the pain coiling around my heart. "I . . . I know who took the Lich Lord's amulet." I don't look up at Natharius. Horrifying images of Nolderan's fall continue swirling in the lake's waters.

"The necromancer," Taria murmurs beside me. "Arluin."

I lift my head in a small nod. "That night, he had a powerful amulet hanging around his neck. The darkness which poured out of it was unlike any other." I finally tear my eyes from the lake, instead glancing across at Natharius. "Even yours."

I shudder in memory of how terrifying that dark presence felt. I should have known that it couldn't be Arluin's alone; his father's felt a fraction of its power.

Is the amulet responsible for corrupting his soul? For poisoning the last traces of his humanity?

No, I can't think like that. Arluin is long gone. The amulet alone isn't responsible for his actions. Only a monster would seek such a wicked artifact.

Yet a part of me longs to believe that the amulet and the Lich Lord's soul are entirely to blame. Not the man I once loved.

I shove away those thoughts, not allowing them to take a hold over me.

Natharius is silent, staring into the lake's depths. What does he see inside the water? Does he also see images of the destruction of his home? Though he claimed he sold the souls of his entire kingdom to the Void King in exchange for power, I wonder if there's more to the truth. Like the Lich Lord.

Taria stands with her hands clasped behind her back, staring up at the branches above as though they may offer her some guidance. Caya is a few paces away from us on a boulder and gazes down at Juron's sword, her hands stiff as they clutch it.

"What does this mean, for Arluin to have a portion of the Lich Lord's soul?" I whisper, turning to Natharius.

"I might know what this necromancer of yours seeks in Gerazad."

"What?"

"When he attacked Nolderan, did he seek anything in particular?"

"Death? Destruction? Revenge?"

Natharius shakes his head, sending his long, silver hair tumbling through the wind. "No. I mean an object. A ring." He raises his hand, drawing on the shadows. Dark magic hums inside his palm. It swirls, taking on the silhouette of a ring.

Though the phantom ring has no color, I would recognize it anywhere. I've known it for my entire life.

"That's . . ." Grief chokes my throat, making it almost impossible to force out words. "My father's."

"This ring has belonged to every Grandmage for as long as Nolderan has stood." He closes his hand and the shadowy ring disappears. The dark magic drifts into the wind. "When your father died, what happened to his ring? Did the necromancer take it?"

I lift my head in a feeble nod. Father always wore it, so it would have been on his finger when he was risen as a wight. Since he's now in Arluin's clutches, the ring must be too. But I don't know what use Arluin has for it, and it certainly didn't seem important at the time. Not when my city was being destroyed and everyone I knew was being murdered.

Natharius lets out a heavy sigh. "I suspected as much. Then it begins again."

"What begins again?"

"Only the destruction of Imyria," he says. Despite the effort he makes to look unbothered by his own words, shadows lurk in his eyes.

"What do you mean?" I ask. By now, Caya has left her rock to join us. She stands beside Taria, her gaze on Natharius.

"I am certain the necromancers are acting under the will of Kazhul Nightbringer, whose soul communicates with them through his amulet. And it seems they already have one of the three rings necessary to break the Lich Lord's seal and unleash his wrath upon this world."

Caya frowns. "And there is another ring located in Gerazad? That's why the necromancers travel there?"

"Correct," Natharius replies. "A thousand years ago, Lagartha the Old was one of the three sorcerers who sealed the Lich Lord inside his frozen tomb. She was of the White Rock Tribe, who made their home in the area that Gerazad now stands today."

"And so, they seek the ring of Lagartha the Old?" I ask.

"I would bet my soul on it."

If Natharius is right, that means Arluin annihilated Nolderan not only to avenge his father but also for this dark purpose. And as it stands, he's on track to succeeding with his heinous plan.

Vengeance, I can understand. It's what fuels me to keep drawing breath, to keep taking one step after another. But I can't understand what motivates Arluin to free the Lich Lord and let him obliterate Imyria. What if the amulet's power has corrupted him, warping his own ambitions with Kazhul Nightbringer's?

Now reaching Gerazad before he and his necromancers do is even more vital. If we fail, if Arluin retrieves Lagartha's ring, it'll be much more than my vendetta at stake. The entire world will be crushed by the Lich Lord's wrath.

"The Grandmage of Nolderan at the time—"

"Lothar Ashbourne," Natharius interrupts.

"Well," I continue, "Grandmage Lothar Ashbourne was one of the three sorcerers who sealed the Lich Lord. Lagartha the Old was another. Before you mentioned that the most powerful sorcerers from the races of man, orc, and elf sealed the Lich Lord away. So, the third person involved would have been the High Enchanter of Lumaria?"

"Indeed." Natharius's eyes glint, swirling with unfathomable power. "He would have been."

"It was you, wasn't it?" I whisper. "You were the High Enchanter at the time, and you were one of the three sorcerers who sealed the Lich Lord?"

He lifts his head in a nod.

I glance across to Taria. As I expect, the priestess doesn't look surprised. Is this what she meant about the Mother rarely smiling upon a demon? Out of the three sorcerers who sealed the Lich Lord away, he's the only one left alive. Even if he's now a Void Prince, his knowledge may be pivotal in saving the world from destruction.

"You sold your soul to the Void King for power," I say quietly. "Power to defeat Kazhul Nightbringer." My mind flashes back to one of our earliest conversations, when Natharius sat at my dining table and we discussed how I could defeat Arluin: *Do you have one hundred thousand soul-gems? Are you willing to sacrifice an entire kingdom worth of souls to summon my demons?*

My mouth falls open as the realization strikes me. I stare at Natharius, somehow seeing him for the first time. As something other than the wicked demon I've always seen him as.

"You sacrificed your entire kingdom to summon the Void King's army from the Abyss," I continue, the words spilling from my mouth before I can stop them. "A hundred thousand mortal souls for a hundred thousand demons—"

"That's enough," Natharius hisses.

The dangerous edge to his voice stops me from saying more.

"I have no wish to discuss these matters with a puny, good-for-nothing mage," he spits. "They are far beyond your mortal comprehension."

Instinctively, his wrath makes me step back. Yet beneath his rage, I catch the flicker of something else. Perhaps pain, but it's hard to tell since the fleeting shadow is gone in mere instants.

Despite all his fury, I don't see a fearsome Void Prince. I instead see an injured wolf lashing out to hide his vulnerability. He doesn't succeed in hiding all of it.

His emotion is raw. And so very mortal.

"I'm sorry," I say. Not that I owe him an apology. I haven't forgotten how he laughed at Nolderan's fall, nor have I forgiven him for it. But the words tumble from my mouth all the same.

Natharius holds my gaze for a moment, his jaw twitching. Then he whirls around and storms past the lake, toward the trees ahead. "We'd better get moving, or else the necromancers will retrieve Lagartha's ring and awaken the Lich Lord."

CHAPTER 27

OUR FOOTSTEPS ECHO THROUGH THE trees. I stare at the back of Natharius's silver hair as he leads us through the Ghost Woods. I can't think clearly. My mind swarms with all he revealed a few hours ago.

That Arluin possesses a part of the Lich Lord's soul. That Natharius is one of the three sorcerers who sealed the Lich Lord inside his icy tomb. That if we don't reach Gerazad before Arluin does and recover Lagartha the Old's ring, then all life will be obliterated from Imyria.

It's all too much. The worry of reaching Gerazad first weighs heavily on my mind.

What visions did the Mother Goddess reveal to Taria? Did she witness undead armies waging death across Imyria? She's quiet as she walks behind me. From her contemplative expression, it's clear she's also wrapped up in her own thoughts. Caya is just as quiet, but perhaps for other reasons. Since leaving the cave, she hasn't relaxed her grip around Juron's sword.

I reopen my eyes and sigh. No one comments on it. With the wind howling through the trees, I doubt they'll have even heard it.

The Void Prince's shoulders are taut beneath his dark tunic. Though hours have passed since we left the lake, his temper hasn't lessened. Rage fuels his every movement. His boots stomp on the twigs and leaves littering our path, crushing them into dirt, and he shoves stray branches out of his way with so much force they snap from the trees. Once or twice, I have to murmur *ventrez* to blow the branches away before they slam into me. I don't think Natharius is purposely trying to hit me with them, though. I'm not sure he even notices me casting spells behind him. His eyes remain on the path ahead.

This anger can't only be from my questions about his past. Surely even Natharius can't maintain such a burning rage over something like that for this long. I suspect his initial reaction at the lake has much to do with his current temper. Shock and horror were plastered across his face, turning his alabaster skin several shades paler.

The Void Prince is terrified. And it seems he's trying to hide his fear by turning it into anger. Maybe he doesn't realize what he's doing. Maybe he doesn't recognize this emotion as fear.

Though I'm certain his anger is due to fear, I'm not entirely sure about the actual reason behind it. He can't possibly be concerned over Imyria's fate. He would probably be amused if all of us mortals perish.

While I'm curious, I decide not to ask. It would only further incite his wrath. My guess is his anger is linked to the measures he took to defeat Kazhul Nightbringer. If the Lich Lord returns, won't that make all his sacrifices be for nothing?

I suppose now the Lich Lord is involved, Natharius is motivated to defeat Arluin. Beneath his anger, I see purpose in his strides as he marches onward through the trees. If he were not accompanied by us mortals, I think he would instead sprint the entire way to Gerazad. Or fly. Though I don't know how long flight in his demonic form can be sustained.

Another hour stretches on. Our pace remains swift, and we don't stop to rest. I'm not sure how long it'll be until dusk falls, but I'm determined to walk until morning, despite the fact I didn't sleep last night. None of us did. Neither Taria nor Caya suggest we take a break, and Natharius could probably keep on walking for eternity.

Despite my initial resolve, I only last what around another two hours before I am forced to ask the others to take a break. Though the aether in my veins has begun to replenish itself, I feel weakened from when the wisps drained my magic. And my soul.

I shudder as I plant myself on a fallen log, its bark covered in frost, and Zephyr flutters down beside me. With Juron's death and the knowledge Natharius shared at the lake, I haven't even had the chance to process what happened in the wisps' cave. How close I was to death. To becoming one of them.

The thought of becoming an undead nauseates me far more than the prospect of death itself. Over the last few weeks, I've brushed closely with death many times, and the fear of dying is familiar. A part of me feels so weary that death almost seems inviting. If not for defeating Arluin and freeing Father, I might welcome it. After all, what else do I have left in this world other than vengeance?

If I kill Arluin and free Father, what will I do then? I have nowhere to return. No one to welcome me back. My home was destroyed. My family and friends were murdered. I am alone in this world.

I shiver.

Maybe the priestess can sense more than just the future, since her golden eyes sweep over me. "Are you all right?" she asks, her white brows knitting together.

I cast her a hurried nod. Nolderan's fall was well over two weeks ago, whereas Taria and Caya lost Juron barely over two hours ago. I'm not the one who should be grieving. Nor do I deserve anyone's concern. "I'm fine, thank you." I turn my gaze in Caya's direction and hope Taria will do the same. Fortunately, she does.

Caya leans against a nearby tree, staring down at Juron's sword as she plays with it in her hands. She doesn't seem to notice us watching her. Her attention stays on the blade.

Zephyr nudges my shoulder, and I tear my gaze from Caya to look at him. His talons claw at the satchel at my side.

"All right," I say, reaching into my satchel. "I'll get you some now."

He sits on his hind legs and watches me as I rummage through all the glittering orbs in search of the pouch of aether crystals.

When I find the orb I need, I hold it flat on my palm and close my eyes. The wisps drained so much aether from me, and I haven't had the chance to replenish my magic. Even casting a minor spell such as *acoligos* will be challenging, but at least it will be easier than casting *crysanthius* to summon fresh crystals. And since my faerie dragon has a very strict diet of aether crystals, he will only turn his nose up at any berries I offer him. Not that I'd contemplate letting him eat anything that grows in these accursed woods.

Zephyr lets out an impatient growl as I hesitate, but I don't break my focus to scold him. I do my best to draw on the dregs of magic left in my veins and direct it to the orb in my palm.

"*Acoligos*," I murmur.

The orb expands into a pouch, and I retrieve a handful and hold them out to Zephyr. My hand is barely out of the pouch before he swoops down and licks them all off my palm, leaving a slobbery mess in their place. I shake my head at him and wipe the saliva from my robes.

I go to tie the pouch, but my fingers pause on the drawstring, and I peer down into the twinkling crystals within. Casting *acoligos* to expand the orb into the pouch cost me the little magic I have left, and I need to compress the pouch again so I can return it to my satchel. With how fatigued I feel, I fear I might not be able to cast the spell and then I'll have to leave them out and they'll be gone as soon as I turn my back, thanks to Zephyr.

Consuming aether crystals is dangerous, unless you're a faerie dragon, but I've done it before. I have so little aether in my veins right now that even swallowing the entire pouch probably wouldn't cause me to implode. Though I don't plan on trying it.

I take only a few crystals, barely enough to fit on my little finger, and lift them to my lips. The crystal's sweet taste bursts on my tongue, and they fizz in my mouth until they dissolve. Instantly, I feel a little more energized, and casting *coligos* to compress the pouch into an orb is easier than expanding it.

Once the pouch is away, I look up to see what everyone else is doing. Taria is in meditation, and Caya is staring at her brother's sword. As for Natharius, he leans against a nearby tree and stares up at the tangle of branches, looking very much bored.

Though swallowing those aether crystals has returned a small amount of my strength, I'm far from my usual self. We aren't out of the Ghost Woods yet—in fact I don't know whether we're even halfway through—and we could face monstrosities far worse than the wisps before we make it to the other side. I need to replenish as much as magic as I can.

I slow my breaths, trying to sense what aether I can in the surrounding air. Little remains beneath the suffocating shadows, and it's hard to guide it away from the dark magic. I fall into meditation, oblivious to the world around me. My attention is solely focused on locating what aether I can and drawing it toward me, replenishing the magic flowing through my veins.

It feels like only minutes pass before a hand gently taps my shoulder, but it could be hours.

I open my eyes to see Taria peering at me. "We should keep moving," she says softly. "It will do us no good to linger here."

I blink, my senses adjusting. Caya has torn herself away from the tree she was leaning on, Juron's bow and quiver strung across her back. While I was meditating, she must have asked Natharius if she could instead carry them, and I doubt the Void Prince protested at that request.

Natharius stands a few paces away. His foot taps restlessly against the frozen earth, and judging by his impatient expression, I must have meditated for longer than I intended.

I stretch my arms and roll my shoulders. My muscles do feel rather stiff. I suck in a breath.

More aether hums within me now, and I feel less tired than before. Hopefully it'll mean I can keep going for longer before needing to stop.

I'm not sure whether Taria rested, but she looks far from fatigued. Maybe her energy comes from all the holy magic radiating within her. Caya also doesn't look too weary, aside from her grief, but I suppose her lean muscles aren't as exerted as mine.

"All right," I say, pushing myself onto my feet. "Let's keep moving."

We continue to follow Natharius through the trees. I'm not sure whether it's my imagination, but the air seems to grow colder the farther we walk through the woods. The layer of frost clinging to the branches and leaves thickens.

The trees creak as the howling wind slams into them, and I'm not surprised we've passed so many fallen trees on our way through the Ghost Woods.

Natharius's strides are as furious as before, though the tension in his shoulders has lessened and he doesn't look quite as enraged.

We come to a patch of trees where the gnarled branches aren't as dense. A glimpse of the sky is visible through the gap. The clouds are orange, streaked with shadows.

"How much longer now before we reach the end of the Ghost Woods?" I ask Natharius.

"Another day, perhaps."

"And once on the other side, how long will it take for us to reach Gerazad?"

"Maybe two days."

I give him a quick nod, and we continue past the patch of amber sky.

The shadowy trees dance around us. I swear once or twice the branches coil together like snakes. I can't wait until we leave these eerie trees behind. Every rustle and crack jolts my senses until my nerves are tightly wound.

Rustling comes from the left. I initially brush it aside as nothing more than the wind blowing through the bushes. And it seems the others also do, seeing how none of them turn to look.

Footsteps sound.

We come to a sudden halt, each of us staring in the sound's direction.

A low, guttural growl echoes through the trees.

No one says anything. Caya draws her sword, and the rest of us draw on our magic. The purple glow of aether dances in my palms, waiting until the enemy shows themselves, and sparks crackle from Zephyr's mouth. Golden light radiates from Taria's hands, and shadows swirl between Natharius's fingers.

Skeletons burst through the trees.

"*Ignira!*"

"*Narliva!*"

Our magic slams into two of the skeletons. Bone disintegrates, turning to ash.

We raise our hands, ready to unleash another barrage of attacks on the three remaining skeletons. But before any of us can conjure another spell, a hollow voice echoes from the trees.

"I wouldn't do that again, if I were you."

A blue light emerges from behind the branches, the same unearthly glow as the wisps. But this isn't a flickering orb. It's a translucent, floating silhouette.

A wraith.

The figure is short and has long, pointed ears, dressed in furs and leather. Its head is at least twice the size of its body, and a few strands of thin hair sprout from its otherwise bald head. Its oversized nose is hooked, and talon-like nails extend from its bulbous fingers. Despite the creature's grotesque appearance, there's a strange femininity to it.

The phantom goblin woman grins at us, revealing rows of razor-sharp fangs. I don't want to imagine how many lost travelers her teeth tore through before she died and became a wraith.

Zephyr lets out a squeal and darts behind the safety of my robes. I dig my heels into the frozen earth, refusing to allow myself to be intimidated by the wraith's terrifying appearance. The three skeletons surround the phantom goblin, their bones rattling as the wind threatens to blow them apart.

"Give me one good reason why I shouldn't blast you all into oblivion?" I growl, flames already flickering in my fingertips.

The wraith's grin doesn't lessen. "The Master warned you might be uncooperative." She nods to the skeleton on her right, and it steps forth, bearing an obsidian box. A skull is featured on the lid, matching the altar hidden in the lake's depths.

The skeleton extends the box toward me. I watch the undead creature through narrowed eyes. Its bony fingers uncurl from around the box, holding it flat in its ivory palms. I hesitate longer before taking the box from its grasp. The motion is swift, and my fingers are nimble, not wanting to touch the skeleton's bony hands. Fortunately, my fingertips only brush over the obsidian box.

I take a step back, wanting to put some distance between me and the undead creature. I stare down at the metallic box. Despite its small size, it's heavy in my hands.

"Open it," the wraith urges, her thin lips curling into a heinous smirk.

There's something in the goblin's expression that makes my stomach knot with dread. My fingers hesitate around the silver clasp.

The others all watch me intently, waiting for me to open it. With a deep breath, I undo the clasp and swing back the box's lid.

When I see what's inside, I scream and slam it shut. My hands tremble around the box, and it almost falls from my grasp. The wraith throws back her oversized head and cackles. The jaws of the three skeletons clatter.

"What is it?" Natharius asks, his brows furrowing as he examines the box's exterior.

I frantically shake my head at him. I can't answer that question. Saying the words out loud will make it real. It's better to convince myself I imagined what I saw inside the box.

Taria gently lifts my fingers from around the box, freeing it from my grasp. I offer little resistance, glad for the horrific object to be out of my hands.

The priestess slowly raises the box's lid until its contents are revealed. She doesn't scream like me but stares down at the inside, frozen in place.

Caya approaches, peering at the contents, but Taria slams the lid shut before she can glimpse what lies within.

Taria raises her head, her expression hardening as she looks at the wraith. "Where did you get this? Who does it belong to?"

The wraith grins. "The Ghost Woods are filled only by the dead. If it hasn't come from yourselves, how else do you think we've gotten such a fresh eye?"

I choke at the word. The image of what I glimpsed flashes through my mind. I'm sure I sway in the wind, unable to shake away the nausea drowning me.

Taria's gaze falls on the box once more, and her hands tremble like mine did. The priestess doesn't seem to notice as Caya yanks the box from her hands and tears off the lid.

With an anguished scream, Caya swings her golden sword at the nearest skeleton and severs the head from its spine. The skull falls, landing on the ice-covered ground and rolls downhill to the left. The rest of the skeleton collapses in a heap of bones, the enchantment severed by the light magic singing through Caya's holy sword.

She thrusts her blade at the wraith. "What have you done to my brother?"

The undead goblin clicks her tongue at Caya. "Now, now, there's no need for that attitude."

"You gouged out his eye!" Caya roars.

"He's perfectly alive," the wraith replies. "Well, maybe not perfectly."

Caya snarls, clutching the box to her chest. Her hand tightens around the hilt of her sword. "Where is he? What do you want from him?"

"My master wants nothing from him," the wraith says. "What he wants is the one that failed him all those years ago." Her spectral head snaps in Natharius's direction.

"I failed him?" the demon scoffs. "I think Mulgath will find that he is the one who failed himself. Though I am the Prince of Pride, that doesn't mean that I am granted with the miraculous ability to prevent mortals from dying."

The goblin wraith only offers him a thin smile. "I am but a messenger. You can discuss such matters with the master himself."

I frown at Natharius. "Do you know who's taken Juron?"

"Likely Mulgath Kharak," he says, "an orcish necromancer who vastly overestimated his own abilities."

"The one that sought the Amulet of Kazhul and died inside the lake?"

"Indeed."

"Where is he?" Caya demands, her attention returning to the wraith. "Where have you taken my brother?"

"To the master's fortress, of course," the undead goblin replies. "If you wish to be reunited with your brother, I can show you the way." She raises her translucent blue hand, gesturing to the trees from which they appeared.

"Absolutely not!" Natharius roars, before Caya can take a single step in that direction. He whirls around to face me, his crimson eyes blazing. "Don't tell me you think this is a good idea?"

While following a wraith back to the fortress of an undead orcish necromancer isn't the wisest of plans, I'm not sure what other options we have. "Well, I agree it isn't the best of ideas, but—"

"But what?" Natharius growls. "In case you've forgotten, there is a necromancer on the loose who possesses part of the Lich Lord's soul and seeks to free him from the icy tomb I sealed him inside a thousand years ago."

I can also hear the words he leaves unsaid: That Arluin seeks to undo what he sacrificed everything for.

"No, I haven't forgotten," I snap, placing my hands on my hips and returning Natharius's ferocious stare. After all, how can I forget that Arluin, the man responsible for destroying all I loved, draws breath? That my home, my people, are unavenged? "But I can't leave someone at the mercy of a necromancer! An undead one at that!"

"Why not? He's mortal. All you mortals are destined to die."

"I wouldn't expect you to understand, demon."

"You're even more useless than I thought. Useless and stupid. Only a fool would fail to see this mortal's life is not worth saving. Some sacrifices are necessary."

I fold my arms across my chest and stand my ground, refusing to let myself be riled by his insults. "Is that what you told yourself when you sacrificed your kingdom for an army of demons?"

Fury rages across his alabaster face, far more volatile than it was back at the lake. In fact, I'm certain the Void Prince is moments from bursting into flames. "I wouldn't expect you to understand, mortal." He hisses the final word as though it's the gravest of insults. "But know this: Had I not made the choices I made, had I not sacrificed all I sacrificed, you would never have been born. Nor your father, his father, his grandfather. Only thanks to me do you mortals draw breath."

The Void Prince's furious stare doesn't relent. I glare back at him, unwilling to yield. For a moment, I'm so focused on scowling at Natharius I almost forget the others are there. And the goblin wraith and its skeletal companions.

"Natharius isn't wrong," Taria says, stepping between the two of us. "Though it pains me to say, one life cannot be deemed more important than the lives of the entire world."

Horror flashes in Caya's eyes, soon replaced by pain. She stumbles back, clutching her chest as though Taria shoved a blade through her heart. "You . . ." She chokes on the word. "You can't mean that? He's my brother! He sees you as family too! We can't abandon him!"

Taria closes her eyes, heaving out a deep breath. "I am the First Disciple of Grand Priestess Elunar. I have no family, except the Mother and all of Selynis." Taria chants the words like a prayer. They seem more intended for herself than for Caya.

Caya shakes her head. "No, you can't mean this. Not after all these years."

Though Taria opens her eyes, she doesn't look at Caya as she speaks. "All of Imyria is at stake. If we fail, if the necromancers recover all three rings and unseal the Lich Lord from his tomb . . ." Taria doesn't need to finish that sentence. We all know exactly what the consequences will be if Arluin and his necromancers succeed: Imyria will no longer be known as the mortal plane of existence but instead the realm of the dead.

A solemn silence falls over us. Even Natharius doesn't speak. His jaw remains clenched.

The goblin wraith glances between us and shrugs her translucent shoulders. "I'll tell the master that you won't be visiting him then. I'm sure he'll find some use for the prisoner."

I swallow down the bile surging up within me. Everything about this decision screams wrongness, but I can't argue with what Taria and Natharius said. We don't know what will happen if we follow this wraith back to its master's fortress, nor do we know how much time we will lose, even if we are successful in rescuing Juron from the necromancer's clutches. Saving him could mean losing everything. The entire world.

I lower my head, the burden of the decision weighing on my shoulders.

Sometimes sacrifices need to be made. But is this sacrifice one too great? Will I be able to live with the guilt of knowing that I left someone to die, even if it was for the sake of the world?

The wraith waits a moment longer before slipping through the trees. "Very well," her hollow voice calls. "I'll tell the prisoner myself that his friends abandoned him. Before we kill him, of course."

"Wait!" Caya cries. "I'll meet with your master!"

The wraith pauses, and the two skeletons halt as she raises her spectral hand. "You can come, but the master will have no interest in you, other than your corpse. At least you'll be reunited with your brother in undeath."

Caya's fists tighten. She glances back at us, desperation plastered across her face. Her dark eyes silently beg us to join her.

What am I doing, forcing someone to abandon their brother? I know all too well the agony of losing those I love, of having their corpses reanimated as undead. How can I subject Caya to the same torture I have suffered?

I grit my teeth, my decision made. I can only hope this won't prove a mistake. That this choice won't cost me everything.

"Is it the Void Prince you want?" I demand, my eyes narrowing as I gaze at the goblin wraith and her skeletal companions.

"Yes, along with the sorcerer who summoned him from the Abyss and bound him to their soul." The wraith's pale eyes flicker across us as she examines us all. "Which appears to be you."

"Very well," I say. "We'll come with you to your master's fortress."

CHAPTER 28

Natharius glares at me as we follow the wraith and two skeletons. Deeper through the trees, icicles hang from twisted branches, and the Void Prince has to duck a few times to avoid them. The rest of us don't have this problem, however, seeing how Natharius stands almost a foot taller than us all.

"Please tell me you have a plan up your sleeve," he hisses across to me, quietly enough that only I hear his words, "and that this isn't what I fear it is."

"And what do you fear this is?"

"A suicide mission."

As much as I wish I have a clever plan, I unfortunately don't. Most likely, Juron's rescue attempt will end up with us all dead.

Or undead.

I don't look at him as I speak. "Think about it like this," I begin, shoving the twigs of a large bush out of my way, "you'll probably return to the Abyss before the night is over."

Natharius snorts. I'm not sure he's pleased about the idea, seeing how the sound lacks any humor. He's more concerned about ensuring the lich he sealed away one thousand years ago doesn't escape than he is about returning to the Abyss. What a change that makes.

He says nothing more, though his stare doesn't relent.

Zephyr was as reluctant as the Void Prince about following the wraith to her master's fortress. He stares at me with a pleading look in his jewel-like eyes and refused to move an inch until I scooped him into my arms and carried him. Now he flutters closely behind me.

As for Taria, though she initially opposed rescuing Juron and risking Lagartha the Old's ring falling into the hands of Arluin and his necromancers, she doesn't protest even once. Her face is emotionless as always, but the tension has dissipated from her shoulders. Perhaps a part of her wanted to save Juron but, as the future Grand Priestess, she was unable to justify doing so. But now I've made the decision, the choice is out of her hands.

Caya walks ahead of us all, directly behind the wraith and her skeletal companions. She's placed the obsidian box safely inside her saddlebags, and she marches through the trees with her sword gripped tightly in her right hand. Her jaw is clenched, and determination powers her every stride.

I hope, for her sake, that Juron is alive. That the undead didn't kill him after gouging out his eye. If he's already dead, we're risking everything for nothing.

I sigh as I step over an overgrown root which has burst through the frozen ground. All I can do is pray we aren't putting the world at stake for a man who is long dead.

The fortress isn't as far away as I expect. It soon emerges through the trees, dark spires towering high above. No grass grows this close to the fortress. Even the gnarled trees shy away from this place.

As we draw near the fortress, dark magic slams into my senses. The intensity momentarily disorients me, and the ominous spires spin around me. The air smells rotten in my nostrils and clings to the back of my throat. Even when I cough, the vile aura won't leave me. The dark magic seems determined to choke me from the inside out, but I force myself to continue forward into this maelstrom of darkness.

Crows perch along the spires. Some are decayed, while others are nothing but bones. Despite their lack of feathers, the skeletal crows manage to fly. As our footsteps echo across this barren patch of land, undead crows let out piercing caws and swoop high into the air. They dance above, keeping a watchful eye as we approach.

The fortress's entrance is marked by an arch, though I'm not sure it can be called an arch, seeing how half of it has collapsed. We pick our way over the fallen stone, climbing the steep hill which leads to the fortress's gates.

The incline is sharp, and the walk takes several minutes, though it feels far longer. With every step I take, my heart pounds more furiously in my chest. While I know of the enemy we face—Mulgath Kharak, an undead orcish necromancer who once summoned Natharius from the Abyss—I don't know of his power. Even if Mulgath was defeated by the undead guarding the Amulet of Kazhul beneath the lake, his strength may have grown substantially during undeath.

At least I'm in the company of the Void Prince of Pride and the First Disciple of Selynis. Few others are more powerful than them both. If they can't defeat this necromancer who fell to the Lich Lord's undead, then we have little hope of vanquishing Arluin.

A narrow bridge leads across to the gates. The ferocious gales have worn parts of it away, and much of the bridge has fallen into the chasm below. A gush of wind blows a loose stone over the edge. My throat dries as I watch it tumble into the darkness. I don't hear it land.

I swallow and remind myself that I'm a mage who can manipulate the winds, no matter how fierce they might be. And I also have the option of murmuring *laxus* and teleporting to safety.

Having said that, I can feel little aether in the surrounding air. If I need to cast any spells, I'll have to rely on the magic within me. And the aether flowing through my veins is yet to be entirely replenished from the wisps' attack.

I try not to dwell on that thought for long.

The goblin wraith drifts over the bridge and glances back at us when she's halfway across. "Mind your step," she hisses with a smirk.

Natharius doesn't hesitate before starting over the bridge. He has even less reason to fear falling than me, seeing how his demonic form comes complete with draconic wings. Taria is just as unfazed and follows him. I suppose Taria trusts the Mother won't allow one of her most treasured priestesses to fall to her death and will somehow offer divine intervention should she slip.

Despite her determination to rescue her brother, Caya briefly pauses at the bridge, staring down into the shadowy chasm. But barely a heartbeat passes before she hurries after Natharius and Taria.

That leaves Zephyr and me.

My treacherous faerie dragon glances between me and the others, and seems to fancy his chances with them more than he does with me—even if it means approaching the ominous fortress.

I sway as a rush of wind hurls into me and fix my heels into the ground so it doesn't blow me over. The wraith and the two skeletons are almost at the fortress's gates now. Natharius glances over his shoulder. His crimson eyes narrow at me.

Even with the distance between us and the roaring wind all around, I hear the growl which rumbles from the back of his throat. His expression reveals the words he would snarl at me if I were any closer: That saving Juron is my decision. That if my hesitation causes the Lich Lord to be freed, he'll torture my soul in far more painful ways than he's ever promised.

In the next breath, I'm hurrying across the bridge. The consequences of failure terrify me far more than the chasm below.

As I fall into step behind Caya, I keep my eyes fixed on the obsidian gates ahead. My palms sweat despite the frigid winds slamming into me. The dread of the unknown, of what lies beyond those dark gates, churns in my stomach. Once more, I remind myself of Taria's and Natharius's vast power.

The gates shudder open as we reach them, and Zephyr darts up and coils around my shoulders. A putrid stench fills my nostrils as I step into the fortress. We'd be cast in complete darkness if it not for the pale orbs floating along the corridors. They remind me of wisps, though they don't make a tinkling sound as I pass.

A few paces into the fortress, the obsidian gates slam shut behind us. I jolt and whirl around. There's no one, or nothing, by the gates. They've shut of their own accord and must be enchanted with dark magic.

I shudder and turn back to the corridor ahead. The others are already disappearing around the next corner, and the undead escorting us are long out of sight. Not wanting to be left alone in this ghastly place with only Zephyr for company, I sprint down the corridor until I catch up with Caya. The warrior doesn't seem to notice my brief hesitation, her gaze on the undead ahead and her fingers curled around the hilt of her sword.

Our footsteps echo through the empty corridors, and the shadows whisper around us. We weave our way through the fortress until we arrive at the courtyard at its center.

Moonlight shines down on us, silvering the withered bones of the many undead gathered here. Skeletal feet clatter against the stone floor. The undead come in a variety of shapes and sizes. Some are humanoid: humans, orcs and goblins. I don't think there are any elven skeletons lurking amid the fortress's shadowy courtyard, but I'm not sure I would be able to distinguish them from the human undead. Goblins are short, with over-sized heads and sharp teeth. Orcs are tall and broad, with tusks jutting from their lower jaws, while elves appear much closer to humans, aside from the fact they are often taller and slenderer.

Though many of the undead are of humanoid remains, most are the bones of various animals. There are bears, foxes, hawks, and even squirrels. They make me shiver as much as the humanoid skeletons.

The goblin wraith escorts us through the fortress's courtyard, and all undead turn their attention to us living beings. My mind is soon frozen by the dozens of empty eye sockets staring at me. The only thought which remains is that of taking one step after another until I reach the large iron doors on the other side of the courtyard.

Like the gates at the fortress's entrance, the iron doors swing open by themselves. The goblin wraith doesn't pause before striding through, nor do the others. But I do, glancing back at the courtyard. All the undead now surround us, blocking our path to the fortress's gates. If we wish to flee, we'll first need to defeat the masses of undead standing between us and freedom.

The undead draw closer. Their hands, talons and claws reach out for me, as if trying to push me through the doors.

I stumble back, Zephyr almost flying from my shoulders, and narrowly escape the grasp of an undead orc. The skeleton stands at nearly twice my height. With the hordes of undead almost upon me, I whirl around and follow the others through the iron doors and into the hall.

CHAPTER 29

Our footsteps thunder through the hall. While the fortress appears derelict, the inside of this hall is a stark contrast. A polished onyx floor stretches out before us, its surface so clear that when I gaze down, my own reflection stares back at me. The braziers lining the stone walls are filled with the same pale light which illuminates the fortress's corridors.

A vaulted ceiling climbs high above, dwarfing even Natharius. At the far end of the hall stands an enormous obsidian throne, a hulking figure sitting on it. The braziers' light doesn't reach them, and I can't make out their features from the darkness. But I have no doubt this is the wraith's master: Mulgath Kharak.

The necromancer isn't alone in his hall. Undead lurk in the shadows, ivory claws and fangs glinting like the monstrosities outside in the courtyard. Though the surrounding undead clamor as we pass, Mulgath himself doesn't stir. He remains hunched over in his obsidian throne, as still as death.

The undead fall silent as the goblin wraith halts before the throne, and we stop a few paces behind her.

Now I can better discern Mulgath's features. Though he isn't small by any means, his figure fails to fill the enormity of the obsidian throne. Natharius said the Lich Lord once made this place his foothold in Talidor. This fortress must have belonged to him, and judging by the throne, Mulgath's size was a fraction of the ancient lich's.

The necromancer's skeletal form is draped in dark, tattered robes, and the torn fabric reveals many discolored bones. Shadows swirl around him, ebbing and flowing in a steady rhythm. His loose-fitting robes drift through the darkness.

Mulgath's head remains lowered. The empty sockets of his eyes stare at the few steps leading to his throne. The bones in his fingers twitch, and if not for that slight movement, I would think him nothing more than a heap of bones.

"Master," the goblin wraith hisses, her voice piercing the silence. "I have brought you the demon you seek. Along with the three mortals."

Mulgath's head lifts slowly. The tusks jutting from his jaw glisten in the pale light. Shadowy orbs ignite in the empty sockets of his eyes, and the necromancer's deathly gaze sweeps over us. His stare fixes on Natharius. It's impossible to read any emotion on Mulgath's skull, but the shadowy orbs in his eye sockets intensify. They look like flickering flames, barely containing the necromancer's wrath.

"Natharius Thalanor." Mulgath's hollow voice reverberates off the onyx walls. The sound is deafening. Inescapable. "Long have I awaited this day."

Natharius meets the necromancer's gaze with a bored expression. "Mulgath Kharak," he drawls. "The most incompetent necromancer I have ever met."

Mulgath leaps from his throne. He throws his skull back and bellows a blood-curdling roar.

I draw back. But there's nowhere to flee. All the undead inside the hall surround us.

Caya unsheathes her golden sword, and Zephyr darts behind me. Even Taria flinches. Natharius is the only one who doesn't wince.

A smirk dances on Natharius's lips. "How can a necromancer pride himself on being a master of undead if he allows himself to be slain by them?"

I cast Natharius a silent plea, desperately urging him to stop taunting our enemy, but he doesn't notice. His gaze remains on Mulgath.

"You failed me," the necromancer spits, descending the steps leading to his throne. "It is because of your weakness that I was defeated."

Natharius raises a silver brow. "Is that what you've been telling yourself all these centuries?"

A growl rumbles in the necromancer's skeletal throat. As it stands, I wouldn't be surprised if Mulgath ordered his undead to attack us at any moment. And we're not here to provoke the necromancer. We're here for Juron.

If he's alive . . .

A sudden burst of courage blooms in my chest. I step in front of Natharius, and Mulgath's gaze flickers down to me.

"We came here because your wraith claimed you've taken our friend captive," I say. Despite my bravery, I don't meet the necromancer's shadowy eye sockets. I stare at the throne behind him, focusing on that instead. "Where is he?"

The necromancer's teeth grind together in what I think is a wicked grin, though it could be a toothy grimace. Since his skull is void of flesh and muscle, it's hard to tell. "Bring forth the prisoner!"

Three undead slip into the chamber on the left. They return moments later with Juron. A strip of dark cloth is wrapped around his right eye but aside from that, he remains very much alive.

His left eye sweeps over the four of us, and then his mouth falls open, seeming to forget the skeletal hands urging him forth. "Caya!" he gasps. "Taria!"

"Juron!" Caya exclaims. "You're alive!"

"You . . . you shouldn't have come for me."

Natharius scoffs. I glare at him before he can tell Juron exactly what he thinks about this rescue mission.

"How could we not?" Caya says.

Juron doesn't reply, and Taria remains silent. The priestess's expression is contemplative.

Caya whirls back to Mulgath. "Release my brother."

The necromancer lets out a bellowing laugh, and the hollow rumbling echoes around us. The undead join their master's laughter, dozens of jaws clattering.

"The demon in exchange for this mortal," Mulgath growls.

I tighten my fists. While I want to save Juron, handing Natharius over wasn't part of the plan. Without the Void Prince, how will I defeat Arluin and the necromancers?

"Not a chance," I say through my teeth.

"Then this mortal dies."

In the next instant, the necromancer is beside Juron, pressing a gnarled blade to his neck.

"No!" Caya cries. Though she looks as if she wants to charge forth, her heels remain fixed on the polished floor. "Don't!"

"The bargain is simple," Mulgath snarls. "The Void Prince in exchange for your mortal friend."

Caya glances back at me. Desperation fills her dark eyes.

If I don't hand over Natharius to Mulgath, Juron will die. But if I hand Natharius over, I will lose my greatest weapon against Arluin. And it's unlikely the necromancer will let the rest of us leave freely even if I comply with his demand.

But refusing Mulgath means sacrificing Juron. And I lack the heart to make that awful choice.

Natharius turns to me, his crimson eyes narrowing. "Don't tell me you're considering exchanging me for that pathetic lump of a mortal."

Surprisingly, no one comments on the insult Natharius pays Juron. The others must be more focused on the impossibility of our situation.

Mulgath glares at me. "You will order the Void Prince to stand inside the binding circle." With his free hand, the necromancer gestures to the markings to the left of the throne. I didn't notice the binding circle until now, my attention otherwise preoccupied with Mulgath and his undead, and the shadowy markings also blend into the onyx floor. "If you refuse, I will slit this mortal's throat." The bones of his right hand tighten around the hilt of his gnarled dagger as he presses the blade more firmly against Juron's neck.

"Reyna!" Caya shrieks. "You can't let my brother die like this! Please!"

"Don't listen to her," Juron says, his shoulders rigid. "My life isn't worth it."

"Juron!" Caya cries, desperation thick in her voice.

I clench my jaw and turn to Taria, hoping she might reveal some guidance as to what choice should be made, but the priestess's golden eyes are devoid of emotion as they flicker back and forth between Caya and Juron.

"Damn this," Natharius curses, pushing past the hordes of undead blocking our way to the doors at the end of the hall.

Mulgath's teeth glint. His skeletal hand twitches, preparing to slice through Juron's neck. "So be it."

"Natharius, stop!" The words spill from my lips before I can realize. My heart is in my throat. Am I making the right decision?

The Void Prince has no choice but to obey my command. Against his will, he's forced to halt and turn back around.

I ignore his glare, my attention returning to Mulgath. For now, the necromancer has stilled his hand. "Let's say I agree to your demands and order the Void Prince to enter your summoning circle," I begin. "What's there to stop you from slitting Juron's throat the moment Natharius enters the circle?"

Mulgath flashes me a menacing grin. "Nothing."

"Then I don't see why I should agree to your bargain. Regardless of the choice I make, it seems our friend will die either way."

"If you refuse," Mulgath replies, "his death is certain, and we'll see how many of my undead it takes to defeat you all."

"If you are so confident in your ability to defeat us, why haven't you struck us yet? Why are you delaying by bargaining with us?"

Mulgath glowers. His glare is as venomous as the one Natharius offers me.

"That's what I thought," I continue. "You fear you and your undead can't defeat the Void Prince unless he's secured inside your binding circle. If you kill Juron before Natharius is restrained, you'll lose your bargaining chip."

I know I'm playing with fire. I can tell that much from the shadowy orbs burning inside Mulgath's otherwise empty sockets.

Though my game is deadly, I have no choice but to play it.

"So, I'll accept your offer for our companion in exchange for the Void Prince. However, you will remove the dagger from Juron's neck before I order Natharius to stand inside your binding circle."

Mulgath pauses, watching me with his deathly gaze. After a moment's hesitation, he lifts the dagger from Juron's neck. If only by a few inches.

Still, the small amount of air between the blade and Juron's throat will mean a few more seconds for him. A greater chance at survival.

My eyes flicker across to Taria. The priestess gives a small nod. Though the movement is slight, it's filled with determination and tells me she's ready for what's to come.

"The Void Prince," Mulgath snarls. His skeletal hand gestures toward the demon.

I turn to Natharius, my lips drawing into a firm line. His scowl hasn't lessened in ferocity. Will he forgive me for this choice? Doubtful. But why do I care whether I can earn a demon's forgiveness?

"Natharius," I grind out, "you will stand inside the binding circle. Now." I point to the shadowy markings etched onto the floor, my sleeve flicking out with the movement.

"You will regret this," Natharius seethes.

I dearly hope I won't. I can only pray the hasty plan forming in my head will somehow succeed.

I don't allow any doubt to betray my expression and simply nod over to the binding circle.

Natharius has no choice but to obey the command. With one heavy stride after another, he drags himself over to the binding circle, offering as much resistance as he can. Though his efforts slow his movement, they don't prevent him from reaching his destination.

Mulgath's gaze fixes on Natharius, as does everyone else's—both the living and the undead. All await the moment that Natharius enters the binding circle.

As his leather boots step over the markings, I draw on all the aether I can. Obsidian chains surge up from the binding circle and shackle Natharius to the floor.

The Void Prince's furious growl rumbles through the hall. I'm certain the walls tremble around us.

Mulgath's jaw clatters together in triumphant laughter. With Natharius safely restrained inside his binding circle, he returns his attention to me. His fleshless fingers tighten around the dagger, and his laugh only grows as he reaches for Juron.

Caya's scream roars through the hall, drowning out the spell-word I murmur.

"*Ventrez.*"

As the blade nears Juron's neck, my spell rushes forth. Aether whirls into wind, and a gale sweeps Juron from his feet. It blows him toward us, narrowly avoiding Mulgath's dagger as it arcs through the air.

There's a slight thud as Juron lands beside me, his boots hitting the polished floor.

A brief stillness falls upon the hall. The brief silence is filled with my ragged gasps. My uneven breathing isn't because of the sudden burst of magic. It's at the realization of how close my plan was to failing. At how close Mulgath's dagger was slicing through Juron's neck.

Though I've freed him from the necromancer's clutches, that doesn't mean that danger is past us. Far from it. Natharius is trapped in Mulgath's binding circle, and the rest of us are surrounded by legions of undead.

"Kill them!" Mulgath snarls. "Kill them all!"

CHAPTER 30

THE UNDEAD CLOSE IN ON us. Withered hands and decayed teeth lunge toward me. I draw back until I collide with Caya and Zephyr. More undead swarm into the hall, stretching into a sea of skeletons around us. They're so close their bony fingers almost scrape my flesh.

Before they can reach me, a burst of golden light erupts from Taria.

"*Zire*!" she cries.

A shield of light wraps around us. The undead who touch Taria's barrier burst into golden flames. Their unearthly shrieks echo through the hall, piercing my ears.

My heart drums in my chest. Aether and adrenaline pound through my veins.

Somehow, we need to navigate out of this mess. We have Juron, but Natharius is shackled in Mulgath's binding circle. Abandoning the Void Prince isn't an option. But right now, I don't know how we can free him and fight our way to freedom.

My thoughts are interrupted by Mulgath's growl.

"*Rivus.*"

He spins the shadows in his skeletal hands, forming a bolt of dark magic. The blast surges toward us.

The attack slams into Taria's shield. Cracks form in the golden light. She grits her teeth, holding the shield in place. Despite the damage Mulgath has inflicted, her spell still causes nearby undead to burst into flames.

Mulgath doesn't hesitate to prepare another shadowy bolt. As strong as Taria is, I doubt her shield will withstand a second attack.

And when the barrier falls, we will be left to the mercy of the ravenous undead. Even with Taria's strength, we won't be able to defeat them all.

We need Natharius. If I can free the Void Prince from Mulgath's binding circle, we'll stand a chance at escaping this fortress.

Despite her concentration, Taria seems to notice my gaze on Natharius. Or perhaps her thoughts merely echo mine.

"Fire," she rasps. "Fire will extinguish the dark magic."

I nod. If I can clear the markings of the binding circle from the floor, Natharius will be freed. And fire stands the greatest chance at washing away dark magic.

Not that I've ever tried obliterating a binding circle.

Swallowing down hard and doing my best not to consider the consequences of failure, I draw on aether and mutter: "*Conparios.*"

Father's staff materializes in my hands, and I close my eyes, using it as a focus to draw on more aether than I naturally can.

Magic hums through my entire being, extending into the staff. When I open my eyes, the pale purple light of aether radiates from me. Magic fizzes and bubbles in my veins, desperate to be unleashed.

Another shadowy blast crashes into Taria's shield. More cracks form in the golden light, and I fear the shield will fall apart around us like paper. Yet it doesn't. Somehow it holds fast. New golden light forms over the cracks, mending the damage Mulgath's second attack caused. But the shield isn't fully repaired: The spots where cracks formed is thinner than the rest.

I have to hurry. Or else we'll be overwhelmed by the undead.

Once more, I close my eyes. In my mind, I picture the binding circle within which Natharius stands and imagine myself at the very edge of its markings. As the spell takes shape, the aether within me flows more violently.

"*Laxus!*"

Magic bursts free. Purple energy flashes through the dark hall like lightning.

In the next instant, I'm standing upon the spot I envisioned. My boots lie just before the boundary of the binding circle. Stepping even a hair's breadth closer will cause me to be shackled by the same obsidian restraints as Natharius.

I don't have time to examine the Void Prince's expression. Now I'm beyond the safety of Taria's golden shield, the hordes of undead are already swarming toward me.

I clutch my crystalline staff in both hands and squeeze my eyes shut, trying to draw on even more aether than I did for the previous spell. I don't have long to destroy the binding circle and free Natharius. My first spell must succeed.

More aether pours into my body. Somehow, even in this shadow-infested place, aether rushes toward me like a thundering waterfall. My skin must radiate with sheer power.

"*Ignir'quatir!*"

I slam the staff against the onyx floor. Flames explode, swarming across the binding circle. In my haste, I don't consider Natharius's safety. But I assume that the Void Prince can withstand the fiery blast.

The flames lick away at the dark magic and, bit by bit, wash away the markings.

"*Nozarat!*" Mulgath roars from behind.

I whirl around to see a phantom knife hurling at me. I clutch my staff and pull aether around me to form a hasty defense, but there's no time. The dark blade is already upon me. Within mere heartbeats, it will pierce my chest.

All I can do is watch death hurl at me.

But death doesn't greet me.

Before the phantom blade reaches me, an arm wraps around my lower back, pulling me to safety. My forehead slams into what feels like a solid wall.

Barely a heartbeat later, the stable wall jolts, throwing me back. But I don't hit the polished floor. The arm holds me tight.

I didn't realize I was squeezing my eyes shut but they open, the impending threat now having passed. My mouth falls open as I understand what just happened.

Natharius's arm is wrapped around me. He pulled me to safety. And he took Mulgath's attack in my place.

I tilt back my head, straining my neck to get a look at the Void Prince.

The obsidian shackles which bound him are nowhere in sight, nor are the markings beneath our feet. My fiery spell succeeded in obliterating the binding circle.

Natharius's jaw is clenched, and his brows are furrowed. Pain glints in his crimson eyes.

His gaze flickers down to meet mine. In this moment, a thousand questions burn on my lips. Why did he save me when I hadn't commanded him to do so? Why didn't he leave me to die so that he can return to the Abyss? Is it because he wants to ensure Arluin doesn't release the Lich Lord from his icy tomb?

I'm not sure whether the demon can read the countless questions in my eyes. But even if he can, he has as little time to answer as I have to ask them.

A growl rumbles from his throat. He releases me, his arm withdrawing. I stumble back, only now realizing how tightly he was clutching me.

Shadows envelop him, growing with intensity until they cover the entire hall.

A hulking figure emerges from the cloud of darkness: Natharius's demonic form. His onyx horns almost impale the vaulted ceiling and glisten in the pale light emanating from the many braziers lining the hall. In a deadly rhythm, his cloven hooves clatter across the polished floor. Draconic wings sweep out, their leathery surface the color of the midnight sky. Crimson markings glow across his alabaster skin, the eerie light reflecting off the obsidian walls, and his eyes burn the shade of vehement flames.

I instinctively withdraw behind him. His fearsome size alone acts as a barrier between me and the hordes of undead around us.

Despite his terrifying appearance, three undead charge toward him. Perhaps those who are already dead have little to fear. Except for Mulgath. I'm certain his expression is that of fear, though it isn't easy to read a skull's face.

Natharius raises his enormous sword. The dark steel glints wickedly as he holds it overhead. In a swoop, it descends on his enemies. The behemoth blade crushes through bone and stone alike.

Though the skeletons' limbs are cast into dozens of tiny fragments, I half expect them to reassemble themselves. They don't, however. I suppose the dark magic whirring inside Natharius's blade has shattered the spell reanimating their decayed corpses.

"*Yanli*!" Taria's voice echoes through the hall. The golden shield explodes. Blinding light flashes through the darkness, causing the undead to stumble back. Those nearest erupt into flames. The holy fire consumes their decayed bones, leaving only ash.

The intensity causes even Natharius to stagger back. But the Void Prince soon recovers, his attention returning to Mulgath.

Natharius strides forth, his blade swinging toward the necromancer. His attack leaves me exposed to the surrounding undead, since I'm no longer safely behind his wings. Fortunately, Taria's spell keeps them disoriented a moment longer, providing me with the opportunity I need.

"*Laxus*," I say.

In the next breath, I'm standing beside Caya and Juron, Zephyr safely behind us all.

Then the undead recover from Taria's explosion, their rotten hands reaching out for us.

"*Ignira!*" I cry, using the aether remaining from my teleportation spell to conjure a swift fireball. I hurl the flames at the nearest undead.

A thud sounds as Caya's blade beheads a skeleton. Its skull falls onto the onyx floor.

"*Mizarel!*" comes Taria's shout. A beacon of holy light shines in her hands. She holds her palms out to her enemies, and a golden beam shoots forth. The light slices through several undead, and they wither away, their decrepit bodies unable to withstand a powerful attack of holy magic.

Behind, Natharius's sword slams toward Mulgath. Before the obsidian blade can reach the necromancer, he conjures a shield of dark magic. It cracks under Natharius's sword, but the barrier holds fast.

Though both Taria's and my attacks obliterate several of the undead, more stalk forth to take their place.

"Ignir'alas!"

Wings of fire burst from my fingers. They soar upward through the vaulted ceiling before plummeting down to the hordes of undead. A dozen undead are destroyed by the spell.

Taria releases another barrage of holy fire. She too defeats many of the undead. Our attacks continue, steadily plowing through our countless enemies.

Though I haven't yet recovered from the wisps siphoning my power, there's no choice but to keep drawing on aether and conjuring spells. In the back of my mind, I feel fatigue gnawing on my consciousness. But I fight past the exhaustion, knowing if I falter for even a moment then the hordes of undead will consume both me and my allies.

A piercing crack rings through the hall as Natharius shatters Mulgath's shield. Before the demon's blade can reach the necromancer, Mulgath sends a blast of dark magic hurling forth. Natharius steps away, narrowly avoiding it.

Too busy glancing back over my shoulder at Natharius, I'm slow to notice the undead nearest me. It's the reanimated bones of a bear, its claws sweeping toward me.

Before the bear can reach me, Juron's blade crashes into its paw. His sword shatters the bones, leaving the undead bear critically wounded. Juron's attack offers me plenty of time to mutter *ignira* and hurl a ferocious fireball at the bear. The flames slam into it and obliterate its bones.

I glance across at Juron and lift my head in a silent thanks. He doesn't have the chance to acknowledge the gesture, too busy slashing his shining sword out at the next undead.

I turn back to my own enemies, continuing to blast through skeleton after skeleton. Maybe it's only my wishful thinking, but it seems that the hordes of undead are finally waning.

Though my enemies seem to lessen, so is my energy. Already the dark walls are spinning around me, and my aim is growing clumsier. A few spells miss, and many more barely strike their target. The ferocity of my attacks is also rapidly decreasing. My fireballs are little more than flickering flames. I don't know how I'll keep holding off the undead.

Taria seems to be faring only marginally better. The priestess's once blinding magic is now so faint that the shadows threaten to consume it.

But before the remaining undead can overwhelm us, a crash thunders through the hall. As do Mulgath's piercing howls.

The floor shakes. I stumble, struggling to find my balance as the ground beneath trembles. Only when all falls silent does the floor stabilize.

I glance over my shoulder to where Natharius and Mulgath fight before the obsidian throne.

The Void Prince's blade is wedged within the onyx floor, and Mulgath lies beneath it.

Defeated.

CHAPTER 31

THE UNDEAD FREEZE AT THE sight of their master defeated by the Void Prince's sword.

Mulgath's remains don't so much as twitch, not even his finger bones. He lies lifelessly on the onyx floor, his torso split in half by Natharius's obsidian blade. The shadowy orbs inside his eye sockets flicker out, confirming that Mulgath is now well and truly dead.

Taken aback by Mulgath's defeat, the remaining undead offer less resistance than before. Or maybe it's the fact we're now stronger. Determination pounds through my veins, somehow conjuring more strength when I thought I was spent. And with Mulgath defeated, Natharius is able to help us destroy the remaining undead. His enormous sword carves through their ranks, and soon the entire fortress is devoid of all undead.

Only when the hall is empty does Natharius shed his demonic form, shrinking back to the guise of a moon elf.

I draw out a shaky breath and lean back against the dark pillar behind me. Now that adrenaline is wearing off, exhaustion claims me. The hall spins. Within moments, my back is sliding down the pillar, and I feel the onyx floor beneath my legs. The polished surface is cool to the touch. Zephyr joins me, curling up beside me.

I rest Father's staff in front of me, staring down at its glistening crystalline surface. Aether hums within from the many spells I conjured tonight. I would safely return it to my satchel, but even the thought of weaving a minor spell like *coligos* is overwhelming.

Though the priestess used up much strength in fighting the undead, she doesn't rest like me. Instead, she strides over to Caya and nods at her satchel. Somehow, Caya knows what Taria means without the priestess uttering a single word. She flips open her satchel and rummages inside until she retrieves the obsidian box the goblin wraith offered us.

Taria is silent as she takes it from Caya and starts over to Juron. He peers at the obsidian box and then at Taria in confusion.

"Sit," she says, gesturing to the few steps leading to the throne.

His confusion doesn't fade, but he does as she says. "Why?"

"Remove the cloth," Taria replies, pointing to the dark fabric running across his right eye.

Understanding dawns on his face. "You already used much of your power to save me tonight," Juron insists. "You should rest or else you'll be hurt if you push yourself too far past your limits."

Taria shakes her head. Her fingers tighten around the obsidian box. "This can't wait. If we don't act quickly, I'll be unable to restore your sight. Already I cannot be certain I'll succeed."

"Then leave it be. I have one good eye. That's more than enough."

Taria's jaw tightens. "I can't leave this be. I am a Priestess of Selynis. Healing others is my duty." She reaches for the dark cloth around Juron's eye. He catches her wrist before she can.

"Taria," he says softly, "I won't see you hurt because of me. You've already done enough tonight. You all have."

Taria's delicate features harden with determination. Juron doesn't release her wrist.

"Are you sure about this?" Caya asks Taria, stepping toward them.

Taria gives a single nod. "Of course I'm sure. I know my limits."

Caya watches her for a moment longer before turning to her brother. "Juron," she says, "let Taria heal you before it's too late.

She's the First Disciple of Grand Priestess Elunar, chosen by the Goddess Herself. It's wrong of you to underestimate her."

"You're right." Juron lowers his head and releases Taria's wrist. "Forgive me. I was wrong to doubt you."

"There's nothing to forgive." Taria tugs the dark cloth from his face.

I avert my gaze, staring down at my crystalline staff. I can't bear to look at the empty socket of Juron's eye, especially not when I've seen the contents of that box. Though with all the death and destruction I've witnessed, perhaps I should be able to.

From the corner of my eye, I catch the flash of golden light as Taria begins her spell. The holy magic reflects off the dark walls, banishing all shadows. I dare to raise my head and look over at Natharius. He's turned away from the blinding light, his eyes squeezed shut as if in pain.

"*Onirya!*"

Taria's holy magic intensifies. All I can see is golden light. Beneath the radiance, I can't make out the outline of my hand. Even when I close my eyes, I can't escape the blinding light.

Juron's screams soon follow. It sounds more like Taria is torturing him than healing him. Though considering how uncomfortable this holy magic is for me, I doubt it can be pleasant for the one it's directed at.

Eventually, his cries of pain fade. As does the golden light. Once more, we're cast in darkness and the shadows return to dance around us.

Now that Taria's spell is complete, I turn to look at them. Juron's right eye is entirely healed, as if it was never gouged out and placed inside the obsidian box. He stares up at Taria, both gratitude and admiration shining in his dark eyes. The priestess sways to either side, as if she's a leaf in the wind.

"Thank you," Juron breathes, his words barely audible. If we weren't otherwise in silence, I doubt I would have heard his words.

A slight smile flickers on Taria's lips. In the next moment, her golden eyes are falling shut, and I'm certain they don't shine as brightly as they did before healing Juron. It's clear the spell cost her a great deal of strength.

Then Taria topples toward the floor. Juron catches her before she can hit it and clutches her tightly, as if she will shatter into a thousand pieces if he lets her fall.

"Taria!" he exclaims, gently shaking her. But she says nothing, and her eyes stay shut. Her chest rises and falls in a steady motion. Even when Juron calls her name again, she remains deep in her slumber.

"She'll be fine," Caya says. "She just needs to rest. As do we all."

Juron gives a slight nod, but the hesitance in his expression is clear. There's something in the intensity of his gaze that makes me turn away. He stares down at the priestess as if she's the most precious treasure in all of Imyria, and his dark eyes are filled with both worry and longing.

Juron lays Taria on the floor and drapes a blanket over her. Even when he steps away from her and sits on the steps leading to the throne, his gaze doesn't leave her.

The Void Prince's eyes are closed, though not as forcibly squeezed shut as they were from the intensity of Taria's healing spell. He sits cross-legged, his back pressed against the pillar behind him, and the shadows swirl around him. It's only then I remember he was injured from Mulgath's attack. That he saved my life.

I'm about to get to my feet and head over to him when Caya speaks.

"She will need time to rest." Caya's gaze is on Taria as she speaks. "I doubt she will be well enough to travel again before the morning."

"We should all rest anyway," I whisper as to not wake Taria, though her sleep is likely too deep to hear my voice. "We'll spent the night inside this fortress and leave at dawn." While the dark walls are far from comforting, at least they'll keep the frigid winds off our backs.

Caya dips her head in agreement. "As you say."

"Though we seem to have vanquished all the undead here," I continue, "we don't know what other monstrosities reside in these woods. I'll take first watch—"

Natharius's eyes flicker open. "I'll take it."

I frown, surprised the Void Prince would make such a generous offer. Caya seems equally taken aback.

"You mortals require more rest than I do to recover," he says. "In case you've forgotten, I am the most powerful demon of the Abyss, second only to the Void King himself."

"But you're injured," I protest. At least, I think he's still wounded. Since Mulgath's attack struck his back, I can't see how his injury is faring. Has it already mended?

"I am fine."

I haul myself onto my feet and start over to him. "Let me see."

"Let you see what?"

"Your injury."

"I have no injury."

I stop in front of Natharius and stare down at him. "You were wounded by Mulgath's attack. I saw it with my own eyes."

Natharius only snorts. "You must have imagined it."

"Stand up."

He raises a brow. "Is that an order?"

"It is, yes."

He draws out a sigh but has no choice to stand up. Though he has returned to his elven form, he towers over me.

"Now turn around."

Natharius does, though only slightly. Yet it's enough for me to see the wound carved into his shoulder. His blood is black and smeared across his pale skin like ink. It hasn't stained his tunic, however, seeing how the cloth was dark. Shadows swirl from the open wound. I can't tell whether that's Natharius's own magic trying to heal him, or whether it's the remnants of the spell which struck him.

"Have you finished staring?" Natharius drawls. "Or can I turn back around?"

"You . . . you can turn around." My voice is barely a whisper, yet Natharius hears me. He turns and glares at me.

I lower my gaze, not meeting his scowl. Guilt claws at my heart. Why, I don't understand. After all, Natharius is a demon. The weapon which is bound to me, enslaved to my will.

"Can I sit down?" he demands.

Though I hear him—his growl is hard to miss—his question doesn't register in my mind. My brows are knitted together as I struggle to understand the unpleasant feelings churning within. I tell myself I shouldn't care about a demon being injured, but it does nothing to banish the guilt gnawing on me.

"I'm sorry," I finally say, my voice quiet.

"For what?"

"You were injured because of me."

"I was injured because of Mulgath," he replies.

"But that attack was intended for me," I say. "You could have let it strike me. I gave you no order to save me."

"If the spell had struck you, then you would have died."

"And if I died, you would have returned to the Abyss. So, why did you save me?"

"Because if I return to the Abyss, then that necromancer of yours might succeed in unsealing the Lich Lord."

"You're a demon of the Abyss. You despise mortals. Why would you care what happens to Imyria?"

Natharius's jaw clenches. "I do not care about what happens to Imyria. But I do care about ensuring that what I have done isn't undone and that the sacrifices I have made are not in vain."

"Like your kingdom? Your family? Your soul?"

"My soul matters not."

I can almost hear the words he doesn't speak. That though his soul doesn't matter, both his kingdom and his family do. How does it feel to be consumed by guilt for a thousand years? Does Natharius often contemplate what happened? Is he regretful over the choices he made?

I suppose that enduring guilt for a millennium explains the Void Prince's volatile temperament.

"Besides," he continues, catching me off guard. "Even if it were not for the Lich Lord, I would have no choice but to save you. When you first summoned me from the Abyss, you commanded me to keep you alive. Since the spell would have killed you had it struck you, I therefore had little choice in the matter."

"Oh. That's right."

He casts me a bored look. "Now that we have settled this matter, can I sit down?"

"Yes, of course you can."

Natharius doesn't hesitate to sit down and lean against the pillar behind him.

I remain in front of him for a moment longer, mulling over my thoughts.

"Is there something else?" he asks, peering at me and examining my expression.

Indeed, there is something else: the matter of reaching Gerazad before Arluin and his necromancers do. Though I try not to reveal my worries, I can't help my hands from wringing together.

Even before we entered the Ghost Woods, the chance of us arriving at Gerazad first was slim. Now we have strayed far from our path, and I've lost track of how long we've spent here.

Is reaching Gerazad before Arluin now an impossible hope? Will we arrive long after the necromancers have besieged the orcish settlement and stolen the ring of Lagartha the Old?

I sigh and turn away from Natharius before he notices my expression. I have no desire to ask him whether or not he thinks we will succeed, because I know his answer will only confirm my suspicions. And I have to believe there's hope we will reach Gerazad first, no matter how foolish it may be. I can't bear the burden of the alternative.

"It's nothing," I murmur as I start away from Natharius, returning to where Zephyr is curled up. My father's crystalline staff lies beside him, and I crouch to retrieve it. I clench the staff and stare into the aether-infused crystalline surface which ripples in the low light. Though Mulgath has been defeated, the braziers lining the hall flicker with ghostly lights. The dark magic in the air must keep them illuminated.

When we reach Gerazad, provided we aren't too late, will I have the opportunity to free Father from Arluin's shackles? Will I be able to avenge everything I've lost?

I grit my teeth, trying to convince myself that I will. Because vengeance is the only thing I have left in this world.

"*Evanest*," I mutter, and the staff dissipates into glittering dust.

With that, I sink to the floor and lean against the pillar. Though I'm tempted to rest like Taria, I need all the power I can muster for when we reach Gerazad. Tonight I used much of my strength to defeat Mulgath and his undead, and my magic was already low from my encounter with the wisps. I must use this time wisely and ensure I recover to full strength.

I sit cross-legged, my hands resting on my knees and my palms facing the vaulted ceiling. I close my eyes and steady my breathing, focusing on what little aether drifts through the air. As I fall into meditation, the floor and pillar fade from my senses. My consciousness transcends, and even my worries and thoughts of vengeance slip away.

Only aether remains.

CHAPTER 32

Dawn arrives too soon. I've barely recovered a fraction of my power by the time sunlight filters through the hall's open doors. That's mostly to do with the fact I fell asleep while meditating. At least I feel refreshed, even if I'm lacking in aether running through my veins.

Caya and Juron are both already awake when my eyes open, as is Natharius. The Void Prince hasn't moved an inch from his pillar, unlike me who fell to the floor during the night. The cool surface presses against my cheek like ice. I roll over and push myself to a sitting position. At least I'm not the only one who's overslept. Both Taria and Zephyr are fast asleep. I expected the priestess to be meditating already. Healing Juron has certainly taken its toll on her. And she also used much strength to defeat Mulgath's hordes of undead.

I stretch my arms high above my head. Every inch of my body aches. Though I suspect that has to do with physical exhaustion, I doubt sleeping on the stone floor has helped. "It's dawn already?" I say with a yawn.

"It's long past dawn," Caya replies. "We must be well into the morning now."

I glance behind at the open doors leading out of the fortress. The morning rays are so bright I have to shield my eyes. It seems day has long been upon us. "You didn't wake me?"

"You and Taria were fast asleep," Juron answers. "We thought it best to leave you sleeping a while longer. You both used up a great deal of strength last night."

As much as I wish they woke me sooner, I suppose exhaustion would only slow our pace. Hopefully the extra time we've spent resting will allow us to make greater haste for the rest of our journey. "We should leave as soon as we can. We've already delayed enough."

"Indeed," Natharius says, leaning back, "we have wasted much time here in the Ghost Woods. I'll be surprised if the necromancers haven't already reached Gerazad and taken Lagartha's ring."

Blood drains from my face, casting me a shade of ashen white. Though I suspected arriving at Gerazad before Arluin is now a hopeless endeavor, hearing Natharius say it so bluntly is like a blow to the chest. "You really think they might already be in Gerazad?"

"It's hard to know," Natharius says with a shrug. "If we had another object belonging to the necromancers, I could locate them and say for certain. However, I believe we should prepare ourselves for the possibility the necromancers will be long gone by the time we arrive at Gerazad. It is the likeliest outcome."

"So, you think there's little point in continuing to Gerazad?" I ask. "Where will the necromancers head after they have Lagartha's ring? Will they seek the third and final ring? The one that used to belong to you?"

"Correct," Natharius replies. "After they retrieve the ring of Lagartha the Old, they will head to Lumaria in search of the elven ring. I suspect it should be in the possession of the current High Enchanter of Lumaria, whoever they might be."

"Should we head there instead?"

"Though it's unlikely that we will succeed in Gerazad, there's a chance we might. Seeing how close we are to it, turning back now makes little sense. It's best to continue and hope we can retrieve Lagartha's ring first. Or else everything will depend on the final ring."

"Then every second we delay could mean the difference between stopping Arluin from retrieving Lagartha's ring or failing."

"Leaving now would be for the best," Natharius replies, pushing himself onto his feet. His crimson eyes sweep across to the sleeping priestess, silently accusing her of being the reason we continue to delay. Why we might fail and enable the Lich Lord to be unleashed.

Caya, who has been quietly observing our conversation, offers me a swift nod. "I'll wake her now."

"Do you think she'll be strong enough to walk?" I ask. Though we need to leave now, if an extra hour of rest means Taria can match our pace without needing to stop, it'll be worth it.

Natharius scoffs before Caya can answer. "If she will prove a burden, then leave her behind. We can't afford to carry dead weight."

Caya glares at him. "She is the First Disciple, the future Grand Priestess of Selynis!"

"She might even be the king of a thousand nations but if she is too weak, she must be left behind."

"How very dare you—"

Before Caya can draw her sword or Natharius can conjure a spell, I step between them and hold out my arms to hold them at bay. Neither edges any closer. "Nobody is going to be left behind." I cast Natharius a pointed look.

The demon snorts.

"So," I continue, "we'll wait if Taria needs longer to rest. She was the reason we all escaped Mulgath's clutches last night. Even you must see that, Natharius."

Natharius doesn't respond. The Prince of Pride is far too arrogant to admit that a priestess might be a worthwhile ally.

"If Taria is too weak," Juron calls over, "I'll carry her until she has recovered."

"Then it's settled," I declare, "we leave immediately."

Juron gives a quick nod and heads over to Taria. He nudges her arm, and it takes several minutes before she wakes. Though he offers to carry her, Taria insists she's well enough to walk. She claims her strength is restored, but I'm certain her golden eyes are a shade fainter than usual.

Once we've had something to eat and I've fed Zephyr aether crystals, we gather our belongings and leave the hall. Since the fortress sits atop a hill high above the gnarled trees, the sun's rays are free to shine down on us. We pass swiftly through the courtyard, none of us having any desire to linger. I didn't notice last night, but various statues stand around the courtyard. All are orcs, depicted in armor so heavy that if they were real, I doubt they could move. These statues must have stood for centuries, seeing how weather-worn they are. Some are broken, missing limbs and heads.

"Was this once the Lich Lord's fortress?" I ask Natharius, looking at the statue nearest us. This stone orc is missing an arm.

"It was."

"Then why build statues of orcs? He was a mage before becoming a lich. Unless Mulgath had these statues built?"

"They were here long before Mulgath. And the Lich Lord as well. This region was once part of Jektar before the undead tainted it."

I stare at the armless statue for a moment longer before continuing across the courtyard.

Though the morning rays shine gloriously upon the courtyard, these corridors are cast in darkness. Only the pale, flickering orbs illuminate our way through the shadowy maze. Though the fortress is now devoid of undead, it doesn't make these corridors any less foreboding. Zephyr crawls up my arm and wraps himself around my shoulders.

Our hurried footsteps echo around us, bouncing off the dark walls. I would mutter *iluminos* to conjure a brilliant orb of aether, but I don't want to use up more magic than necessary. I don't know how long it will be before we reach Gerazad, and whether I'll have the chance to replenish my magic. I must reserve all I have.

Eventually, the maze of dark corridors brings us to the fortress's gates. They're shut, like we left them.

Natharius steps forth, shadows swirling in his hands. With his back facing me, I can see the injury on his shoulder. Though his flesh isn't fully mended, dark magic no longer oozes out of the wound.

Wordlessly, he unleashes his magic upon the fortress's gates. The shadowy vortex rushes forth, slamming into them. They shudder and burst open, flying from their hinges. With the intensity of the blast, I fear the shoddy stone bridge ahead might also be damaged.

Fortunately, when I step beyond the gates, I see that the bridge isn't any more ruined than when we entered the fortress last night.

Though I'm wary of crossing the bridge, I have no desire to linger inside the fortress. Especially not alone. I hurry across the bridge, not daring to look down into the dark chasm.

The rest of the way out of the fortress is a sharp incline downhill. Our pace is brisk, and the Ghost Wood's murky haze soon descends on us. Toward the bottom of the hill, the trees tower over us again, their gnarled branches banishing all sunlight. Finally, the fallen archway greets us, marking the end of the fortress. I only spare the ominous spires behind us a momentary glance before passing beneath the fallen archway.

We press onward through the trees, saying very little to each other as we walk. Though we've rested in the fortress, it seems everyone is weary. Either that, or everyone is so anxious to escape the Ghost Woods they don't dare to waste their breath on words.

Perhaps it's my imagination, but the trees somehow seem less eerie. I no longer have the same prickling sensation that we're being watched. Maybe Mulgath's eyes were on us from the very moment we entered the Ghost Woods, and that was how he found the opportunity to capture Juron. Maybe the wisps were even in league with him.

Still, I don't lower my guard. Though we've already defeated two enemies inside these woods, I don't know whether any others lurk amid the shadows, waiting for the opportune moment to strike. The sooner we reach the other side of the Ghost Woods, the better. We can't afford another delay. The odds against us are already close to impossible.

Despite the futility of our plan, we have no choice but to keep putting one foot after another and pray the Ghost Woods will soon end. That we will somehow reach Gerazad before Arluin and his necromancers. Because if we don't, the Lich Lord will be one step closer to unleashing his wrath upon Imyria.

And Father will remain shackled to Arluin's will for eternity.

CHAPTER 33

IT ISN'T UNTIL THE FOLLOWING afternoon that we put the last of the Ghost Woods behind us. Without the dense canopy of gnarled branches overhead, the sun is free to shine down on us with all its radiance. The suffocating shadows fade with the sinister trees, and I find I can breathe easily again.

Beyond the Ghost Woods, more aether hums in the air, and its presence brings me comfort. The wind is no longer frigid, and the sun warms us as we traipse across Jektar's sprawling plains, though the temperature isn't scorching like in Selynis and seems closer to what I'm used to back home in Nolderan. I'm not sure whether this is typical for the rest of Jektar, however, since it's an extensive region which spreads far to the east and we're currently at its western border.

We walk onward across the grassy plains, and the Ghost Woods grow fainter until it vanishes. The sun sinks in the horizon, dusky hues streaking through the sky, and before long darkness descends on us.

We continue for most of the night, the twinkling stars illuminating our path. Only when the moon is long past its apex do we stop for the night, much to Natharius's annoyance. He doesn't protest about us taking a break, but his expression alone is evidence of his opinion.

Though the sun was warm while walking today, the air has since cooled considerably. The twins gather firewood and I use the spell *ignis* to ignite it, and then we all huddle around the campfire. Except for Natharius, that is. He sits away from us, gazing at the moon.

I retrieve some aether crystals for Zephyr and beef jerky for myself. It isn't particularly appealing, but wildlife is scarce here since we're close to the Ghost Woods. The dried food Taria and the twins pull out of their bags doesn't look much more appetizing.

Once we're finished, I yank off my boots and lie back on my blanket and stretch my toes, Zephyr nestling into my side. My feet ache from all the walking we've done today, though not enough to warrant the use of Ice Honey, but I much prefer traveling on foot to horseback. However, I can't deny that the latter is much quicker, and I don't know how deep Gerazad is into Jektar.

I frown and look up at the twins. "Do you think we'd be best stopping at a nearby village and buying horses and fresh supplies? If there's a village nearby, that is."

"We won't find horses in any orcish village," Juron says.

"We won't?"

Caya shakes her head. The flames highlight the scar stretching across her cheek. "Orcs ride wolves, not horses."

"Oh," I say. "What about supplies, at least?"

"They would sooner cross blades than trade with us," Caya says.

My frown deepens. "Humans and orcs are at peace."

"That doesn't mean they like us," Caya replies.

"If not for the Grand Priestess's power," Juron adds, "along with the combined forces of every human nation, they would have long attacked our borders."

"Even being here on their territory breaches the peace treaty," Caya says.

"Surely just anyone crossing their border can't violate the treaty?"

"We aren't anyone," Caya says, nodding over to Taria who's already deep in meditation. A golden aura radiates from her. "We're traveling with the future Grand Priestess of Selynis."

If the orcs are as hostile as Caya says, how will I convince them of the threat Arluin and his necromancers pose to them? As soon as High Priestess Ahelin discovered my connection to Natharius, she stopped believing my story. It's possible the orcs won't believe me at all. But nothing can be done about it until we reach Gerazad. Hopefully when we arrive, I can think of a way to convince them of the truth—or that they're willing to be reasoned with.

In an attempt to lift my spirits, I rummage through all the humming orbs inside my satchel until I find the bottle of moon blossom wine I packed, along with the two crystalline goblets from Father's cabinet. Juron watches me curiously as I pour the wine out into both goblets, so I cross our camp and hold one out to him.

"Here," I say, "help yourself to some wine."

Juron takes the goblet from me and peers down into the glittering surface. "I've never seen wine like this before." He dips his finger into the wine and tries a few drops. "It's so sweet. And . . . tingly. Is there aether in it?"

I nod. "There's a reason moon blossom wine is Nolderan's most treasured wine." I hold the other goblet out to Caya.

"No, thanks," she says. "Juron's the one with a sweet tooth, not me. I couldn't think of anything worse."

"What about Taria?" I say, though I'm not sure how the aether in the moon-blossom wine will react to the light magic in Taria's blood. "Will she want any?"

"I doubt it," Caya replies. "She'll be busy meditating for a few hours, and she isn't the biggest wine drinker."

I start back over to my blanket with the goblet but catch Natharius's gaze and head toward him. The Void Prince probably doesn't deserve such kindness, not after all the insults and threats and taunts he's ever paid me, but now he's determined to defeat Arluin—even if it's for his own agenda— and so it seems politeness is the best approach. Besides the nicer I am, the less he'll torture me in the afterlife. Whenever that will be.

The demon doesn't look at me as I near him. His gaze remains on the stars.

I hold the goblet of moon blossom wine out to him. "Do you want some?"

He glances back at me. "No."

"You know, it is customary to say 'no, thank you' when one is offered something for nothing in return."

He stares blankly at me.

I wonder whether manners are respected in Lumaria as much as in Nolderan, or whether Natharius has lost them during his past millennium in the Abyss. Though it also wouldn't surprise me if he never had them to begin them. He was a prince, as well as the High Enchanter. I doubt either breeds humility and good manners.

"Don't you like moon blossom wine?" I ask, withdrawing the goblet. "I thought all moon elves loved it, especially enchanters."

"Do I look like a moon elf to you?"

I bite my tongue to stop myself from reminding him of the dozens of times he's referred to himself as a moon elf. "Only a little."

It must be a rhetorical question, since his glare intensifies.

"What? You asked me a question, and I answered. Your ears are pointy, and your hair is silver. Aside from your eyes, I'd say you do very much look like a moon elf."

Natharius says nothing. I turn to my blanket, where Zephyr is already sprawled out.

"Wait," Natharius says after a few steps. "I will drink it."

I refrain from saying that a 'please' would go a long way, since manners seem a foreign concept to him, and wordlessly hand over the goblet.

The Void Prince stares down at the glittering liquid, his eyes shadowed. "It has been long since I last tasted moon blossom wine."

"How long is 'long'? Before you became a demon?"

"Indeed."

I tilt my head as I examine his contemplative expression. Maybe the reason he initially refused the wine was because he has drunk none since he was a moon elf and it reminds him of his mortal life.

"You shouldn't sit all the way over here," I say as he lifts the goblet, nodding to where Juron and Caya sit before the campfire.

He pauses, the goblet stopping at his lips. "Why not?"

"Isn't it lonely?

"I'm a Void Prince of the Abyss. Why would I experience such pathetic mortal feelings?"

"Who knows? You were mortal once. Did you experience pathetic mortal feelings such as loneliness before you became a demon?"

Natharius drinks instead of answering my question.

I narrow my eyes, silently willing the answer from his lips.

"I was mortal a millennium ago," he replies. "I do not remember such trifling matters."

"If you say so."

"I was the High Enchanter of Lumaria, and the son of King Vastiros Thalanor. Why would someone of my station experience loneliness?"

"With how defensive you are, I'm becoming convinced that you were a very lonely moon elf."

"I wasn't lonely. I merely did not see the point of wasting time with others. Books are far better company."

"All right," I reply. "From the sound of things, you definitely weren't a lonely moon elf."

Natharius scowls.

"What's the Abyss like, anyway?" I ask, ignoring his glare. I only realize now that I've yet to ask him that question, though it intrigues me greatly.

"Cold," he says. "And dead."

"Like the Ghost Woods?"

"No. In the Ghost Woods, the trees are alive, even if they are diseased by dark magic. In the Abyss, there are no trees. Only illusions of them."

"Illusionary trees?"

"Indeed," he replies, "among other things. Some Void Princes craft illusions to fill their realms. The Prince of Lust is known for her extravagant gardens, filled by illusionary black roses. Their petals are like ink and their thorns like poison."

"What about you? Do you have illusions to decorate your realm?"

"Some," Natharius says. And that's the only answer I receive. His gaze returns to the stars, and he sips at the moon-blossom wine. It's clear the Void Prince is done talking for the night.

I shrug and start back to my blanket, the half-empty bottle of moon-blossom wine where I left it. The dusky liquid shimmers in the moonlight, beckoning me forth.

CHAPTER 34

MAYBE MY TOLERANCE TO WINE is already waning. Though I'm certain I drank little moon-blossom wine last night, I wake to a splitting headache. Losing my tolerance to alcohol makes little sense, since it was only a few weeks ago I was drinking atop Nolderan's cliffs with Eliya.

That thought makes me pause. It's hard to believe barely over two weeks have passed since Nolderan's fall. Already it feels like a lifetime ago. In some ways, at least. My pain is as raw as the night Arluin seized everything from me.

My headache lessens throughout the day, fading to a dull ache by the afternoon. The grassy plains soon turn into a rugged landscape of crags, and our journey becomes much more arduous. On several occasions, we have to scramble up rocky faces, and more than once I consider using magic instead of my hands. I don't, however, knowing Natharius will only mock me for it. Even Taria, who's draped in flowing golden robes, has no difficulty in climbing the rocks with her usual elegance. Besides, using magic would waste the aether flowing through my blood. After last night's indulgence of moon-blossom wine, my magic seems to have finally returned to its usual strength, ready for the battle to come.

"When do you think we will reach Gerazad?" I ask as I fall into step beside Natharius. My breaths are uneven from all the climbing, but I do my best to hide my fatigue.

The Void Prince doesn't turn as I speak. Not that the path ahead is particularly interesting; it's filled only by cliffs, trees, and grass. At least the fact he keeps his gaze fixed ahead means he doesn't see the reddening of my face from all our trekking. "Maybe this evening," he says. "Or maybe tomorrow."

"You're certain?"

"I am."

"You don't sound very sure," I reply. "It sounds like you're guessing."

That gets the Void Prince to look at me. "Why do I sound like I'm guessing?"

"There's a difference between arriving this evening or tomorrow. A difference significant enough to determine whether or not we make it to Gerazad before Arluin."

"I am the Prince of Pride, not your personal map."

"But you've been this way before?"

"I have."

"And you're certain you remember the way?"

"It was centuries ago I was last here."

"So, we could be walking in circles right now?"

Natharius says nothing, and I'd panic if not for the slight curling of his lip. The expression means the Void Prince is teasing me. Or at least I hope so.

Before I can order him to tell me the truth, Natharius points at the path ahead. A ring of stones looms on the horizon, though I have to squint to make them out.

"What's that?" I ask, my brows knitting together as I squinted in the distance.

"The Ring of Thunder," Natharius replies.

The menhirs become clearer as we draw closer, and I can soon make out the glowing runes etched into their stone surface. They're polished and gleam like swords in the noon sun.

We stop at the center of the hulking stones, and their enormous height blocks out the sunlight, casting us in shadows.

I whirl around, gazing at the surrounding stones, and I count seven altogether. The energy rippling across the standing stones and illuminating their runes looks like aether. Yet there's an unfamiliarity about it. "The Ring of Thunder?" I mutter under my breath, echoing Natharius's words. "What do they do? Why are they here?"

"Long ago, this place was sacred place to the orcish stormcallers," Natharius says.

"And it isn't anymore?" The entire area is alive with energy, and I'm sure I can see lightning sparking off the standing stones. Why would a place so rich in magic be abandoned?

"Not since the first king sat upon his throne and rebuilt a broken Jektar after the Orcish Wars," Natharius replies.

"Wasn't this once a meeting place for the tribes?" Taria says.

"Indeed, the orcish tribes would gather here biannually, on Summer and Winter Solstice. They would also meet here to discuss any matters of importance, as their sacred stones were considered a place of peace."

As Natharius speaks, I step toward one of the enormous stones and press my palm against the polished surface, feeling the energy hum beneath my skin. A sudden rush of electricity jolts through me, and I leap away, rubbing my now numb palm. I glance back to see the Void Prince raising a brow at me, as if to ask whether I really am that stupid. The others are watching me too, though their expressions aren't condescending like Natharius's.

"Is it aether flowing through them?" I ask him. "Or something else?"

"Aether, but not the kind you magi are used to."

"I figured that much," I reply. "Would you care to explain?"

"The constitution of each race differs. Orcs were once goblins, warped by the Void King into their current form. Though aether flows through their blood, so does dark magic—far more than elves and men. Their magic is tainted by shadows, even when drawing on aether."

"But dark magic consumes and corrupts aether," I interrupt. "How can dark magic and aether both exist harmoniously within their bloodstreams?"

"Even magi can harbor a small amount of dark magic alongside their aether. You should know that firsthand. Orcs can merely withstand significantly more, due to their origins."

"And what of elves? Are they able to resist the corruption of dark magic for long?"

"No," he says, "we cannot."

Before I can question him further, he turns and continues through the ring of standing stones.

We continue after Natharius, weaving our way through the ragged landscape of crags. We encounter a few more rocky faces to scramble up before the terrain finally flattens. The wind now blows stronger than it did this morning, and I suppose it's because we're on higher ground. Before long, the sun dips into the horizon and sinks entirely. The moon rises, and the stars twinkle. With every step, my heart beats a little more restlessly.

Natharius claimed we would likely reach Gerazad either tonight and tomorrow. Maybe we'll arrive in the next few hours, or maybe tomorrow morning.

Dread tightens its grasp over me. I don't know what to expect when we finally reach Gerazad. Will Arluin be there? Or will he be long gone, having already besieged the orcish city days ago? Or maybe, just maybe, we will arrive there before Arluin does and have plenty of time to warn the orcs.

And if we do meet Arluin in Gerazad, will Father also be there? Will I finally free his soul from Arluin's shackles and allow his body to be put to rest?

The questions gnaw on me, suffocating all thoughts. I stare blankly at the path ahead. Though my eyes see my surroundings, my mind doesn't. Once or twice I stumble over a stray stone, and Caya steadies me, preventing me from crashing into Taria. Realizing Caya is the one assisting me is the most conscious thought which has passed through my mind in a while.

"Maybe we should stop," Caya suggests, her gaze on me.

"No," I say through clenched teeth. I won't be the reason we stop. Not when we're so close. Stopping now could mean failing to reach Gerazad before Arluin. Besides, it's my mind that is exhausted from my thoughts. Not my body. I must keep myself walking for as long as I can.

"There is little sense in stopping now," Natharius agrees, glancing back at us. "Gerazad isn't far now. We should keep walking until we arrive."

A fresh wave of determination surges through me, shaking away the exhaustion clouding my mind. "It isn't far now?"

Natharius dips his head. "Passing the Ring of Thunder earlier this afternoon means we're close to Gerazad. I am certain we will reach it before this night is over."

My body trembles in a concoction of emotions: fear, determination, fury, and hope.

Even if we reach Gerazad soon, I don't know what will await me. Whether everything will be in vain.

I suck in a sharp breath and focus on putting one foot in front of the other. The promise of vengeance drives me onward. It marches me across the grassy landscape. Justice is so close my fingers can almost touch it. I will not give up now. I have to believe that it won't be too late. That Gerazad won't already look like Nolderan. Broken, cold, and lonely.

Arluin. When I find him, I will destroy him. With his blood, he will pay for all he has taken from me.

With such vengeful thoughts consuming me, I barely pay attention as the terrain shifts. Out path climbs higher into the cliffs, and the ferocious wind whips across my cheeks. I'm slow to notice the amber lights flickering in the far distance, a stark contrast to the surrounding darkness. Natharius halts, and so do the rest of us.

The outline is faint, but I'm certain I can make out the silhouette of city walls.

I whirl around to Natharius. "That's Gerazad? We've arrived?"

"Indeed," he replies, "we have."

Juron frowns as he peers into the distance. "It seems the necromancers aren't here yet."

Caya's eyes narrow. "Or at least, they are yet to begin their attack."

Taria gives a slow nod of agreement. "At any rate, we mustn't delay. The necromancers could be among the streets as we speak, preparing their attack."

I grit my teeth. From experience, I know that's a likely possibility. At any moment, Death Gates could open, allowing hordes of undead to swarm into the city. "Will the orcs have wards placed around Gerazad?" If they don't, they will be easy prey. Nolderan fell the moment Arluin forced Father to deactivate the Aether Tower, rendering all magical wards placed around the city useless.

"Their stormcallers will have crafted some magical defenses around the city," Natharius replies. "From what I know of the orcs, their wards will be runes carved into standing stones similar to the ones at the Ring of Thunder."

"And these wards will offer protection against Death Gates?"

"Most likely, yes."

"That's what they will target first then, before they launch their assault on the city. The necromancers also have orcs among their ranks, so they'll be familiar with the city and where the wards are placed."

Taria strides forward, her golden robes swishing in the night wind. "If the necromancers are already present, we must make haste before they strike. Or else it will be too late to warn the orcs of the threat they face."

CHAPTER 35

THOUGH GERAZAD'S WALLS ARE CRUDE in their architecture, they certainly appear robust. And towering high.

We come to a stop before the hulking iron gates, which are sealed shut. The orcs must have a curfew for travelers entering and leaving their city.

"Who goes there?" a gruff voice demands from atop the walls, his voice echoing through the night.

I strain my neck to peer above. Dozens of archers line the walls, their arrows pointing at the six of us below.

The others look to me. I glance at Natharius, but the Void Prince remains silent. As does Taria, though I hoped the priestess would take charge, seeing how she is the future Grand Priestess of Selynis. I can't fathom how I've ended up as the leader of our party, especially since I'm by far the least qualified for the role as a mage who has barely graduated from the Arcanium.

But there's little time to protest over my designated role. Countless arrows threaten to rain on us. And if we don't hurry, Arluin could launch his attack before we enter the city. At least the security of these gates brings some reassurance. Then again, Arluin and his necromancers will no doubt find a way to bypass them. Unless they already have.

With a deep breath, I take a step forth. The straining of wood and string rings out as the archers' bows grow tauter. "We've come to speak with your king!" I raise both palms, hoping it will demonstrate my peaceful intentions.

The orc who called down to us leans further over the edge, staring at me. He's broad, and the steel shoulder-pads he wears makes his figure even wider. Heavy armor covers all of him, except for his head. Large tusks jut out from his square jaw, and his skin is the color of moss. The top of his head is shaven, but some dark hair is left untouched at the back, and he wears the remaining strands in a short braid. I'm also certain his brows are thicker than my fingers.

A sneer emerges on his face. "You, a human, wish to speak with our king?"

The archers around him burst into laughter. Hopefully none will laugh so much they accidentally shoot us.

"I've never heard anything more absurd!" the orcish captain continues with a scoff. "Five humans coming here to talk to King Agzol himself."

"Are you blind or just stupid?" Natharius spits, coming to a stop beside me. Annoyance flickers like flames in his crimson eyes. "I am no human, orc."

The orc only shakes his head. "An elf then. What difference does it make? You look the same, except for your pointy ears. Your kind are as unwelcome here as humans, elf."

Natharius's fists tighten. I expect him to correct the orc and his true identity as the Void Prince of Pride, but he wisely keeps his mouth shut.

"Please!" I call. "There isn't much time left. We must speak to your king at once!"

The orc's eyes narrow. "There isn't much time left for what?"

"Before a cult of necromancers besieges your city. Before they turn each and every one of your people into mindless undead, like they did to my homeland. They obliterated our city, leaving no survivors in their wake."

His lip curl around his tusks. "If they left no survivors, why do you draw breath?"

I open my mouth to speak, but the orc continues before I can utter a single word.

"I've heard enough lies for one night." He scans across us, lingering on Taria in particular. "Spies, the lot of you. Sent by Selynis to gauge our weaknesses. You can scurry back home and tell your masters orcish cities are built without weaknesses."

I dig the heels of my boots into the ground, refusing to retreat.

"Go!" he roars, his voice echoing like thunder. "Or I will send you back to your masters in pieces!"

"You don't understand what doom awaits you," I continue. "We can leave, but the fate awaiting your city won't change. When the end comes crashing down on you all and your king looks for one to blame, it will be your head he claims. All your men gathered here are witnessing your refusal to heed my warning. Your failure to serve your king."

The orc grips the edge of the wall, the veins in his temples throbbing. Rage blazes across his expression, and for a moment, my stomach knots with fear. Have I pushed the orc too far? Will he order his archers to release their arrows on us?

"I should order my archers to strike you where you stand, human," the orc snarls. "Do not dare threaten me again."

Once more, I raise my hands in surrender. "I am not threatening you. I am only warning you of the events which will follow if you turn us away. Allow us to at least speak with your king. Let him decide the truth in my words. At the very least, if a disaster is to follow then you will not be blamed for it."

The orc pauses. I squeeze my fists together, praying with all my heart we won't be refused entry. If the orcs won't let us through the gates, how can I defeat Arluin? How can I avenge Nolderan and free Father?

"Very well," the orc grinds out through his teeth, as if uttering those two words causes him physical pain. "You may enter, but you will do so blindfolded and without weapons. You will be surrounded by guards at all times. One wrong move, and you die. Do we have an agreement?"

My heart skips a beat, barely believing his words to be true. That he is really granting us entry; that everything won't be in vain.

"Yes," I breathe. "Yes, we have an agreement." As long as we speak to the Orc King, it doesn't matter how we enter the city. Natharius won't be thrilled by the prospect of being blindfolded, but I don't care for the demon's thoughts on the matter. The Void Prince's injured pride is the least of my concerns.

The sound of metal grinding against metal rings out as the heavy iron doors open.

"Good speech," Natharius murmurs, his words barely audible over the gates.

I turn and blink, my brows furrowing as I try to read his face. I'm certain such words can only be sarcasm when coming from his mouth, yet he wears no smirk.

"Orcs were bred for destruction and understand only two things: strength and fear. Any reasoning with them must involve both."

His tone sounds serious. Does that mean the Void Prince is actually complimenting me? And if he is, should I thank him for it?

I instead settle on: "I see." It's probably the safest option.

I stride through the gates and into Gerazad, the others close behind.

On the other side, the orcs waste no time in blindfolding us. All I catch is a glimpse of stone buildings before my vision is cast in darkness. They tie the rag tightly around my head, and the coarse fabric scratches the skin around my eyes. Fortunately, Natharius doesn't protest about this arrangement, though I doubt he looks particularly pleased.

"What should we do with this creature?" one orc asks. Though I can't see, I suppose he must mean Zephyr.

"Put him in a sack," the captain replies.

The squeak which comes from Zephyr confirms they're definitely talking about him.

"Zephyr," I say, "do as they say. It won't be for long."

He must obey me since he doesn't let out any more squeals of protest and the orcs say nothing more of the matter.

"This way," the commanding orc's gruff voice comes from ahead. A firm hand on my shoulder shoves me forward. I almost stumble over the stones, my feet struggling to find grip.

The orcs march us through the city. As we pass through the streets, chatter drifts around us in a guttural language my ears can't decipher. But I don't need to understand orcish to know the surrounding civilians will be chattering about the outsiders their guards are escorting through the streets.

More than once, I find myself wishing I could see the city. With the blindfold secured around my eyes, I'm left to imagine what the streets might look like. Perhaps the orcish houses will be built out of the same crude yet robust stone as the city's gates. I wonder whether they have many taverns here and how they compare to Nolderan's. Most likely, they will be closest to the taverns sitting on Nolderan's docks, frequently filled with drunken sailors. I imagine the orcs probably use as colorful curses in their own language and have as few manners.

It might be minutes or hours later that we reach stairs. The orcs don't bother warning me, and I trip over the steps. The only reason I don't fall flat on my face is because the guards are keeping a close hold on me. I also don't want to know how many blades are pointing at me right now.

I'm more than glad when we reach the top of the steps, and our path remains flat for the rest of the journey, and we soon come to a stop. I open my eyes as best I can with the blindfold, and amber rays filter through the coarse fabric.

"You stand before King Agzol, Son of Udrod, Son of Bashag."

As the orc captain speaks, the guards untie the blindfold from around my eyes. The sudden light makes me squeeze my eyes shut, and I blink until my vision adjusts.

We stand inside a hall, braziers casting fiery light all around us. An iron throne stands opposite us, framed by two enormous tusks from creatures I'm unfamiliar with. An orc sits on the throne, red paint smeared across his murky face, forming foreign symbols which are likely of the same language as the runes marking the standing stones in the Ring of Thunder. His head is bald except for the white beard sprouting from his jaw. Most of his hair is woven into braids and secured by iron beads. His tusks gleam in the amber light, making them look as if they're forged from gold. He's also clad in heavier armor than the captain. Perhaps orcs show off their social status by wearing as much armor as they can. I imagine it's even less comfortable than a corset.

"Lhorok," Agzol begins, his narrowed eyes on the orc captain who escorted us. The Orc King's voice reminds me of the grinding of metal. Though his words are slow, they carried an unfathomable weight. "Who do you bring before me?"

Lhorok pays his king a deep bow before answering the question. "These humans arrived at our gates and demanded to speak with you."

The Orc King rises from his throne, chain-mail clinking as he does, and his movement is measured yet deliberate, reminding me of a river. Mighty, unhurried, and ancient. As he stands at his full height, I realize how tall Agzol is. Though Lhorok is far from short, the Orc King is a giant in comparison. It's no wonder he can wear three times the amount of armor as his captain.

"They asked to see me, and you accepted their request?" Agzol doesn't roar these words, but they're nonetheless terrifying. "Tell me, should I carve off your head from where you stand? Are you worthy of the rank I have bestowed on you?"

"Apologies, my lord," Lhorok replies, dipping his head in reverence to his king. "I cannot deny their suspicious nature. Normally I would not entertain such foolishness, but their claims were bold. They warned of a great threat to our city, and I could not risk inaction."

Agzol gives a slow hum, the sound reverberating off the hall's stone walls. He scans across us more carefully, lingering on both Taria and Natharius. I suppose I look less formidable than the priestess and the Void Prince. Even Juron and Caya receive more attention than me. Maybe the Orc King doesn't recognize what my purple robes stand for. Or maybe he doesn't care.

"Lhorok, you are mistaken," Agzol finally says, his eyes fixed on Natharius. "We have four humans and one demon."

Lhorok frowns. "A demon?"

The Orc King inhales deeply, his nostrils flaring. "A powerful demon of the Abyss. Can you not sense the great darkness within him?"

"No, my lord, I did not until now."

The Orc King turns to us, though his attention is mostly directed at Natharius. "Why have you come here?"

With a deep breath, I take a step forward. Somehow I persuaded Lhorok to allow us into the city, though it seemed impossible. In the same way, I will convince the Orc King the threat to his city is real. I have no choice but to succeed.

"King Agzol," I begin, bowing my head, "we've traveled here to warn you of the grave threat your kingdom faces."

He strokes his white beard. "And what threat would this be? From Selynis? Tirith? Or from our orcish neighbors in Dromgar?"

"None of them," I reply. "A group of necromancers of all races march on this city. They could already be here, plotting their assault."

"How many necromancers?" Agzol demands.

"Twelve—"

"Twelve necromancers?" Agzol barks out a rumbling laugh, which echoes through the hall. "You call twelve necromancers a grave threat? Do you humans really think that little of us orcs?"

I tighten my fists. "Twelve necromancers and hundreds—no, thousands—of their undead minions. Enough to raze an entire city to the ground, no matter how well-defended it might be."

"Thousands of undead you say?"

"All hungering to consume the living."

"Where are these thousands of undead?" the Orc King says. "Why are my scouts yet to report an army so large marching on this city?"

"I don't know where the undead are right now," I admit. "But I do know the necromancers themselves are headed here. They can summon their undead through death gates, portals channeled through dark magic."

"The defenses of this city are more than capable of preventing the opening of portals. Though our magic is different to yours, mage, that does not mean it is inferior."

"It doesn't matter how strong orcish magic is. The necromancers will find a way to bypass your defenses. That's how they destroyed Nolderan."

"Nolderan? Defeated? Your story becomes even more absurd by the minute, human!"

I grit my teeth. "Yes. Nolderan was defeated. The necromancers forced my father to deactivate the Aether Tower, rendering every magical ward in the city useless. Then they unleashed their hordes of undead on us and obliterated the streets."

"Your father?"

"The Grandmage of Nolderan."

The Orc King laughs again. "And now you claim your father is the Grandmage of Nolderan!" He turns to Taria, a sneer forming as he looks at her golden robes. "And I suppose you're also the daughter of the Grand Priestess of Selynis? The daughter of a celibate priestess!"

"Actually," Taria says hesitantly, "I am her first disciple, and the future Grand Priestess of Selynis."

"By the Thunder God, it gets even better!" The Orc King's gaze sweeps across to Natharius. "And you, demon? What ridiculous identity would you like bestow on yourself?"

As expected, Natharius doesn't hold back.

"I am the Prince of Pride, the mightiest of the Void King's seven lieutenants," he says, returning Agzol's stare.

The Orc King throws his head back and laughs so hard I'm sure I see tears rolling down his face. "While I can sense you are a powerful demon," Agzol says when he recovers from his laughter, "I hardly think that such a scrawny band of travelers could summon and bind a Void Prince of the Abyss. At least you did not claim to be the Void King himself! Or else my side would split from laughter."

"You must believe us!" I exclaim, taking a step closer to the Orc King. A step too close, apparently, seeing how dozens of guards soon surround me. Countless blades are at my throat faster than I can blink.

"And why must I believe you?" Agzol rebukes, starting down from his throne. "What evidence do you have for these ridiculous claims?"

I swallow.

"That's what I thought."

"Wait!" I cry, my racing mind constructing a clumsy plan. "Nolderan is destroyed. That is evidence enough."

"And you expect me to take your word for it?"

"No, I can prove it. I can teleport you to Nolderan. Then you can see the state of the city with your own eyes."

Agzol only sneers. "I am the King of Jektar. Do you really think I would agree to such a proposition?"

"Then choose someone you trust, and I'll teleport them to Nolderan in your stead. When they return, they can tell you whether it's true my home has fallen. Would that at least not confirm my story?"

Agzol pauses, stroking his white beard. "Magi are well known for their enchantments and illusions. What is to say you won't cast a spell over the chosen witness and cause them to see that which you wish them to see?"

"I thought we were only a scrawny band of travelers who aren't capable of summoning a Void Prince," I reply, folding my arms across my chest. "If you send someone experienced with magic, they'll be able to sense a spell being cast over them. Unless we really are as powerful as we say, which would make our identities true."

The Orc King pauses. I chew on my lower lip as I anxiously await his response. I glance across at Taria and the others. The priestess's expression is as worried. If King Agzol won't agree to this suggestion, I don't know how else I'll make him believe me. And if he remains convinced that my warning is false, then the entire city will be left to Arluin's mercy. And I know firsthand he has none.

"Lhorok," the Orc King finally says.

My heart thumps in my chest. My palms are slick with sweat. Agzol can't refuse. He can't.

"I would have you as my witness. But only if you are willing to be teleported to Nolderan by this mage. I have no desire to force you, if it is not what you wish."

Lhorok doesn't hesitate for even a moment before bowing his head to his king. "I am willing to serve you at any cost, my lord. I could think of no greater honor than to confirm whether our kingdom truly faces a great threat."

"If you are certain."

"I am."

"Then Lhorok, captain of Gerazad's guards, shall accompany you to Nolderan in my place. Are you in agreement, mage?"

I give him a swift nod. While I'd prefer for the king himself to visit Nolderan and realize the gravity of the threat Gerazad faces, the captain of the guards isn't at all a poor substitution. As long as King Agzol trusts Lhorok's word to be true, it will be enough. "Of course."

"Very well then," Agzol says. "Lhorok will accompany you to Nolderan to see if what you say is true."

CHAPTER 36

LHOROK STEPS TOWARD ME. Though King Agzol has agreed to my idea, I'm far from relieved. Never have I teleported across such a great distance. While this feat is possible for experienced magi, I'm uncertain I'll succeed. It will take a great deal of strength and the toll on my magic will be costly. Teleporting Lhorok and myself to Nolderan and back could very well mean I'll lack the strength to defeat Arluin if he begins his assault soon. And that's assuming I succeed. If I fail and my teleportation spell is misdirected, we could very well end up at the bottom of the ocean.

I turn to Lhorok and pray my face doesn't betray my fear. If the Orc King realizes how inexperienced I am, he won't entrust me with his valued captain.

"We won't be long," I say, hoping my voice sounds firmer than it feels. "We will be gone for an hour at the most."

King Agzol gives a slow nod before striding up the few steps and sitting on his throne once more. "We will await your return."

I dip my head and turn back to Lhorok. The captain's expression hardens. Not from fear, or at least I don't think so. He looks ready to rush into battle and face his enemy head-on. Hopefully he doesn't see me as his foe rather than the true enemies we all face.

"Ready?" I ask, my voice small against the enormity of the stone hall.

Lhorok clenches his jaw. "Ready."

I hold out my hand. *"Conparios."*

Violet light stretches into my staff's silhouette, becoming solid in my hands. My fingers grasp the smooth crystalline surface, and it glistens in the amber light of the braziers.

The staff is heavier than usual. I can't fail with this task. If I do, Nolderan will go unavenged. My father won't be laid to rest.

With a deep breath, I close my eyes and draw on all the aether around me. Magic rushes into the staff, spilling into brilliant purple light. I seek more and more aether, until my blood is boiling with power.

When more magic bubbles in my veins than I can contain, I focus my mind and envision the streets of Nolderan as vividly as I can. I picture them as I left them: silent and still. It's the fountain in the upper city's square I imagine myself standing in, and in my mind's eye, I craft the ornate white benches surrounding it. I sharpen the image with so much detail I see the water trickling from the fountain. I hear it.

I remove one hand from my staff and reach out for Lhorok beside me, sensing his presence through my magic. I clasp his armored shoulder, allowing my magic to wash over him, and continue to craft the image of our destination in my mind.

Teleporting over such a great distance requires precise targeting, as well as an abundance of aether to fuel the spell. Only when the image is fully formed do I finally unleash my magic.

"Laxus!" I cry, my voice reverberating off the stone walls.

The floor fades from beneath my feet. As does the echoing of my voice. The tinkling of magic sounds all around us, and we're swept from time and space, floating through the planes of existence. I feel as fluid as water and as light as air. This spell takes far longer than usual to complete, and I have more time to experience the effects of teleportation.

My heart thunders against my rib cage. Will this teleportation spell work? What if we never materialize again?

No, that's impossible. I've never heard of a mage remaining dematerialized forever from a teleportation spell. The worst that can happen is that we could teleport to an unfamiliar location, maybe even to the bottom of the ocean. At least my magic can prevent us from drowning. Magi lost to teleportation spells always turn up in the end. I remind myself of that over and over, drowning out the shouts of my doubts.

Ground emerges beneath my feet. My eyes flicker open to see the silhouette of Nolderan's streets crafted from purple light. The fountain stands before us, gradually solidifying.

My shoulders sag in relief. We are here—exactly where I intended.

A dome of violet light appears high above us, the protective barrier which now surrounds Nolderan. Beyond it, I can scarcely make out the night sky and the stars' twinkling light.

The buildings of the upper city materialize. In the distance, I see Nolderan's Aether Tower. Activated, like I left it.

The city is silent, aside from the night wind sweeping through the streets. The rubble around remains untouched.

Lhorok scans across the square, his brows furrowed. "This is Nolderan?"

I dip my head, a lump swelling in my throat. The loneliness of the city makes my heart shudder. "Yes," I reply, my voice breaking, "this is Nolderan."

Lhorok says nothing as he stares at the rubble scattered through the square. His gaze trails upward to the Aether Tower, and his eyes narrows as he examines it.

"That's the Aether Tower," I explain. "It powers all the wards here. Before I left, I used it to activate a shield which prevents anyone but me from entering the city."

Lhorok's frown deepens. "Though the city is ruined, there is no trace of death."

"You mean there are no bodies?"

"Indeed."

"That's because the necromancers reanimated all the dead, leaving no corpses." Except for Eliya. But that's only because I clung to her body, refusing to let the necromancers take her away. And Arluin apparently instructed them to spare her to use her as bait for me. At least he underestimated my ability to trick him with an illusion. I suppose the Reyna he once knew was a far more useless mage than the Reyna of today.

"I have never been here," Lhorok says after a moment. "While I cannot deny the state of this city, I am unable to confirm whether it is Nolderan."

"Shouldn't the fact that this city has been destroyed and has no corpses be evidence enough of the necromancers I speak of? Shouldn't this be enough for you to tell your king that the threat Gerazad faces is very much real?"

"Perhaps," Lhorok replies, "though there is the possibility that this city belongs to an ancient, lost civilization."

I let out a sigh. We have so little time. If Lhorok refuses to believe me, despite seeing Nolderan with his own eyes, how else will I convince him of the impending threat?

"An ancient city would not be this well preserved," I counter. "Time would have left its mark on the stone."

"There are spells which would preserve the city," he replies.

"And can you detect any such spells?"

The orc pauses, turning his head either side. "No, I cannot."

"And if we are not in Nolderan, where else would we be?"

Lhorok shrugs. "Maybe you have teleported me to the far reaches of this world."

I run a hand down my face. Are all orcs this stubborn? How can I prove this city is Nolderan to someone who's never been here?

I press my lips together, thinking for a long moment. Then an idea strikes me.

"The Arcanium," I say.

Lhorok casts me a confused look. I don't bother wasting my breath to explain how the Arcanium is Nolderan's academy for magi.

"Can you read the alphabet for the common language?"

"I can," he answers. "Why?"

"Because I know how to prove this is Nolderan."

With that, I hurry down the street, ushering Lhorok to follow.

The Arcanium is only a few corners away from the Upper City's square and we are soon greeted by the grand archway at the entrance. The statues of all famous magi stand sentry over the forlorn gardens.

I don't waste any time examining them and head for the statue at the very end of the path.

The statue of Grandmage Delmont Blackwood is situated at the foot of the steps leading to the Arcanium's pillared entrance. He wears majestic robes and grips the same crystalline staff as the one in my hands. His nose is so sharp I suspect it would pierce my fingers if I placed them on the stone.

I stop at the base of the statue and point to the golden plaque. "Grandmage Delmont Blackwood," I read aloud, my voice ringing through the emptiness. "Founder of Nolderan and the Magi."

Lhorok edges closer to the plaque, reading for himself the words etched into the metallic surface. Surely he can't continue to dispute the fact we're in Nolderan?

After a long moment, the orc withdraws. "Very well. I will report to King Agzol that Nolderan has indeed been destroyed."

I frown at him. He's strangely calm. I've proven Nolderan's destruction, so isn't he worried the rest of my claims may also be true? "What about the necromancers? Do you believe me when I say that they're the ones responsible for the destruction of this city? That they march on your city with the same intentions?"

Lhorok trains his gaze on me. "I believe what I have witnessed first-hand: that this ruined city is Nolderan, and that its streets are void of the dead. That is what I will report to my king, and it is up to him to evaluate the implications of my observations."

I suppose that means there will be more discussion and deliberation, wasting precious time. We need to act now, before Arluin makes his move. Otherwise, it will be too late.

"There is one thing I don't understand," Lhorok says, interrupting my thoughts.

"What?"

"The entire city was destroyed, and it appears everyone was killed. Why is it you alone survived?"

I hesitate.

"Are you in league with these necromancers? Were you sent to divert our attention while they are busy preparing an ambush?"

"Of course not!"

"Then how did you survive the massacre?"

Blood drums in my ears. Arluin spared me because for some reason, despite all his wickedness, he could not bear to kill me. I don't know how to explain my relationship to Arluin, nor the part I played in Nolderan's fall. And I suspect trying to explain any of it will only cause Lhorok to suspect my motives even more.

"I was out of the city when they attacked," I lie, the words spilling from my mouth before I can think them through.

"Yet the way you speak of Nolderan's destruction is like you witnessed it with your own eyes."

I flinch and turn away. "That sounds like conjecture to me. You said that you would allow your king to evaluate the implications of your observations."

Lhorok grunts in response.

Though I've evaded Lhorok's questions for now, I will need to deal with King Agzol's interrogation.

I heave out a breath. "We should head back to Gerazad. There is little time before the necromancers strike. Of that I am certain."

Lhorok nods. "There are wards placed around the city, so you will be unable to teleport directly inside."

"Should I direct my spell to the city's gates?" I ask.

Lhorok pulls a medallion from around his neck, and the dark iron has been wrought into a circle with a thunderbolt and hammer carved into the center. From my studies at the Arcanium, I vaguely recall it as being the symbol of Jektar. "This will allow you to bypass the wards and teleport into King Agzol's hall."

I take the medallion from him and feel the same familiar yet foreign hum as I did when pressing my palm to a menhir in the Ring of Thunder. Aether tainted by a trace of dark magic. I hold out my staff, close my eyes and draw on all the surrounding magic.

Aether floods into my staff and my body far quicker than it did in Gerazad. I suppose that's thanks to the Aether Tower humming high above. While my concentration is weary, I hope the abundance of magic will allow me to teleport back to Gerazad. If I misdirect this spell and we end up somewhere far from our intended destination, I'm not sure I'll have the energy to teleport for a third time. By the time I've recovered, Gerazad may have long been defeated.

I clasp Lhorok's shoulder and picture the Orc King's hall as vividly as I can, envisioning the flickering amber light of the many braziers inside and feeling their warmth brush over my cheeks. The image of the hall grows clearer in my mind, until I can hear the air whispering across the tall walls.

"*Laxus!*" I call, releasing the spell over Lhorok and me.

Nolderan dematerializes, and then we're racing through radiant purple clouds. Light blurs around us. It traces the outline of the Orc King's hall, complete with his throne and many braziers. The silhouettes become concrete, stone and metal replacing the purple light.

The hall isn't as we left it. King Agzol promised he would await our return, but the hall is entirely empty.

Well, almost entirely.

Natharius is sprawled across the Orc King's iron throne, his head tilted back as he examines the ceiling above him with a bored expression. As we emerge from aether, his gaze trails down to the two of us. I also note that Zephyr is cowering behind the brazier to the left of the throne. My gut twists with dread.

Before I can demand to know what the Void Prince is doing on the Orc King's throne, he speaks.

"Took you long enough," he says, his tone too dark for my liking.

My stomach knots a little more. "Where is everyone?" I whirl around, searching the empty hall and hoping to find someone else.

Yet I see no one. Not Taria, the twins, King Agzol, or any orc other than the one beside me.

Have we returned too late? Have we somehow spent so long inside Nolderan that Gerazad has already been destroyed?

Beyond the hall, the clanging of steel rings through the night. It sounds like swords striking bone and stone.

A shadow descends on Natharius's angular face. "Your necromancers have arrived."

CHAPTER 37

My heart thunders in my chest.

Arluin is here. Along with his necromancers and hordes of undead.

I tighten my fists. Teleporting away has meant I've missed the moment of his attack, and taking Lhorok to Nolderan has proven completely pointless. King Agzol can now see his city being attacked with his own eyes. All I achieved was wasting precious time. And magic.

"Wait here," I say to Zephyr, who peeks at me from behind his brazier. "If any of the undead come in here, then make sure you hide."

Zephyr gives me a nod, and I whirl around and head out of the hall. Lhorok's footsteps are frantic behind me. I glance back to see Natharius peeling himself from the iron throne. In the next heartbeat, he's close behind us.

"Where are Taria and the twins?" I ask.

"Assisting King Agzol," Natharius replies. "I said I would wait in the hall and explain the situation when you returned."

The night air slams into my face. I stop at the stone steps leading down from the Orc King's hall and to the street. Anguished shouts and unearthly howling ricochet through the darkness in a cacophony of noise. Bolts of ghostly white light reach up into the sky, marking where the necromancers have cast their death gates.

Countless undead swarm the streets, and many dead orcs have already risen from their graves. Lhorok and I were away for half an hour at the most. How has Arluin caused this much devastation in such a short time?

Lhorok is frozen in place. He stares down at the chaos unfolding beneath us.

"We need to find Taria and the others," I say to Natharius.

"The priestess's plan is that she sees to defending the city with the orcs and to destroy as many death gates as possible before the streets are overrun."

I glance around at the hordes of undead. It already looks as if the streets are overrun, and the orcish forces are vastly out-numbered. "And what about us?"

"We have the important task," he replies. "Finding your necro-mancer and stopping him before he finds the ring of Lagartha the Old."

"Do you know where it is?"

"I do not."

"And you didn't think to ask the king where it might be?"

Natharius glares at me.

I sigh. Of course he didn't bother to ask King Agzol where we can find the ring Arluin seeks.

I turn to Lhorok instead. "Do you know where we might find the ring? A thousand years ago, it belonged to an orcish woman called Lagartha the Old."

To my dismay, Lhorok shakes his head. "I don't recognize the name."

I draw my lips into a grim line. With the city being ravaged by undead, we can hardly stroll through the streets and ask the citizens if they've heard of such a ring.

"He wouldn't be familiar with the name," Natharius says. "Orcish culture has changed much over the last millennia."

"So, that means no one here will know anything about the ring and where we can find it?"

Natharius ignores my question and raises his hand, darkness billowing out. The shadows settle into the outline of an iron ring with a dark, jagged stone at its center. I think it might be onyx, but seeing how the image is formed from shadows, I can't tell whether there's meant to be any color.

Still, it's enough for recognition to flash across Lhorok's face. And horror.

"That's . . ." He chokes on the word, stumbling back. "That belongs to my wife."

"You're sure it's hers?" I ask.

"She is the Chief Stormcaller. It was passed to her when she assumed her position."

Maybe Chief Stormcaller is a similar title to Grandmage and High Enchanter.

"The necromancers seek this ring?" Lhorok says.

"They do," I reply.

"And will they know where to find it? That it belongs to Olra?"

"There was an orcish woman among them," I answer. "With long, white hair."

Something in Lhorok's expression makes my chest tighten. "Did you catch her name?"

"They called her Grizela."

His next pause makes my skin shiver. It only lasts a moment. In the next, Lhorok is racing down the steps and into the chaos below.

Judging by his reaction, it seems he knows that orcish necromancer very well indeed.

I glance at Natharius. The demon raises a brow.

"Well," he says, "I suppose we ought to find the orc's wife before the necromancers find her first."

I nod and hurry after Lhorok who has been swallowed by the masses of orcs and undead ahead. I glimpse his armor and sprint toward him, desperate not to lose him in the chaos.

Skeletal hands lunge from the right.

"*Ignira,*" I snarl, blasting the undead with a hastily crafted fireball. Though it's far from my finest attack, it's sufficient to incapacitate my enemy.

I push on through the masses, carving a path of fire through the undead. Natharius guards our flanks, holding our enemies at bay with blasts of dark magic. With our combined strength, it doesn't take us long to catch up to Lhorok.

The orc grips a giant axe. He wasn't carrying it before, so he must have retrieved it from one of the fallen orcish warriors.

Lhorok cleaves through the undead with his axe. Dark lightning sparks from the blade as he strikes each enemy.

"Do you know where your wife is?" I call over to him. The clamor of death and destruction drowns out my voice, but Lhorok hears me all the same.

"Home." He glances back at me. Fear clouds his eyes. "Grizela, she knows where we live. She will know where to find Olra." His words are uneven as he swings this way and that at the undead.

I grit my teeth as I launch another fiery attack into a nearby ghoul. Though I'm curious as to the history Lhorok and his wife share with the orcish necromancer, now is not the time to ask.

"Are you sure she will be at home?" I ask as we push onward through the street. "You said she's the Chief Stormcaller, so won't she be helping to defend the city?"

"I don't know," Lhorok replies between breaths. "She shouldn't be."

An undead charges for me, pulling my attention from Lhorok. I blast it with flames.

"She's . . ." Lhorok continues, his words laborious. "She's with child."

My lips part with horror.

Not only is his wife at stake, but also his unborn child. I was wondering why the Captain of the Guard is pursuing Arluin with us rather than leading the city's defense, but a pregnant wife explains that decision. Though it probably can't be called a decision. I'm not sure Lhorok is thinking right now. Fury, panic, and horror all rage in his eyes.

We break free of the first street and turn down the next. More undead swarm here, but at least there are more orcs to fight them. With how crowded it is, it'll be a struggle to reach the end of the street.

Unlike me, Lhorok doesn't hesitate. He charges at the nearest undead, his axe arcing through the air. Bolts of shadowy lightning spark. After another blow, the skeleton falls to the ground.

I follow Lhorok as his axe slices through the undead. Natharius brings up the rear, preventing any of our enemies from ambushing us.

We reach the end of the street sooner than I expect.

A death gate lies ahead, channeled by a necromancer. Two others stand guard.

Countless undead swarm out. I don't know where they come from beyond the dark portal, but their masses are endless.

Golden light slams into a row of undead pouring out of the ghostly portal. Taria's molten robes billow around her from the impact of her spell. King Agzol is with her, wielding a massive sword. Lightning hums across the blade. Whereas sparks ignite from Lhorok's axe, full bolts surge from the Orc King's sword. Agzol is almost as terrifying as Natharius in his demonic form. But his enemies aren't capable of feeling fear. They're already dead.

"Reyna," Caya calls, the first to notice our arrival. "You're back!"

Taria glances over at us. Not for long, though. An undead nears the priestess. Juron cuts it down with his shining sword.

"Find Arluin!" Taria shouts. "Leave the city's defense to us. We have already destroyed one of their portals. We will soon close this, and then the rest!"

Though they've destroyed one death gate, many more are scattered around the city. Beams of white light pierce the night sky, and the streets are being overrun by undead. I pray Gerazad won't fall like Nolderan.

King Agzol is too frenzied by the battle to notice us. His attention is fixed on a necromancer, and he sends shockwaves rolling through the earth.

"We must find your wife before the necromancers do," I say, turning back to Lhorok.

Lhorok doesn't need telling twice. He hurries away from the death gate, continuing through the streets. With every corner we turn, his pace becomes more frantic. As do his attacks. The closer we draw to his home, the more he must fear for his wife's safety. Even if she is the Chief Stormcaller, this part of the city is crawling with undead, and each street is more overrun than the last.

"Here," Lhorok rasps as we turn the next corner. "Our house is—"

The street comes into view, and the words die in his throat.

A strangled noise escapes me. I don't even realize it comes from me until long after the sound bursts through my lips. My breaths come out like snarls, and blood pounds through my veins.

Before me stands Arluin. The man I hate most in this world. The man I have sworn to destroy.

Grizela, the white-haired necromancer, is beside him. An orcish woman lies dead at their feet.

Arluin raises his hand, examining the object he holds.

An iron ring.

CHAPTER 38

LHOROK ROARS WITH ANGUISH AND fury. He falls to his knees, his armor slamming into the stone.

Arluin turns, and so does Grizela. A cloud of confusion passes over Arluin's expression. He frowns at me, as if he doesn't believe I'm really here. But he quickly smooths out the wrinkle of emotion.

"Reyna," he says quietly, "I wasn't expecting to see you here."

My entire body shakes with uncontrollable emotion. For a moment, I'm returned to Nolderan. To the Aether Tower, where Arluin murdered Father. To the upper city's cathedral, where I lay Eliya to rest inside a crystalline coffin.

I clutch my staff as if it's the only thing keeping me upright. From falling to the ground like Lhorok.

"You," I snarl, my words so thick with emotion they come out as hoarse breaths, "you stole everything from me!"

I can hear the pain in my voice, and I loathe how vulnerable it makes me. That Arluin can see how much he has hurt me. Yet I can't hold my emotions at bay.

"I didn't steal everything from you," Arluin says. "I spared you."

Blood drums so loudly in my ears I can barely hear him. "What you did," I gasp, barely able to draw breath, let alone force out the words, "was no mercy."

Arluin pauses, tilting his head as he regards me. "Then you would have preferred me to kill you? To raise you from the dead with your father?"

An animalistic growl rumbles in the back of my throat.

I hate him.

I hate him so damn much there are no words to describe the extent of my hatred. My muscles spasm with rage, unable to withstand the ferocity of my emotions.

Of course I prefer it that I wasn't risen from the dead to serve his tyrannical will, and it disgusts me that I can't deny his words. But it doesn't mean he showed me mercy. Mercy would have been killing me and leaving my body and soul to rest, so that I neither have to serve him in death nor live out such a lonely life consumed by vengeance and anguish. Except then, I wouldn't be able to bring Arluin to justice.

And that is what I'm going to do. Right here. Right now.

He will face my wrath.

For Nolderan.

For Father.

For Eliya.

My blood bubbles with magic. I didn't realize how much aether my fury has summoned. And like my emotions, it is impossible to contain.

It screams to lash out, to obliterate Arluin. To burn him with the heat of a thousand suns. Until not even ash remains as proof of his existence.

The aether escapes my hands. I utter not a single spell-word. There's no need. My magic thoroughly understands my burning will.

My need to destroy.

Flames explode from my fingers, surging toward Arluin. Sparks crackle from the intensity of the fireball, scalding even the air in its wake.

Arluin's mask falls for the briefest of moments, revealing his surprise. He doesn't expect such power from me, the useless adept who brought about the destruction of her own city. I hope he fears me and what I am becoming—if he is alive enough to feel fear. With Father's staff and my rage, I will show him the extent of my power.

Despite his surprise, my attack doesn't catch him entirely off-guard. Before the fireball reaches him, he wraps a wall of shadows around himself.

"*Ekrad!*" he shouts. And so does Grizela beside him.

My spell collides with their dark magic. A shock-wave shudders through the air, causing me to stumble. Even Natharius and Lhorok are driven back. And my enemies are also shaken by it.

The raven curls atop Arluin's head are tousled from the force. One sweeps into his gray eyes. He brushes it away with the back of his hand. His other clutches the iron ring he pried from Lhorok's wife.

He doesn't appear bothered by my attack in the slightest. "It seems granting you mercy was a mistake."

"Arluin," I spit, "I will destroy you, even if it's the last thing I do."

"Come then," Arluin says. "Come and destroy me." He tears his gaze from me and examines my two companions. Natharius says nothing, his crimson eyes fixed on the iron ring Arluin holds. His jaw is tightened and his expression is hardened, ready to fight. Lhorok, however, remains on his knees. He stares down at his wife's corpse, barely blinking.

I pray the orc will find the strength to fight. Even with Natharius, I don't like our odds.

"A demon?" Arluin asks, his voice rising. "You summoned a demon?"

"A Void Prince," Natharius growls with a venomous glare. "And I grow tired of your words, mortal."

In the next breath, shadows swirl around Natharius, draping him in a cloud of darkness and warping his form into a monstrous size.

Large draconic wings beat, the resulting wind almost blowing me down the street. Gnarled onyx horns glisten, and crimson light radiate from the demon's markings, reflecting off the nearby stone walls. A maddened grin spreads across his face, revealing glinting fangs, and his knuckles twitch with eagerness as he grips his obsidian sword.

Never have I been more grateful to witness such a terrifying sight. Even if Natharius's demonic form chills me to the bone.

"Let me teach you the true meaning of doom," his voice booms through the empty street.

Natharius's blade descends on Arluin.

"*Farjud,*" Arluin mutters, the shadows spinning around him.

He merges with the darkness, slipping past Natharius and reappearing behind him.

Natharius's sword crashes into the street, and the ground quakes with the tremendous force. With a snarl, the Void Prince tears his sword from the street, leaving behind a deep gash in the stone, and he whirls around, preparing to attack Arluin again.

Arluin slips the iron ring inside his pocket and reaches for the amulet beneath his tunic. He inhales deeply, and the icy stone hanging from the skull's jawless mouth glows brighter and the same light fills his gray eyes. The intensity of his magical presence grows tenfold, and the air becomes as suffocating as it was inside the Ghost Woods.

Natharius pauses for a beat. His brows furrow as he regards the Amulet of Kazhul. Rage burns in his gaze, and his crimson eyes flicker like blazing flames.

"*Gavirk!*" Arluin calls.

Crows burst from his hands. With razor-sharp beaks, the shadowy birds dive toward Natharius.

The Void Prince swings his sword at them. The murder of crows is shredded apart. Feathers scatter through the air, disintegrating with the spell.

Natharius laughs. It's a wicked sound which makes me shiver with fright.

"Is that all you have, necromancer?" Natharius says with a sneer. "From all Reyna has said, I expected more of a challenge than this."

Despite Natharius's taunts, Arluin doesn't flinch. "I wonder what your father would think of your newest pet," he says to me.

Natharius snarls, gripping the hilt of his sword. "You will regret belittling me, mortal."

Arluin pointedly ignores him, as if he were an ill-tempered hound wrestling against his leash. "Why don't we ask him?"

My breath catches in the back of my throat.

My father.

Is he here?

I grip the staff, the crystal creaking beneath my grasp.

The memory of his dead eyes and reanimated corpse makes me tremble with grief and fear.

Arluin's eyes shut for a moment, his lips moving as if uttering a silent command. It must be intended for Father. Or at least the undead which wears Father's corpse.

A part of me prays he won't appear. But he has to. If he doesn't, I'll never be able to release his soul and lay his body to rest.

If I don't free him, he will remain shackled to undeath for eternity.

There's no choice but to be brave.

"*Rivus,*" a shout comes from the right.

A bolt of darkness hurls at me.

Grizela.

With my attention focused on Arluin and the possibility of meeting Father's corpse, I all but forgot about the orcish necromancer.

Panic shoots through my nerves. I hurriedly draw on all the aether I can. But the shadow bolt is already upon me. I don't have time to shield. Or teleport away.

Lhorok's axe meets Grizela's attack. Lightning sparks off the blade as it absorbs the dark magic. For a moment, I fear that the axe will break. That Lhorok will be left defenseless against the brunt of the dark magic. But the axe holds fast, devouring the shadows. The lightning humming through the steel blades darkens, tainted by the magic. Instead of being weakened by the shadows, the energy coursing through the axe intensifies, as if the dark magic fuels the weapon.

"I'll deal with Grizela," Lhorok says. His expression is as grim as his voice. "You help your demon deal with the other one."

I give him a hasty nod, my gaze flickering across to Arluin. He and Natharius are locked in battle.

"You will deal with me?" Grizela sneers. "You are not even a stormcaller, Lhorok. How could you ever match my strength?"

"You will pay for what you have done to Orla." Lhorok's words shake with rage, grief, and hatred. All the emotions which churn within me.

I don't turn to look at the two orcs. My attention is reserved for Arluin.

Natharius curls his hand, warping the shadows. Dark flames rush for Arluin.

"*Ekrad!*" A shield forms around Arluin, preventing the attack from reaching him.

The shadowy flames lick at his defenses, threatening to gnaw holes through it. He grips the amulet more tightly, and the jagged blue stone glows brighter.

"*Uzrit.*"

His shield explodes. Dark magic sweeps out, causing even Natharius to step back. I fight to keep my feet fixed to the ground.

I clutch my staff, summoning all the magic I can.

"*Ignir'alas!*" I call.

Aether ignites into flames. Fiery wings spread upward, descending on Arluin.

"*Farjud,*" Arluin says the moment before my blazing attack is upon him. He merges with the shadows and reappears a few steps away.

The fiery wings slam into the ground, burning the street. Where they touch, the stone is left charred.

I grit my teeth, preparing another attack while Natharius holds his attention. I don't maintain my concentration for long.

Footsteps sound behind. They're slow, dragging across the stone.

I glance back. My focus broken, the spell I was forming withers in my hands, returning to raw aether.

My father stands there, his head bent at an unnatural angle. And his dead eyes pierce through my soul.

CHAPTER 39

"F-father," I stammer.

My father says nothing. He only stares at me with that hollow gaze of his.

He still wears his magnificent Grandmage's robes, now tattered and dirtied. Defiled, like the rest of him.

"It's me," I choke. "Reyna."

I'm not sure why I bother. I know he won't recognize me. His corpse is an empty husk, enslaved to Arluin's will.

Yet I wish that he wasn't entirely gone. That a part of him remains somewhere deep beneath the dark magic reanimating his corpse.

"Your . . . your daughter."

I long to see recognition flashing through the shadowy orbs of his eyes. But there's nothing, only the twitching of his fingers which are held in a rigid claw.

My hands tremble around his staff. I lift it, hoping he might recognize it. He does not.

His lip curls into a snarl. He raises his hand in a stiff movement that looks as if it will snap his arm from his shoulder. Shadows gather. Though my eyes see what he's doing, the thought takes several heartbeats for my mind to process.

"*Rivus,*" he croaks. His broken voice grates through my ears like gravel.

A bolt of darkness spins toward me.

"*Muriz!*" For a moment, my voice sounds distant. As if it is not my own.

Aether wraps around me. Just in time before Father's attack reaches me.

Shadows slam into my glittering shield. The surface flickers as it withstands the force of the blow. Though he is a shell of his former self, Father's strength is as tremendous as always.

The dark magic gnaws on my shield. I clench my jaw, holding the aether in place as best I can. Willing it not to be corrupted.

Sweat beads on my forehead as I fight the shadows. I begin to fear that my shield isn't powerful enough to stop the attack from reaching me. But then the shadows dissipate into sooty clouds.

I let my shield collapse around me and suck in a shaky breath. Though I've sworn so many times to free Father from Arluin's shackles, I now fear I lack the power to defeat him. And the strength of will to cut down my father. Even if he is a wight.

I am the most awful mage Nolderan has ever known. My Mage Trials were supposed to prove I possess the strength of heart, mind, and magic that is necessary of a mage. Yet I am weak, cowardly, and stupid enough to allow the man I once loved to destroy everything.

And maybe the fact that I refuse to admit certain defeat makes me even more stupid.

Though my last spell left me fatigued, Father appears entirely unaffected by his. More shadows whir in his hands. His attacks are unrelenting.

"*Nozarat.*"

His dark magic forms a phantom blade, and he launches it at me.

I must turn my heart to ice. I must stop feeling. If I continue allowing myself to feel, there will be no chance of defeating Father. I must make my heart as cold and dead as Arluin's, just for this one battle. This is why he summoned Father here. He knew my emotions would weaken me.

So, I force myself to stop feeling. I focus on the magic humming through my veins, through the crystalline staff. There is only aether, and nothing else.

"Laxus."

My mind works faster than I can register my own thoughts. It's as if the magic is controlling me, guiding me will. I'm not even sure whether I imagine the spot behind Father. But that's where I end up.

My magic whispers to me, showing me which spell to cast next.

I slam the staff into the street. Aether shudders through the ground.

"Magmus!"

Stone turns to molten rock. A wave of lava hurdles toward Father.

"Ekrad," he calls in that blood-curdling voice of his. The shadows wrap around him, protecting him from my attack.

Or at least, they try to.

The spell is more ferocious than I expect. I have surrendered myself to aether, and the Grandmage's staff acts as my focus, bolstering my power to heights I have never dreamed of.

My father's shield only withstands a fraction of my spell. He's flung backward from the force and slams into the wall. The building shudders. I'm certain his bones rattle and break, but not even the slightest flinch of pain flickers across his face. He lies crumpled in a heap against the wall, his limbs twitching.

I briefly tear my attention from Father to see how my companions are faring.

Lhorok swings for Grizela with his lightning fueled axe, while the necromancer has conjured a dark, phantom sword and uses it to counter his attacks. Both are covered in blood.

Arluin and Natharius fight on, neither showing any sign of injury or exhaustion. While I'm relieved Natharius matches Arluin's strength, I was hoping the Void Prince would prove far more powerful than him. Then again, Arluin is wielding the Amulet of the Kazhul, which houses a fragment of the lich's soul. All I pray is that because Arluin himself is mortal, he will eventually tire whereas the Void Prince won't.

I turn back to Father. He's hauling himself back onto his feet. His shoulder sticks out at a horrible angle, the bone protruding through his tattered robes.

I know what I must do. And yet, as I stare at his mangled corpse, I fear I'm too cowardly to do it.

The shadowy orbs of his eyes meet mine. There's nothing in his gaze except an insatiable hunger for the living. This isn't my father. This is Arluin's undead minion. And if he knew I'm allowing him to suffer this humiliation, he would never forgive me. I can't allow his memory to keep being defiled like this. I must end it now.

He staggers upright, swaying in the breeze like the ghastly puppet he is. Though I attempted to banish all my emotions, they now crash into me like an all-consuming tidal wave. Yet I ground myself, refusing to be washed away.

I draw on aether, a tear tracing my cheek. I weave it into an inferno, grief blurring my eyes. Though my sight is hazy, there's no mistaking the flames crackling and sparking in my hands. My breaths are shaky, but I hone my fury, my hatred, my anguish into a weapon. The flames intensify from my raging emotions, so wild and deadly they threaten to explode in my fingers.

"*Ignira,*" I whisper.

And with that word, I kill my father.

He releases an unearthly howl as the flames consume him, licking his rotting flesh from his bones. He doesn't scream in pain, but in anger.

The staff falls from my hands. It bounces onto the street, clinking with the impact. I clutch my ears, desperate to silence the sound of Father's shrieks. But the sound isn't muffled by my palms. His howls are deafening, drowning out all else in my mind. I think I might be screaming with him too.

Finally, he falls silent.

Slowly, I open my eyes. The flames consume the remains of Father's corpse, and there is little left of him beneath the amber glow. He stares at me, and I stare back, lifting my hands from my ears. A ghost of a smile flickers on his face. His eyes twinkle with magenta light.

I am sure I see my name on his lips. Hear it ringing through my mind.

Reyna.

My lower lip trembles. "Father," I gasp, reaching out. "Father!"

His smile grows, illuminating his entire face with warmth.

And then he's gone.

Ash scatters through the wind. The flames die.

A shimmering cloud of purple light drifts over me, sweeping across my face. For a moment, it feels as if Father's fingers are brushing over my cheeks.

The cloud of aether soars upward into the night sky. Then it fades, taking Father's soul with it.

I fall to my knees. I don't feel the impact. I stare at the spot where his reanimated corpse stood moments ago. The stone is blackened where my fireball struck.

The world sways. Even remaining on my knees seems impossible.

I don't know what I expected to feel in this moment. Maybe relief as a burden slips from my shoulders. Maybe fury over what Arluin did to Father. I expected to feel hatred, but not toward myself.

My limbs feel like ice. I try to move them, but they refuse. All I can think about is killing Father. Even if he was already dead.

I know I must move, that I'm currently in the midst of battle, but I can't.

"Reyna!"

The shout of my name jolts my senses. I glance back to see Natharius shouting at me, horror on his face.

Shadows race toward me. Arluin's hands are raised.

Adrenaline pounds through my veins. I scramble to my feet, but there's no time. The crystalline staff lies several paces away from me.

I will die.

Natharius's draconic wings beat as he glides toward me. But even he won't reach me in time.

There isn't even time to mutter *muriz* and conjure a shield to protect myself. Not that it will do me much good. The bolt of shadows racing toward me is far more powerful than my magic.

I lunge to the side. The shadow bolt alters its course.

There's no escaping it. I watch the spell close in.

Shadows crash into me. They throw me backward, my head slamming against the stones beneath. Darkness clouds my vision. My lungs empty of air.

I expect to feel pain, but I feel none.

Is this what death feels like?

Am I dead?

Hands shake my shoulders. Frantically. Natharius stares down at me. His onyx horns glisten in the starlight. His crimson eyes are filled with concern, strange though that is.

"Reyna?" he shouts when I don't stir. He's at least thrice my size in his demonic form and when he shakes my shoulder again, I fear he might accidentally tear me apart.

"Ow," I complain, tugging my shoulder from his grasp. He releases me, his brows furrowing in confusion.

"You're . . ." he says, "you're shining."

I blink, my mind taking a few heartbeats to realize what he means. I lift my hand and examine it.

He's right. I *am* shining. My skin glistens with aether, as if my flesh is crafted from thousands of tiny crystals. The spell surrounding me feels as comforting as a blanket.

And I immediately recognize whose magic this is.

Father's.

I choke at the realization. Fresh tears swell in my eyes.

When his soul was freed, he must have used the last of his magic to place a protection spell over me. If he hadn't, I would be dead.

Arluin would have killed me.

At that, I push myself upright. "Arluin," I rasp to Natharius.

The Void Prince whirls around.

But Arluin is already gone. Along with the iron ring.

CHAPTER 40

"WE MUST FIND HIM BEFORE he can escape the city," I say to Natharius.

The Void Prince doesn't need telling twice. He straightens himself to the full towering height of his demonic form. Then he closes his eyes and inhales, his nostrils flaring with the force.

"He has melded with the shadows," Natharius says, reopening his crimson eyes. "I can sense his magic in the air."

My heart skips a beat. "Does that mean you can track him?"

"If we are quick," he answers. "The trail will not last long."

I nod and turn to Lhorok and Grizela who still battle each other. Lhorok is soaked in blood—his blood. I doubt he will hold out much longer. We must deal with Grizela before pursuing Arluin. Or else Lhorok will be dead when we return.

It means giving Arluin more time to escape, but if we can take Grizela prisoner then at least we might have a way of discovering his whereabouts. Though I don't know what horrifying torment it will take for the necromancer to talk.

I glance back at Natharius, who is already turning away. Clearly the Void Prince is more anxious about locating Arluin than ensuring Lhorok isn't killed. "Can you subdue this necromancer?"

Natharius casts me an impatient look, but doesn't waste time arguing with me. Dark magic spins in his hands, and he hurls the spell at Grizela.

The attack catches her by surprise. The shadows slam into her, shoving her against the nearest wall. Obsidian chains spring from the stone, holding her captive.

"Our young lord is already long gone," she cackles. "You will never catch him now."

Natharius ignores her and instead turns to Lhorok. "Keep a close eye on her and see to it she does not escape. The chains will hold until we return."

Lhorok gives him a stiff nod, and then his mournful gaze falls onto his wife.

"Ready?" Natharius asks me.

"To find Arluin?"

His response comes without warning. He scoops me into his arms and clasps me to his chest. Then we're soaring into the air, his leathery wings beating behind us and propelling us forth.

Though he remains in his demonic form, his height has diminished to that of his elven guise. His grasp is still unbearably tight, and I half worry he might accidentally snap my spine.

We climb higher into the night sky, the city shrinking beneath us. The undead crawl through the streets like insects, and the orcs fighting them beneath remind me of toy soldiers. We're dizzyingly high now.

"Don't drop me," I warn.

Natharius chuckles. "Don't tempt me."

I consider reminding him that I'm a mage and that dropping me will achieve nothing but inciting my rage, but it'll only tempt him to drop me and I'm far more concerned about finding Arluin before he escapes the city.

A burst of golden light flashes below. Taria. I can almost make out the priestess's molten gold robes from this height. I'm glad to know that Taria is safe and hope the same can be said for Caya and Juron.

Only one death gate remains now. All the other beacons of ghastly white light have been extinguished. Was that Taria's doing, or what the necromancers intended?

Natharius drifts farther over the city. Wind bites my cheeks. I turn my face into Natharius's chest to protect myself from the gales. His crimson markings glow brightly in my eyes, and I close them to avoid being blinded by their light.

After a moment, I glance back to see where Natharius is taking us. The wind stings my eyes. I blink it away, focusing on the city beneath.

We're flying toward the remaining death gate.

"He's going to leave Gerazad!" I exclaim over the roaring wind.

When I peer up at Natharius, I see his jaw is tightened. I suppose his silence means he already figured out this was what Arluin plans.

Though the streets beneath are still full of undead, the necromancers' army is only a fraction of its size. Far less entered through the death gates tonight than they did in Nolderan.

Today, Arluin didn't seek Gerazad's destruction, only the second ring he needs to unseal his undead master. This was his plan all along. He struck me to distract Natharius, and then shadow-stepped away to the nearest portal.

Now I fear he's no longer in the city.

The final death gate is already closing. The ghostly beam has all but faded into the night sky.

Natharius descends rapidly, but he isn't fast enough.

As we reach the ground, the last necromancer slips through the death gate. I lunge forth, freeing myself of Natharius's grasp. I reach for the necromancer's dark robes, but my fingers clasp only air.

The portal shuts.

I stand there for several long moments, inhaling deep, shaky breaths as the reality of what happened catches up with me.

Arluin is gone. And he took Lagartha's ring with him.

Now he only needs one ring to release his undead master. Then doom will descend on Imyria.

The unmistakable shadow of fear falls on the Void Prince's face. He says nothing. Both his fists and jaw are clenched.

"What do we do now?" I whisper.

He swallows. "I don't know where that death gate leads."

I doubt it's a small thing for the Prince of Pride to admit his ignorance. And I hate it proves how grave our situation is.

"We captured one of the necromancers," I say. "Maybe there is a way we can make her reveal Arluin's location."

"Even if the necromancer talks, it's doubtful we'll be able to reach it easily. You can only teleport to locations you've previously visited."

"Their lair could be closer than we think."

It's something, at least. Something that means hope hasn't entirely been lost.

Natharius offers me a quick nod and wraps his arm around me once more. He casts us both in dark magic and we meld with the shadows.

We drift through the streets, and the buildings pass me in a blur. I wonder if the reason Natharius hadn't shadow melded us to the death gate is because he can't also track a magical trail at the same time. If he could maybe we'd have arrived at the death gate before it closed. Maybe we could have faced Arluin on the other side of the portal, wherever that is.

Natharius soon brings us to a stop. The shadows fade from around us, and the surrounding buildings become less of a blur. They still sway around me, but I suspect that has more to do with my vision.

Lhorok kneels a few paces ahead, cradling his wife in his arms. Her lifeless face is wet with his tears. He looks up as we approach.

Grizela laughs. "It seems you return empty-handed."

Natharius lunges for Grizela, his hand gripping her throat. He presses her more firmly into the wall she is bound to by the obsidian chains. "Where do the death gates lead?" he roars.

The necromancer only continues to laugh. The strain of Natharius's grasp around her throat turns it to a gargling sound. "You do not scare me, demon."

Natharius grits his teeth. He glowers at the necromancer for several heartbeats before releasing her, a snarl curling on his lips.

"Where the death gates lead is inconsequential," he says to me. "We know where the necromancers will strike next."

"Lumaria," I reply.

"Indeed, they will seek my old ring. We cannot allow them to find it first."

His words almost sound like orders.

For a moment, I am cast back to my dining table, where I first begun planning my pursuit of Arluin and where Natharius wished for me to choke on my food. So much has changed since then. Though Natharius started out as a reluctant weapon, now a tentative alliance has formed between us. A partnership of sorts. And even if his words sound like orders, I don't care. All that matters is finding and destroying Arluin before he can destroy Imyria.

"Then we must go to Lumaria and find the ring before they do," I say with a nod.

My gaze drifts across to the blackened spot on the street where I obliterated Father. I breathe in a shaky breath. The thought of what I've done nauseates me. And yet, there was no alternative. My father would have urged me to do what I did, but it makes the burden no easier to bear.

Natharius places a hand on my shoulder, his brows furrowed and his face drawn into a similar expression to when Arluin almost killed me.

"He was already dead," he says softly, both his words and tone surprising me. "There was nothing else left to be done."

A part of me longs to throw his hand from my shoulder, hating that even Natharius pities me for my weakness. Yet another part of me cannot deny the slight comfort his presence brings—is grateful for it even.

I tilt back my head and gaze up at the twinkling stars.

Tonight, I was so close to defeating Arluin. To avenging Nolderan. And yet, I've failed once again.

I squeeze my eyes shut.

I will face him again—of that, I am certain. And the next time I do, I will not fail.

Reyna's story will continue in...

TEARS OF TWILIGHT

To learn more about TEARS OF TWILIGHT (Legends of Imyria, #3) and find out how to get a copy, you can visit here:

www.hollyrosebooks.com/tears-of-twilight

You can also subscribe to my newsletter so that you never miss out on new releases, giveaways, cover reveals, or other fun things (like bonus scenes!)

www.hollyrosebooks.com/subscribe

ABOUT THE AUTHOR

Holly Rose has been obsessed with high fantasy since the age of 5, when she first watched The Fellowship of the Ring (her parents raised her right). After realizing she couldn't become an elf, she decided to start writing about them instead. She also grew up on World of Warcraft and copious amounts of anime.

She was born and bred in Wales, United Kingdom, where she currently spends her days terrorizing teenagers with mathematical equations (and sometimes teaching them useful things). When she gets home from school, her real work with writing about magic and mayhem can begin.

You can find her online at:
http://hollyrosebooks.com/
https://www.instagram.com/hollyrosebooks/
https://twitter.com/hollyrosebooks
https://www.facebook.com/hollyrosebooks

CPSIA information can be obtained
at www.ICGtesting.com
Printed in the USA
LVHW110725120822
725756LV00004B/101

9 781914 503047